ELUSIV

As an African t
towards indep
men come down from their villages to
seek their fortune in the capital city.
Their ambitions vary but all three see
how, in different ways, independence
will mean great opportunities for them.

Evans has the clearest vision, of
progress through engineering; Malachi
simply wants to make money; and
Dipra sees politics as his way to the
top.

They experience condemnation
and praise, hatred, envy and love as
their careers diverge and converge in
intricate patterns. They learn in
different ways how to relate to the
wider world and how to handle moral
problems. They fight and make up as
success and failure alternate at various
times for all three. Their love lives
are marked by both tragedy and joy.
And through it all their loyalty and
friendship survive.

For
Sule Ajiboye and Nat Araoye

... the world cannot be really sad
if one has a friend .....

By the same author
One Death For Freedom

ELUSIVE AMBITIONS

JOHN DORRELL

Hillside Publishing, Orion's Orchard, Hallett Road,
Ansford, Castle Cary, Somerset, BA7 7LG, U.K.

Published in Great Britain 2005 by
Hillside Publishing, Orion's Orchard, Hallett Road,
Ansford, Castle Cary, Somerset, BA7 7LG, U.K.

British Library Cataloguing-in-Publication Data.
A catalogue record for this book is available
from the British Library.

ISBN: 0-9551283-0-7
ISBN-13: 978-0-9551283-0-1

Produced by Manuscript ReSearch (Book Producers),
P.O. Box 33, Bicester, Oxon, OX26 4ZZ, U.K.
Tel: 01869 322552/323447
Printed and bound by MWL Print Group Ltd., South Wales.

ONE

The first hint of daylight penetrating the cracks around the hangar doors was enough to wake Evans. He guessed it must be gone six already, time for him to stir and hunt for some breakfast. There were still two shillings left from his weekly wages, a small miracle on a Thursday. As always he had put five straight into his savings bank last Saturday morning but he did sometimes wonder if he was overdoing it. But better that than be poor for life.

Stretching to his full height, or length, of five feet nine inches - he seemed to have stopped growing now, he had noted with regret - and reaching above his head, he could just touch the two ends of the bucket with feet and hands. Looking across the half-light he could discern no movement from either Dipra or Malachi, asleep in the other two machines. Lazy devils, Evans thought, they'd be asleep when the manager arrived if I left them.

Not for the first time he wondered whether he'd made the right move in coming down to Henry City with them. He'd been doing well at school, much better than either of his friends. But they'd persuaded him of the great opportunities in the capital. Well, at least they had jobs and they were all still together. If only Dipra was not so wrapped up in the politics and Malachi so impatient to make his fortune. Every man to his chosen path, he thought – now where did that quotation come from?

The biggest problem in getting up was clambering out of the bucket. He heaved himself up on to the lip, a corner of his blanket firmly gripped in his teeth so that he could retrieve it and fold it away in some obscure corner of the hangar for the day. Then came the drop to the floor. He stood back to read once more the large black lettering standing out boldly on the front of the bucket against the bright yellow, INTEREARTHMOVE. A little surge of pride ran through him before he sprinted across to the other machines.

Selecting a large spanner he gave three sharp taps on the

first bucket's end wall, to be rewarded by reverberating clangs and a sharp cry of pain from its inhabitant. Dipra.

A pair of black hands appeared over the bucket lip, followed by a sleep-ravaged face, two eyes squinting evil at him. "Can you not find better ways to wake me?"

"Sun up. Manager coming soon. Need to move quickly."

Evans moved on to the third bucket to repeat the exercise but Malachi forestalled him. "O.K. O.K. Evans. We are awake." We, noted Evans, so she'd stayed with him. That might be dangerous. He'd talk to Malachi later.

"Give me a push," came the girl's voice. "It is too hard for me!"

"Better hard than soft," giggled Malachi. "Use my hands for step."

The girl appeared above the rim. Evans watched, fascinated. A sudden squawk as she was heaved on to the rim from behind, just clinging on by one arm and one leg.

"Go on," came Malachi's voice. She pulled the leg over, Evans averting his eyes, and dropped down to the extent of her arms.

"It is only a foot drop," said Evans sympathetically.

"O.K. You catch me." She was beginning to exploit the situation. These girls were all alike. "Right," he agreed.

She let go and Evans moved smartly back. "You never help me!" she complained. "No need," he said.

Malachi now heaved himself on to the bucket lip and rolled over to drop down. He's getting fat, Evans thought, the girl is feeding him too well. From her mother's kitchen, he had little doubt. His own stomach was now knotted in hunger. For a shilling he should be able to get a fried plantain with his nshima and an orange. Evans had read about the importance of fruit in the diet.

Dipra now came alongside. "When we go find somewhere better to sleep? In proper bed?" he demanded.

"Dipra, nowhere in Henry City just yet. You want bed, you go home to village. Wait till we earn more money."

Malachi butted in. "We should ask manager for more. He not paying enough for such hard work. You the clever one, Evans, you ask him."

Dipra frowned. "No. For money we talk to him each on own. We ask together, he think we a cheeky gang. Maybe he sack all three of us." He cut short Malachi's attempt to speak again. "And we never can tell him we need money so as not to sleep in machines! Get nightwatch into trouble too."

Evans took command. "Yes, right. Let's go now, come back half past seven. Watch the Bank clock to come on time." He looked significantly at Malachi. Then turned.

"Where is your blanket, Dipra?"

Dipra swore. Now he would have to clamber in and out of the bucket again. That Evans, he too clever.

*

Dipra was not the only person to notice. The foreman, Joshua, soon realised that all three lads were a bit out of the ordinary, but only Evans could really be trusted, in his view. Evans was quiet. Malachi seemed to think he would soon be the General Manager - no chance, not ever - and Dipra was always on about "freedom".

Send Malachi to the market to buy a few pots of paint and he'd take all morning. Then he'd come back saying how difficult it was to find and how hard he'd had to haggle to get four five-litre cans for the money he'd been given. He'd have a piece of paper showing the price he'd paid but that didn't fool Joshua. He guessed Malachi had made a bob or two on the side, but what can you expect from the slave wages we paid? Dipra was right about that. But it wasn't worth making a fuss. They were all lucky to have jobs.

Just as there was no point in telling the manager how the lads slept in the buckets each night. Probably safer than relying on the nightwatch, who might be anywhere. Joshua just hoped they wouldn't start bringing girls in. Girls were trouble in an engineering shop, with their damn curiosity.

That Dipra, now, right little firebrand. He'd heard it said

that Dipra Forfpi went to all the rallies, both for the Democratic Peoples Party and for the One Bishgad Alliance. Both parties were a joke in Joshua's eyes but OBA at least had initials that said something, Oba being a respectful term of address. Joshua couldn't imagine the colonial government taking any of these people seriously, but you never knew. Other parts of Africa were getting Dipra's precious "freedom" if the papers were telling the truth.

Evans was different. He seemed to be reading all the company brochures when the others were reading the daily scandal sheets. He'd had an intelligent conversation with that visitor last week while waiting for the manager to come back from town. The man had commented to the manager that Evans seemed to know a lot about the machines. Full marks. He would ask the manager if Evans could work as an apprentice, not just a yard boy.

*

Malachi had never been to such a huge rally. He didn't know there were that many people in Henry City. People seemed to fill the pitch, if you could call this litter-strewn stretch of waste ground a pitch. But there were the remnants of white lines among the dust. And that three tier wooden stand from which the speaker was bellowing was a reminder of the original purpose.

Surely this crowd couldn't all be party members? It was a bit frightening and he began to wish he hadn't let Dipra persuade him to come. Evans had said he "didn't want to get mixed up in all this politics". "Don't blame me if you have to spend the night in a prison cell," he'd said, "the whole Jamesland Police Force will be there!"

"You too cautious," Dipra had responded. "Come to rallies and when Jamesland gets freedom, we be big men in Bishgad. I see dat. Malachi and me, we aim for de top! Kilimanjaro, highest mountain in Africa, not so? An' if we get put prison, it help us when freedom comes. We be martyrs, heroes of de struggle!"

Evans merely smiled. "I think I'll just aim to be a good engineer. Both Jamesland and especially Bishgad if it comes will need lots of engineers. Especially if we do get this freedom, because I expect all the Europeans will go home."

Malachi found that thought rather encouraging. If he could trade in the market for a couple of hours with just the money the manager gave him to buy paint and make half as much again in profit, what could he do when he was the manager himself? He began to think that while both Evans and Dipra seemed to be on to good things, they were their own things. Not his.

He himself might set up a stall on Sundays with his own small savings to practise trading. Grace had expensive tastes like ice cream and chocolate, even if she did bring good food from home, which saved him money every day.

Dipra was just in front of him, bellowing the slogans in response to the speaker's rhetorical questions, along with the crowd. 'What do we want? Free-dom! When do we want it? Next year! How shall we get it? Strike and fight! What do we want? Free-dom! When do we want it? Next year!'

Would the chanting never end?

Malachi looked around the braying crowd and noticed a section not responding, simply looking at each other as if waiting for some alternative stimulus. Then he caught sight of Grace, her face screwed up with worry, her lips spread beyond clamped teeth, fervently beckoning him. She glanced either side of her and then mouthed something, which could have been "Come away!"

Suddenly he understood what was going to happen. He pushed through, grabbed her now trailing hand and pressed on to the edge of the crowd. Behind him, the roar was changing, losing its discipline. Ahead was a line of riot police, shields and batons at the ready. Grace dragged him running, right up to the line, face to face with the apparent leader.

"We are not part of it! Let us through," she pleaded. For a few seconds the senior policeman impassively inspected Grace and Malachi. Two fat teenagers, he thought, innocents abroad from their middle class enclosures. He waved them through and with an almost continuous movement waved his squad forward.

"What about Dipra?" panted Malachi, when they had run another hundred yards through scrub and bush.

"What about him? What can we do? He goes to both OBA and DPP rallies and now they are fighting and he will not know which side to fight on. Better for him if he gets arrested quickly, but I think they are not looking to make arrests, just to beat a few people to scare them away from rallies like this. It is a silly game, this politics, like Evans says. Good job I followed you tonight. That Dipra is not a good influence on you!"

Malachi was wide-eyed at this diatribe, the longest speech he had ever heard Grace make. But she was not finished.

"And Evans is right about my not sleeping in the bucket with you. Someone will catch us and then all three of you will be in trouble. Evans is a sensible boy, even if he only nineteen. You two could learn from him."

Malachi was silent, thinking about this as they hurried across town. "Where we going?" he suddenly asked.

"You are taking me home, where it is safe. Then you can go back to your works, across the new building site. But first I can introduce you to my parents. You can be the hero who rescued me from the riot."

Oh God, parents, he thought. I'm not ready for this yet. Then he brightened. Perhaps there would be food.

*

"So where is Dipra?" demanded Evans as Malachi sleepily clawed his face above the bucket rim. "He has not been here tonight!"

"Perhaps he got caught up in the rally. It got a bit rough. The police stopped it."

"But you were with him!"

"At first. I left early; the crowd was too big and noisy for me. Anyway, I not sure I want to get involved."

"Could you not have dragged Dipra away?"

"Oh, no. You have to see Dipra when he excited about something. The OBA leader was making the crowd very excited and Dipra was shouting like a madman. They were all madmen.

I think you wise to stay away."

He looked slyly at Evans. "Where did you go last night?"

"I went to the Technical Institute, to get some information on study courses. Maybe the manager will pay some fees." Evans realised he had been diverted. "No Grace in there last night?"

"No. We took your advice. But I met her people. Nice people, nice house, she an infant teacher, he a doctor, good job at Karle Mo hospital. Grace says she wants to do medicine too. I had to pretend I am staying with relations. Grace backed me up. Maybe I marry her."

"Marry her? Foolish idea, Malachi. She won't want marriage if she wants to study medicine. Not for years. Who are you - a twenty-one-year-old yard boy with no qualifications? Get some studies yourself. English to start. Then business. If you want to be a big businessman, you better understand marketing, accounting, all that sort of thing. It will take a few years, but without qualifications you will always be a petty market trader. Me, I shall study engineering, then maybe go into the construction business. Have you seen the pictures of the new dam where our machines are working?"

Malachi saw the fire in his eyes and heard the steel in his voice. Evans would get on, he knew. He should stay friends. But where was Dipra? He struggled over the bucket rim and dropped down in front of Evans. "Should we go seek for Dipra, you think?"

"We could ask around before work. But we must be on time. Losing our jobs won't help Dipra. Besides, I want to ask manager for help with my studies, so I need him to think me reliable. You've forgotten your blanket."

With that, Evans quietly slid open the hangar door just wide enough to get through, while Malachi looked around for a box to use as a step in scaling the bucket again. That Evans! He didn't know whether to admire him or hate him.

*

Evans nervously faced the manager, steeling himself to ask his question. But the manager spoke first. "What happened to

11

Dipra today then?"

"We don't know, Sir."

"Was he mixed up in that rally last night? He's a bit of a troublemaker, isn't he?"

"No, Sir," protested Evans. "Not troublemaker. But he does have strong political views, independence and all that."

"Well, I expect it will come in time, but not before I'm enjoying a life of leisure in Dorset, I shouldn't think. But what are you going to do with your life, Evans?"

"I want to be an engineer like you, Sir, if you will help me. The country will need engineers whether it is independent or not. Especially if you going home."

"Good thinking" said the manager grudgingly. "Engineer, eh? Do you know how much hard work is involved? For years? Any good at Maths?"

"Yes sir, but I have to get my Oxford. I was wondering ...."

"Wondering what, laddie?"

"Wondering if the company could advance my fees for an evening course at the Technical Institute, Sir. I could pay back weekly from my wages."

"Hmmm." The manager contemplated the idea. "What courses do you have in mind?"

"Maths and Technical Drawing to start, Sir. They cost about fifty shillings a term for the two, Sir, and I could pay back four shillings every week."

"Four shillings? Don't be daft man. How will you eat? Where do you live?"

Evans was discomforted. He paused while integrity battled with ambition. "I have free accommodation Sir and I already save some every week in my savings book."

The manager looked at him carefully. "Do your friends enjoy free accommodation too, Evans?"

"Yes, Sir." What else could he say? Had he given the game away?

A gleam of understanding flashed in the manager's eyes,

followed by the merest hint of a half smile on his face. "Was the free accommodation found by you or by one of your friends?"

"By me, Sir." The game was up. He'd confessed his secret and betrayed his friends.

"Right," said the manager, "I've been getting good reports on you from Joshua who wants you as his apprentice. So," he paused, "I'll do a deal with you. I'll advance the money for your courses and you will work very hard to do them successfully. You fail the exams and you have to pay me back. You pass, we call the fees a prize. Roger Brown at the Institute is a friend of mine, so I'll know how you are doing. Meanwhile you can work with Joshua. I'll get the cheque made out for you to collect at the end of business. All understood?"

Evans was flooded with gratitude. "Yes, Sir, oh, thank you very much, Sir, I'm really very grateful Sir..."

"OK, OK, don't overdo it. Off you go." Then, as Evans was opening the door, "By the way, one of the big machines will be on its way up to the dam tomorrow. You'll be helping Joshua get it ready. Anyway, I believe you know a bit about them already. We'll be glad to get another one out of here, earning a bit of money. Maybe you shouldn't look too hard for Dipra. OK, go and find Joshua."

*

Malachi wanted to spend the evening hunting for Dipra but since their morning search had yielded nothing, Evans argued, they'd be wasting their time going over old ground so soon. Funny how they couldn't find a single person who had been at the rally. Malachi had thought the entire population of Jamesland had been there. "Anyway," Evans said, " I have to register for my courses at the Institute this evening and you could come with me and find out what the Tech could offer you."

"Manager is not going to pay my fees," grumbled Malachi.

"Perhaps not, but you could ask. Though I don't want you to, because it might spoil my own arrangement. Listen, you've made enough money in the markets - with company money anyway - to pay for your own. Better than spending it all on Grace."

Malachi wondered how much Evans knew about his trading activities. The boy was as sharp as a pin. But he was still worried about Dipra. Couldn't they go to the police station to see if they had any record of Dipra?

"And if he's in prison, you want a big Lembe policeman to know you are his best friend? After last night, three people killed, one of them a police, and thirty injured? No, leave it for a few days, Malachi, let things cool down. Perhaps our manager has a friend high up in the police. Not that he cares for Dipra much but he might enquire for us."

So Malachi found himself scanning the courses at the Tech, and at Evans's urging decided to sign up for English and Accounts. The Registrar explained that the two courses would cost fifty shillings a term, unless, with a slight smirk, Malachi proposed to pay for the whole year in advance, only two hundred and twenty five shillings altogether.

Malachi took offence at the smirk. "Give chance, five minutes," he said fiercely, "Must go to toilet" and rapidly left the room, leaving an abashed Registrar and a wondering Evans. Four minutes later he was back, flourishing a wad of notes and slapping it down on the desk with an air of triumph, "Two hundred twenty five! You count 'em!"

The Registrar counted, recounted, and reluctantly gave Malachi a receipt. "First English lesson tomorrow evening, half past six. Lecturer is Mrs. Stephenson, room forty two."

"There you are," said Evans as they left the room "Now you are really working towards being a big businessman. Where did you get the money so quickly?"

"Secret pocket in my underpants! Nowhere else to keep it safe."

Evans sighed. "Malachi, I have to teach you about banks to start. Anyway, Grace will respect you for getting an education. More importantly, so will her father!"

Yes, thought Malachi. Good point. Evans sees these things. But where is Dipra?

TWO

Over the next year Evans progressed steadily under Joshua's tutelage and began taking responsibility on site for some of the smaller machines such as air compressors. The customers' gangs were not always the most respectful or disciplined of workers but Evans often exhibited good command of men twice his age. Although still no taller, his muscular physique also helped.

But one particular gang boss he did not look forward to working with. "What do *you* know, black boy?" was the familiar challenge. "I been working wid dese machines fifteen years. You think you know better than me?"

Joshua was sympathetic. Yet Joshua knew there comes a time in any young person's life when he has to overcome the challenges if he is to make his own way. "The old days are gone, Evans. You can't sit back and leave it all to the elders any more, like they do in the villages. If nobody under fifty can be heard, we shall be ruled by old men who live in the past.

"Look at the young expats who come out to manage us - see how they take control. Our manager started here when he was twenty-five. When he goes back for the last time he will be only fifty, and a rich man. I hear him talking to his friends and they speak of houses with five bedrooms and two bathrooms. If we want to get rich like that we must give young people more power, I think. But young people must be ready to use it and use it well. How're your studies going?"

"Well, Joshua! I think I should pass my next exams, so again I will not have to pay my fees back to the company."

"Good. Manager wants you to succeed. He doesn't want the money back. What of Malachi?"

"Malachi will pass his exams too, I think. Once he puts his money down, he makes sure he gets good value!"

They both laughed. "You don't envy Malachi his comfortable office job?"

"No. I suppose we each enjoy what we are good at. It was

Malachi who found us the flat and came up with the deposit money."

"So you still good friends, even after living together for six months?"

Evans just smiled and nodded.

"You had some practice," continued Joshua. "The flat must at least be better than the buckets. Now, tomorrow you have to go back to the Korle Mo hospital site, change the oil in the compressors, take some new spade bits for the drills. Watch that foreman. And stand up to him."

Evans was still contemplating the buckets remark and realised Joshua did not wish to pursue the subject, just to let them know he *knew*. He focussed his mind on the obstreperous foreman. Yes, he'd have to stand up to him.

"Get some of the workmen behind you," was Malachi's advice. "Isolate him."

"Not easy, Malachi. He's old enough to be my father and his workmen respect him. But he doesn't always understand how the machines work. After all, that's why the company sends me."

"So explain that to some of the leading workmen. If you had a white skin, with your knowledge and skills they would all listen to you. We have to learn to respect our own people's progress, tell them."

"You sound like Dipra!"

"Yes, some of Dipra's ideas made sense. I wish we knew what happened to him. You think he dead?"

"No, I think he ran far away. Maybe Russia. OBA seemed to have good contacts there. But he wouldn't understand a word of the language. Still, wherever he is, I somehow think we shall see him back in Jamesland again. Or more probably Bishgad, as he wants to call it."

*

"I need to take this machine to the other end of the site, beyond the hospital main entrance," said the foreman.

"OK. Let's find six men."

"Six? Ridiculous. You can have three men. Two at back, one in front."

"Look, it's a single axle machine. Three won't be able to balance it, especially across all that rough ground."

"*Four men*, with you." The foreman turned on his heel.

"No, I won't move it. Six men."

"You go to hell, book boy. I move it myself."

"If you move it against my advice, you will be completely responsible for mistakes. I shall report to my manager. Your company will have to pay for any damage."

The foreman came back and thrust his darkened face inches from Evans's. "You cocky young book boy," he snarled. "You just watch. We move machine. I complain about you not co-operating on site. You in big trouble, book boy."

Evans steeled himself. In a quiet voice he said, "You touch that machine and I will recommend we never hire to your company on this site until you are off it."

The startled foreman backed away a little. He became aware that all the workers had downed tools to watch this struggle. Then he burst into laughter. "Just watch us, book boy. Amos, Micah, Gabriel, over here!"

The three shuffled reluctantly forward. "We going to move this 'pressor to far end. Amos take tow ring with me. Micah and Gabriel push back end, pressing down to keep it level."

They took up positions. "I lift stand first," said the foreman, loosening the lever, shortening the jackstay and retightening.

"Not tight enough," shouted Evans.

"Shut up. We doing this."

They set off, the wheels bumping across ridges, the back pair pushing with their shoulders while desperately pressing down with their hands to maintain the balance and keep the standpipe, the jackstay, at the other end clear of the ground. The front pair were heaving on the great iron tow ring.

Having reached a smooth driveway, they accelerated until they hit a speed-bump which caused the momentum to tilt the whole machine forward. The jackstay held it momentarily and

17

then the clamp slid juddering down the standpipe. At the back, Micah and Gabriel were lifted bodily. Down went the tow ring at the front, with the foreman screaming, "Hold it! Hold it!"

Amos let go a split second before the ring hit the concrete. The foreman was too slow. His scream turned from anger to agony as he raced blindly across the site. Every workman stopped to watch him pass. Only Evans bellowed, "Catch him!" galvanising three men to tackle the demented foreman. "Get him into the hospital, fast!"

Having seen six burly men restraining and carrying the still screaming foreman across to the casualty department Evans walked back to examine the ring. Bloodily protruding into its centre were the tips of three fingers.

*

"Tell me exactly what happened," demanded the manager.

Evans recounted it, as calmly as he had confronted the foreman the day before.

"Why didn't the jackstay hold it?"

"Not tight enough, Sir." With sudden and total recall, he blurted out "That's exactly what I shouted, Sir. 'Not tight enough,' I shouted. And he shouted back: 'Shut up. We doing this.'"

"Witnesses?"

"I expect only the three men - Amos, Micah and Gabriel - saw the whole thing, but everyone on the site must have seen the machine tipping over, because the foreman was screaming so loud, screaming for them to 'Hold it!' I'm sorry Sir. He just wouldn't listen to me."

"Well, I'm sure he wishes he had now. You seem to have done all the right things, Evans. I don't think the contractor will sue or anything. Trouble is, I can't even send a 'get well' card without it seeming an admission of guilt. Stay away from him, Evans. Heard your exam results yet?"

"No, Sir. This morning. I will go up to the Tech in my lunch hour."

"Do that, laddie. You won't be disappointed. A little birdie

18

told me you did rather well."

*

Malachi had done rather well too. Another year and they would both have diplomas, the manager pointed out. Perhaps now that Malachi had shown commitment the company should have the same arrangement with Malachi as it had with Evans. Both fees would be paid for them upfront and diplomas would cancel out the debt. Agreed?

Malachi beamed. "Very good arrangement, Sah. You see how good it make Evans work. I will work just as hard for you, I promise."

"Not for *me*, Malachi. It's *your* future, not mine. Get your diplomas and later on I'll see if we can get you some UK experience. If you're going to progress out here you're going to need a better understanding of the world picture. No promises, mind you, but I'll see what I can do. Engineering and Accounts diplomas might just put our masters in the right frame of mind. But that's all in the future; there's another year of hard work in front of you."

*

Malachi was still seeing Grace, who had got good enough "Highers" to start on a medical degree at Henry City University.

"You should get yourself a girl, Evans, then we can go around in a foursome. Grace likes you, you know, why don't I ask her to find someone for you?"

Evans thought girls would distract him from his studies. "This is our final year, Malachi, we must keep working hard."

"OK, OK, but I *am* working hard. And so is Grace. We only go out Saturday nights, just down to the Kakadu for a few beers and dancing under the stars. More fun in a group. Let me ask her."

"All right. No silly promises though. Don't want the girl expecting Harry Belafonte. Tell Grace. And it's for one evening, remember. I'm not looking for a permanent relationship, not like you and Grace."

Malachi shook his head in wonder. "You got to let yourself

19

go, man. I better warn her she'll be dancing with a slide rule."

Evans gave him a playful punch. "Grace will understand better than you do! You're a lucky man to have Grace, but I don't know why she puts up with you."

*

Saturday night turned out really well. Grace brought a friend, a nurse she'd met at the hospital during her practical work there. Evans was acutely aware that Mercy was several years older than himself, but Grace had told him not to let on. "You are a very mature young man," she told him. "Mercy won't know if you don't tell her."

They danced and drank, drank and danced, sometimes with their own, sometimes with their friend's partner. The tiny dance floor and the ground around it had dried from the earlier rain but the place still had the fresh smell which followed it. It was a warm evening and they were glad of the occasional light breeze stirring the palms.

Despite the beer, Evans maintained sufficient control not to give in to his preference to dance with Grace. She was Malachi's. And anyway, Mercy was nice, quite pretty if you ignored the small cicatrices on each cheek. When were we going to abandon this barbaric habit? Mercy probably didn't regard them as disfiguring, since she'd certainly had them from a baby.

She was a good conversationalist. They discussed the effects independence might have on the development of their country, whether British nurses would want to go home, whether enough local medical staff could be trained up in time to fill their places. "Good heavens," said Evans, "it's not as if independence is coming next year. I'm sure the British will start preparing us for it in good time. And lots of British will stay on for a while."

"I'm not so sure," said Malachi. "Not all British managers are like ours."

Mercy and Grace now began to swap stories about patients in Karle Mo. "One of my people some months back had lost three fingers of his right hand in an accident on the hospital site.

He was swearing revenge on a kid who made it happen. Reckoned he'd kill him when he got out."

Malachi looked sidelong at Evans. Three mouths clamped shut as Mercy looked wonderingly around the group. "Have I said something?"

"When *did* he get out?" queried Malachi.

"Oh, about a month back. He needed a lot of physio. Why? He didn't really mean it, of course. Just a way of shifting the blame and comforting himself."

She looked around the group again. "What is it? Do you know about this?" Her eyes widened. "Was it one of you? He said 'a kid'."

"I'm the kid," volunteered Evans. "But it wasn't my fault, it was really his own fault for contradicting me."

"But he said you made him..."

"Nobody made him," butted in Malachi. "Evans told him about safety procedures and he ignored them. He was the site foreman and should have known better."

"Time to be going, I think," said Grace, trying to warm the sudden chill that had descended. "Let's walk to my place and we can have some good coffee."

*

Saturday nights became regular dates but it was some weeks before Mercy raised the matter of the missing fingers again. During one of the waltzes played by the band as a short respite from the energetic Highlife, and primarily for the benefit of expatriate couples, they were close enough for her to murmur the question. "What exactly *did* happen on the building site?"

Evans spun her round a couple more times while deciding on his strategy. She looked keenly into his eyes.

"Let's go over there, away from the crowd, and I'll tell you."

She giggled softly. "Grace and Malachi will wonder what we're up to."

"Do you want to know or not?" he asked her fiercely. In reply she simply took his arm and led him off.

When he'd finished, she stroked his hair. "Poor you, it must have been a nightmare. Some people just hate education, don't they? Especially in a youngster."

He looked up, warily. "Oh, it's all right," she said softly. "I know you're only about twenty-one. But you're nice. Though not the man for me. But I'd love you to be my brother. I'd be really proud of you." She kissed him lightly on the cheek and stood to go. "Shall we get back to the others?"

*

They were leaving at eleven o'clock as usual, huddled in pairs to use the narrow footpath running alongside the big storm drain which paralleled the ring road coming down from Grace's parents' district around the edge of town. Occasionally they paused while other people negotiated past them. Young people perched on the edge of the big drain reading their homework books by the big sodium lights.

Evans was sympathetic. "Lucky we have better facilities than they have, Malachi!"

A single man loomed up in the gloom and stood aside while Malachi and Grace stepped past, closely examining their faces but without recognition. Then surprisingly he stepped back onto the path between the two couples. And shone a torch directly into the faces of Mercy and Evans.

"You!" he gasped. "You takin' out dis nurse who make my hand better. I get you soon, bookboy. You never enjoy dis nurse, 'less you have her tonight. I got sharp knife ready for you. I come for you very soon."

And disappeared into the night.

*

Grace tried hard to persuade Evans that he should continue with their Saturday night dates but he argued that he still had too much work to do for his diploma.

"Anyway, it is too dangerous, especially for Mercy. If my foreman does attack, he may bring friends to help, and if I'm with Mercy, he may have a go at her too, even though she helped him so much. The man seems a bit mad."

"Why don't you tell police?" suggested Malachi.

"You think they will worry about some personal ill-will like this? They are too busy watching OBA and DPP to bother with me."

"At least tell manager. He has police friends who might keep an eye open. This foreman is a thug; they might know him from other things. We know his name. And he's very easy to identify. Please tell manager, Evans. He already knows how it happened."

"True. All right, I'll tell him about that meeting on the path. But no more Mercy. Sorry, Grace, I know she's your friend."

"And not yours?" Grace asked.

"She's nice. She's lovely. And she's intelligent and fun. But we're not right for each other. We've agreed that. But I'm fond of her, enough not to want to put her into any kind of danger."

He looked at Grace and caught the faintest glimmering of a smile.

*

Malachi was bursting to tell the manager that they had got their Diplomas but Evans calmed him. "I think Mr. MacDonald probably knows already. He has many friends at the Tech."

"Well, anyway, we have to tell him officially." Malachi's eyes suddenly lit up at a new thought. "Maybe he'll give us a good rise?"

"Don't rush your fences, Malachi; let's not put any pressure on. Remember we owe our Diplomas to him anyway."

"Rush your fences? What dat mean?" Malachi put on his most innocent, white-eyed surprised look.

Evans laughed at the face. "You know very well what it means, Malachi. But I wonder where it comes from? Maybe from hunting in UK where they have to jump fences all the time."

"How can you hunt in a country with fences? Surely the fences keep the wild animals out and the useful animals in?"

"Foxes, I think they hunt. Can get through fences and under

hedges. I read a novel about it once."

"Books. You waste too much time reading, Evans. Should be more dancing, more fun in your life."

"But books *are* my fun, Malachi. Don't tell me now you've got your Diploma you're going to do nothing but dance and drink beer."

"No, but I'm not going to stay in every night reading books."

Mr. MacDonald greeted them next morning with the expected question. "Something to tell me, boys?" He smiled quietly as Malachi poured it all out and exchanged a knowing glance with Evans. I really think I begin to know this man, thought Evans.

"So now we are qualified *professional* people," concluded Malachi.

MacDonald smiled enigmatically, raised his eyebrows and sent a questioning glance up at Malachi; while Evans discreetly tapped his shoe against Malachi's. There was a moment of silence. Then MacDonald burst out laughing while they stood in embarrassment.

"OK OK I get the message," chortled MacDonald. "Yes, you each get a fifteen percent rise, in recognition of your efforts. Don't let it go to your heads. And I'll think about UK for you. Off you go and get down to work."

*

Heathrow airport seemed about a hundred times larger than Henry City. "A thousand," argued Malachi. "It looks more people here today than go through Henry James airport all year."

They were chagrined to see the long queue for non-EEC passengers. "We don't make people wait like this at home. I know, I have met my uncle off the plane and he came through in a few minutes."

"Patience," counselled Evans. "They have a lot more people and a lot more nationalities to deal with here. We'll get through. The manager made quite sure we had the right entry visas and letters about our stay here. His friend Mr. Richards was very helpful when I went to the British office - did a careful check on all the papers. Look, we're moving forward now."

"Where have they taken that man who was holding up the queue?"

"Don't know. Perhaps his papers weren't right. That seems to be a Customs man who's gone with him. I hope *you* haven't brought anything you shouldn't."

"I'm not that silly, Evans. Only some Betel nuts - they'll know about them, won't they?" he asked, suddenly anxious.

"Yes, I'm sure. But don't make a song and dance about them. Your turn, go forward."

"Can't we go together?"

"No, you first."

As they dithered, the immigration officer looked across. "Next," he shouted pointedly. Evans eased Malachi forward, his pristine passport in hand. The officer leafed through it to find the visa on page one. "First visit, eh?"

Malachi nodded. "There is a letter from our company in there. My friend is next."

The officer looked up, beckoned Evans across the red line. "You are together?"

"Yes. A training course for our work."

"OK, looks alright to me." He stamped both passports. "Sixty days max. Don't disappear." He made a note on a report sheet of the two names and the employer before handing back the passports. "Enjoy your stay."

As they walked away, Malachi asked what 'disappear' meant.

"Too many people come in on a short visa and then stay on illegally. I read about it in one of the manager's magazines - The Economist, I think it was called. You ought to be reading that too, Malachi. Especially if Bishgad comes. Trading will be much more international then, when we aren't a colony any more. Maybe we should both learn some French. They speak French in Astrica, you know. Which of these belts has our baggage on? I think it tells you up on that screen."

Malachi scanned the television screen at the entrance to

the hall. "Henry City, channel four. Where do these trolleys come from, will we have to pay like at Henry James?"

The two boys looked up and down and identified the source of trolleys. "You collect one and I'll look out for our bags. I think trolleys are free." Evans moved towards the belt while Malachi dashed off to the trolley park. He was back in seconds, scared of losing Evans in this hubbub.

"There's your bag," exclaimed Evans and moved to heave it on to the trolley. "Much heavier than mine! What have you got in it?"

"Lots of warm clothes. And a few souvenirs ... for friends of my family here."

"But you've just declared to Immigration that you have no family or friends here! If Customs ask you, what will you say?"

"Gifts! Gifts for our hosts. If I'm asked. We'll go through the Nothing to Declare channel. Coming from Jamesland, they won't stop us. We have no gold, no diamonds, no drugs. We a well run colony!"

As soon as they were outside Malachi declaimed, "What did I tell you?" "Shut up, Malachi or we'll be back in there," Evans muttered. "See our names on anyone's board out there?"

They wandered down the line to find INTEREARTHMOVE in large red letters. Evans approached the driver. "That's us, Sir."

The driver looked at him. "Welcome to England. No need for 'Sirs' here. I'm Fred. You?"

"Evans. And this is Malachi."

"What? I've got Goodwill and Watanero."

Evans grinned. "Right. Malachi and Evans are our first names. You'll get used to them! Nice to meet you Fred."

THREE

They had never seen so much machinery in their lives, row upon row of diggers, scrapers, graders, backhoe loaders, pile drivers and half a dozen types they didn't even know the names of, every one in the familiar company yellow. For Evans it was like a visit to paradise. For Malachi, it represented more money than he dreamed existed in the world. InterEarthMove must surely be the biggest company in UK.

"Impressive sight, isn't it?" commented their guide. "Most of those are already ordered, the far ones for the UK market, the nearer ones for overseas. Of course those will have to be dismantled again and crated ready for assembly in Kuala Lumpur or Stockholm or wherever, perhaps even in Henry City." He led them back into the offices.

"I'm going to put you, Evans, on the gang dismantling and you, Malachi, will work in the accounts department for a couple of weeks. Then you'll be together for a few days each in design and production, marketing, purchasing, quality control etcetera. By the time your four weeks is up you should have a pretty good picture of the operation. Settled in at the hostel?"

*

The twenty-four-bed hostel was a new experience for them both. Australians mixed with Arabs, French with Filipinos, Irish with Iranians. InterEarthMove had agents and distributors all over the world and one of the best training programmes in modern industry. The two Africans found themselves befriending a black American who expressed amazement at their "snooty British English."

They in turn were confused by some of his American expressions but his very blonde Swedish friend explained in his own clipped tones that "America has not had the benefit of proper English teaching since seventeen seventy something!" earning himself a playful cuff around the ear.

The shifting population of the hostel was like a mini United

Nations, Malachi opined. "But they all speak English! Why should we bother to learn French, for instance?"

"Because one day you may want to visit France and I don't think they speak English there."

Halfway through their stay a new arrival, from Hong Kong, swept Malachi off his feet. Celine Brandt. Slender and beautiful, she was of quite indeterminate race, though Malachi classed her as Chinese.

"More complicated than that," she laughed when questioned. "My mother was 'Portuguese,' which is what we call people from Macao, really a mix of Portuguese and Chinese, and my father German from his father and Chinese from his mother. So I am two parts Chinese, two parts different European. My friends joke that I should look for a British/African man for husband so my children will be even more international."

The boys cast their eyes down at such open discussion of race. "What's wrong?" she asked. "Have I embarrassed you? I'm sorry. It is only a joke."

"In our country there is very little inter-marriage between whites and Africans."

"Oh. But white boys must sometimes go with your lovely girls? No coffee coloured children? I read there are many in South Africa."

Evans took charge. "Most expatriates come out with their wives and families. I think any British who got involved with a local girl would be sent home. Bad girls don't seem to have babies."

"You mean prostitutes?" Evans blushed and lowered his head. How could she be so outspoken? And changed the subject. "You speak Chinese at home?"

A clear little bell of laughter gently acknowledged his embarrassment. "Yes, with my mother most of the time. Sometimes Portuguese, but I don't like it much. Much prefer English, but it is not good for her. I can use German with my father and French with my boyfriend who comes from Vietnam."

"You speak *all* those?" Malachi was stunned. "What are

you studying here?"

"Oh, I'm topping up product knowledge, especially the new range of diggers and hopefully learning some advanced marketing skills. When I get back to Hong Kong I shall be regional Marketing Manager."

"Part of Hong Kong?" asked Malachi, displaying his total ignorance of her country.

Again that tinkling laugh. "Hong Kong is just less than four hundred square miles though our population is several million. No, my region will be East Asia, from Japan down to Indonesia and west to Thailand. How big is Jamesland?"

Malachi, in awe of this tiny brilliant girl, despaired. He had no idea. Evans came to his rescue. "About one hundred and fifty thousand square miles, but most of it rain forest. Population about seven million."

Looking to his saviour with a mix of emotions, Malachi added: "Must be half in Henry City." Evans nodded agreement though he knew it was nearer a quarter. "Are they Chinese in Vietnam?"

"I think you must learn much more about the world," she said, then seeing his downcast response, added sympathetically, "Most of it you learn in your late twenties and early thirties, I think. If you read properly."

"So how old are you?" Malachi blurted.

She gave him a coy look. "Gentlemen don't ask ladies that question!" Then she smiled, breaking his heart once again. "Let me just guess five years older than you. Then we don't have to tell each other anything!" A soft chuckle.

"Would you two like to take me around the sights in London on Saturday? I haven't been yet and I'm dying to see the Houses of Parliament and Big Ben and St. Paul's Cathedral and all that."

"Yes, good idea. We haven't been either. You probably know more about it than we do. You can be our guide and we'll be your escorts. Deal?" Evans had once again taken charge. Malachi hated him and loved him.

*

London terrified them, but Celine took it in her stride. She bought a tourist map showing all the famous landmarks and showed them how to read the bus and underground network map. They trailed from the City to Marble Arch, from the Tower to Buckingham Palace. They bought sandwiches and coffee from a tiny kiosk in a small park and Celine later suggested they try some beers in a Fleet Street pub.

"Won't they think two black men ....?" Malachi let the sentence hang in the air.

"Oh, come on, this is London, Malachi. They won't even think a yellow girl strange! There have been black and Chinese communities here for centuries!"

Nonplussed by this beautiful, dynamic, uninhibited lady, they followed her meekly inside, trying to disturb the sawdust on the floor as little as possible.

"What shall we drink?" she asked.

"Planet beer?" ventured Evans. The barman looked puzzled. "Is that a beer in your country? Don't keep that, sorry. Got a very good Ruddles."

"OK, Ruddles," said Evans. "Celine?"

"G and T please. And I'm paying, for your escort services."

The boys looked at each other. What was a 'G and T?' They carefully observed the barman dispense the drinks and buried their faces in the great pint tankards in which theirs was served. Careful swallows were followed by puckered faces. "Bitter!" exclaimed Malachi.

"Of course it's bitter! What do you expect from real ale? Oh, I suppose you were reared on lager. Coloured lemonade!" The barman could not keep the contempt out of his voice. "Your Planet beer - made by one of these continental brewers?"

"Probably like Tiger in my country." Celine came to their rescue. "My people are not keen on English ale. Only British expatriates drink it. Good experience for you," she said, turning to the boys. "British men think it is manly!"

They struggled through it and began to feel light headed. Evans fell against Celine as they left the pub. She pushed him upright, laughing. "I hope that is only the beer working! Maybe we should walk down by the river to clear your heads." She consulted her map. "Yes, over Waterloo Bridge first and then along the bank."

By the end of the day they were exhausted but Celine seemed as energetic as ever. As they walked through Belgravia, she spotted a flag. "That is my country's commercial office! Will your country have one too?"

They expressed doubt. "Never mind, let's see how many flags we can recognise - that one is China, that one Turkey, that one Indonesia -"

"Ghana!" burst out Malachi. "First independent African country!"

"So," said Celine, "a black star, eh? You two should be the black stars of your country, when the time comes. You think it will be soon?"

"Some years, I think," said Evans. "We shall need many more qualified people. Like us, I suppose," he added after a moment's thought. "But the politicians will all be people who have fled the country, I'll bet. A friend of ours disappeared a few years ago and I guess he is in Russia or Cuba or somewhere."

"More likely in a British jail!" exclaimed Malachi. "It is the one thing Evans and me disagree about."

"Evans and *I* disagree about," interjected his friend. "You still have work to do on your English!"

Celine gave her tinkling laugh. "You boys are very funny, but I think you are good people. Maybe we shall meet from time to time on the InterEarthMove circuit - that would be nice. You are the only African men I know."

Malachi's heart missed a beat.

*

"She is very beautiful, Malachi, and very clever, and very sophisticated and five years older than you! And engaged to a Vietnam man."

"She never said 'engaged.' She just said 'my boyfriend.'"

"Let's look in the atlas, Malachi. I think Hong Kong is

about ten thousand miles from Jamesland. You'd better stick to Grace. She's beautiful and clever too. And same skin colour. You are missing her, that's why you fall for Celine."

"What has skin colour got to do with it? When we are free, we shall be able to have white girlfriends. I remember Dipra telling me. Or yellow ones."

"Malachi, Celine is leaving this weekend, back to Hong Kong, her new important job and her man. A different world from yours. Just concentrate on being good at *your* job. Make yourself worthy of Grace. You can be at the top level in Bishgad when it comes. Remember Dipra's Kilimanjaro."

"When it comes! I tired waiting. All these committees and reports about our constitution. Sometimes I think Dipra was right - we'll have to seize independence with guns, or never get it."

"Steady, Malachi! If guns are used, people will die or be crippled. And they won't all be white men. Guns breed hatred - and what we shall need most when we are free is the support of white men."

"Germans and French will help!"

"Yes, but they won't know us and understand us and ... love ... us the way the British do. Unless we use guns."

"Love?!"

"Yes, love. Why else are we here now? Hasn't our manager tried his best for us? Didn't he overlook our sleeping in the buckets until we were better off? The British will need us as much as we need them. InterEarthMove won't have a monopoly in Bishgad - but I'm sure they will be hoping we stay loyal to them. And I hope we will too."

*

Back at Heathrow, they were glad to see a few more black faces in the queue for their ticket desk. "Not many from home, though," commented Evans. "Mostly they will be going to Accra or Lagos, I'll bet."

Having passed into the airside lounge, they hunted for their gate number among the signs. "I can't see fifty-two anywhere.

I think the girl made a mistake." Malachi was his usual apprehensive self. But Evans was carefully scanning above the heads of the milling crowd in this huge concourse.

"There. Fifty to sixty-nine. I expect it's quite a long way. Better start walking." He led off, Malachi in close attendance. An announcement about their flight over the loudspeakers caused them   both to quicken their pace. They passed down a maze of walkways, sometimes seeing passengers arriving, walking in the opposite direction on the other side of glass walls. They were doing this, with Malachi constantly checking the overhead notices, when they passed Dipra Forfpi travelling inward.

"Dipra!" shouted Malachi. He banged on the glass and walked back to stay level, causing some confusion to the traffic flow. The man may or may not have heard him through the heavy glass but he certainly inclined his head the other way and carried on walking.

"It *was* Dipra!" Malachi insisted to Evans. "I'm sure it was! We should run back and catch him."

"Yes, I think it probably *was* Dipra. But I think he did not want to be recognised. We'd never catch him anyway; and how could we get back through immigration?   And even if we did, we'd never find him in the crowds. Come on Malachi, we don't have much time."

"Why should he not want me to recognise him?" demanded Malachi, hurrying to keep abreast.

"Don't know. He might think - he might be travelling under a false identity. We don't know anything about him, where he's coming from, what he's up to."

They reached Gate 52, which was steadily filling with passengers. Malachi was still agitated.

"Listen," said Evans, to comfort his friend, "I think Dipra probably did see you but needed to avoid you. We must leave it to him to contact us when he's ready. Did you notice how very smartly dressed he was?"

"No smarter than us, man!"

"No, perhaps not, for today, because we're in our best.

Something about him tells me he wears suits like that every day."

*

They gave the manager the letters from the British head office. He read them carefully, looking up from time to time. "Well, it seems you have given a good account of yourselves. These reports are excellent. You seem to have worked well and found your way in a new country and a new culture. Well done. I have good news for you both. From the first of next month you will be in full charge of the air compressors section, Evans and you Malachi will take over the bought ledger. All right?"

"Great!" said Evans, "Thank you, Sir."

"Very good," said Malachi. "Will there be an increase?"

The manager smiled. "Yes, of course. You will each get two thousand shillings a month."

They were silent for a moment, overwhelmed by such figures.

"Of course," added the manager, "you will have to pay tax out of that. But it should improve your lifestyle. You still share a flat?"

"Yes, Sir."

"Good. For your job, Evans, you will need a car. I could insist you keep it in the yard, but I think I can trust you to be sensible so I will let you keep it at home. Then Malachi can share it in the evenings. But if I hear of you quarrelling over it, I shall take it back. Understood?"

Malachi nodded vigorously. "No problem, Sah. Evans and me good friends."

Evans smiled. "Thank you, Sir. You have been good to us."

"I want to see you two moving up the ladder so you're ready when independence comes. It will be some years, but I rather think it is inevitable. Work hard and be honest. No more market trading, Malachi, you are beyond that now. In ten years time either of you could be sitting behind this desk, if you keep your noses clean and hard up against the grindstone. Right, off you go!"

They left. "What grindstone does he mean, Evans?"

*

A few months later a small paragraph in the Henry City Recorder caught Evans's attention.

London: Police sources yesterday confirmed that they had arrested a group of men in Brighton, a seaside resort on the south coast of England, thought to be associated with a rebel movement in Jamesland. Immigration officials had become suspicious when one young man entered UK on a clearly forged visa. They informed the Special Branch who tracked the man to a hotel in Brighton where he rendezvoused with a number of known political dissidents. Police kept careful observation for some weeks, then raided the hotel and detained six men in all. They have yet to be charged.

He read it to a stunned Malachi.

"You think that was Dipra?"

"Highly probable. It would explain why he turned away from us. We have to wait now for some more reports to be sure."

But the manager was ahead of them, summoning them to his office. "Did either of you meet Dipra Forfpi while you were in England?"

"We thought we saw him but not to meet. He was going in at Heathrow as we were leaving. We saw him through a glass wall, but he didn't acknowledge us. Perhaps it wasn't him. Why do you ask, Sir?"

"You haven't seen this item?" He handed over a British newspaper, which Malachi took and scanned. An indistinct photo of four of the men, clearly taken from undercover at long range dominated page five. Evans peered over his shoulder, gave a shrug of resignation and turned to the manager.

"Yes, Sir, one of them does look like Dipra. But we can't even be quite sure it was Dipra we saw. He was past in a flash and he turned away when Malachi shouted. Of course he may not have heard."

"Well, I'm glad he didn't. Because I'll bet my pension it

was him, and that he's the young man in this report. He always was a hothead. You don't know what he's been doing these last few years?"

They shook their heads.

"No postcards from sunny Tripoli? Or snowy Moscow?"

"No word, Sir."

"Good. Look, I know he was your friend, but he's trouble and you're better off without him, at least for the next few years. Get yourselves senior positions here and if he does wind up as a minister or something, he'll be glad to have you on his side then."

Evans was astonished. "You think he might do that, sir?"

"In politics, my son, anything is possible and impossible things are probable. Now, how many compressors can we put on the by-pass project, Evans?"

*

Dipra Forfpi soon hit the headlines again. All six men were charged with conspiracy to undermine Her Majesty's Administration in Jamesland, by shipping in seditious material printed in various East European countries. In court, Forfpi was defiant, claiming to be a freedom fighter, not a terrorist.

"We fight till my country is free of the barbarous yoke of British government," he is reported to have said from the dock.

The Recorder's circulation almost doubled. There was much hilarity in Henry City, among both black and white, about the barbarous yoke and what a barbarous joke it was.

Even InterEarthMove's manager enjoyed it. "Come in, Evans, put on this barbarous yoke and order another twelve compressors from UK will you, please?"

Evans smiled. "Dipra was always a bit dramatic, Sir."

"Well, he's going to be cooling his heels in a British jail now for at least a couple of years. Then I expect they'll let him out and put him on the negotiating team for your independence."

"Only two years? And you really think they might put him on the Bishgad team, Sir, after a conviction like that?"

"Bunch of naughty children, Evans, caught drawing plans on the backs of envelopes. But give Dipra ten years to grow up and he'll be President. I should go into the astrology business. Have you got *our* plans for next year completed yet?"

*

Dipra got five years. The manager comforted Malachi by explaining the curious system in England where five years probably meant four and with good behaviour it could be even less.

"Good behaviour, Sir?"

"Just means doing what he's told, eating up all his dinner and keeping his cell clean. He might get a job in the library, or on one of the prison farms. Or he might play a lot of snooker and table tennis. It wouldn't surprise me if they transferred him to an open prison after a bit."

"How can you have an open prison? Won't the prisoners all run away?"

"If they did and were caught again they would be facing much longer sentences in proper prisons. No, Open Prison people don't run away. It's usually for prisoners convicted of fraud or embezzlement or some other non-violent crime. If the authorities want to talk to these people about the future of this colony they may well soften them up with civilised treatment."

Six months later The Recorder was able to report that Dipra and his colleagues had indeed been transferred to an open prison. Unconfirmed stories suggested that high-ranking civil servants had visited them there and that even the next Governor of Jamesland had visited before taking up his post. When approached, the present Governor was unable to comment. He had very much enjoyed his time in Jamesland and now looked forward to a leisurely retirement in Hertfordshire with more time to pursue his watercolour work, though he would certainly miss the many exotic flowers in the Mansion Garden.

The new Governor was rather more forthcoming. He called a press conference soon after his arrival, to explain that her Majesty's Government was looking carefully at all the options for the future of Jamesland and would have discussions with many interested parties to ensure a smooth handover of responsibility in perhaps five or ten years time.

"It is of course very important to ensure that we leave behind a secure economy in the hands of properly qualified people and a democratic system which is free and fair. To this end I shall soon be announcing a scheme to enable twenty of Jamesland's brightest students each year to take up places at British universities for three year undergraduate courses in selected subjects."

"They will all come from Karle Mo Grammar," said Malachi contemptuously. "All good book boys."

"You and I are book boys, Malachi, that's what the foreman called me. No, I'm sure they'll spread the net wider than one school, however good it is."

"You want to go?"

"Maybe, but I'm not at all sure. We are doing so well here, it would be a difficult decision. Even if we did get the chance."

"Perhaps I could get a degree in economics." Malachi was suddenly enthusiastic. "Nobody else in Jamesland has one. They can't run a government with three doctors and five lawyers. And no engineers - you should go for it, Evans."

"I'm not sure. But I certainly wouldn't argue with your going if you want to. But are you going to leave Grace for three years?"

Malachi's face fell. "I could come back from time to time." A new thought struck him. "I could marry her and take her with me. She can earn money as a nurse in England."

"Wait and see, my friend. You don't even know she *will* marry you." He held up a hand to stem the protest. "Sorry, Malachi but you don't actually *know* till you ask her. Especially if you're going off to London. And anyway you have no idea who will be offered these scholarships yet. Or what the terms will be. They might only allow younger people. Or single people. You'd better just keep watching the papers for more news."

Malachi nodded morosely. "Life never simple."

"Come on, cheer up, Malachi, we've got a better life than we've ever had, with our flat, the car, good jobs and money for the pictures. I think we will both do well if we keep on like this, whatever happens to these scholarships. Or to Jamesland."

*

Grace was trying to persuade Evans to join Malachi and herself for their usual Saturday evening out at the Kakadu where they could dance under the stars and enjoy a good meal quite cheaply. And she would get Mercy to come too.

"Mercy? She is not married yet?"

"No, she's waiting for you, little man!" Grace was forever teasing him.

"That I know is not true. We agreed a long time ago. Still, I haven't seen the nasty foreman for a long time. OK, I enjoy Mercy's company, anyway. If she'll come, I'll come. But not without her. I'm not coming to play gooseberry."

"Play gooseberry?" queried Malachi.

"An expression I learned from Celine. Don't know why, but it means being the third, odd man out."

"And just who is Celine?" demanded Grace.

"Did he never tell you about the lovely Celine? The Hong Kong girl who showed us all over London?" Evans grinned as he observed Malachi's crestfallen face.

"It's all right, Grace. She was just a lady in our hostel and we agreed to tour London together one Saturday. An older lady, very senior in the company but as new to London as we were. No competition for you!"

FOUR

The Kakadu was throbbing and they could hardly hear each other. Evans momentarily wondered about the effect of the noise on nearby houses. Perhaps the occupants all came to the Kakadu anyway, especially on Friday nights. Or perhaps they all threw barbecues in their gardens and danced to the music coming over the walls.

They filled their plates at the buffet and returned to their table, Grace making a great point about the seating arrangements being boy, girl, boy, girl. It was a very small table, leading to much hilarity about "playing kneesy" underneath. For most of the evening they danced in the African manner, each individually yet as part of a team, but later they danced in couples, Malachi with Grace and Evans with Mercy.

Grace and Mercy went off to the Ladies and the two boys to the Gents. As the girls returned, Grace hesitated before sitting down, took Evans by the arm and said, "Come on, let's mix it."

Evans looked at Malachi for permission but was forestalled by Mercy who crooked her arm ready for Malachi to take it. As they hit the floor, Evans queried Grace. "Is this some kind of plot?"

"Don't be silly! I just want to know all about this Celine."

"Nothing to know, Grace. We told you, she was a Hong Konger - if that's what you call them - going to be Area Marketing Manager for InterEarthMove for a large area of the Far East. Clever, she speaks about six languages, because of her mixed parentage."

"And you both fell for her!"

He smiled. "She was lovely, lively, charming, very well educated and about twenty years older than us!"

"Twenty?" They turned just in time to avoid crashing into a table.

"All right, ten perhaps. Five even. We never knew. How can you judge age in another culture? I can't even tell how old European expatriate wives are, they never seem old enough to have children of nine and ten."

"How old am I, Evans?"

He wondered momentarily where this was leading. "I've never asked Malachi. But I guess - from your Highers days - and life in the buckets -" She blushed a little. "You must be about twenty-seven." He pretended to duck.

She grinned. "Not bad. And you are twenty-six?"

"Yes."

"And Mercy thirty-one."

The music stopped but Evans delayed her on the floor. "Grace, what's all this talk about ages? It's never bothered me, or Mercy. Are you plotting again?"

"No." She paused. "Have you had a woman yet, Evans?"

*

They left the Kakadu and called the last, dilapidated two-door Nissan taxi from the rank. Evans held open the single door and pushed forward the front seat for the girls to squeeze in behind. He joked with Malachi: "Lucky me gets in the back with both girls and you share the front with the driver."

Then he saw the gun in the driver's hand. "Your friend can walk!"

The taxi screeched away, the open door swinging shut with the impetus and the driver shouting at the top of his voice. "You move and I crash the car. He waved the gun across his shoulder at Evans. "I let the girls out in a minute. You, bookboy, I got plans for."

They sat uncomfortably rigid on the back seat. Mercy said: "I nursed you back to health all those years ago. You can drive a car now. What have you got against us?"

He ignored her. "You had dis nurse yet, bookboy?"

"No. She is not my lover, just a friend."

The driver continued in silence, while Evans wondered whether an opportunity might arise to tackle him. Perhaps if they ran into traffic and he had to stop. On an open stretch of road, the driver turned to look at them, the car wandering across the lanes.

"Keep your eye on the road, man."

"Maybe you have her tonight, eh? I watch you. Den I cut you and you know what you missing for rest of life. Like me wid de fingers."

He pulled the car off the road, along a muddy track. And brought it to a shuddering halt, leaping out of the door with the gun still waving at them. "Get out!"

They extricated themselves from the tiny car through the passenger door. "Go over there!" They followed his instruction.

"OK. Now you," he indicated Mercy, "lie down and take off knickers."

"No!"

He fired a shot at her feet. Both girls screamed.

"Man, this is inhuman!" shouted Evans.

"You rather have the other one? " He turned to Grace. "You want bookboy? He yours if I say so."

Grace's mouth opened but no words escaped.

"Shut up, you swine!" Evans was incensed. "Have you no humanity left? All because of a silly accident years ago?"

The driver's response was another shot into the ground, close to Mercy's feet. "One of you get down for him! I give you five... Five, four, three..."

In a sudden overwhelming rage Mercy leapt forward to attack their tormenter. "Let us go, let us go..."

He tried to push her away and saw Evans converging on him too. There was another, curiously muffled, shot and Mercy collapsed at his feet.

The driver stepped back. "I warned you!" he screamed at Evans. "Get back!"

"But she is wounded, you fool!"

"I no fool, bookboy, I am the foreman here."

But Grace was already crouching over the inert Mercy.

"She is not just wounded," she said in a quiet voice. "Mercy is dead." She looked up at the driver. "You have murdered her, you ungrateful bully!" And with that she flew at him, pounding at his face and pushing him off balance.

As he fell, Evans launched himself on top, smashing his wrist against the ground so that the gun fell free. Evans kicked it away. "Grace, get the gun!"

She retrieved it and handed it to him.

"Are you quite certain Mercy is dead?"

"Certain." The tears streamed down her face and her body shook with grief. "My good friend is dead. She saved his hand and he took her life."

Evans put his free arm around her. "Sshh.. Try to keep calm, Grace. Go for the police and an ambulance. I will keep this beast here until you come back."

*

The police Sergeant and his constable were suspicious. Was this just a lover's tiff? Evans was holding the gun. How did they know it was not he that fired the shot?

"It was, it was!" shouted the driver. "He killed her and now tries to blame me! She was my girl, nursed my hand better when dis man make me lose t'ree fingers. I love her, now he kill her."

Grace protested. "Lies, all lies. He tried to make Mercy...." She could not continue.

"We would like to explain to a senior police officer, please." Evans was taking control. "We need to have my friend Malachi Goodwill with us too. You can ask Mr. MacDonald, the manager of InterEarthMove for references for us. Can we all go back to the station?"

The constable looked to his Sergeant for guidance.

"Handcuff dis man to the girl and yourself to him," he indicated the driver, still lying on the ground.

"How we go sit for car?"

"You four squeeze in back. I drive. Where de keys?"

The constable indicated the car. The Sergeant sighed. "How many times I have to tell you, always bring keys? Get on with it."

They were kept waiting on a narrow bench at the station, still in their handcuffs, while every other policeman came out to have a look at their colleague Amos and this strange group who had killed one of their number.

Eventually Malachi arrived, full of questions. They began to explain until the Sergeant saw them and bellowed at his duty constable, "Keep them apart! They can be making up a story! Take this one," indicating Malachi, "and put him for office. This one in a cell; Amos, you take him. The boy and girl can remain here still handcuffed."

Malachi protested. "But I have done nothing wrong! You can't lock me up!"

"Shut up," said the Sergeant. "We not locking you up. You may be witness. We get the Super soon."

Chief Superintendent James Holland listened carefully as the Sergeant told him the story. "Where is the body now?"

"In Karle Mo Hospital, sah. The woman outside claims to be a doctor and she says her friend was a senior nurse there."

"Right, I want to talk to her first."

Grace was seriously upset. Holland called for tea and added plenty of sugar. She steadied her hands with a supreme effort and sipped at it as she explained the relationships between the four and the driver. Malachi was her boyfriend. Evans was his best friend, whom she'd known for years. Mercy was.... had been.... a very good friend and colleague in Karle Mo. Evans had joined them for foursomes before.

Gently, Holland led her into an account of the evening's happenings. This was an educated young woman, of good family. But she was holding something back, he knew. Probing carefully he went back over the shooting incident. Why was Mercy so incensed at that particular point? Grace hung her head.

"It is too shameful."

"Did he assault her? These things happen, you know. You should know, you are a doctor. Was he insulting?"

The story poured out in a barely discernible mumble. The shots had unnerved them all. Only Mercy had the courage-

"Or sufficient rage," Holland interjected. "That will do for now, Miss Endoman. I want you to wait in the reception area for now. I will arrange more tea for you."

Evans was next in. Holland looked at him keenly. "I have seen your picture in the newspapers, haven't I, Mr. Watanero? What was it about?"

"Malachi and I were sent to England on a training course for InterEarthMove a while back. We were the first to go from here and we have quite important jobs now. Our manager has helped us a lot."

"Duncan MacDonald?"

"Yes, Sir. I am Division Manager for compressors and Malachi manages the Bought Ledger."

Holland was impressed. "Yes, I think I may have heard Duncan mention you. Now, tell me what happened tonight. Start with an accident five years ago."

"Grace told you about that?"

"She did. But I want to hear your story. And remember I can check it with Mr. MacDonald."

Evans gave a calm account of events, the accident, and the previous threat.

"I thought it had all gone away, it was so long ago. Then tonight..." He paused for a moment and took a deep breath to gather control again. "I think he was waiting for us. Maybe he has waited for weeks. Maybe he waited at the front of the taxi queue and let others go until he saw us."

"Conjecture, my son, but we can talk to some of the other drivers perhaps. Go on. Why did he leave Malachi?"

"Too many people perhaps. He only knew Mercy and me but I had put the two girls in the back, so he had no choice but to take the three of us."

Evans reported events as if he were writing a report on the mechanical condition of a compressor. Holland could almost hear the subheadings, the scene, the orders, the varied reactions.... "I blame myself for not having a go at him earlier."

"And you would be lying on a mortuary slab instead of her. Or possibly all three of you. No, you were in the grip of events; I have little doubt of that. With training, you could have spread yourselves around him, but I don't suppose survival training is included in InterEarthMove's book. You were not in love with Mercy, then?"

"No, Sir. We were good friends, I liked her and she was fun, witty...."

"Grace?"

Evans hesitated. "My best friend's girl. Not for me."

Holland let it go. It wasn't relevant to his enquiry, he decided. Malachi next, before he talked to the suspect. The suspect didn't seem to be in their class. His story about Mercy being his girlfriend seemed pretty unlikely.

Malachi was still indignant at his treatment. Bit of a firebrand, Holland decided. Patiently he extracted a similar story to Evans's. Malachi was astounded when the taxi just pulled away. There wasn't another taxi to chase them in; that was the last on the rank at the time. He had walked to the nearest police station to report it. They hadn't believed him because he was just a little – well, he'd had a few drinks. But just as he was giving up and going to leave they got a phone call and pulled him back. He knew the driver was a madman. Poor Mercy, such a nice girl, and Grace's best friend.

He wasn't that upset, concluded Holland. Now if it had been Grace? No, Malachi was more interested in career than people. He'd probably go far. These two might well be the future of Jamesland, or of Bishgad if that ever came to life.

The driver was brought in and sat down. Holland searched his face in silence for several minutes. "How could you drive a car with a gun?" he suddenly asked.

"I got plastic fingers, gives me good grip on wheel." He held up his right hand to demonstrate, wriggling the digits.

"But you couldn't fire a gun with those."

"No, I use left hand...." In a moment of recognition, he jerked to his feet. "You trick me!"

"Sit down, Mr. Adunbi."

*

"Murder is very difficult to prove in this case," said Chief

46

Superintendent Holland. "It is true that he threatened to kill you, Mr. Watanero, but he didn't actually do it. He killed Mercy, whom he had no intention of killing. The correct charge will be manslaughter, but I'm inclined to think that he was not of sound mind; that the loss of his fingers had deranged him and he spent years nursing a terrible grievance against you, which gradually corroded his spirit.

"If we were in England there would be a great trial with expert barristers and conflicting medical opinions, which would drag on for weeks. For once, gentlemen, you may be glad we are in a simple colony where justice is less complicated. A judge will almost certainly commit him to protective custody for life, that is, to a secure mental hospital."

*

Duncan MacDonald was relieved that his two protégés were totally exonerated of blame in the "affair of the mad taxi driver" as the press quickly christened it. He urged them to get on with their careers as if nothing had happened.

"How is Grace taking it now?"

Malachi was concerned. She seemed more distant, distracted. No, this wasn't the time to be whooping it up in the Kakadu but surely they might go to the cinema occasionally? But she was working harder than ever at Karle Mo, long hours, often covering for friends. She seemed to be drowning herself in work.

After six months of this, Malachi discussed it with her father.

"I am really concerned now, Dr. Endoman. You must see how hard she is working in the hospital. Can't you persuade her to relax a little? Change her shifts perhaps?"

The good doctor had no influence on the shift patterns in Accident and Emergency. He was the Orthopaedic consultant. Grace was also studying to become a consultant in orthopaedics. That was taking much of her time. Still he did realise she needed a break.

"Why don't you ask her to marry you, Malachi? Isn't that

what you want? I am sure you can afford it now, and if you were married you would have each other's company without taking her away too much from her studies. You would both be happier."

Malachi discussed the idea with Evans, who was cautious with his advice.

"Yes, you can certainly afford to be married now and with Grace's salary you could probably live very well. But is it too soon after Mercy? You told me she seemed a little distant lately. You haven't been out much recently. Perhaps she is still grieving too much. I don't know, Malachi. I can't really advise you."

But the idea began to grow on Malachi. A flat of their own. Grace had been his girlfriend for six years now. What difference would it make, being married? Only more comfortable. They would spend their evenings discussing each other's day's work. No more begging for an evening together, no more taxis across town to her home when Evans needed the car. They could plan their lives around each other. And a married man would command greater respect in the business. "I was telling my wife the other day..." sounded good. "My wife is a great cook."

It was another fortnight before Grace would grant him an evening. They would see the picture at the Orion, the new one about the family in Yorkshire. It was romantic, touching, all the papers said. People came out with tears of happiness on their faces, he read. Just what he would need. Grace was reluctant to give up an evening's study, but she had also read about the film and she would go. He was like a puppy, frisking around her when he collected her from Karle Mo.

The film worked beautifully. She was so moved she cried into his shoulder before they even left the cinema. A quiet coffee was called for, in his own flat, which Evans had discreetly agreed to vacate for the evening. He put on some mood music and made the coffee in the new percolator they had just invested in. Grace approved the aroma and was impressed with the hot milk routine. They settled back on the sofa.

"Grace," he began. "We have been going together now for nearly seven years, you know? I have been loyal to you all that time, because I really do love you. Isn't it time we were married?"

"Married?" She looked startled.

"Of course. Don't tell me you are surprised. I want us to have our own flat, to have you with me every night. Evans teased you about Celine, I remember, but you knew really you had nothing to worry about. Please marry me. I know your father would approve."

"My father?" A huge cloud gathered on her face. "You have discussed this with my father?"

"Not discussed. I told him I was going to ask you. He was keen. He thinks it would be good for you, help you to relax a little."

She was on her feet now. "You men, you think you can tell us what to do with our lives. We have never talked of marriage. Maybe I just want to be a very good doctor, like you want to be a top businessman. Maybe marriage is not for me at all. Certainly not with you, Malachi. You are busy telling me there are no other women in your life, but I'm not sure. And how you know there are no other men in mine? We don't know each other very well these days, Malachi."

He recoiled. "But I thought it was understood we would be together. Before now, I could not afford it. Now I earn more money than you do. Are you saying there *is* another man?"

"No, I'm not. But if there were, you wouldn't know. Yes, I have been with you since I was a girl, but that was just a foolish affair. We have grown apart, with our jobs. And mine is as important as yours, even if it is not so well paid. I love my work so much I think I have to marry another doctor, someone who understands. Or someone quieter, like Evans. Where is he, tonight, without the car?"

"Evans? You have a thing for Evans? Well, he doesn't think of you! He stayed out tonight to give us space. Forget Evans."

"Will you take me home please? My answer is no. Maybe

I should pay for my cinema ticket."

"Maybe you should! If I take you home now, we finished. I am not begging any more. You keep me dangling for too long. Try your luck with Evans, but you'll get nowhere." He stormed out of the room, shouting over his shoulder, "Come on, get yourself in the car."

They made the journey in complete silence.

*

"Have you been seeing my Grace?" Malachi had been waiting up for Evans for an hour.

"Seeing her? What do you mean?"

"She turned me down. Said you might be better for her. She was mad that I discussed marriage with her father."

Evans was shaken. He remembered some odd remarks of Grace's. Surely she didn't ... "It's nonsense Malachi. You know it is. I did warn you she might not be ready. But it's nothing to do with me. We have never met without you being there. I hope you haven't spoiled your chances for ever."

"I don't know. Maybe I have. We got any beers in the fridge?"

"It's gone midnight, Malachi, and you said you had to have your budget figures ready by noon tomorrow. Beer is not a good idea."

"Beer is a very good idea, the way I feel. I'll look myself."

Evans shrugged. "I'm off to bed. Take it easy Malachi. If you can't get Grace back, there are other cats in the forest."

FIVE

Duncan MacDonald had already overstayed his original plans by some years. The earlier idea that he should spend his last five years back at the company's HQ seemed to have got lost in the bureaucracy. His company, a tiny part of the world wide InterEarthMove empire but one the Board thought had considerable growth potential, was growing nicely, his salary was rising – and along with it his final pension – so he had not been inclined to make a fuss about it. Jamesland had its compensations, like year-round golf, tennis and a decent cultural and social circuit. His wife enjoyed the warm climate and occupied herself with part time teaching and sundry charitable works.

But Independence loomed. It had seemed rather slow coming, but it could not be long now.

So the letter from London suggesting he might like to take early retirement on advantageous terms had not been entirely unwelcome.

Duncan MacDonald now made a curious decision; he even wondered himself, after the act, if it had been a wise move. Having informed London that he would accept their offer he called Evans and Malachi into the office.

They stood before his desk, directly under the ceiling fan, which had not moved for months. MacDonald was a stoic who seldom worried about creature comforts while he was working. An open window provided sufficient breeze and had the advantage that he could hear what was going on in the yard. But he was never impolite.

"Sit down gentlemen. I'm going to tell you something ahead of everyone else in the company, because I believe it will affect you two almost more than any other member of staff."

"However I have first to tell you that I haven't been happy about the relationship between you lately. What's wrong, do you still share a flat?"

"We do still share, sir." Evans stared ahead.

"Girl trouble between you?"

"Yes." "No." They spoke simultaneously.

"Which is it, then? Look, you have to learn to keep any trouble out of the office. Your progress in this company depends upon it. And on each other. I can understand you missing Mercy, Evans-"

"Not that, Sir, Malachi imagines I put Grace off him. I didn't. I have nothing to do with her. She turned him down."

"Because you interfered..."

"Quiet, the pair of you. This isn't the Marriage Guidance Council. Keep it out of your work. I have been rather proud of you until now; you have both been doing so well. And I want to hand you over with confidence."

"Hand us over, sir?"

"To your new manager. That's what I want to tell you. I'm leaving in about six months. But that, for the time being, is top secret. London have offered me slightly early retirement on very good terms, because it suits their personnel promotion plans."

They were agog, fearful. MacDonald had been with them all their working lives. Their guardian and benefactor. Always a little distant but helpful, encouraging.

"Who will the new man be, sir?"

"Woman, Malachi. You have to give her the same respect you give me, of course. She is very talented, has a great reputation in the company. You may even have met her in UK when you were there. I understand the dates of her last course partly overlapped with yours. Her name is Celine Brandt. Did you?"

Evans recovered first. "We did, sir. We toured London with her. She is very clever, very beautiful."

A smile crossed MacDonald's face. "She can't help that, Evans. It is her brains and determination she's being promoted for. In Hong Kong she's been responsible for marketing across a wide region. Jamesland will be her first taste of general management. She'll probably be on a three-year contract.

"Nick Barmby will be coming home with me, he'd already

planned to leave at the end of this tour, because it's a good point for him to make a move, but he doesn't know I'll be going too. So you, Evans, will report directly to Miss Brandt for the operational side.

"I shall recommend that Joseph keeps working with you because I know he respects you and will not be upset about you being promoted beyond him. Malachi, you will take over the sales ledger as soon as I make my announcement, alongside your present responsibilities, plus all the buying and importing. You'll have to work very closely with Evans, but you'll report to the chief accountant. Keep it clean, Malachi, or Roger Waddell will be on to you. Now, not a word of this until I announce it all formally."

"But how long will that be, Sir?" Evans could hardly believe his ears.

"Probably a couple of months. Keep it to yourselves until then. And for goodness sake, forget any disputes between the two of you and put your back into the work. Right. Off you go. And good luck to you both."

Outside the office Malachi questioned Evans. "Why does he tell us ahead of the others? Is this some kind of trap?"

"I think it's a test, Malachi. He's told us we can have great futures, but he's put us on trial by giving us early warning. If we break that confidence, he might withdraw those plans."

*

A long ten weeks followed until MacDonald made his announcement. Evans and Malachi feigned the surprise they knew was expected of them. But they felt a curious pride that they'd known all along and not divulged a word. A pride that MacDonald shared in.

"Well, you passed the test, boys, you've earned your promotion. You'll need a lot more of that discretion as you become senior managers."

*

"Evans! I hoped it might be you meeting me. Is Malachi still with you?"

Celine Brandt was as excited as a schoolgirl about her new position in a new and strange country. She chattered about the deserts over which she had flown, about the great river deltas emerging from rainforests, about the mud huts they passed with women outside pounding something in big wooden bowls - "What are they doing, Evans?"

He smiled. "Yams, perhaps. Could be rice or wheat. Mr. MacDonald will meet us at your hotel."

"And you will be my number two! This time it must be you and Malachi who show me around. Remember London? I found it fascinating."

"I remember, with pleasure." He skilfully skirted around a donkey cart while she shrank back in her seat. "There are not many Chinese in Henry City. But I expect you have been warned about that. A few restaurants are springing up. I think your people are looking forward to our independence and getting in early!"

"Oh, I shan't worry. I have two good friends here already. Malachi couldn't get away?"

He nodded silently and she looked at him closely. "You two not friends any more?"

"Not the very best of friends. We still share a flat." He paused while she waited expectantly.

"It's OK. Just a little misunderstanding. Nothing to worry about."

Celine cocked her head on one side. "I can't have two senior managers engaged in a civil war, Evans. What caused this 'misunderstanding?'"

Evans negotiated a roundabout in silence, before giving in.

"His girl turned him down and he blames me - but he was wrong. He should have known I wasn't seeing her. But it's all in the past now. Anyway, Malachi can tell you his own story. I am looking forward to working with you, Miss Brandt."

"Celine, you ninny! Just because I'm the boss doesn't mean we can't be friends. I shall rely on you and Malachi, Evans. Please don't let this personal dispute affect your work. My appointment is important for several reasons. One, it shows women can make it to top positions."

"That will be a major problem for you here in Jamesland, Celine, getting people to accept a woman as the boss."

"I can handle that, Evans. The second point is that it will be the first InterEarthMove company in Africa to be left to run without Brits. Well, at senior level, only one Brit anyway. It is just as important for *you* to succeed as it is for me. You do see that?"

"Yes. I shall do my best."

"Maybe you should think of marrying; it would give you extra gravitas - you still look so young. Malachi's girl wasn't keen on you, by chance?"

He pondered this. "No. No girl in my life yet. Too busy with work and study. Anyway, you haven't married!"

She laughed. "Touché!"

She saw the puzzled look and explained: "French word, acknowledging a hit in fencing, but used in English for verbal scoring. No, I haven't married. Too busy with work and studying! But I think Hong Kong society may be more easygoing than Jamesland. I suspect a man in your society ought to be married to establish his status. Not so?"

"In general, yes. This is your hotel. We'll find Mr. MacDonald in the lounge, I hope. You'll like him - he's been a very good manager."

"Well, I hope you'll be saying that about me in three years time!"

*

Malachi was not as keen on Celine as he had been in London. A glamorous companion in London was one thing; a female boss at work was another. And he wasn't as close as Evans, who was a rank up on him now.

Celine understudied MacDonald for two weeks before taking over and he stayed on for another two weeks as her adviser. She got Evans to organise a proper farewell party for Mr. MacDonald, with all the staff. They had a collection and bought him a large copper wall plate and a scroll on which were written all their names.

"Make sure everyone is on there, Evans, even the yard sweepers. It has to come from *all* the staff, even if they can only contribute a few coppers." Celine knew about good personnel relations. It was rumoured she had slipped the odd small note to the lowest paid so that they *could* contribute, but no-one was admitting it.

The party was an emotional affair. MacDonald had been a strict but fair manager all his career and he was well respected. Evans and Malachi had particular debts and both felt his departure keenly. But they were not the only ones with tears streaming down cheeks as MacDonald made his final speech.

The copper plate was duly presented to "our manager" and a huge bouquet to his wife. Celine led the clapping to bring the little ceremony to a close.

"What is it about British managers?" she asked Evans later. "I have seen scenes like that in Hong Kong too. As if you were all losing your father. Will they lose a mother when I leave do you think?"

"That depends on how good a manager you prove to be," said Evans. "I think you have started well. Everybody likes you. Some of the men are rather dazzled by your beauty. Maybe you should...."

"Yes?"

"Well..."

"Wear shapeless clothes and no make-up?"

He summoned his courage and faced her squarely. "Skirts without the slit, or trousers would be good, and your hair tied back perhaps."

She laughed. "What an old fuddy duddy you are, Evans! But I can see you may be right. I'll give it some thought. I'm glad *you* aren't dazzled by my beauty! Hasn't it occurred to you that *all* Hong Kong girls look like this? It's the attraction of an exotic race. Trouble is, it can easily turn into *dis*traction. And I need to be friends with female staff too. OK. Keep telling me home truths, Evans. I need one man I can absolutely rely on. You will make a good number two."

*

Celine moved into MacDonald's old bungalow and carefully took control of the company. For six months she did little but continue the existing systems, observe staff performances and monitor sales and expenses. Then she made her first bold move, albeit one not directly related to business.

With the coming of the hot season, she circulated a memo to senior staff that their wives and families were welcome to use the bungalow swimming pool on Monday, Wednesday and Friday afternoons, two till five, and they could come themselves in their holidays or when there was a public holiday.

Malachi was horrified. "Don't you know some of them have three wives and twelve kids?" he asked her. "You could at least suggest one wife at a time."

She consulted Evans. "Yes," he said. "Malachi has a point. It's a lovely gesture but - still, I don't suppose many of them swim anyway. It will be very popular for two weeks and then settle down to one or two families."

"But you may not be popular with other expatriates!" Malachi interjected.

"I'll meet that problem when it arises. So I don't need to send a new memo restricting it?"

"No." Evans was firm. "That would make it a big disappointment. Most of them will only want to see how you live. When their curiosity is satisfied they won't bother again."

"Thank you, oh wisest of advisers! Will you come yourselves? Bring a lady friend on the bank holiday Monday? I hear you are back in favour with Grace, Malachi."

She saw him glance at Evans. "You were seen in the market together last Saturday."

Malachi shrugged. "I could suggest it."

"Good. Evans?"

"I could come, but on my own."

She raised her eyebrows and cocked her head

57

interrogatively. "Not taking my advice yet, then." He smiled and Malachi wondered what the advice was.

*

Both Evans and Malachi proved correct in their forecasts of the reactions to Celine's offer. On the first Wednesday of the offer, hordes of women and children turned up, to the undisguised disgust of Amos, Celine's steward, who thought these people should not be allowed into a nice house. When Celine returned from work at 6.30 that evening there were still six mums lying around the poolside in their day clothes taking full advantage of the free cokes and some twenty children splashing about in the water, mostly in just their knickers, some completely nude. The pool was of an even depth and Celine had with some foresight reduced the water level to three feet for the occasion.

She quickly changed into a swimsuit and joined them, delighting in their joy, but finding it impossible to swim her customary twenty lengths. The mums, embarrassed now in the presence of the mistress, soon departed, dragging protesting children with them.

And on the Friday, the steward reported only four families had turned up.

"Why so few, today, Amos?"

"The Muslims cannot come, madam, and many of the others came just to peep inside the house. They will not come again."

"And everyone has gone now."

"Yes, madam, I tell them you like to swim when you come home. And I refill the pool to five feet ready for you," he added proudly.

Celine paused. Well, he was protecting her interests, she shouldn't fight it. "Thank you very much, Amos," she said, and he beamed.

For the Bank Holiday Monday, despite the promise of a free barbecue, only three staff families turned up, plus Malachi and Grace, and Evans on his own.

"You see," he said, "the novelty has worn off, but they will all be boasting for evermore that they were once your guests. It is enough."

Celine simply nodded, before going off to greet an older grey-haired and distinguished looking Chinese gentleman.

"This is Charles Teng, a friend of my father's," she introduced him to the boys. "He is the general manager of Hong Kong and Shanghai bank here."

"Sadly, you bank with Barclays DCO," Mr. Teng joshed them. "I keep mentioning our bank to your chief accountant but he seems to be wedded to a UK based bank. Why isn't he here today?"

"He has taken his family to Lombe National Park for the week-end," answered Celine.

" Maybe when you are the chief accountant," Mr. Teng joshed Malachi, "I will come calling again."

"Charles, you are not to talk shop at my party!" Celine jokingly admonished him. "I shall report you to my father!"

"Oh, no, please not that," he pretended horror. "He will have me barred from Happy Valley!"

She laughed, that tinkling laugh which reminded Evans so much of London.

"Happy Valley?" he queried when Teng had moved away.

"Hong Kong's top racing club. Horse racing. Very exciting, I wonder the British didn't bring it here."

"I don't think horses do well down here. But they could have done it in the North. Our people up there are famous horsemen. And I read they have camel racing in the Middle East. We could do that very well."

"Do make our other guests feel at home, Evans. Charles tells me that my swimming pool offer has put some expatriate noses out of joint, just as Malachi forecast, but it's done now and they'll soon have something else to moan about – or they'll go back to the perennial subject of unreliable servants! Anyway, people who come must be made welcome. Let's go and talk to Micah and Mrs. Adejunle, he's a very good storekeeper, isn't he?"

"The best," said Evans. "Perhaps we should tell that to his

wife. Is Mr.Teng not married?"

Celine looked at him rather curiously for a moment. "His wife died three years ago. Very sad for him, out here on his own. I try to bring him into society a bit, otherwise he'd sleep at the bank, I think. I go round and cook him a meal now and then and we listen to music. His taste is very classical …"

"So he's keen on you?"

"Evans, you don't understand our society. Yes, I think he is keen on me, but being a wife to a man of his generation would be like pure slavery for me. He has to accept me just as a helpful friend, whatever hints he drops to my father!"

"I apologise. It is not my concern. I hope Roger Waddell and his family enjoy the Park. The elephant population is recovering well now that the Wildlife Service has got a grip on the poaching business."

"Well, rather him than me in this heat. I think it's time I took a dip. You coming in, Evans?"

"I'm afraid I can't swim. Pathetic, isn't it?"

*

First thing on the Tuesday morning, Celine received a call from Chief Superintendent Holland. "There is a rather urgent matter I should like to discuss with you personally, Miss Brandt. May I come round?"

"Not very convenient, Chief Superintendent. We have our postponed Monday morning meeting just about to start. Can it wait till say eleven?"

James Holland was firm. "It would be better if you saw me now Miss Brandt. The matter may impact upon your meeting."

"Really? What can it be? Can't you give me an idea on the phone?"

"I can be with you in ten minutes. I take it you are in your office?"

"Yes. All right. I will put my meeting back an hour. See you soon."

The super was as good as his word.

"Coffee?" she offered. "No thank you. Please sit down,

Miss Brandt, I have unhappy news for you."

She sat and looked at him with lips slightly parted. "I am not easily upset, Mr. Holland. Tell it to me straight."

"Last night, on his journey back from Lombe National Park, Roger Waddell crashed his car into an abandoned lorry. I am sorry to have to tell you he died in Holy Martyr Hospital, Jamestown early this morning. Mrs. Waddell is severely injured and is being brought by ambulance to Karle Mo Hospital for surgery. The two children escaped serious injury but are obviously very shocked. They too are coming in the ambulance."

Celine was silent for several minutes while she contemplated the horror of it all. And the consequences. "What time is the ambulance expected here?"

"It has probably arrived by now. I was advised that surgery will take several hours. Could you perhaps help with the children?"

"Yes, of course, I'll get over there now. But I'm sure Roger and Jane had some good friends among the expatriate community here. I feel bad now that I didn't get to know them better myself. I'll ask my own staff and then perhaps around the Henry City Club. Don't *you* know their friends?"

"Afraid not. I'm a Bridge addict and they aren't in that scene. The Tennis Club might be your best bet. I hear Roger is – was – an ace." He rose to go.

"I shall have to complete an enquiry of course, but there's not much to go on. Another expatriate couple also visiting the park came across the wrecked car on their way home. They think he just hit the back end of the lorry sticking out into the road. Probably abandoned earlier in the day. No lights or markers of course. Typically irresponsible driver probably high on a weed." He sounded bitter. "I think you are better disciplined in Hong Kong."

Celine got up to show him out and found herself placing a comforting hand on his shoulder. "We shall look after the family, Mr Holland. Good luck with your investigations."

He brightened a little. "How are Evans and Malachi?"

"You know them?" She was surprised.

"Just a little adventure we all got involved in a couple of years back. Give them my regards." He climbed in beside his driver and was gone.

*

Malachi was charged with finding out what procedures were necessary for the shipping of the body back to England, while Evans accompanied Celine to the Tennis Club. Ignoring the battered 'Europeans Only' sign at the entrance, Celine led the doubting Evans into the main hall, to find its bar was shuttered and there wasn't a soul to be seen. The courts immediately outside the hall were similarly deserted.

"The families will be around the pool," she said. "Come on."

Sure enough, half a dozen young mums were splashing in the pool with kids and some older women were draped over sun-loungers absorbed in paperback novels. Celine approached one of these.

"I'm sorry to disturb you but could you perhaps tell me if the Waddell family have any particular friends here?"

The woman surveyed this slip of an Asiatic girl and the accompanying African. "You are not supposed to be in here," she addressed him. "This is a European Club."

Evans turned his head away and Celine ignored the taunt. "The Waddell family, who *are* Europeans, badly need some help and we have come to find their friends."

"The Waddells have their own pool. They come here only to play tennis. I believe he's the Club Champion. You might find Barbara over there knows them a bit; her husband plays too, I believe. But you," she turned her gaze on Evans, "should not be in here."

"Mr. Watanero is a valued member of my management team, working alongside Mr. Waddell," Celine spat back. "I will talk to the lady you indicated." And walked away.

'Barbara' acknowledged that she knew the Waddells, but they weren't close friends. "Although he's a damn good player, the family aren't great socialites. Why do they need help?"

Celine explained. Roger had been killed in a road accident, his wife was in Karle Mo and nurses there were looking after his kids.

"My God!" Barbara gasped. "A road accident. This place is too bloody dangerous to live. We aren't going any too soon!"

Celine was persistent. "There must be somebody in the British community who could help out?"

"Trouble is, my kids and I are due to fly home tomorrow. You could try the Vintners, they live next door to the Waddells. Angela Vintner isn't here this morning so she'll probably be at home. I take it you know the Waddell residence? George Vintner works for Chempharm."

"Thank you, yes, I'm Roger's MD. And Mr. Watanero here is a close colleague. We'll find the Vintner house. Have a good flight back to London." Celine swept away with Evans in her wake.

They located the Waddell bungalow and noted the sign for the Vintners next door. Celine drove up to the gates and the watchman challenged her.

"I have come to visit Mrs. Vintner," she said firmly, and he reluctantly swung one gate open. Celine waited and stared hard at him until he opened the other half.

Angela Vintner was sitting by her own pool reading as Celine approached, with Evans close by her side. A slight frown crossed her face but she managed a welcoming smile.

"Mrs. Vintner, I'm sorry to disturb you but wonder if I can ask you for some help for the Waddell family." Celine came straight to the point.

Puzzled, Angela asked, "What help do they need? Have they got stuck in the Game Park or something?"

"Worse, I'm afraid. They have been in a road accident. I'm sorry to have to tell you that Roger was killed, Mrs. Wadd-"

But she was interrupted by Angela's scream. "Killed?"

"I'm sorry, I'm sure it's a shock. Penny is in Karle Mo

63

undergoing major surgery, the kids are there too, but not badly hurt, except of course it will be a terrible shock."

The tears poured down Angela Vintner's face as she sobbed uncontrollably. Celine put a comforting arm around her while Evans watched in embarrassment. Gradually, Angela regained control.

"I must have the kids of course. I'll drive across to the hospital now. Will Penny be conscious? You must be Roger's boss, he's mentioned you."

"Yes, Celine Brandt, and this is Evans Watanero, our Operations Manager." Evans extended his hand, which Angela shook limply.

"Yes I've heard of you too. Roger was rather proud of your company and staff, Miss Brandt. My husband would often josh him about his views on Independence, if they ever get it, but Roger was a firm believer in local staff development.

"Would you like a lift or shall we go in convoy to the hospital?" suggested Celine.

SIX

Penny Waddell was still unconscious but the operation had been successful and the surgeon expressed his hope that she would make a good recovery, though he thought she might have a slight limp for the rest of her life. And she had yet to learn about the death of her husband.

"She will need a lot of comfort and rest for the next six weeks or so," he warned. "Will she get plenty of family support?"

"We don't know the situation in England, but the firm will help here. Where are the children, do you know?"

"We gave them a couple of shots to calm them when they arrived, but they'll be out of those by now. Their injuries were only minor. The nurses are looking after them. There's an annexe to the children's ward and you'll find them there."

"That is Grace's father," explained Evans as they walked away. "He doesn't know me, of course."

"You don't think Grace will have mentioned you at home?"

"Who knows? Probably not. If she has, Dr. Endoman senior hasn't made the connection."

The kids were beautiful – a little boy of three and his sister five, covered in iodine and sticking plaster. A long scar on the girl's head seemed the worst injury, exaggerated by the shaving of her hair away from it.

"Auntie Angela, is Mummy better? And where's Daddy?"

Angela's eyes filled with tears again. Celine looked at the nurses who shook their heads. Then she stooped down to put an arm around each child and ask in a low voice, "Do you know who I am?"

"Daddy's boss lady," offered the girl. "You're nice."

"And what are your names – Mary and ...?" She found her voice choking.

"Joseph!" said the little girl. "Mary and Joseph, just like in the Bible."

Celine hugged them more tightly while Angela put a hand

on her shoulder and Evans had to turn away to wipe the tears from his own cheeks.

"My name's Celine." She took a firm grip on her emotions. "I'm afraid your Daddy has gone a long way away and won't be back for a very long time."

Angela gave a small cry and fled from the room.

"You mean he's dead, don't you?" demanded Mary. "And he's *never* coming back!"

Celine could only nod, mute. Mary began to cry and Joseph joined her. Evans was moved to lay his hands on the little heads in sympathy.

"You still have your Mummy and you must be very brave for her," he murmured. "Your Daddy would have wanted that, I know."

Celine looked up at him in gratitude. "Now I think we all have to go home, maybe to my home, let's talk about it."

*

Penny Waddell plunged into a deep depression as soon as she heard the news of her husband's death and the doctors were concerned that this would delay her recovery. "The sooner you can get her back to England the better, Miss Brandt. Have you contacted her parents?"

"She is an orphan, but she has a sister, who is making a career in Hong Kong. I have asked my own contacts there to find her and I have offered to pay her flight out here – she can come via Johannesburg – then she can advise us what to do."

Angela Vintner felt she could not after all have the children staying with her. Her husband was not keen.

"But I thought they were good friends, your husband and Roger?" queried Celine.

"Yes, but it's not the same as having three and five year olds disrupting your life, is it? If you can have them staying at your place, I'll entertain them during the day and take them in to see Penny every day. It's only the evenings George would object to."

So Celine took in the children and Angela called round for

them every day at eight in the morning, delivering them back promptly at six in the evening, whether Celine was home or not. Her steward could take charge for half an hour, she reasoned.

The arrangement worked well for a few days, but inevitably Celine had a function coming up which would present a particular problem. She discussed it with Evans.

"Could you fill in for me, just for Thursday evening? I really ought to be at the Chamber of Industry's dinner. I hoped my friend Lilly might be able to do it but she has an engagement that evening too. Penny's sister will be coming from Hong Kong over this weekend, which will ease the situation, I hope."

Evans considered it. "The children hardly know me. But perhaps if I was to visit Mrs. Waddell at the same time as they do today."

"Good idea, Evans. Yes, go in at three this afternoon. Talk to Penny and Angela and the kids. I'm sure they'll love you."

He was terrified. This pretty European lady was sitting up in bed in a flimsy nightgown, her hair all dishevelled, her eyes still red from weeping. He was intruding; he had no right to be here. But the children chatted to him freely.

"You are not the one who works with my Daddy are you?" The girl was curious. "He has a funny name, I think it is Michael Good Wall."

"Malachi Goodwill," corrected Evans, "he is a good friend of mine, we share a flat."

"And your name is the same as a friend of mine, but she is Sally Evans."

"Yes, I have heard it is usually a family name in England. Here it can be a first name too. I'll bet you don't know any Watanero families in England."

Penny smiled. She liked to see her children relating to a man, even if he was an African. Roger had been full of praise for his Malachi and this Evans. The thought of Roger made the tears come again but she blinked them back and turned to Angela, who had been listening in silence.

Angela had been curiously distant, despite coming in every

day. The children seemed more of a burden than a pleasure, though in the past she had always enjoyed them, having none of her own. Penny wondered about that. Perhaps George was against kids; that was why Mary and Joseph had to live with Celine Brandt. Thank God for Roger's colleagues, whatever race they were. But she did look forward to her sister June's arrival.

*

The children had an uproarious time with Evans the evening he was in charge. In the hot humid evening they wanted to swim. He was ashamed to admit he couldn't.

"Anyway," he said, "I don't have any swimming things."

"That doesn't matter!" declared Mary. "You can swim in your shorts. Daddy did sometimes. We'll get our costumes." And off they went into the house before he could protest further.

"But I still can't swim," protested Evans when they emerged.

"Course you can! Even Joseph can swim, can't you Joseph?"

"Yes," said the monosyllabic Joseph, jumping in to demonstrate a doggy paddle.

"You see, it's only three feet deep. Celine has it lowered for us. You can't drown in it. You can have my ring so you can learn. Go on," she insisted, giving him a push.

"OK. Let me get my shirt and shoes off first." Evans capitulated and gingerly descended the steps.

"Get your arms through this inner tube and then let your feet come off the bottom," Mary instructed. "Doggy paddle like Joseph."

Slowly, tentatively, Evans began to move across the pool. "Now kick with your feet," Mary commanded. "You'll soon be swimming."

Taking his feet off the bottom required an effort of will. But he managed it. And he found himself floating in the ring. Doggy paddle, Mary had called it. Ten minutes later he tried just holding the ring in front of him. Mary instructed him to put his face down into the water and open his eyes. "It won't hurt, really it won't."

Another ten minutes and he was swimming unaided. It wasn't the way he'd seen other people swim but it felt like the greatest achievement of his life. He wanted to swim and swim, end to end, side to side forever. This little girl had given him a great new power and he would be eternally grateful. Only when the light began to fade did he realise how late it was getting.

"My goodness, it must be gone seven. We have to go in and I have to get you some tea, don't I?"

"Yes, that will be easy." Mary was full of confidence as always. "I will find you some of daddy's shorts for you to change into."

"And will you read us a story in bed?" queried Joseph, in his first full sentence of the evening.

"Of course he will," pronounced his sister. "Celine always does and I'm sure she has told Evans to read too."

He had to admit that was true.

*

Celine was reassured to see his car in the driveway when she got home, rather later than she'd intended. The boring old expat who'd spent earlier years in 'The Colony' as he insisted on calling Hong Kong would have kept her till dawn if she hadn't made a determined move.

Evans was fast asleep in one of the big chairs. She placed a gentle hand on his shoulder to arouse him. His eyes flickered open, then he sprang to his feet. "Sorry, I didn't mean to sleep, what time is it?"

"Gone midnight. My fault, I got caught up in a ridiculous conversation. Kids behave?"

"They were wonderful." He paused and then let it out in a rush. "Mary taught me to swim! Really swim. Something I never thought I would do."

Celine smiled her broadest smile. "Wow! Better than a babysitting fee, eh? You know, you're really good with kids. In fact you relate well to many people. Even Penny Waddell said how nice you were to her. One day, they'll welcome you to the Tennis Club, you see. I'd love to see the expression on that crabby woman's face the day you swim in *their* pool!"

"No chance," he said making for the door. "I'd certainly have to learn tennis first."

"So come round here to learn. I'll teach you the basics and then we'll get a couple of friends in to make up a double. Charles is a nice steady player. Lilly Bell plays me once a week."

"Lilly Bell?"

"My best friend here. She's a bit Hong Kong and a bit Trinidadian, brought up mostly in the West Indies." She saw the puzzled look on his face. "You'll have to get used to mixed race people, you know, Evans. We are all going to be citizens of the world. You're good with people, you'll take to it easily."

"Well," he said doubtfully, "perhaps. I'd better be going now. That big new consignment is coming in tomorrow."

"OK. Thanks a million for doing duty tonight. Did you read to them?"

"Until I nearly fell asleep in their bedroom!"

"Aaah! Little girls can always twist men around their little fingers. Wish I still had that power!"

He unaccountably blushed. "See you in the morning. Good night."

"Good night Evans. We'll fix the tennis date tomorrow."

*

Malachi sat uncomfortably in the visitor's chair, wondering what he'd done wrong. A summons from the boss lady on a Monday morning before the meeting was pretty unusual.

"Malachi," she began, "I've been talking to London about the replacement for Roger Waddell."

"Yes, we need him badly. It is four months now and I have to work very long hours to try to keep up."

"I know. Me too. You've done very well. So I suggested to London that we promote you...and they have agreed."

He was astounded. Then elated. "Thank you. You sure I can handle it?"

"I'm sure you'll need help, but you'll grow into it. After all, you have been doing most of it since Roger…that was the argument I put to London. Of course we'll have to promote someone to fill your present role. Jackson, you think? He's not that accurate at times but if you keep a watchful eye on him-"

"Not Jackson, Celine. Amos Andanero is better."

"But he is more junior, surely?"

"Yes, but better at his work. More conscientious."

Celine maintained silence for a minute. "OK. It will be a brave move, Malachi. But if you are to be a good Chief Accountant you will need to make brave moves. And I need to trust your judgement. Just don't let me down. Or let *him* let me down. *You* have to handle the protests of Jackson and you have to ensure your *protégé* makes good."

"Protégé?"

"It means literally protected one, but in English it has come to mean a junior person you favour and help towards achievement. People's own status in society is partly determined by the success of people beneath them. Remember that, Malachi. Just as my success is determined by how well you and Evans do. Right, I shall announce your new position at the meeting. Better get your books, you've got fifteen minutes."

"OK. Will I get more money?"

"Of course. We'll pay you sixteen thousand."

"Not as much as Evans."

"Evans has been longer in the job. Be grateful for a good rise. Off you go, Malachi."

Evans led the applause when Malachi's promotion was announced. After the meeting he suggested they both go out for dinner the next evening to celebrate. "Can you get Grace to come?"

"I never know, with Grace. And if I bring some other woman she will hear about it and get cross again. What is it with women, Evans?"

"Come on, ask her. She'll be pleased to hear your good news and that will soften her up. Is there a time when you can

71

ring her at the Hospital?"

"Yes, lunchtime. Who will you bring? Shall I ask her to find someone for you?"

A wild and improbable thought struck Evans. It would be a sort of thank you for the promotion. Could one do that? Would she feel it was cheeky?

"I'll make an enquiry myself," he responded, and Malachi was left wondering. "You just line up Grace. Let's make it the Flower Garden. I'm told it's the best Chinese in town."

At lunchtime, while Malachi phoned Grace, Evans plucked up his courage to visit his boss with some manufactured query about stock levels.

"We agreed to take some risk of over-stocking last week, Evans." Celine was mildly irritated. "What did you really come for?"

"Malachi and I want to celebrate his promotion with a dinner tomorrow night and we are going to the Flower Garden and I wondered," he paused and let it all come out in a rush, "I wondered if you might be free to act as our guide. We don't know anything about Chinese food."

Celine was amused and her eyes sparkled a little. "Well, that would normally be my night to cook for Charles, but I'm sure he would forgive me if I offer tonight instead. Yes, OK. Thank you for the invitation. Will you let *me* eat dinner too?"

Evans looked puzzled.

She smiled at him. "I shouldn't tease you, should I? But you don't need to be afraid to ask me out to dinner, Evans. I am honoured to be included. Is Malachi bringing Grace?"

"He's phoning now."

"Good, I hope she'll decide she can make it. If not, perhaps I could ask Lilly Bell to join us. By the way, I've booked her and Charles for tennis next week, which means you have to come round for some basic lessons one evening or over the weekend."

*

Grace pleaded pressure of work to get out of the evening. Secretly she felt it was a bit brash so soon after his boss man died. A despondent Malachi reported back to Evans.

"Don't worry, we have two Chinese ladies to help us. Celine can fix it. And Grace can't complain about that, can she?"

"Two? You mean Celine? And..?"

"Yes, Celine and her best friend here, a lady called Lily Bell. It will be a thank you to Celine."

Two local lads dining with two Asian ladies drew considerable attention from the other diners at the Flower Garden. Muttered conversations at many tables tried to define the dark skinned Asian and the semi-European look of the other. They could all be from the same company, of course. Wasn't the new boss of InterEarthMove from Hong Kong? So who were the locals? They paid the bill, too; you could see them splitting it. This was going to be a funny country when they got independence.

"That was a wonderful evening," pronounced Lilly when they emerged from the restaurant. "I haven't had such a good meal for ages. Thank you very much, boys."

"We were just very glad to have two experts with us," said Evans, "and I think I shall now develop a firm taste for Chinese food."

"You won't often find it as good as here," warned Celine, "but I'm glad we've educated you both a bit. Can I give you a lift home, Lilly?"

They saw off the girls and climbed into their own car. Evans, on a high until now, felt unaccountably disappointed. He was quiet on the way home.

"You hoped you might get off with Lilly?" queried Malachi.

"No, no, foolish idea. Anyway I will be playing tennis with her next week."

"Tennis?? You don't even have a racket! You mean you have dated her for tennis when you don't know the first thing about the game?"

Evans explained the arrangement Celine had made.

"Why not me?" demanded Malachi. "You will be one African and three Asians. I would make a better balance."

"You don't have a racket either. I bought one today; it's in the boot. If you want, I will mention your interest to Celine. But you'd better be serious. Let me see you buy a racket and proper clothes before I ask her."

"Maybe, maybe, I must think about it. Perhaps I'll watch you play first."

"Not on my first game, you won't! I'll let you know how I'm getting on."

*

He got on well. Celine proved a hard-driving but sympathetic coach, showing him time and again how to perform the throw for service, how to begin by concentrating on accuracy rather than power, how to vary the direction from the centre line to the corner, how to strike a return at the correct height, how to slice without sending the ball into the neighbour's garden. She seemed infinitely patient and he concentrated furiously to be worthy of her confidence in him.

"Well?" demanded Malachi when Evans returned from his second evening's coaching. "You entering for Wimbledon this year or next?"

Evans ignored the sarcasm. "The game requires a lot of concentration, a lot of careful control. I'm going tomorrow morning again for a final session before we take on Charles and Lilly next week."

"You got something going with Celine?"

"Don't be silly. As I told you in London, the likes of Celine are not for us. But she's a good friend and a helpful teacher. We have a lot to learn, Malachi, in every sphere of life. Look how little Mary taught me to swim. I'm glad to have friends among other people. You think Bishgad is coming. When it does, we'll have to deal with people all over the world, learn new systems, new games to be sociable. Golf has always fascinated me. I can't think how they ever hit such a tiny ball with such a long stick."

"You," interrupted Malachi with acerbity, "are selling out to the expatriates. You have no African friends. You will need them when Bishgad comes."

"I have you, Malachi. And Dipra, when he comes home. And Joshua. I may not be special friends with my staff, but I think they respect me."

"And mine do not respect me?"

"Of course they do. Don't be so sensitive, Malachi. And don't be jealous of my meetings with Celine. I think she needs extra friends here. Have you bought your tennis kit yet? Shall I mention your interest?"

"No. Tennis is not for me. It is for social climbers. I know you aim to join the club, but they won't let you in until Bishgad comes."

"No, maybe not, but when it comes there will be a social as well as a political revolution – you've said that yourself – and I want to be part of it. Join me, Malachi. I'll ask Celine if you can come and watch next Tuesday evening. That'll show her how keen you are."

Malachi lapsed into silence. "Grace is still freezing me."

"I'm sorry. If you have nothing to lose, find a new girlfriend. Not difficult for you, surely? You have money. You are clever and have a good position. Maybe you should find a separate flat now. Give both of us more freedom."

"You want to get rid of me?"

"No, it isn't like that. Just that we are grown men and perhaps it's time to be a bit more independent of each other."

Malachi lapsed into silence again. He had to admit to himself the awful truth that he had always left the organisation of domestic life to Evans. Could he manage on his own? Was this Evans's way of telling him to grow up? He was a big man at the office, but Evans was the boss at home. Evans hired and fired the staff, told them what to buy in the market, checked the money carefully. He smiled to himself. If Evans had been in charge back in the old days, he would never have made any money in the market.

"OK." He came to a sudden resolution. "I'll start looking for another flat. Give me some time."

"Of course. No hurry. You want me to help you?"

"No. I can find my own flat. My choice. To my taste. But you will be left with twice the rent."

Evans nodded. A small price to pay, he was thinking, to avoid this constant bickering. They would be better friends when they lived separately.

SEVEN

Celine was gratified by the way the two boys settled to their new jobs. MacDonald had been absolutely right about their innate abilities, she mused. This must be the most senior local management team in Jamesland and she was proud of them.

She was therefore astonished by Malachi's announcement.

"Have you discussed this with Evans?"

"No. I come to this decision on my own. We talked about these scholarships when they were announced some time back but took it no further. Evans is more clever than me, but he is content to continue his engineering studies at the Tech and I believe he is going to apply for that system they have in UK; I think they call it Open University. I would not have the willpower to do that. But I write to British Liaison Office and London School of Economics and I think they offer me a place."

"You *think*, or they *have* offered?"

"British Office tell me they sure I would qualify."

" Sit down, Malachi. This needs careful thought. You are only one year into your new post. You have a good salary and a nice flat. Can you go from that to being a poor student in London? And I cannot keep that job open for three years, you know."

"I must take my chance, Celine. I have savings, too. When I come back with good degree I will be the only African economics graduate in Jamesland, or it may be Bishgad by then. Can you see me *not* getting offers of jobs? Seriously?"

"Has your dispute with Evans brought this on? Even now you are living separately? Are you still seeing Grace?"

"Grace is nothing to me now. That was schoolboy stuff. I know I have a good job now and I am grateful to you for it, but I need more...sophistication...like Evans. He mix well with different kinds of people. I will learn that in London."

"You think I am more friendly to him than to you?"

"Yes. But that is not all of it. He speak better. He reads books I do not understand – not just engineering, but books about society, about education, history and stuff. You like him better because he is easy with you, relaxed. I am nervous. He offer to ask you about my coming to tennis but I refuse. I know I will not fit. Not yet. When I finish London I will be ready for top society."

She smiled at him. "You know, I'm sorry if I seem to have made a favourite of Evans. I didn't mean to. I have tried to give you each a fair chance. At least I can see you are well able to speak your mind. And you seem to have it made up. But let me be quite sure. You really want to give up your well paid job in a leading company full of prospects and go off to London?"

"Yes. I'm quite sure."

"Well, I suppose I must accept that. OK. You do have to give me three months notice on your contract, you know."

"Oh, plenty of time. I shall not leave until end of September. Easy for you to find someone in that time."

"Not in Jamesland, it isn't. We shall have to go back to an expat. Shame. You were leading the field, Malachi. Still, perhaps you're right and when you come back you'll catch up. You should tell Evans first. Shall I call him?"

Malachi considered this. Telling Evans quietly after work might be better. But it might make a big quarrel. Would Evans approve? He wouldn't like it that Malachi had made all the arrangements without even mentioning it to him. They still had to work together for some months. He came to a decision.

"Yes. I think it better you tell him while I am here."

"No, *you* tell him while *I* am here."

So Evans was summoned. He absorbed the news in silence and without a flicker of emotion. Then after a pause he turned to ask Celine: "Do *you* think it is a good idea for Malachi?"

"I understand Malachi's motives and I recognise it is a risk. There are arguments on both sides. But the choice is his. It is *his* life Evans. I just pray that *you* won't catch the same bug."

"So you think it is a disease?"

"No, Evans. An enthusiasm. I think it is like falling in love. There is nothing he or we can do about it. So we should help him enjoy it, help him make it successful."

Evans looked across to Malachi. "I shall miss you," he said

quietly. "But I wish you luck." He stretched out a hand, which Malachi shook, both of them moist eyed. And Celine heaved a huge inward sigh of relief.

*

"So what do I do now, Evans? I do not think there is anyone in the company capable of taking over Malachi's job."

"No. You could ask Roger Brown at the Tech if he knows anybody. But I myself have not met anyone there experienced enough to do the job. There might be someone in the United Africa Company but would he leave a good career path for an industry he knows nothing about?"

"Probably not. So I'll have to ask London again, you think?" Celine enjoyed these man-to-man discussions with Evans. And this one confirmed that at least *he* had no thoughts of leaving.

"Yes."

She pondered the situation for a moment or two. Evans's success was important to her and he was the only horse in the race now. And she had to admit to herself, his friendship equally important. London would mean another expatriate but she didn't want one who might succeed her, pushing Evans aside.

"That could be a problem … or perhaps..." She brightened a little, "perhaps it is really an opportunity."

"Explain that to me please."

"For the post of Chief Accountant they will undoubtedly offer me a choice of young Englishmen. Or more probably Scottish men." She smiled at the concept. "You would have to come with me to choose."

"Me? Go to London to help choose an expatriate?"

"Yes," she said. "Intriguing, isn't it? Important though, if you are to have the title General Manager some time in the future. Don't you think?"

She gave her little tinkling laugh at the stunned look on his face. "Don't tell me that hadn't occurred to you!"

"You are teasing me, Celine. They will send another expatriate when you go, even if it is another Hong Konger, or perhaps an Indian. Anyway, you are not going for years."

"Now there you are wrong, Evans. I shall leave at the end of my three years, which is next May. Perhaps June or July if they need that. But there will not be another Hong Konger or an Indian, if I have my way. You will succeed me, Evans. And by taking you to London, I shall show British management my intentions."

Evans simply stared at her while conflicting emotions raged through him. Losing Celine would be like … he couldn't think of a sufficiently significant comparison. She was so lovely, sitting across the desk there with her beautiful smile, her long glossy black hair bouncing out of its ribbon behind her, her eyes twinkling. He could easily imagine himself in love, stupid as it would seem.

But General Manager? GM of the largest British company in Jamesland? Evans Watanero from Ijebodwe? At thirty something? He suddenly realised he was not only staring, but tears were gathering in his eyes.

"Won't you like that?" she asked, so softly he could hardly hear it above the newly installed air conditioner.

"Yes," he gulped. "I shall like that very much. But I shall hate losing you." This confession of his feelings made him blush deeply, darkening his face so that even Celine could not miss it.

"Oh," she said, rather weakly. "We shall miss each other, I expect," blushing in her turn. "But we have months before that. And London to look forward to again. An adventure, Evans. Enjoy it. I'll talk to London tomorrow. But say nothing to Malachi until he has absolutely finalised this LSE business. I think he actually knows he will be awarded one of these scholarships."

*

Malachi was duly awarded a full scholarship, all expenses paid, to read economics at LSE, with even a decent living allowance. He confirmed it first to Evans.

"So my new place will be free. It a better flat than yours, Evans, and rent is the same. You interested?"

"Yes, I may well be. Have you told Grace?"

"She not interested any more, Evans. Thinks only of her work. I do not think there is even another man." As he thought of this he smiled.

"Maybe she will still be single when I come back with my degree. She will be impressed, she was always telling me I should educate myself. And I shall get top job in the new Bishgad government when it comes."

"*When* it comes, Malachi. These things don't happen overnight."

"Neither will my degree. I will take bet with you; Bishgad will be independent in the year I take my finals – just right timing! What will Celine do about my job?"

"Recruit another expatriate, I think. Nobody locally as well qualified as you, Malachi."

"See? We have come a long way, my friend."

"Yes. And don't forget that we owe a lot of it to Mr. McDonald and to Celine."

*

Heathrow airport was its usual organised chaos and Evans and Celine were glad to get through immigration and customs procedures. To their relief, the InterEarthMove card dominated the line-up of greeters. And to Evans's joy it was Fred holding it.

"Welcome back, Evans. And Miss Celine. They tell me you work together now."

"Miss Celine is the boss and I make the tea, Fred."

Celine gave Fred her broadest smile. "That's when he's not running the rest of the company, of course. Fred, I can't wait to get in one of those hot baths at the hostel, let's go."

"Oh, but they've put you in the Intercon. Miss Celine, both of you. Here's a letter for each of you." He handed over two bulky packages. "I think it explains where you will be doing your interviewing."

They settled into the car, Evans sitting alongside Fred and Celine in the back. As they pulled out on to the M4 she leaned forward to say, "The Intercon, eh? We *are* honoured, Fred.

InterEarthMove must have had a good year."

"Ah, you haven't heard. We are bidding for European Contractors Hire. Looks like a done deal too, given the strength of our shares."

Evans looked at him with renewed respect. "How does that work, Fred?"

"I'm sure Miss Celine knows. Too long to explain in all this traffic. She can tell you in the hotel."

An hour later they were booking in and agreed to meet in the bar at 7.30 for a drink before dinner, having read their letters. A small suite had been reserved for two days for interviewing and there were six short listed candidates. They were to select two for a second interview on the second day, at which InterEarthMove's Personnel Director would be present.

"So we'd better pick two top-notch men, Evans. Mind you they all look great on paper, don't they? We aren't to know that two of them have convictions for fraud, one speaks such heavy scouse nobody can understand him and one is only four feet tall."

He smiled. "What's scouse?"

"The language of Liverpool. Impenetrable. Worse than Micah on a bad day." This reference to the company storekeeper set them both off giggling.

"Isn't there a law against accent prejudice? And one that says midgets must have equal opportunities?" asked Evans.

"I expect so. Except for dance instructors in a tall ladies club. I hope they've got a law to cover prejudice against slanty eyes."

He looked up at her keenly. "You can't legislate for or against beauty, can you?"

"Evans, I do believe you meant that as a compliment."

"You have lovely eyes," he muttered in confusion. "All these young men seem to be very good looking from their photos," he added, trying to change the subject.

"Evans," she leaned across the table towards him, "no competition! Let's order, shall we?"

They ate well and confined themselves to a demi-carafe of the house white wine, Celine advising Evans at each step.

"I haven't drunk wine before," he whispered.

"Lots of things you haven't done yet, Evans. This trip will be an education for you."

They lingered over coffee in the lounge, Evans reluctant to take his leave, yet by now desperately tired. Where did Celine get her boundless reserves of energy from?

Celine was having an internal debate. He was a lovely man but it would be foolish to start an affair with him. It was unprofessional and would spoil their excellent business relations. Perhaps even spoil their friendship. In a year she would be gone anyway, there was no chance of anything becoming permanent. On the other hand, a big anonymous hotel like this presented opportunities they could never have in Henry City.

"I really have to turn in," he was saying. "Long hard day tomorrow, isn't it?"

She had to agree. They rose together and made their way to the lifts. Funny, she thought, six-two-four and six-two-five; there'd never be a better chance. But they still had four nights ahead. Maybe she'd put off a final decision till later.

"Goodnight, Celine," he said. Did she detect sadness, disappointment? Or was that just her own hopes overwhelming common sense?

"Goodnight, Evans," she responded, and firmly closed the door behind her.

*

There were three candidates they could easily agree to eliminate: the bombastic one who'd never been outside Walsall but felt he knew all about Jamesland because he'd been reading it up in his library; the timid one from Midhurst who nervously asked a thousand questions about the people and the food and the climate and the hospitals and would Evans be his boss? ; and the London man who'd clearly invented his degree – how did Personnel let *him* through?

Which left – as Celine had forecast – the three Scots, for

whom they had the shorthand titles Aberdeen, Glasgow and Edinburgh. And not a whisker between them.

"But we have to eliminate one," Celine insisted. "We are asked to choose just two for the Director to look at tomorrow. Well, you are going to have to work with the new man for some years so it should be your choice really. I'm really glad I brought you, Evans. The Director will want to consider the prospects of the man in the longer term, of course, beyond Jamesland."

Evans glanced over the papers again. "There's nothing between them on academic or experience grounds. I liked all three. But perhaps a single man would find it more difficult to settle. Better a family man in a strange culture, don't you think?"

"Not necessarily. Remember the Waddells and the Vintners? Who would have thought Roger would go off the rails like that?"

"Off the rails? What do you mean?"

"Oh, come on Evans. Didn't it strike you as odd that Angela Vintner left her husband to come home to England so soon after Roger's death? Didn't you see how devastated she was?"

Evans looked at her wonderingly. "You mean they..? Did Penny Waddell know about it?"

"No, of course not. And never will, I hope. Roger was a decent chap and a good family man and that's the image she should keep of him. But I'd like to bet George Vintner knew what was going on."

"But Mrs. Waddell was such a pretty lady – and they were such a happy family, too. I will always be grateful to little Mary for teaching me to swim."

Celine shook her head. "You are too nice, too honourable and too innocent for your own good, Evans. OK, never mind, let's put the two family men forward. And hope they are absolutely devoted to their wives. Perhaps we should ask them that tomorrow."

Her eyes sparkled with mischief as she observed Evans's discomfiture.

"Come on Evans, lighten up. I promise not to embarrass

you tomorrow. I'll do the negative call and you can have the pleasure of making the two invitation calls."

*

"Oysters!" exclaimed Celine as she examined the dinner menu. "Poverty and oysters always seem to go together, according to Dickens. But he was wrong; they're now an expensive dish. I prefer 'oysters is amorous'. I don't know where that comes from, sounds like a Dickens character to me though it can't be, but oysters are very popular in Hong Kong for that reason."

"What does it mean?" enquired Evans innocently.

She gave a broad smile. "Aphrodisiac."

"Afro what? An Afro is that big bushy haircut some people...."

"Ssshh ... Aphro a-p-h-r-o disiac. From the Greek goddess Aphrodite. Supposed to make you feel sexy."

He dipped his head in embarrassment.

"Maybe," she said blandly, "we should have half a dozen each. They're delicious. And if anything happens, we can always blame it on the oysters."

Evans didn't know where to look.

She stretched a hand across the table to touch his. "Can I be serious with you for a moment?"

He looked up, catching a new tone in her voice.

"You and I have quite a few more months to work together. We respect each other and I think we are fond of each other. I could very easily fall in love with you, but I'm not going to let myself. It wouldn't be sensible for either of us."

She broke off as a waiter approached. "Oysters for both of us for starters and then rack of lamb for me. Evans?"

He was confused and forgot what his original choice had been. "Rack of lamb for me too, please," he muttered. Then, gathering himself, "And a demi-carafe of the House White please."

Celine resumed in a low voice. "We have just a few nights together in this hotel. When we get back to Henry City we'll have to continue as before. Anything that happens here need not affect our future relationship. But for these few nights, well … I'm offering. No strings."

She paused while the demi-carafe was delivered.

"And I won't be hurt or offended if you turn down the offer."

Liar, liar, her brain was screaming. But she was already frightening him. Please God give him the courage to sin just a little.

They sat in silence for a while before Celine drew his attention to another diner. "Evans, isn't that Aberdeen over there? Staying overnight, ready for tomorrow?"

Evans focussed on the solitary diner against the far wall. "Yes, it's him. But he's booked into the Midland, down the road. That's where I phoned him. Probably he just fancied dining here this evening."

"Can't be the oysters that attracted him," she said mischievously, enjoying his blush. "Not with his wife up in Aberdeen."

"He's my front runner, I think," said Evans in another attempt to divert the conversation.

They lingered over the coffee and After Eights in the lounge, refilling their cups from the sideboard.

"Well gone ten," she finally declared. "I should be going up. Coming?" The trouble, now that she had declared her hand, was that every conventional remark had a double edge. But Evans just nodded and got up with her.

Coming from the lift, they arrived at her door first. Inserting her card in the lock, she turned to him, eyes as wide and innocent as she could manage. "Come in for a nightcap?" Celine saw the puzzled look on his face. "The last drink of the day."

Saying which, she walked through. And Evans followed.

EIGHT

The telephone rang. "This is your wake up call," announced a robotic voice.

"Thank you," responded Celine automatically, replacing the receiver.

Evans put an arm around her and she snuggled up to him. She loved the contrast of his dark copper skin against her own light olive.

"Now," she said, "you are nearly ready for Grace. But you still need a little more practice."

"Grace?"

"I see it in the stars. Come on, we have work to do today."

*

Evans was surprised at how fully at ease he now felt with Celine. All the barriers had come down. Now he understood why the Bible always said Isaac or whoever 'knew' his wife. They were a great team. They would impress the Director with their business acumen and their shared psychological insights. Evans was on a high.

The three spent two hours in the morning with Edinburgh and two in the afternoon with Aberdeen, promising each of them they would make their decision that evening and telephone. Edinburgh opted to travel home overnight but would be waiting by his home phone at eight next morning. Aberdeen would be 'in the Midland again'.

"Nothing to choose between them," pronounced the Director, when Aberdeen had left. "The choice should be yours, since you have to work alongside him. But if it helps any, I will certainly consider the other for future vacancies as they arise. And if as you say the young chap from Glasgow is equally good – and I have to trust your judgement on that – he'll be in the pot too. Indeed we seem to have struck a rich vein of talent here. Now, who will you go for?"

Celine gave the slightest of nods to Evans. Like a green light.

"Aberdeen, Sir. Very down to earth, practical man. I know the two children make him a bit more expensive but they will give him stability and a certain standing in our community."

He tried not to blush at Celine's enquiring sidelong glance.

"Right," said the Director, who wouldn't know when a black man blushes anyway. "He's yours if he passes the medical. And he looks pretty fit. Andrew Maitland. Good strong name too and I like the way he sticks to it in full. Better not try to 'Andy' him, Evans. He'll be a stickler. Now I must be off. We'll send his contract from Head Office and send you a copy when he's signed. OK?"

"Just a point, Sir."

"Yes, Celine?"

"May I take it we would have your approval to promote Evans to my job when I leave?" Evans was startled.

The Director smiled. "Ah. Well, he would have *my* support, but that's a long way ahead, and would be a Board appointment. Still after your performance here, I think if things continue as they are, you could be pretty confident the Board will accept my recommendation."

He grinned. "That's why you brought him, wasn't it? Smart move, Celine." He turned to Evans. "I hope you know how much you owe her."

"Yes, Sir, Celine's been an excellent guide and mentor." He blushed again as he realised what he'd said, but again the Director was unaware of it.

*

The next day was taken up visiting the plant and looking around all the latest developments in machinery. Evans couldn't wait to get his hands on some of this new and ingenious kit. He took lots of pre-release introductory literature to show his major clients back in Jamesland.

The final day they spent revisiting the sights they had discovered together all those years ago. A day of laughter and happiness and just the occasional tear. After dinner in the hotel they walked along the embankment admiring the strings of street lamps against the dark river, like pearls on velvet, as Celine put it.

"And look, there's a diamond," she exclaimed as a jazz boat drifted by in the centre of the inky blackness. "It's all so romantic. Very appropriate for our last night," she whispered.

"Celine," he began, but she put a slim finger to his lips.

"Don't say anything. There is nothing to be said, dear Evans. Speech will disperse the magic. Let's go back."

*

As Henry City came into view in the window, Celine turned to him. "Home. For you, anyway. Sorry it can't be for me too. I just want you to know you have given me great joy to balance the sadness I feel now. Grace will be a lucky girl."

"Grace is nothing to me, Celine."

"She will be, Evans. She will if you just contact her. She will be able to tell you of the love she has felt for years. I mean it. And now, my friend, buckle up. And buckle down to work when we arrive. And remember how your society values a family man."

She turned away to hide her moistening eyes.

Malachi was there to meet them. As they drove down the long avenue into town he was agog to know who his replacement would be.

"I expect he's properly qualified with letters after his name and all that."

"He's a good man, Malachi. A Scot from Aberdeen in the far North."

"But isn't that all just mountains and sheep?"

Evans broke in. "Aberdeen, Malachi, is the centre of the British off-shore oil industry. When you get to England you must read all the papers and magazines more carefully to learn more about the world."

He gave Malachi a playful punch. "And what's been happening in Henry City this week?"

"A machine broke down up at the dam and they need you up there urgently to look at it."

"Couldn't Joshua go?"

"He says it may be something beyond him and he wants to go with you to learn how some new control mechanism works. It only happen on Thursday so not too bad a problem for them. But you better go first thing Monday."

Evans turned to Celine and winked. "Five days away and the company falls apart."

"Not so," protested Malachi. "I sweet talk the foreman up there, telling him how the machines are so modern we are in the front of developments and there bound to be a few running-in problems."

"Good for you, Malachi," said Celine. "And stop teasing him, Evans, you should be grateful he was willing to look after things while we were away."

"Yes," said Malachi, "No more London jaunts when I leave. It will be years before your Scottish man knows the company as well as I do."

"OK Malachi, you win," conceded Evans. "What else? Have we cleared the big spares consignment?"

"Yes. The documents were late, as usual, but you know Samuel, he could clear goods through Customs on a bus ticket."

They all had a little laugh at Samuel's legendary ability to surmount bureaucratic hurdles at the docks.

"Well done, Malachi, while Evans is up at the dam he can talk about the new equipment we've seen being developed in England. Get in early, Evans, and stir up their interest."

"Your house first, Celine? I can cut off at the ring road and avoid the traffic. You would think Saturday they'd all stay at home. So early in the morning too." Malachi looked in his rear mirror and she nodded approval.

"You can both come in for a nice cup of coffee while we talk more about work. In London, you know, Evans and I went over the old places again. It was lovely but they are building huge tower blocks all over the city – it will soon look like Hong Kong."

Malachi was surprised. "You mean Hong Kong is more

modern than London?"

"I don't know about more modern, but we certainly got into tall tower blocks on a grand scale earlier. Of course we've nothing to match the antiquity of the Tower or Westminster Abbey."

"What else did you do? How was the hostel?"

Celine paused and Evans took up the reins. "They'd put us in a hotel this time so we could have a room for interviewing. It was hard work, Malachi, interviewing all day for two solid days, keeping notes and all."

"Aaah." Malachi was sounding sceptical. "You think it was easy back here?"

"No, I'm not making comparisons. Just that I don't want you to think it was all a bit of a holiday."

Celine felt the need to give Evans support. "We had comfortable rooms and we ate well but we also worked hard to get the right person. Apart from the one day touring the sights again it was a working week."

Why should they have to defend themselves? she wondered.

"One day was up at Edgware of course, looking at developments, as I said. I expect you missed Evans."

"I managed OK. Here we are. Someone has left your gates open Celine!"

"I expect Amos calculated when we would arrive and opened them ready."

But the front door was open too and there was no Amos to welcome them. Celine made her way in and the men followed her.

The living room was a scene of devastation, a bare sideboard with its drawers pulled out, a television stand boasting only loose wires, bits of crockery everywhere. Celine pressed on into the kitchen.

And there was Amos, lying on the floor in a little pool of blood.

Celine kneeled down to him. "Call an ambulance, Evans. The burglars have hurt him badly."

*

Chief Superintendent Holland came along with his Chief Inspector.

"First significant burglary we've had for some time, Padmore. I want to get hold of this one fast, whether it's a gang or an individual. The last thing Jamesland needs now is a spate of attacks on expatriate houses. There'll be enough uncertainty, with Bishgad looming, without this."

"Yes, sah. You think all the expatriates will want to go home?"

"No. But some of them will and they're all bound to think about it. A few episodes like this and they'll leave in droves. But I have no plans myself, in case you're thinking my job might be up for grabs." He smiled to take the edge off it.

"One day, I hope, sah. But I still need to learn plenty from you. You should stay for a couple of years after independence." Padmore Watabenje said it with such serious mien that James Holland was quite moved.

"OK. Next house left," he said gruffly. "You know this lady?"

"Only from picture in the paper, sah. But I know Evans Watanero a little. From my village."

"Good. So do I. Remember the mad taxi driver?"

An ambulance swept in just ahead of them and two white clad figures jumped out.

"Just a minute," called Holland. "I'd like to take a look at the victim before you move him."

"If he's suffered head injuries we need to get him back to hospital as soon as possible," responded the female white coat, who seemed to be in charge. " Doctor Grace Endoman, from Karle Mo. Do you remember me?" Grace held out her hand and Holland took it.

"Of course. A pity we meet again in bad circumstances. I only want to view him in situ. Gives me a clearer picture of what went on. After you, doctor."

Evans and Malachi were standing about helplessly wondering if there was anything they could be doing for Amos

92

while Celine bathed the wound on his forehead with warm water.

"No, leave him," commanded Grace, "any movement might be harmful. Let me take a good look at him."

"Perhaps," Evans offered to Celine, "we could help you tidy up a bit?"

"No, don't touch anything," Holland ordered. He looked down at the supine Amos on the kitchen floor.

Grace looked up at him for permission to proceed and he nodded. The male nurse hurried out for a stretcher while Grace examined the wounds to Amos's head. Evans wandered closer.

"Hello Grace. Will he be OK?"

"We shall need to do some tests. X-Ray and perhaps a scan on our new equipment. We are grateful to InterEarthMove for the money."

Working together the two medics swiftly but carefully lifted Amos on to the stretcher and carried him out. The ambulance bell was soon fading into the distance.

"What money, Celine?" Evans was very curious.

"Our charitable gift for last year," interjected Malachi. "Celine didn't want to make a big thing out of it."

Perhaps, reflected Evans, he didn't know Celine as well as he thought.

"Was that to help Malachi's relations with Grace?" he asked, when he could talk to Celine alone.

"No, of course not. It was our company's wish to make a contribution to Henry City society. £50,000 if you want to know."

"Phew! And you never told me anything."

"Full marks to Malachi for being so discreet, even from you. I knew of course that you would notice it when you take over. But Malachi was the only person locally who needed to know at the outset."

"Excuse me, people, but I have some questions for you." Chief Superintendent Holland raised a hand to head off any protest Evans might have wished to make, while turning to Celine for information on the scale of the burglary.

"I could make up a list of things missing for you but Malachi could more easily provide it from company records. Virtually everything in the house belongs to the company, of course. And I think it's all insured." She looked to Malachi for confirmation.

"But your own personal effects, Miss Brandt?"

"Oh, nothing important in here." She gave a sharp intake of breath. "I haven't even looked in the bedroom yet!"

She dashed off to the rear of the house closely followed by Holland. Her bedroom was strewn with clothing, one set of wardrobe doors agape, drawers half out or abandoned on the bed.

Biting her lip, she opened the second wardrobe. It was completely empty. She gave a little sob and sat down on the bed.

"Every last dress!" she complained. "They've left me nothing but jeans and T-shirts."

Malachi and Evans, hesitating in the doorway, were struck dumb. Holland moved forward and took Celine by the arm.

"Come on, Miss Brandt. I think we should get you into a hotel for a few days while we examine this more closely." He looked to the waiting men.

"Of course," said Evans. "Come on Celine, this is only upsetting you. Malachi will drive us down to the Tropical House. We'll book you in until Monday for now and then we'll see how things turn out."

"Good man, " said Holland. "Padmore and I will give this place the once over. Were they … *Chinese* dresses, Miss Brandt?"

"Many of them Cheong sams," she confirmed.

"Then they will stand out in Jamestown. We'll keep an eye out for them, Miss Brandt. "

Evans put an arm around the sniffling Celine and led her to the car. Holland was moved for the second time in an hour, as he observed the stocky African gently leading away this tiny frail beauty.

And Malachi wondered at Evans's presumption in putting

an arm around her shoulders. Brass neck, he thought, a phrase he'd only recently learned on the telephone from the dam foreman.

*

"You have settled Miss Brandt into the hotel?" Grace had come down to the hospital reception area to see Evans.

"Yes, she's still a bit upset, mostly by the beating Amos got, presumably protecting her interests. I promised her I would check with you and phone her with the latest situation. How is he, Grace?"

Grace bit her lip. "He needs some surgery on his skull to release the pressure on his brain. My father is a good surgeon but he has no direct experience of such an operation. However he has been on the telephone to London for advice and he will lead the best team we can get together. Pray for a good outcome, Evans. Tell Miss Brandt we are confident, but you had better know there are real risks. We cannot do nothing."

"Of course not." Evans paused. "You know about Malachi?"

"Going to study in England? Yes, he told me on the phone. Only last week, though he must have known for some time." She shook her head a little. "It is no concern of mine, but I wish him well. And I hear that rogue Forfpi is likely to come back to us."

"That rogue Forfpi will probably eventually be a *minister*, Grace. We'd better learn new respect!"

"He is not half the man you are, Evans. I must go back and get ready for this operation. Pray for Amos – and my father. Go back to your Celine."

"Not *my* Celine, Grace. My boss, remember? But, yes, I ought to get back to her. How long before I should get back to *you*? About Amos I mean."

"We do not know how long it will take. Don't bother us before six o'clock. If we are still in the theatre I will try to leave a message here in reception for you. OK?"

*

Malachi and Celine were with Holland in a far corner of

the Tropical House lounge, looking over the company records of property in the bungalow. They all looked up enquiringly at Evans's approach.

He shook his head. "Major operation needed. We shan't know how it's gone until around six. Grace will leave a message for me if it isn't over by then."

"I'll catch this blighter if it's the last thing I do in Jamesland." declared Holland. "Were your own things insured, Miss Brandt?"

"Yes, I have always been cautious about property. But what matters really is Amos. He is such a good man. I couldn't bear it if he…."

"Grace is very hopeful, Celine. Let's not worry unnecessarily. You OK now?"

She nodded. Malachi noted the exchange, Evans's tone of voice and the eye contact between them. Could something have developed between them in London? he wondered.

*

Grace and her father emerged from the operating theatre with relief, leaving the closure to a junior surgeon.

"You think he'll be OK now, Dad?"

"We won't know until he comes to, daughter. I couldn't *see* any damage to the brain itself, but then I'm no expert. I don't imagine he was exactly an Einstein, but let's hope his intelligence isn't damaged."

"Perhaps he will be able to remember who attacked him. The police are very keen to talk to him."

"Yes, I know. But keep them at bay for now. And don't let them get too close as soon as he regains consciousness. They can be a bit insensitive, you know. The poor man will need time to gather himself. Did I hear Malachi is going off to London?"

"Yes. To study. He's finally getting some ambition."

"Oh come on now, he's done very well in InterEarthMove, hasn't he? But you have not been seeing him lately. Does that explain his trip to London?"

"No, Dad. We were finished a long time ago in truth."

"And his friend Evans?"

"Oh, I think perhaps Evans will get even more promotion when Miss Brandt leaves. He has *real* ambition. Not just making money, but pushing the country forward."

"You know what I mean. Evans and you. Wouldn't that be a good match for you? Especially since you are such an admirer."

"Dad, you tried to hitch me up with Malachi when I wasn't ready. Why not just let me be a good doctor? Don't you want me to be the next Orthopaedic Consultant at Karle Mo?"

"A woman needs children. And your mother looks for grandchildren."

"And you've got about twenty years for me to provide them in!" she laughed. "Give chance, honourable ancestor."

They saw Evans approaching down the passageway.

"What news of Amos?" he asked.

"The operation was clean and we think successful. Damage to the brain can only be assessed after he regains consciousness. We have good hopes. My daughter was an enormous help."

He didn't have to put that in, thought Grace. He's still trying to get me off with Evans. Sometimes I hate all men, even my own father.

"Then I will tell Celine. Perhaps she can come and see him tomorrow?"

"No, not for several days, I'm afraid. We really don't know what the mental effects may be. Miss Brandt has recovered from the shock?"

"I think so. She's quite a tough lady, even if she is only seven stone!"

Now how does he know that? thought Grace. She makes me feel like an elephant and I'm only nine stone.

Grace was suddenly aware that she would welcome Miss Brandt's – Celine's – return to Hong Kong. Ridiculous really, she told herself, why should I care? When Malachi goes off to London I shall be free of all men. And I intend to stay that way.

NINE

'Aberdeen', Andrew Maitland as they must begin to call him, arrived with his wife and two children on the overnight flight from London, to be greeted initially by Evans.

"The children slept beautifully almost all the way," explained Fiona Maitland in answer to Evans's enquiry, "but Andrew and I hardly got a wink. I suppose the answer is to tell the staff you don't want dinner, or breakfast or any of their silly duty free stuff, put on those shades and retire for the night."

"Och, I wouldna want to have missed the malts at those prices," protested Andrew.

"Malts?" queried Evans.

"Single malt whiskies," said Fiona, "I'm afraid you'll have to get used to my husband's obsessions."

Evans looked from one to the other, but they were smiling broadly so he took this to be a joke between them. Well, he hoped so.

Shepherding them out through the crowds, he gathered them on the forecourt and signalled across the car park to a minivan, which promptly took off and screeched around the circuit to join them.

"My colleague Malachi Goodwill," announced Evans. "I expect the children will want to ride with their parents, Mrs. Maitland, so perhaps you'd all like to climb in the back?"

They were quickly on the road into town, down the Great East Road which rumour had it, explained Evans, would be renamed Independence Avenue when freedom came.

"It will be interesting to be here when that happens," commented Andrew Maitland. "A moment of history of course."

Malachi, sitting now in the front passenger seat turned round to express surprise that he took such an interest in it. "But England has been free for a thousand years," he commented, "according to my history books."

"Aye, but we're frae Scotland, ye ken, and we have yet to gain oor independence. Three hundred years of domination by the English we've had to put up with."

"Och, doan't exaggerate, Andrew," admonished his wife. He smiled at her.

Evans called out, "We tend to think of UK as all one country, of course. Anyway, you're not really a Scottish Independence Party man are you?"

"Noo. I'd like to see us running more of our ane affairs, but I'm a wee bit wary of letting the politicians in Edinburgh and Glasgie loose. We canna be sure they'd be any better than the London lot. Anyway we certainly don't want to break up the UK. That would be ridiculous. Like you trying to break up Bishgad into its tribal areas. I don't know about your tribes, but our tribes are all so mixed up, intermarried and living everywhere that it would be chaos to try to separate them."

Malachi was intrigued. "I didn't think you had *tribes* in England – I mean UK."

"Well, we have the remnants. There are probably folk in the Highlands who still think they are exclusively Scottish and I expect people in the mountains of Wales who are Welsh to the core, but most of us are mongrels. My own father had some Italian ancestors and my maternal grandmother had a suspiciously Scandinavian Christian name! And Fiona here is from the deep south, ye ken, from Edinburgh itself."

Fiona chuckled. "Andrew, stop misleading them."

"I thought mongrels were just dogs!" exclaimed Malachi.

"It's a jokey use, Malachi," Evans said. "This is the hotel we've put you in for now, Andrew. We'll let you settle the children in and get some lunch, then perhaps Malachi can come round for you at about half past two to bring you into the offices. If there's anything you need Mrs. Maitland, please let us know."

*

"Strange man, your Aberdeen," commented Malachi as they drove away, "and I can't understand all his words."

"He speaks quite well, Malachi, with just a bit of accent you'll have to get used to. Anyway, you'll only have four weeks to learn it. But when you're in London among students I'll bet you'll hear a dozen different accents. I heard a Geordie one once – they sort of sing – and that was very difficult."

"Geordie?"

"People from North East England, Newcastle and that area. Think we'd better start calling him Andrew, by the way."

When the new man came into the office with Malachi to meet Celine, she recalled how she and Evans had called the three finalists by their home cities for ease of reference. And Maitland was rather taken by the idea.

"I suppose there'll be a few other Scots in Henry City?" he asked.

"Sure to be," commented Evans, "our last manager was Scottish, though he didn't have much of an accent, his name was Duncan MacDonald, but he's gone to live in Dorset. That's in the South, isn't it?"

"Bit warmer than Skye," commented Maitland, to everyone's mystification. "Isle of Skye," he added, seeing their incomprehension, "where the MacDonalds came from originally. But I'll bet all the other Scots are lowlanders. Never mind, you know, I rather like 'Aberdeen' as a name, easy for the staff I imagine and quite an honour for me in a way. Can I be *Aberdeen* within the company? But Andrew to you, of course."

"Of course!" exclaimed Celine. "I love it. The staff will find it very easy. Don't you agree, Evans?"

"Absolutely. But you'll still get *Mister* Aberdeen from most people."

"OK. I can manage that." He stood and looked at each in turn. "Aberdeen," he announced. "But Andrew to you, Evans, Malachi and ??"

"Celine. Miss Brandt in reference of course. And Mr. Watanero and Mr Goodwill."

"Guid," he said. "I like to know the rules before we start. Do I get introduced to the rest of the staff now?"

He was obviously keen to get on with it.

"This afternoon? After an overnight flight?" Celine was a bit doubtful. "I thought you'd want to take it easy and recover before jumping in the deep end."

"Well, I havena got long to learn how to swim, have I? If Malachi's ready, then so am I."

"Good man," she said. "OK, off you go Malachi, but don't tire Andrew out on his first day."

*

The four weeks of Andrew's overlap with Malachi flew by, but Malachi reported to Celine at their last meeting that the new man had shown an amazingly quick grasp of the systems.

"Well, he *is* a qualified accountant, Malachi. You've done very well from your evening classes and sheer experience but this man's been doing accounts since he was sixteen, remember. Plus he's a year or two older than you. After London, you'll be like him."

"I hope so. He reminds me of previous manager. You and Evans chose well in London." Malachi looked up to see if his reference would cause any embarrassment but Celine was merely smiling.

"We shall be a good team, I think. Thanks for all *your* input, Malachi. I wish you every success in London." She rose and showed him to the door, accompanying him across the curiously empty outer office and guiding him gently to the warehouse door.

He looked at her in some puzzlement, until the door was thrown open and Evans stood there welcoming him. Then he saw the crowd gathered behind.

"A little farewell surprise, Malachi," murmured Celine.

Evans shook his hand and banged a spanner on a small machine nearby. The crowd went silent. "We're here," began Evans, "to wish goodbye to a great and very popular manager, Malachi Goodwill."

Applause. Then Celine stepped forward and mounted a wooden box to bring herself level with her managers. "Malachi, we have a little present here which all the staff have contributed to and which we hope you will find useful in London."

Malachi tore at the wrappings to get at the cardboard box

within, watched in delighted anticipation by the whole company. Inside the box was a splendid black leather briefcase, with his initials gold embossed, which he opened very carefully with the tiny brass key, muttering embarrassed thanks. Inside the case was an A to Z of London and a large fold-out Underground map. He looked up in amazement.

"You can thank Aberdeen for those," said Evans. "He managed to find them at Heathrow."

*

It had taken Amos Ijegbu weeks to come out of his coma, with both Celine and Chief Inspector Padmore Watabenje maintaining an intermittent watching brief. Chief Superintendent Holland noted that his senior policeman visited the hospital so frequently he began to suspect there was a particular attraction among the nurses, but he let that ride. Or was it Celine? Well, it was no business of his. But if it was the Hong Konger, Padmore was way out of his depth.

Finally Watabenje announced that the patient appeared to be awake again but was not making much sense. However Doctor Endoman senior felt he could now allow Holland a brief interview.

Holland was surprised at how well Amos appeared to have mended physically but he was quickly aware from the mumbling responses to his initial questions that some mental damage was still present.

Celine brought in little gifts of fruit and newspapers, which Dr. Endoman had permitted. "At least," Holland said quietly to Celine, observing the tears which sprang to Amos's eyes, "his emotions seem to be fully engaged. Whether he'll ever be able to give us an account of the burglary I somehow doubt."

"Give him another week," said Dr. Endoman. "Some people make remarkable recoveries. Don't give up hope yet, Chief Superintendent. But please don't put him under any pressure."

Celine always arrived back in the office depressed after a hospital visit. "I somehow feel responsible," she explained to

Evans. "There we were in London…." She left the sentence unfinished.

"Come on Celine. The burglary probably happened at dawn, while we were landing at Henry City. You can't shoulder any blame. But I would really like to catch up with the burglars. I'm sure Amos will come out of this and be able to tell us something. And Mr. Holland is a very clever man."

"Maybe. I hope before I have to go home. Only eight months now, Evans."

"Yes. I dread it. Not taking over the company. Losing you."

"Evans! If you would pick up the relationship with Grace, you wouldn't miss me at all. Make some more hospital visits, find out her duty hours and arrange to be there at the right times. She'll soon get the message. And I'm sure she's waiting for you."

She laid a hand on his arm. "What we had was lovely. And our friendship will always be a happy memory. But neither of us should chase a lost cause, Evans. See Grace, please. Have you heard anything from Malachi yet?"

"Only a card to say he's found a nice 'bedsit', he calls it, in Battersea with a wonderful landlady who feeds him well."

"Ah, that will be maximum happiness for Malachi!"

Evans laughed. "Yes, even Malachi will be able to take on London alone, with a full belly. Where will you live in Hong Kong, Celine?"

"In my flat. It's been rented out while I've been here but I had planned for it to be vacant when I returned. If you ever visit Hong Kong you'll be welcome to stay. Why not bring Grace for your honeymoon?"

"You're making assumptions. And anyway, I couldn't afford that!"

"Nonsense. Grace isn't going to marry you next week but in a year's time… We might even be able to call it a business visit. I have three bedrooms, so accommodation is no problem."

"But wouldn't it be, well, you know, embarrassing?"

"If I can put the past behind me, so can you. I would do nothing to harm your future happiness, Evans. Bear it in mind. Grace would be thrilled, I'm sure."

*

Amos made steady progress but it was still another month before he began to make real sense. Only Holland and Celine were visiting when he came out with a first piece of memory.

"They said Watanero."

"Who said, Amos?"

"The men. Watanero house, they said."

"You saw them?"

"No, they were behind me, holding me."

"And what did you say?"

"I said no, not so, and they hit me." He hesitated, wincing at the thought of the blow. "They shouted 'Liar, liar' and kept hitting."

"They thought the house was Mr. Watanero's?"

"Don't know, don't know." The tears came again and Celine held up her hand to restrain Holland.

"Goodbye for now, Amos. Mr. Watanero will come to see you tonight. Now you are getting better I will arrange for your mother to be picked and brought to see you." Celine turned away to hide her own tears.

"Why would they think it was Watanero's' house, Miss Brandt?" Holland was anxious to follow up this first clue.

"I can only think because he has been coming to swim in my pool and comes to play tennis once a week with some of my friends. A casual observer might possibly think he lived there. Or even, " she paused, "well, I expect some people might guess he *will* be living there, and got their dates wrong. But it's months away and anyway the final decision about who will take over from me …. You think this was to do with Evans in some way?"

"I'm not sure, but I shall be making some enquiries. If they were trying to get at Evans, maybe it wasn't a simple burglary." Holland walked off to his car, leaving a mystified Celine.

*

"Padmore, I want you to check with the mental hospital on all visitors to Benson Adunbi. Who goes, how often. Family, I expect. You know the drill."

"Will they allow me to look at the book, do you think?"

"Of course. Flash your badge at them. And if there is a regular visitor, ask the staff who he is, how old, why do they think he visits?"

"What is all this about, Sir?"

"Just following up a hunch, that's all. See if you can work it out yourself, after you've looked at the visitors' book."

Benson Adunbi did indeed have a regular visitor, just the one. Micah Adunbi came every week, regular as clockwork, bringing food to his father. Staff vetted the food because they could not risk anything that might disturb Adunbi's equilibrium. He was volatile enough without stimulants. Sometimes he would bellow all night and they'd have to remove him to the solitary, soundproof cells.

What did he bellow? Usually some tirade about his lost fingers and someone he hated, someone he called 'Bookboy.' No, of course he'd still got his plastic fingers, though sometimes in his rage he would hurl them through the bars. Still, he usually seemed glad to have them back later.

Chief Inspector Padmore Watabenje puzzled over it on his way back to the station. Who was 'Bookboy?' What had this to do with any of the cases he was looking at just now? What was the Super up to?

Holland listened to his report in silence and then broke into a large smile. "Bingo, Padmore, my hunch was right. There's the clue to the burglary at Miss Brandt's."

Padmore considered, then the light dawned. "'Bookboy' is Evans Watanero?"

"Exactly, Padmore. We are looking at family revenge for

the poor deluded Adunbi. Father asks son to keep his ears and eyes open. Son picks up some wrong clues about the house and conveys them back. Father is probably furious that Watanero seems to be so successful, wants to take him down a peg. What better than a good burglary, something I'll bet his son is no amateur at.

"I'd also bet they got a shock when they found all Miss Brandt's dresses. But they weren't going to let slip opportunities like that. Anyway, poor Amos gets caught in the middle. Let's go back to the hospital and see if Amos can do any better."

Celine and Evans were with Amos. "Isn't it good?" she greeted Holland, "Amos can come out tomorrow. I shall be so glad to get my steward back, and he's keen to start straight away."

"Has Dr. Endoman approved that?"

"Oh, yes, of course. I shall go very easy on him for the rest of my time here. And after that Evans will too, won't you, Evans?"

Evans wondered if Celine was wise to assume publicly that he would be the next occupant but nodded his agreement. Holland cut in: "Does he remember anything else, now? About the break-in?" He looked across to Amos.

"Two men. But only one talking. I see the other one but only back view while he stealing things, putting them all in big sack. Talking man has arm round my neck, nearly choking me. He shouting in my ear. 'We know this Watanero house!' I say no and each time he hit me. 'Liar, I see him come in!' he shout. 'All this Bookboy's. All swindle.' When I still say no he hit me so hard I faint. Next thing, Missee Brandt leaning over me. Then I think ambulance, I remember pretty doctor lady. Then faint again."

Amos looked up for approval.

"Well done, Amos! Now we have something to go on. Take it easy when you get out. And Miss Brandt, make sure all the security is in place every night. We can't be sure he won't try again. But not if I catch him first."

Chief Superintendent Holland strode off down the ward, stopping only to greet Grace Endoman, on her way to check up on Amos. "He seems to be doing very well, Dr. Endoman. You and your father have done a great job on him. I'm sure he'll be very grateful."

Grace pressed on to see Evans at the bedside. The little flutter she felt despite herself was quelled by the sight of Celine Brandt on the far side of the bed. Did he only ever come with her?

Celine saw Grace approaching and rose to her feet. "Hello, Dr. Endoman. I'm so pleased Amos will be out tomorrow. I was just leaving but I'll send a car to collect him in the morning. We are all really grateful for what you and your father have achieved. Goodbye for now." And the little dynamo with her willowy figure, almond eyes and long black hair trotted off on her tiny feet. She left Grace breathless.

TEN

Malachi had taken time to accustom himself to London. He just wished he had Evans alongside him again. On his first visit all those years ago he'd turned away from Celine to remark to Evans on the Underground that everybody seemed to be ignoring them.

And Evans with his customary insight had said, "Look around you Malachi, *everybody* is ignoring everybody else. This is one of the biggest cities in the world; people don't expect to meet friends much on the Underground. Though I'll bet many of them catch the same trains every day and 'know' people by sight. But they are British. They don't speak unless there's some kind of emergency, or so I have read."

Malachi thought this time he could break the mould.

"Rotten weather today," he remarked to a man he guessed to be about his own age, and immediately kicked himself for making such a stupid comment down here on the Central Line.

"Ugh," muttered his neighbour, nodding his head.

Malachi studied the advertising cards opposite. "Does that really work?" he asked, indicating a cough medicine advertisement.

"Shouldn't think so," muttered the neighbour, unfolding his previously abandoned Evening Standard and burying himself in the sports pages.

Rebuffed, Malachi turned to his other neighbour, a young woman with six shopping bags at her feet restricting the gangway.

"You've been busy," he said, smiling.

She froze him with a look and took a tighter hold on the handles of the bags.

Perhaps not, he said to himself. Maybe I'll offer to carry some if she gets off at my station. And maybe not. It was difficult to know what these people liked or wanted. Fortunately both neighbours got off at the stop before his. Perhaps, he thought, I'll have to find some black friends. Not many Jameslanders in London, though. Wonder what we'll call ourselves when the country is Bishgad? Bishgadians? Sounds a bit peculiar. Plenty of Nigerians of course but they can be a bit, well, overwhelming.

No, why should I feel overwhelmed? I'll bet not many of them have had jobs as important as mine. Perhaps it was a mistake to abandon it? Still, it was obvious Evans would always be one step ahead of me. No, I've got to sweat this out, make friends through LSE perhaps. The landlady's OK but she doesn't have any black friends. When I think about it, I suppose it's a bit surprising she took me in. But my money's as good as anyone else's, isn't it? Anyway, Mrs. Baldock does a great dinner. And the cakes! I'll get fat as a … 'pig', said Evans's voice in his ear. Yes, thanks Evans, fat as a pig. Must learn to refuse second helpings.

Malachi soldiered on for a couple of terms, making a few acquaintances at LSE but never forming proper friendships. He began to sense an age gap and also something he had never experienced before – he actually felt as a black man more mature than his white fellow students. One or two he got chatting with seemed sceptical of his stories about his previous work. He guessed they simply didn't believe him but were too polite to challenge him outright. Instead they quietly avoided him.

He was invited by a Jamaican to come along to a 'social' but soon learned that his new acquaintance's idea of a relaxing evening involved dabbling in a drug of some kind. He hastily backed off, imagining how well that would go down with his paymasters.

Malachi wrote occasionally to Evans and always received a prompt reply but the gaps in their correspondence grew ever wider and in the final term he didn't write at all. Anyway, he had so little to write about. No new friends to speak of, no adventures outside his studies.

Mrs. Baldock began to be concerned that her handsome lodger seemed never to go out. And he wasn't even going home at the end of terms. Perhaps he couldn't afford it.

She resolved to ask him about it. Or would he think she was getting nosey? But it couldn't be healthy for him, spending every evening working up in his room. Perhaps he'd go home to Jamesland at the end of his first year. She would wait until that time came. Meanwhile she did wish he would take her up on the occasional invitation to watch something on the television. But he always pleaded pressure of work.

In late June, Malachi pre-empted any questions she might have raised with him. "Guess what, Mrs. Baldock, I got such a good result in my first year exams they are talking about a First for me! See how my studies have paid off?"

"Oh, many congratulations, Malachi. I really am very pleased for you. You deserve to do well after all that studying. But shouldn't you relax a bit now and take it easy before starting the second year? Are you going home for the summer? *Is* it your summer in Jamesland?"

He smiled. "Only dry and rainy seasons in Jamesland, Mrs. Baldock. But no, I'm not going home, I'm going to travel round England and see more of your country and your cities. Perhaps I can .." he struggled for a moment. ..."You call it hitchhiking don't you? That means it will be cheaper. And anyway, I shall have the money saved on my airfares. I want to see as much as possible over here, make myself more ... sophisticated ... like my friend Evans back home."

"Well," she said doubtfully, "if you think you can manage, I suppose it will be good experience for you. But remember you can always have your room at any time. You don't have to take everything away with you, you know."

"Mrs. Baldock, I shall pay you rent for the room for the whole vacation."

"Oh no need for that when you aren't here, dear boy. After all, I shan't be feeding you."

Malachi grinned. "Then you make a little profit on me, 'stead of the losses I expect my appetite gives you!"

They had a little laugh together. "I like a man who appreciates my cooking!" she declared. "Don't waste away while you're travelling, will you?"

"Waste away?" Malachi looked puzzled.

"Get thin," she explained.

"No chance, Mrs. Baldock!"

*

Malachi's efforts at hitchhiking were singularly unsuccessful. He had not realised he would be competing with dozens of fellow students, not to mention the tramps who seemed to inhabit every main road and motorway slip. He was never the one picked out by the drivers to pull alongside. Maybe his black skin counted against him. They seemed always to pick girls first and if there were no girls, they might not stop at all.

He noticed the young white men often put a girl to the front and when a car or lorry stopped, emerged from a bush or from behind some convenient cover. Sometimes, he was amused to see, when the car driver saw the boy coming, he'd accelerate away, leaving the pair of them shouting abuse. Still, sometimes it worked. Could he find himself a girl as bait?

Not in a foreign country, he mused. I'll never pick up a white girl here. Dipra's ideas about all the races mixing were impractical. Malachi, who could pick up a girl back home just by winking at her, was out of his depth here. Perhaps he should have gone home after all. No, he was determined to see the country and if that meant paying to go everywhere, he'd pay. Hadn't he seen some advertisements for cheap coach fares? Where did you catch such long distance coaches?

Trudging on foot to the nearest town, he knocked on the doors of five houses showing B&B signs before he found a place to stay. Three of the earlier ones had vacancies signs outside, but claimed on his approach to be full, and they'd 'just forgotten to change the notice.' The fourth had claimed they weren't in B&B any longer. "Must take that notice down, sorry, it is a bit misleading isn't it?"

The people at the fifth place were quite welcoming but clearly puzzled. "You're a student, are you? Which college?"

"LSE"

It obviously meant nothing to them.

"London School of Economics, a part of the University of London."

"Oh. But you're a bit older than most students, aren't you?"

"Yes, I suppose so. Maybe I have left it a bit late to take a degree but I have been very busy with my business career."

"Oh, yes?" They clearly didn't believe him either. They asked him to pay in advance. But the room was OK and the bathroom along the landing not too inconvenient. He booked for a couple of nights and asked what time dinner would be.

"Oh, we don't do evening meals, dear. This is just B&B you know. The George, in the High Street, does a very good bar meal. Steak and kidney pudding, fish and chips, all sorts."

These were at least familiar sounds. But as he wandered down the street looking for The George, he was assailed by a longing to be back in his own digs, consuming Mrs. Baldock's Shepherd's Pie with Bread and Butter Pudding to follow. Funny how that felt like home now.

He came to a pub called The George and Dragon and assumed this was what the B&B people had meant. At the door he hesitated, then heard Evans's voice. "Go on," it whispered in his ear. "You've made it this far. Press on, my friend."

He entered the huge open space beyond the door and the hum of conversation died away as every face turned towards him. "Evans, help me," he pleaded silently, and walked up to the bar as boldly as he could manage. "I'm told you make good bar meals," he said to the man he assumed was the manager.

"The best in Middletown," claimed the barman. "Here cast your eyes over that while I get you a drink. Beer?"

"Coca Cola, please," responded Malachi, burying his head in the big menu while the hum of conversation resumed around him. There were eight pages in the book. He didn't really understand some of the items.

The barman put his drink in front of him and said kindly, "I expect it's the bar meals you want, just on the last page. You from Jamaica?"

"Jamesland," said Malachi. "I'll have the plaice and chips please."

"Right-o. Where will you sit? There's a little table in that corner might suit you. And where's Jamesland when it's at home?"

*

Using the disciplines he'd learned from his studies, Malachi next day visited the local library, approached the girl behind the counter and asked for information about public transport services in the area. He learned that a bus went through to Oxford every hour from the war memorial in the centre of town. And in Oxford he could get coaches to many towns, the young lady assured him. She waxed eloquent on the beauty of the Cotswolds, the elegance of Cheltenham and the splendour of the Welsh mountains beyond. Malachi was entranced.

"Good luck," she said wistfully as he left. "Enjoy your travels."

He felt he had made a breakthrough of sorts. He would go on to see as much of England and Wales as possible. And next year he would try Scotland.

*

A letter from Evans greeted Malachi on his return to Battersea. It was full of news about the growth of InterEarthMove and how well Aberdeen had settled in and how well Celine was running the company. And just in passing mentioned a film they'd all been to see recently, Andrew and Fiona, Celine, Grace, Charles Teng and himself. Malachi permitted himself a small smile. He had been right all along about Grace. She had really been waiting for Evans. But the boy was so slow. He might be a great engineer and manager but Grace would have to push hard if she wanted him. Or would she lose out to Celine?

He wrote back quickly, ignoring the reference to Grace and recounting in some detail his summer vacation travels. He felt better for getting it all down on paper as if he thought nobody would believe him from word of mouth. The letter also forced him to re-live his adventures, recalling all the people he'd met,

113

all the sights he had seen. So pleased was he with the result that he made a copy of the whole letter on the students' copier at LSE before posting off the original. Now he had experiences that even Evans could not match.

He wondered how Dipra was getting on, and idly considered whether it might be worthwhile trying to see him. Could he have visitors in prison?

Malachi postponed the thought and buckled down to the second hard year's work on his degree. But the resumed flow of letters from Evans raised his mood and Mrs. Baldock noticed he was much more relaxed. She thought it must be that the dear boy was coming to terms with this strange new culture at last.

*

It was the trip to Scotland that changed Malachi's life in England. He had learned about Youth Hostels and cautiously tried one at Ambleside in The Lakes. Finding them cheap, comfortable and best of all distinctly multiracial, he resolved to use them whenever possible.

So just a week later he found himself trudging up a path in the Cairngorms in search of the local hostel, in the company of a young Scottish lady from whom he had enquired the way in the town centre.

"I'm goin' there m'sel," she'd said. "Let's walk together."

"I'm studying down in London," Janet volunteered. "But I've come home for a spot of fresh air and exercise. What do you do?"

Malachi was anxious to impress. "I'm at LSE," he said and it came out a little more pompously than he had meant. "Just finished my second year."

"Tremendous!" she exclaimed. "I'm there too, but only just finished my first year. You on some kind of scholarship?"

*

Back in London, Malachi made an effort to keep in touch with Janet, meeting her for coffee each Saturday in the students' bar. Mrs. Baldock was very interested in his new friend and suggested he should invite her home to dinner one evening, but he again felt that would be intruding on Mrs. B's privacy too much.

"No, I'll try to invite her to a meal in the bar, I can't ask you to cook for my friends, Mrs. B."

Mrs. B shook her head. What friends, she asked herself? This Janet was the only one she knew of and Malachi wouldn't even invite her home. Perhaps it was too much like taking your girl home to mother. But he was too old to worry about things like that, surely?

The following Saturday, Janet did indeed join Malachi for lunch in the students' bar. Because she had an idea to put to him. Why didn't he join their amateur dramatics group? It so happened they needed a mature black man for a particular part in the next production.

He was doubtful, could he spare the time? How often did they meet?

"Rehearsals every Tuesday evening. Surely you can afford *one* night off, Malachi? You must be really well up on studies now, into your last year with prospects of a First."

"OK," he said, "I will try it."

*

The Director thought Malachi would be splendid for the part. "But you'll have to improve your diction," he warned Malachi. "Perhaps Janet can help you."

Malachi enjoyed the tutoring of his little redheaded friend who spoke such beautiful English with the merest touch of Scottish accent.

Janet urged him to lighten the tone of his voice, to open his mouth properly and to declaim. "The audience needs to *hear* you, Malachi."

Enchanted, he followed her every word and after a couple of weeks she pronounced him "making great progress."

"Yes," agreed the director, "we'll have you speaking like Martin, yet."

Malachi was flattered but when he was alone with Janet later asked who 'Martin' was. "Martin Maclean, the newsreader, of course, don't you have TV at home, Malachi?"

"Mrs. B sometimes invites me to watch downstairs, but I don't like to invade .."

"Her privacy," concluded Janet. "I know. Come round to our flat one evening. The girls would love to meet you."

So Malachi found himself invited back to the house Janet shared with three other girls, an English with a very funny accent, an Indian, he thought, and an African with another funny accent.

"Malachi's come to watch the news," announced Janet. "I want him to hear Martin Maclean."

"Yeah, right, he's another dish," commented the English in a curious whine, while openly admiring Malachi.

"You Kiwis, always on the lookout. I'll bet Martin's married with four kids."

"Well this one isn't, is he?"

"Behave, Daintree, you'll embarrass my guest."

"Kiwis?" whispered Malachi, who hadn't yet moved from the doorway.

"New Zealanders," explained Janet. "Sorry, I didn't introduce you properly, did I? Daintree from Auckland, Reeta from Kampala and Winnie, a refugee from Johannesburg."

"Refugee?"

"Don't you know about Apartheid? Man, it is the most repressive regime on earth." She looked at him enquiringly. "You West Indian?"

He hung his head and shook it. "African, from Jamesland, still a colony. Struggling under a barbarous yoke." He had to smile to himself even as he said it.

"Thet's balls, man. You don't know you're born. British Government scholarship?"

"Yes."

"I should be so lucky. I'm sweating my guts out in a Wimpy forty-eight hours a week just to get enough for my share here and evening classes at the Poly."

"Come on, Winnie, don't give him the full diatribe, it isn't his fault he's got a cushy number. He's come to hear Martin.

Sit down, Malachi and make yourself at home. Time now. Click on, Daintree."

Daintree pushed one of the buttons on a curious little black block and the screen sprang into life.

"Wrong programme, Daintree, we want Martin."

Daintree clicked again and the picture changed. And there was the mysterious Martin, a distinguished looking black man in a very smart suit, with absolutely perfect diction.

Malachi was open mouthed.

"You two ought to listen more carefully too, then I might understand what you're talking about!" Janet ducked as two well-aimed cushions came across the room. "Behave, now, all you colonials."

Reeta giggled softly. "Yes, I suppose we all *are*, in a way. Or ex-colonials. You'll soon be an ex-colonial, Malachi. What is it like in Jamesland? What did you do there?"

She spoke so softly and Malachi's attention was on the screen, so he missed the question. Martin Maclean was introducing an item about Jamesland. The girls noticed how Malachi leaned forward with interest and quiet descended on the group.

"Yes, Martin," an outside reporter was explaining, "it really looks as if the breakthrough may have come with agreement reached in principle on the form of the interim government for Jamesland, or Bishgad, as they want to call it. If all goes to plan, the elections will have to be held within a couple of years. Those elections will of course be carefully monitored and HMG has suggested international observers nominated by the UN should be used. It all looks quite hopeful."

"See?" whispered Reeta. "Sshh…." whispered Janet.

"And who are the people, Hugh, who are likely to lead the new nation of Bishgad?"

"Well, you have only to look at the group photo taken at the end of the conference. Here it is..

"Centre front is Emmanuel Endoman, from a well-respected family in Henry City – his cousin is an orthopaedic surgeon at the main hospital there. Endoman has only recently come to the fore in his party and now he heads the OBA delegation, and next to him is Abel Iffeled, the leader of the DPP delegation. Those two parties will share the interim government but my guess is that the elections will shake one of them out.

"Interesting to look at the younger members; here is Kofi Iffekan, on the DPP side, not yet thirty and considered their best economist and over here…"

Malachi gave a sharp intake of breath.

"Over here is Dipra Forfpi, his rival economist, though his degree is from Russia so I don't know how relevant that will be in the context of a western oriented young country. Forfpi, and several of the other junior delegates now have to return to their open prison while ministers and FCO officials consider the details. However, Jamesland or Bishgad should be in for some interesting times. Back to you, Martin."

"My friend!" exclaimed Malachi. "We used to work together in Henry City. For InterEarthMove."

"Say. Even I have heard of thet outfit. Scraipers and craines and allsorts. What did you do there, make the tea?"

"Winnie! Don't be rude to our guest."

"Matter of fact," said Malachi, sitting more upright, "I was the Accounts Manager."

They looked at him in awe. "Hey, why the hell did you leave that, chuck?" burst out Daintree. "For three years in London? You must be mad. Girl trouble?"

"No." Malachi drew on his reserves of dignity. "I came for my degree. Dipra's Russian degree won't count for anything. And I think Kofi Iffekan is with the wrong party. So I shall be the best-qualified economist in Bishgad, with my LSE degree. *And* I'll have accounts experience behind me."

"Wow. We take it all back, don't we girls. We hev a future prime minister in our ranks. OK Malachi, just remember there'll be a well-qualified black girl looking for a good job in a couple of years. I'll be ready to run your parliament's catering facility by then."

"And Kiwi nurses are the best in the world, you know."

"Come on, girls, give the man a break." Janet hastened to Malachi's defence. "Don't *you* want to work in the new Bishgad, Reeta?"

"Not if they are going to throw out all the Asians two years after independence," she said softly.

"Yeah, right, but listen, they won't do that with Malachi in charge," said Daintree. "He's going to run a multicultural country, ain't yer?"

"You all counting your sheep, ladies. Wait till I get another good job after my degree."

"Counting our chickens, Malachi, chickens. We still have a bit of work to do on your English idiom. Sheep are what you count to get to sleep."

"OK, chickens for future, sheep for sleep. Good. But you never tell me exactly where *you* come from, Janet. Are the highlands really your home?"

"They are, Malachi. I'm from Speyside, a native of Grantown," she answered.

"Och aye, the noo, it's a braw brecht moonlecht necht the necht," intoned Daintree.

"Shut up, Daintree. Malachi won't know what you're talking about."

"But the Highlands are where Aberdeen – sorry, Andrew Maitland came from and I couldn't understand a lot of his words."

"Oh, Aberdeen," commented Janet, " perhaps he's still got some of the old gaelic. Who's Andrew Maitland?"

"The man who replaced me in Henry City."

They were all terribly impressed.

ELEVEN

Malachi tried hard to keep up with world news and current events now. It became customary for him to visit the girls on Thursdays, on the excuse of watching Martin MacLean, but actually because he was rather taken with them all and quite fancied his own role in the multi-cultural milieu.

He sometimes found the tall New Zealander and equally tall South African rather overwhelming, even if he had a half-inch advantage, but Janet he was used to from his amateur dramatics. It was the petite, quiet and gentle Reeta who entranced him. Perhaps, he told himself, because she reminded him of Celine. A darker Celine but with the same lovely long black hair.

To make up for the evenings he was losing, Malachi worked solidly through the weekends, pausing only to scribble the occasional letter to Evans. After all, there was plenty to write about now, particularly everything he'd seen and heard about Dipra.

Dipra was in the news from time to time, along with other members of the delegation; Malachi wondered when he would be going out to Jamesland. The 'details' which had for so long been the subject of speculation on TV seemed to be taking a terribly long time to sort out. So long that the media interest faded and there would now be weeks when Bishgad was never even mentioned.

*

Dear Evans,

My final exams are coming up fast now so I think this may be my last letter for a while. Are you getting any news about Bishgad down in Jamesland? The papers and TV seemed to have lost interest here but I expect a lot is going on behind the scenes.

I have been wondering if I should try to make contact with Dipra after my exams. Can people visit prisoners in an open prison do you think? Maybe I should write to him first. For now, I just have to concentrate on my exams. My tutor thinks if I do well the University might offer me a schol to do some extra qualification. I'll have to think about that, if it happens.

My one break from studying is this play we are working on; the performances will be a couple of weeks after finals of course We seem to be selling tickets for four performances. I hope it's a big success because we've all worked hard on it. Perhaps you will even hear improvements in my diction when I come home. At least it will be better than Dipra's from what I have heard of him on the telly....

*

Dipra Forfpi had been gratified to be included in the negotiating party put together by OBA and the Democratic People's Party for discussions with Her Majesty's Government but he was fretting at the delays caused by the obstacles Whitehall seemed to be able to erect on a whim.

Nevertheless the new Governor of Jamesland had met Forfpi several times during the latter's imprisonment and had been impressed by the lad's enthusiasm. He could hardly believe the boy had been living in Russia for several years but perhaps that explained why his English was so basic and his pronunciation positively painful. Indeed he frequently needed to ask for repetitions of sentences. Perhaps after another year in Jamesland his ear would be more attuned to the local abuse of English.

Still, the records showed he had actually worked for a British company in Jamesland, a significant plus point in the Governor's view. Though there was little information on what he had done there or indeed how long he'd been in Russia. The question was, had he been thoroughly brainwashed?

The meetings in Lancaster House were dragging on but they were always infused with goodwill. Although HMG was obliged to play its cards very close to its chest, it was quite obvious to the Governor that an agreement had to come out of these discussions. But not too quickly. The protection of British interests in the colony was all that really mattered, though the Under Secretary of the FCO had to pay much lip service to the establishment of the proper democratic structures. It was this requirement that underlay most of the delays.

Looking around the table at the OBA and DPP delegations, the Governor thought the chances of Bishgad having free and fair elections for more than four years after independence were negligible. Well, that was their affair. Or at least he hoped it would be.

They had talked, back in the Office, of making him the first High Commissioner, assuming Bishgad wanted to stay in the Commonwealth. A post to be avoided at all costs. He would propose the young Principal of the Central Africa section – a nice leg up for him, he hadn't got past First Sec. Com. in an overseas post yet. And he seemed to get along well with young Forfpi; that might be a useful relationship in the future. He would mention that when he was de-briefed by the Minister.

Over coffee, the Governor sauntered alongside Forfpi. "For whom did you work in Jamesland, Mr. Forfpi? You never did tell me."

As at every previous meeting, Dipra momentarily basked in the *Mr* Forfpi afforded him by this great man, then told himself he had every right to it. Meanwhile he turned over that curious question in his mind, worked it out, and replied with no shadow of modesty, "InterEarthMove."

"I'm impressed. Will you go back to them when you return?"

"No. I have degree in politics and economics now, from University of Vladamir. I 'spec to work for gov'ment like you, Sir."

Damn, Forfpi thought, that Sir just slipped out. The Governor was a Sir of course but Dipra knew that Sir on its own was subservient and he had no need to be that. They were bargaining on equal terms. 'Sir Joseph' was needed. He'd stick to that from now on.

"How you t'ink t'ings going on, Sir Joseph?"

Sir Joseph looked at him closely while his brain untangled the garble he'd just heard. It was clearly a question. He'd have a stab at it.

"Your leaders are doing quite well but you could help them by urging the case for more complete protection of British interests. After all, you worked for the biggest British company in Jamesland. Have you still got friends down there?"

"I not know. Maybe. One Malachi Goodwill and one Evans Watanero were my best friends. If they stayed I 'spec dey quite important by now. Evans particular is clever man. But Malachi good businessman too. I see'd dem once Heathrow, years ago, just before you arrest me!"

Dipra laughed at the memory. "I 'fraid dey identify me an' cause problem, but your police save 'em de bother!" He laughed again.

"Your police so good, I hope you goin' to send lots out to train our people. Only t'ree expatriate police in Jamesland. Not enough for Bishgad. We need very disciplined force."

Sir Joseph reflected on the irony of this little speech, pleased with himself that he had understood most of it. But like the seasoned diplomat he was, he reverted to an earlier subject.

"I will check on your friends through my office, Mr. Forfpi. Perhaps Mr. Willoughby will be kind enough to do that for me, after the session."

"Mr Willoughby the man in charge Africa at FCO?"

"For a large region of it. The Principal. Of course the Minister is really responsible under our system, but Mr. Willoughby has the day to day running of our work here. I have seen you chatting to him."

"Good man, I t'ink, but hard to negotiate with. We need more help from UK. Shall I ask him 'bout my friends?"

"Yes, do. I'm sure he will be most helpful. Mention that I thought it a good idea."

*

Dipra was amazed to hear how high his friends had risen in the company. And even more surprised to hear that Malachi had been studying for a degree in Economics at LSE. Was actually in London now and almost taking his finals in fact.

"Dat will look better dan mine from Vladamir," he

complained. "But I will be in gov'ment first, if you people get on wid it. Can't you raise initial funding a bit?"

Peter Willoughby said he would look into the numbers of scholarships HMG might be able to fund in UK. "But have you the people to take them up, Mr. Forfpi? Some more practical higher education in polytechnics and so forth could perhaps be of more immediate use. A dozen electricians, perhaps? A dozen carpenters and another dozen plumbers?"

Dipra Forfpi was mortified. "We got plenty carpenters. Figure carvings from Jamesland get sold posh shops in London. I see'd 'em."

"Ye .. es. Very artistic. But not quite the same thing as carpentry, old chap. I've been out to Jamesland, you know, and seen your furniture for instance, which is rather ... well ... 'heavy', wouldn't you say? With such splendid timber available to you, I should think a few well trained carpenters – I mean *designers* as well as carpenters - you could build up a good export market for furniture."

Forfpi's eyes gleamed. "Exports, eh? I learn all about exports. OK. It sound a good idea. But we need more doctors too. I know a few trained in Russia but we need people who know western medicine too. And engineers. I t'ink my frien' Evans probably best qualified native engineer in Bishgad – but only one. Why don' we say one hundred scholarships a year, spread across diff'ren' jobs?"

Willoughby spread his hands in a placatory gesture. "Maybe. I can but ask my masters. Do you speak Russian, Mr. Forfpi?"

"Little bit, enuff for my course, though most in English. One lecturer tell me my Russian better dan my English. But he an Englishman from Cambridge."

Discreet coughing signalled the end of the coffee break and they all trooped in to sit around the splendid oval table again.

"See?" whispered Willoughby to Forfpi. "Your people

could make furniture like this. I'll bet the wood came from Africa."

*

"What do you think of young Forfpi, Peter? Got enthusiasm but not terribly bright, eh, perhaps a bit out of his depth here?"

"Well, Sir Joseph, he doesn't give the appearance of high intelligence, but I rather think he is sufficiently endowed with low cunning and certainly political nous to make his way in the new Bishgad."   "Really? Up against all these big chiefs? He comes from a lowly background, he was telling me himself, if I understood him correctly. Not a head man in the family; and you know how their society works."

"Not as well as you do, Sir Joseph, but I understand the point you are making. Don't you think the new dispensation will shake up that society, give more opportunity for merit? Forfpi is just the sort of political animal to make the most of that, in my view."

"Interesting viewpoint, Peter. Do I hear a certain sympathy for the idea?"

"Well, of course once independence is granted I shall do my best to both support and keep an eye on the new administration. But you will be there, Sir, will you not? Change of title to High Commissioner?"

"No, I think not. I fancy a change. And I thought the HC might be a very suitable role for you, especially since you will be on the best of terms with all of them. I'll put in a word for you with our masters."

*

The talks were going well, but never fast enough for Dipra. His solicitor petitioned for early release from prison and the Home Office asked the FCO how they felt about it.

"Better to have him out now, I think, Under-Secretary, the others were released a while back and seem to have disappeared. It was generally agreed Forfpi was the only serious player among them. But there would be the question of accommodation outside.

125

We have funded other delegates for a while and I suppose we'd have to treat him the same. Perhaps the Thames Mansion?"

"Good God, another five thousand a week of taxpayers money down the drain? Well, I suppose we'll have to do it. Tell him to stick to the set menus and not to use the phone – he can make calls from the conference rooms. Keep him on a tight rein, Willoughby."

"Yes, Sir," responded Willoughby, wondering how the hell he would manage that. Make it part of the release bargain, he supposed. He briefed the solicitor. "Your client must understand his release is conditional on behaving himself on the financial front. We don't want him setting a bad example to the others."

"Quite so," agreed the solicitor. "Though what you can do about it if he orders champagne with every meal I can't quite think."

Willoughby blanched. "Do your best old chap. For the taxpayer."

*

"When we going back to Jamesland, Peter?" Dipra was now sufficiently friendly with Willoughby to use his Christian name.

"Now Dipra, you must know that when you do go back, there will be complications. We know from other independence negotiations. We must have the new constitution all cut and dried and indeed announced in Jamesland and in our own press before you can go back. And we still have work to do on that. If only OBA and DPP could see eye to eye on the set-up we could make some rapid progress. It's your people holding this up now, you know."

"Trouble is," said Dipra, "nobody knows how many each party represents."

"That's just the point of elections, Dipra, to find out. Your people have to learn to accept the will of the people, even if they don't get jobs out of it."

"Interim government should be divided equal. I want Industry Ministry, is all. I know I young but who else has

126

economics degree? I do a deal with you."

"A deal?" Willoughby was cautious. "What kind?"

"Simple. You make sure I get Industry Ministry, I talk OBA and DPP into half shares."

"And what makes you think they will listen to you, when I've been trying for months to make them see sense?"

"I neutral. I used to go to both party rallies. OBA get me to Russia, but since den, I get frien'ly with DPP. So dey t'ink each I on their side. And," he added proudly, "I only one with degree. Forget Kofi Iffekan. Vladamir degrees pretty good in Russia, you know."

"Are they?" Willoughby tried to sound convinced, or at least willing to be convinced.

"I propose secret ballot to pick chairman of interim Executive."

"Dipra they are all hardened party men, the ballot would simply be an exact tie."

"Not if it secret, Peter. You don't know dem like I do. You decide who you want, den I work on opinions. If we get enough people t'inking your man going to win, they vote for him, never mind party. Den *everyone* tell him they voted for him. Some liars, some telling d'truth."

"I will ask my masters. But how can I possibly be sure to get you Industry, Dipra?"

"Easy. You work on new chairman. Tell him quietly all my idea to get him job. And I best candidate in HMG's view. He so grateful, he make me minister straightaway. You play snooker, Peter?"

"Yes, a bit. Why do you ask?"

"I learn in prison. Dey got table somewhere in dis house?"

*

Willoughby put it to Sir Joseph, who sounded out junior minister Rodney Forsure, who put it to the Secretary of State in half a page of writing. It came back with a scrawled 'Yes, for God's sake let's get rid of the bloody place a.s.a.p. Tell me when I can announce something to the House."

Roger Forsure carefully filed the response and gave his verbal OK to Sir Joseph who authorised Willoughby to proceed, "strictly between ourselves, young man."

Abel Iffeled, formerly the DPP leader but now pledged to total impartiality was thus duly selected by secret ballot. Peter Willoughby decided it would be best if the actual numbers were also kept secret since Abel's majority was only three and all thirty two members of the delegation would wish to assure him that they had voted for him. Not that he would believe many of them, but you never knew.

A proper sharing out of ministries was then haggled over for some weeks, but agreement finally reached. And Dipra, who had already promised undying loyalty to Iffeled, had his Industry ministry without even calling on Willoughby for support.

Sadly, the news of this caused the expatriate Director of the Public Works Department, when he heard about it in Henry City, to tender his resignation with immediate effect. However after some urgent phone calls from London and a very substantial increase in the said officer's pension arrangements, he agreed to stay on for the first two years of independence, resigning himself instead to button his lip before a thirty-something ignorant bushman who would no doubt drive around all day in a Merc. He'd rather one of his own men with at least smidgeon of experience should get the job. Or better still, he thought, that Watanero chap at InterEarthMove – now he was even younger but he did know his stuff. Best man in Jamesland in the construction game.

*

Malachi thought of trying to make contact with Dipra through one of the television studios but felt uncharacteristically shy about the venture.

"Go on, man, I thought he was your best friend? What's holding you back?" Winnie was her usual aggressive self.

"Tell you what," Daintree added, " your English is a damn sight better than his now. He sounds to me like he just came down out of the trees."

"Daintree! I know Malachi's English has greatly improved, but don't knock his friend." Janet was embarrassed by the remark. "That sounded so racist!"

"Hey, listen, sorry mate. No offence meant. No racism in this house, you know that." Daintree gave Malachi her most winning smile. "We've learned to live with the Maori all right, intermarried like good 'uns. They say there aren't any purebred Maori left in New Zealand, you know. You think that'll happen in your Bishgad?"

This big long-legged blonde with her outrageous ideas could still make him feel very uncomfortable.

"Well, it happened in South Africa, even though the stupid government tries to outlaw it," offered Winnie. "I reckon I'll look for a handsome Swedish ski instructor and hev lots of nice brown children."

"Everyone will eventually finish up my colour," interjected Reeta softly.

"Yeah, that's right and we'll put the suntan people out of business!" The girls all had a little giggle at Daintree's picture, while Malachi smiled and tried not to look shocked.

"So you think I should write to Dipra?" He seized an opportunity to change the subject.

"Yes, of course, Malachi." Janet thought he needed help. "Why don't you invite him to our show? Then we could all meet your friend. I'll get a complimentary ticket for you to send to him."

"He won't come," averred Malachi. "He is too big a man now. He may not even remember me."

"Go on, sport, give it a go. It'd be choice to have him in the audience. And if he doesn't want to know you now, what kind of a friend is he anyway? Fair weather, we call that." Daintree was leafing through the telephone directory. "Here we are, the address of the BBC. They'll be your best bet. Just mark it private and confidential and they'll get it to him, betchyer."

So Malachi promised to write.

He was carefully constructing the letter the next evening,

when Mrs. Baldock came up with the news he was wanted on the telephone. This was unheard of, who knew this number?

"It's your college, dear. A Mrs. Robinson wants a word with you."

She handed over the phone and stood expectantly, while Malachi wished she'd go away.

"Hello, Malachi Goodwill here."

"Mr. Goodwill, this afternoon we had a Mr. Forfpi asking after you. I know he is one of the delegation from your country but we have a policy of not releasing addresses or telephone numbers without the specific permission of students. Do you want him to know?"

Malachi was ecstatic. "Yes of course. He is a very good old friend. I was just trying to contact *him*. Can you give me his contact address or number?"

"No. He said he would phone back tomorrow – he felt sure you'd want to meet. I'll give him this number."

"Thank you, thank you very much Mrs. Robinson. You make my day. When will he be phoning you back?"

"About ten, he said."

"OK. He can ring me right away then, from his digs."

*

He was sitting on the stairs when the call came, getting in Mrs. Baldock's way as she tried to hoover them.

"Dipra, you devil, rising like phoenix from the ashes!"

"What dat mean, Malachi? I not devil, I big man on freedom delegation, you see me on the TV?"

"I've seen you Dipra. Wonderful. I've got a letter to you nearly ready to post but let us meet somewhere."

Malachi wondered what Dipra's digs would be like. His own bedsit in Battersea might not impress Dipra. His flat in Henry City would have been much more prestigious. He'd suggest somewhere neutral.

"Some friends of mine want you to come to a little show we are putting on at the School. First night is next Tuesday, but we must meet before then."

"Is dat London School of Economics? Where I phone? Where is school?"

"In the Strand. I have just finished the finals for my degree. We could meet at a café I know near the school. For coffee, Saturday morning?"

"I have better idea. You come for lunch. Thames Mansion Hotel. Mid-day."

"Thames Mansion? Very expensive, Dipra!"

"It OK. All on my expenses. I told you, big man now. You coming?"

"I'm coming, Dipra."

*

The Thames Mansion Hotel had been only a big doorway until now. But inside it was grander by far than the Tropical House. How many hundred rooms did it have? And how would he find the lounge?

The head porter saw this apparently disoriented African staring around him. "Can I help you, Sir?"

"I am supposed to meet a friend in the lounge. You know where that is?"

The porter smiled. "I do, Sir. Just go up the stairs there and through the big glass swing doors on your left. Or would you prefer I had your friend paged for you?"

"Paged?"

"Called on the public address system, Sir. What is his name?"

"Oh, no, I couldn't have him called like that. He's Mr. Forfpi, an important man on the Jamesland delegation." Malachi couldn't stop himself basking in Dipra's glory and he quizzed the porter's face in the hope this would mean something.

"Ah, yes, you will find him sitting up against the window overlooking the street in the lounge, sir, I happened to notice him there a few minutes ago."

"You know him?"

"We all know Mr. Forfpi, Sir. He is a very *generous* gentleman."

Generous? Dipra? He must be spending someone else's money. "Thank you, thank you," he muttered, making his escape towards the stairs before any more hints about tips could be made.

Through the big glass swing doors he could immediately see Dipra. He hadn't changed much over the years then. But he was *smoking*. A foolish habit, in Malachi's eyes. Evans had explained to him all the harm it did to your throat and lungs. Even the Europeans seemed to be giving it up now, though plenty of the young people at LSE still smoked. And Daintree smoked, though she swore she was trying to give up. Malachi didn't understand 'trying' but it wasn't his problem. He didn't like the smell much though – and Daintree *smelt*.

He approached Dipra and smelt that acrid smell again as he came near. But Dipra was full of bonhomie.

"Malachi! I very glad to see you again. But why you here, when I hear you were big man in Bishgad?"

"Not as big as you in London, Dipra! You going back soon? Evans will be very pleased to see you."

"Evans! I bet he top man now, eh? Your boss? Dat why you leave?"

Malachi seated himself carefully. "No. He *might* have been my boss if I had stayed. But I actually came because I wanted to be properly qualified for the new Bishgad. Like you Dipra."

Dipra smiled. "Actually," he enunciated very carefully and mockingly, "actually you better qualified than me. But I President before you, Malachi!" He laughed uproariously. "Don't tell Abel Iffeled of course."

"What *will* you do when you get back, Dipra?"

"Let's go in to lunch and I give you some ideas. I t'ink better on a full belly."

"Looks to me as if it takes a bit of filling these days, Dipra," said Malachi glancing down at Forfpi's paunch.

"You a cheeky bugger," said Dipra, "good belly shows de world I important man, don't you know? Slap up lunch will do you good, Malachi, you look too much thin to me."

TWELVE

Celine Brandt read the 'Strictly Confidential' letter from London with very mixed feelings.

Mark Tomlinson has persuaded the Board that he still needs up to a further year to complete the integration of European Contractors Hire's East Asian subsidiaries into our network. The Board have agreed that it would be better this should be complete before you take over so he has been granted this extension. I'm sure the delay of eight months or so will be something of a disappointment to you but I'm equally sure you will see the logic of the decision and of course you are doing an excellent job in Jamesland so your extra time there will certainly not be wasted.

You may want to reassure Evans Watanero that he is still the favoured successor to you though we are very unlikely to put anything in writing until perhaps three months ahead of your planned departure. It will certainly do him nothing but good to have a little extra time understudying you out there in Henry City...

Celine had been really looking forward to the top job in Hong Kong though she knew she would hate leaving Evans and Andrew and all her Henry City friends. Especially Evans. She had thought she had only to steel herself for a few more months and meanwhile she had encouraged Grace to join their group outings. The girl needed to be dragged away from her work occasionally. Andrew and Fiona, Charles and Lilly were good for that. She could get Evans and Grace together without it being obvious. She wondered if Evans still had a bad conscience about 'stealing Malachi's girl' though he hadn't actually stolen her yet.

Anyway it was Malachi's decision to go off to study in London. Still, he did seem to be making a success of it, judging by Evans's reports. It seemed they exchanged letters regularly. Celine wondered if Evans ever mentioned their group outings. Ever mentioned Grace's presence.

Her mind switched back to the letter in front of her. Of course she would accept it. The job was still hers if she would be patient. That's what it was really saying. It wasn't offering any alternative. But she now had to break the news to Evans. How would he take it?

*

Evans's feelings were quite as mixed as Celine's. He had tried hard to put their personal relationship to the back of his mind and to respond to Celine's rather obvious machinations to get him alongside Grace. While his friendship with Grace was certainly developing it wasn't easy to put Celine to one side, especially since he was still playing tennis with her once a week. He enjoyed the banter between Charles, Lilly, Celine and himself but had to be careful not to seem keener on Celine than Lilly as his partner.

Celine had tried to widen the tennis group by bringing in Andrew and Fiona and of course Grace, but Andrew pleaded that the different discipline of tennis would ruin his golf swing and Fiona preferred to walk the course with her husband. Grace had managed to get an evening or two off to come and watch but she never joined in the play, arguing they were all much too good for her, she'd spoil their well-balanced game. But she did enjoy being a spectator. "As good as Wimbledon," she claimed.

Celine had suggested that Evans should offer Grace some coaching on the hospital courts, neglected as they were. He'd tried this and to his surprise Grace had taken him up on it. They were to start tonight.

But now the agonised balancing act in his heart between Celine and Grace, which he had thought would be over in a few months, had been extended to a year. At least it delayed the moment of truth when he would be required to take on the sole responsibility for the operation of the company at the same time as he lost Celine. Celine had been steadily introducing him to the additional skills and techniques he would need, but there would come a time ….

"In this extra period, Evans, I want to take more and more

of a back seat in the operational management of the company. I shall try to give you as much freedom as possible to try out your own ideas, make your own dispositions of staff and so on, though I may have to over-rule you occasionally, because London will still hold me responsible. But we have been mostly in agreement over the years, haven't we?"

"We have, Celine. And I am very happy with the arrangement."

"Not cross about the delay in taking over? Disappointed?"

He paused and looked away for a moment before turning back to her. "You must know I have mixed feelings, of course. But I am content to be patient. Which, I suppose you have to be too. What is the job in Hong Kong?"

"Still confidential, I'm afraid. But it is the present man's wish to hand over a clean sheet that has delayed matters. I'm sure it's for the best.. I hope Grace won't be upset."

"Grace? She likes you and is very happy you invited her to be part of our group."

"Yes, I like her too, Evans. She is a lovely lady and I greatly admire her professional abilities. But I feel sure she will be quite glad when I go, all the same. You have never told her...?"

"About London? No." Evans unaccountably blushed at the reference.

Celine examined him over the top of her spectacles. "Sometimes, just now and then, I think it was all a big mistake. Then I remind myself of the love that went into it and I know it was inevitable. It must remain just a happy memory for us both. And the tinge of guilt we'll both have to live with. Maybe," she broke off for a tiny chuckle, "maybe you will be able to tell Grace after your twenty-fifth wedding anniversary."

Evans smiled. "Mr. MacDonald would have said you should put away your crystal ball, Celine."

*

Evans was working in his blue overalls on a particularly tricky piece of the control mechanism for one of the grabbers, with Joshua in close support.

"It isn't right you should have to do this, Evans, but when you have shown me the secret I will be able to train the others."

"It's alright, Joshua, I quite like getting my hands dirty from time to time. Quite like old times really. Remember how you taught me to scrape a straight furrow with a nice smooth base? I bet I could do that better than most contractors, even now."

They were laughing together at the shared memory when a large bearded white man approached them across the yard.

"Where do I find the chief, boys?"

"Dis man the chief," said Joshua. "Unless you want Miss Brandt?"

"*Miss* Brandt?" repeated the man incredulously, ignoring the earlier remark. "A girl? German?"

"Hong Kong lady," interjected Evans, "She's the Managing Director."

"Nah. I want to see a proper manager, someone who knows about these crummy machines."

"Well then, I suppose I'm your man," said Evans, holding out his hand. "Evans Watanero, Mr?"

The stranger ignored the hand. "Look, son, I'm sure you're this monkey's chief, but I want the big organ grinder, the one who writes the music."

Evans stood stock still, while he weighed up the situation, with Joshua watching him carefully.

"Joshua here is probably the best mechanic in Jamesland. His forbears have lived at ground level for at least as long as yours, I expect. Now, can we begin again with respect on all sides? I am Evans Watanero, Operations Manager of the company. And you are?"

"Swanepoel. *You* are the manager?"

"I am."

"Then I must be enquiring at the wrong outfit. I thought this was InterEarthMove."

"It is. Our big sign has just been taken down for repair."

"Ach, stuff it. I'll find some other way to solve my problem.

Bunch of bloody blecks running it." He started off back across the yard before turning. "I suppose your Miss Brandt isn't bleck too?"

"Hong Kong, I told you."

"Bloody hell, you mean Chinese?"

"Sort of."

Hanse Swanepoel turned away again, muttering something that sounded like "Chinks and Kaffirs in charge. Bloody hell. Does anything work in this bloody country?"

"Take no notice, Joshua. A very ignorant man, I think. You know where he comes from?"

"He has that strange accent I have heard from some other white men. I think it from South Africa. I have met some of them up at the mines, but they are usually very polite. One even calls me Mr. Ademanle."

"Quite right too, Joshua. I think I shall report this incident to Miss Brandt. She will know what to do, if anything. But I wonder what it was he wanted. I hope he is not a big chief for one of the mines, needing some equipment. You think I offended him?"

"The bit about my forbears!" Joshua had a good laugh. "He never expect that!"

*

Celine was very disturbed to hear the report. "Swannypool? And you think he is South African? Must be at one of the mines, mustn't he? I'll try the South African Consulate."

The Consul was a man of impeccable manners. "In what way can I help you, Miss Brandt?"

"Is 'Swannypool' a name from your country, Mr. De Klerk?"

"It is, Miss Brandt, quite a common name. Why do you ask?"

"Could you tell me if you have a Mr. Swannypool here at the moment?"

"Yes, I think there is a new man at the Bendu Mine. He hasn't checked in with me yet but I expect he's pretty busy taking over, he's the new General Manager, I understand. I take it the mine is a prospect for your company?"

"Yes, Mr. De Klerk, we think it may well be. In fact we feel sure it will be. But we may have had a misunderstanding with Mr. Swannypool."

"I don't follow you, Miss Brandt. Would you like to expand upon that?"

"Not at the moment, Mr. De Klerk. Shall we just say some bridge building may be needed and bridges of course have to be built from both ends."

"Quite so. If I can be of any service, Miss Brandt, please do call upon me." There was a pause. "It is possible that some of the newer members of our mining fraternity find it difficult to adapt to the rather different culture in Jamesland."

"Mr. De Klerk, I feel you have understood our problem. But please do not intercede until I can brief you further."

"Miss Brandt, I shall await your instructions. Meanwhile, perhaps you would like to be on the guest list for our South Africa Day party. Given the current problems in my country and the prevailing climate in Jamesland, this will of course be a rather low-key affair. But I hope the Governor and certain senior people may be present. And I should add, the General Manager of Bendu Mine, as you might expect."

"Excellent. I should welcome an invitation, Mr. De Klerk. Would it be too much to ask if my Operations Manager Evans Watanero might accompany me?"

"I shall be glad to add his name, if you could just spell it out for me...?"

*

"Are you sure I should go, Celine? Is it not a little... provocative?"

"Evans, in a few months you have to run this company. You will be the figurehead. And you will be working in your own country. You have nothing to be afraid of in accepting invitations from Consuls. That will be a significant part of the company's PR work. Of course you must come."

Evans grinned. "It is not as if I can hide behind you at parties, even now. OK I will screw up my courage. But he'd better not insult me again. I really want to ask for an apology for Joshua."

"Give him time, Evans. He'll probably adapt to your society in a few weeks. But then, I agree, we should suggest he make amends to Joshua."

Joshua himself was intrigued by the idea but very doubtful. "Papers all say white South Africans treat their people very badly. But that is not so at some of the mines here. I told you, very nice people, some of them. But Bendu the biggest mine of all. You need to keep on right side of this Mr. Swannypool."

Celine was firm. "Joshua, we are not going to sacrifice dignity to profit. This is Jamesland. Foreigners need to conduct themselves properly. There is a saying 'When in Rome, do as the Romans do.' You and Evans are the Romans here, Joshua. Let the man recognise that."

Her determination was reinforced within a few days, when she received a signal from London telling her that a Mr. Swanepoel had asked for quotations for certain equipment to be shipped directly to the Bendu Mine. Could they handle this enquiry locally? London would prefer not to enter into direct contracts with customers, with all the credit and shipping risks that would entail. London would respond drawing Mr. Swanepoel's attention to their local company's capacities. Should InterEarthMove Jamesland not have been aware of this likely demand?

"So that's how you spell his name!" Celine exclaimed. "Obviously I shall have to make contact before the party. I'd hoped to make this easy but now he's given us no choice. And you must come with me, Evans."

With some difficulty, she made the telephone call to the mine. The operator said Mr. Swanepoel was actually down the mine at the moment but she would tell him this afternoon. "Who I say wishes to speak?"

"Celine Brandt. InterEarthMove. You can tell him I wish to make an appointment for a visit to the mine."

Several days passed without a response. Celine rang again. The operator was obviously unhappy handling the call. "I did tell um, Miss, he just say 'OK sometime'. Then he go away."

"Tell him I rang again today. And tell him … no, just tell him I will keep ringing until I catch him in the office. But it would be better if he rang me back, wouldn't it?"

"Yes'm. I try for you. He my boss. He tell me what to do."

Celine was moved by the girl's plight. "It's OK. I know you are doing your best. Just say you think I am a determined woman. Because I am. What is your name?"

"Beatrice Chiluba, madam."

"Beatrice, you are doing a good job. Sweet talk him for me."

"I try madam."

*

Evans recounted the situation to Grace and his own misgivings about it. "I do not like it when politics comes into business."

"But Evans, when you are a top executive you cannot help getting involved. Anyway, Celine is quite right to make a stand. I admire her for that. We cannot have white men looking down on us. A few of the British do it and I hate it. But they are mostly good people, I think. Andrew and Fiona are lovely people. And Mr. Holland is a good man. But I read that many South African people are bad. The politics down there are too cruel. The new independent African countries try not to have anything to do with them."

"But from what I read in our house magazines, South Africa is a big strong country, rich from gold and diamonds and still developing fast."

"That may be, Evans, but we don't have to like them. This Mr. Swanepoel of yours sounds a very nasty man."

"So meeting him may not be good. But his company can be an important customer."

"Celine knows that. The judgement must be hers for now,

Evans, but it will be yours in a few months. You must watch carefully how she handles it."

"I shall do that. Celine has taught me a great deal in recent years."

"Not only in business, I think." Grace gave him a sly look, which embarrassed him. Evans blushed and added, "Of course, there was tennis too. And Charles and Andrew have taught me golf."

Grace let it go. His friendship was better than nothing. And why would he discuss his problems with Swanepoel if he didn't regard her as an important friend? He had even asked her for a second opinion after Celine had made her own plans clear.

For two more weeks Swanepoel ignored Celine's calls and London's letter advising him to call their local company, while his foreman was daily complaining about the lack of suitable equipment. Pieter Pullen the foreman reminded him they were not in their own country now. "You will stir up a hornet's nest, man, if you dig your heels in over this. You forget they will soon have an African government. You want to get us thrown out? Anyway, we can't do much more until we get the new gear."

So Swanepoel had to capitulate. "But it goes against the grain," he told Pullen.

"Man, you shouldn't have come here if you can't come to terms with it. This is a bleck man's world."

The first telephone conversation between Swanepoel and Celine was so close to the Consul's reception that she suggested they should leave the arrangements for her visit to the mine until then. "And you can meet my Operations Manager, Evans Watanero, but then, I think you may have met him already," she added archly.

Swanepoel muttered that he might have done. "He's coming to the Consul's reception?"

"He is, Mr.Swanepoel. Mr. de Klerk recognises a future top man when he sees one. Whatever his colour."

"See you there, Miss Brandt," said Swanepoel and quickly

141

replaced the receiver. He hoped the Consul had some decent Scotch ready.

*

Celine was not unnaturally a focus of attention at the reception. Mr. De Klerk was respectful hospitality itself and introduced her and Evans to everyone who crossed their path.

Chief Superintendent Holland grinned and shook both hands warmly. "At last we meet on a pleasurable occasion, Miss Brandt. And you too, Mr. Watanero. You know, I had a letter from Duncan MacDonald the other day and he was asking after you both." He turned to Celine. "Evans was very much Duncan's protégé, you know, Miss Brandt."

She nodded. "Mine too, Mr. Holland. I am only sad we lost Malachi Goodwill, but I hear he is doing well with his studies in London."

The Governor on his third Scotch was extremely affable. "Your friend Dipra Forfpi has mentioned your name several times in London, Mr Watanero. It is a privilege to meet the man behind the reputation."

Hanse Swanepoel watched all this from a distant corner of the room. And then observed that De Klerk seemed to be ushering the pair across it towards him. He wondered momentarily if he should exit through the door, but Pullen was alongside, holding his arm and whispering, "Courage, man. Face the future. It won't be so bad."

De Klerk was saying, "I'd like you to meet Mr Hanse Swanepoel, Miss Brandt, manager of our largest mines here."

Celine offered her tiny pale hand and Swanepoel was careful not to crush it in his great sunburnt paw. "And this," said Celine, "is my Operations Manager, Evans Watanero."

Swanepoel lowered his head a little as he took the proffered hand, "We have met," he said gruffly. "I may have misjudged…."

"Forgotten," said Evans suddenly, not knowing where the word came from. He turned to the man with Swanepoel. "And you are?"

"Pieter Pullen, foreman at Bendu mine." They shook hands.

"My right hand man," grunted Swanepoel. "Says we need your kit damn quick."

"We'll do our very best, Mr. Pullen, won't we Miss Brandt? But it would be good if you could make friends with *my* foreman, Joshua Ademanle. We think he's the best mechanic in Jamesland, but I'm sure your own skills are similar. You may enjoy working with him, as many of the other mine engineers do. We'll bring him with us when we visit."

Celine was astounded at this piece of blatant one-up-manship and told Evans so on their way home in the car. "If I had any doubts at all about your ability to follow me in the top job they would have been set aside after tonight, Evans. It was as if you had planned your whole approach. You *knew* who Pullen was, didn't you?"

"I did. Mr. De Klerk is a very helpful man. And…"

"And?"

"And Grace gave me some ideas to work on."

"You will make a great team, Evans."

THIRTEEN

Despite the delay, Celine's last day at InterEarthMove Jamesland came all too quickly for Evans.

"You know, I'm still not entirely sure I'm up to this, Andrew," he confided to Maitland early that morning.

"You mean losing Celine, or running the company?" asked Maitland, looking intently at Evans.

"Well, both..." began Evans.

"You'll run the company like clockwork, man. Nothing to fear there. But as for losing Celine..." He left the matter hanging.

In the silence that followed Evans found himself blushing, and hoping Andrew couldn't see it. "You've become a good friend, Andrew. Yes, I can manage the company with you alongside me," he said.

"And didn't I see you with Grace the other night, eating in the Peking on your own until Celine and Mr.Teng from the Hong Kong Shanghai came over to join you?"

Evans nodded. "Well, she is an old friend, Andrew. She was Malachi's girl for a long time. "

"Pretty lady, our Grace, and very intelligent. I think Celine's been quietly matchmaking for some time, but before now you seemed always to manage to keep it to the group. Hope that's a change of policy, Evans. Grace would be a good catch for you. And being married would be good for your image here, wouldn't it?" Before Evans could respond, he added, "Take your mind off Celine too, eh?" and rose to leave the room.

At the door he turned. "Old Teng keeps on at me about opening an account with him. It might not be a bad idea to have another string to our bow. I'll drop you a memo about it." And he was gone.

*

Evans ducked out of the responsibility for the farewell speech at Celine's party. He couldn't be sure he'd stay in control of his emotions. And he couldn't be seen to cry in front of his people. It wasn't expected of General Managers.

Andrew declined too, pointing out that he'd only been there 'five minutes.' Why did expatriates always use five minutes as the measure of a short time, even if it was some years?

The warehouse manager Johnson Bedagwe was ' honoured and delighted' to be invited to make the speech on behalf of all the staff. Miss Brandt had been a 'mother to them all.'

His speech ran for fifteen minutes, to the delight of all the junior staff and the considerable discomfiture of Celine and her two senior lieutenants. But one or two of the phrases Johnson used brought a lump to her throat and she was glad when he finally wound it all up with a request to 'our most senior man' to present the small gift to which every member of staff had contributed, something to remind Miss Brandt of happy times in Jamesland.

Evans collected the large brown paper parcel from the corner and handed it to Celine with a tiny kiss on her cheek, a kiss which again brought the lump, for reasons she would have been hard put to define even to herself. For Evans, the kiss represented the edge of the abyss which he now felt stared him in the face. He could not bring himself to add more than the customary 'go safely' to Johnson's long spiel.

The parcel contained a rather splendid copper plate with a central wildebeest in relief and a suitably loquacious farewell carefully etched around its flat edge.

"It shall have a place of honour in my living room in Hong Kong, a lovely reminder of the happy times I have shared with you all." Celine was adept at using the right words for the occasion. Her audience were properly gratified at this evidence of the high esteem in which she held them all.

"Now you must look to the future. Whatever the final outcome of your political institutions here in Jamesland or Bishgad, I know that I leave your company in very safe hands, those of my good friend Evans Watanero. You should be proud that at last one of your own people is in charge of the company's destiny, a man who has done every job from factory sweeper to

Operations Manager as he worked his way up through the company. He is an example to you all. Give him the same loyalty and energy you have given me and this company can be the best performer in the whole InterEarthMove Group."

There was a spontaneous burst of applause, while she turned away to hide the beginnings of tears.

Afterwards, Evans had a quiet word with her. "Your speech was...."

"I know," she grinned. "I over egged the pudding, didn't I? Nearly made myself cry. But they loved it, didn't they? And the thoughts *were* sincere, you know. Just expressed a little more fulsomely than perhaps I would have done in London – or even Hong Kong. You think I have finally got the hang of your culture, Evans?"

He laughed. "You are a very clever woman. I will never meet another as clever as you."

"*Now* who's exaggerating? You will meet many clever women in your life, Evans. You already meet one regularly, in Grace. And she's not just clever, she's beautiful and what's more she loves you."

He looked away with embarrassment.

"I think she may have loved you for years, probably even when she was going out with Malachi. But don't hang about, my friend. Even Grace can't wait for ever."

"Who are you waiting for Celine?"

She smiled. "My career takes up all my energy. But one day, I know, a tiny Chinese man with a brain like Einstein and several million in the bank will sweep me off my feet. No," she cut off the expected protest from Evans, "don't worry, I shan't make any rash moves. Just try to be happy for me, please."

He nodded slowly. "Yes. I shall wish you joy, whatever you do."

Andrew came to interrupt them. "Tomorrow is Saturday, Celine. Don't be surprised if there are a hundred staff at the airport to see you off."

"Yes, I suppose so." She turned to Evans. "It will be just

like Duncan MacDonald's departure."

"Absolutely. You are, you heard, 'our mother'"

*

The airport was its usual chaos. Evans and Andrew shepherded Celine through the throng up to the ticket desk and heaved her baggage on to the scales.

"Good job you are flying First," commented Andrew, "with all that weight."

"Just as well I was burgled," she laughed. "But I only really lost the dresses Evans would never let me wear. Too sexy for his Puritan tastes."

Evans made a wry face. "Come on Celine, they're all waiting for you in the restaurant."

The restaurant was packed with InterEarthMove staff, each with a large bottle of Planet and all full of laughter.

"You'll have to make just one last speech, Celine, as short as you like, but a proper farewell. Then I will walk you to Immigration while Andrew keeps them occupied." Evans looked significantly at Andrew who simply nodded his assent.

Evans assisted Celine as she climbed up on to a chair and from there to the table, amid great hoots of laughter from all around. From this slightly elevated viewpoint she was able to address the crowd, which had now quietened in anticipation.

"That is the second last time I shall call on Mr. Watanero for assistance!" she joked. "The very last time will be when I have to get down again!"

They loved it and banged their bottles on tables to express appreciation.

"I've got up here just to wish you all the very best of luck."

Evans seized a bottle from the nearest bystander and thrust it into her hand. She immediately understood and held it out with a flourish. "I drink to the health and happiness of every one of you. Goodbye, my friends."

Upending the bottle she took a large swig and there was a short period of absolute silence as every bottle in the room was tipped in unison. Swiftly followed by a round of applause.

Celine leaned over a little and Evans put both hands around her waist and lifted her bodily off the table.

"Thank you kind Sir, now I must be off," she muttered. I'm glad tomorrow's Sunday so they all have a day to get over it."

She waved a hand around the room and converted it into a farewell gesture. They were still waving back, led by Andrew, as Evans and Celine left the room.

A rush to follow was checked by 'Mr. Aberdeen', saying, "No, you can't go further, we'll wait here and see the aeroplane take off in a little while."

"How long it take to fly Hong Kong?" asked one man.

"Today she flies to Rome, about five hours I think. Then she stays in Rome for a few days to see the sights and then on to Hong Kong, I think about ten hours."

"What are these sights in Rome, Mr. Aberdeen?"

*

At the Gate, Evans and Celine embraced for a last time.

"Good," she said as they broke off, "I was afraid there would be no chance for that. I want to keep that memory of a strong African man and a very dear friend. Goodbye Evans. Don't forget about the honeymoon in Hong Kong." And she fled.

Could he face going back into the restaurant? He took a deep breath and strode across the concourse. He would watch the take-off alongside 'Mr.Aberdeen' and in the company of his own staff. *His* company staff.

*

They could see the aircraft taxi out to a waiting area just off the runway.

"Why is it waiting, sah?"

"Maybe something coming in. The airport is very crowded, Johnson"

"London flight comes in about now."

They turned to look to the sky above the runway and to hear a roar as the flight from London touched down, accompanied by an announcement that 'flight BA X91 has arrived from London.'

Everyone's attention was now focussed on the parked plane moving out to the runway end. Another deafening roar and it began its slow roll forward, gathered speed and hurtled away until it was a blurred mirage just leaving the ground. In another ten seconds they could see it turning off towards the North.

*

Andrew and Evans left the staff to their carousing in the restaurant and made their way back across the concourse to the exit doors. Outside there was another huge crowd gathered around six of the best taxis Henry City could boast, with police desperately trying to keep them back, while allowing a sole cameraman beyond their cordon.

"Looks like it must be your 'Freedom' delegation, Evans."

A ripple of excitement passed through the crowd as a number of suited men, all wearing dark sunglasses emerged from the doors to be ushered into the taxis. One of them came over to the cordon, took off his glasses and extended a hand.

"Evans, it good to be back. We must talk sometime." He then turned away and hurried back to join his companions waiting impatiently in the last taxi.

Andrew turned to Evans. "Good contacts in the new regime, eh?"

"Dipra Forfpi. He used to work alongside Malachi and me when we first started at InterEarthMove. He went off somewhere after a riot and we didn't hear from him for some years. Then we caught a glimpse of him when we visited London and he was arrested soon after. Since when, he's never been out of the news. I know he made contact with Malachi in London, but Malachi rarely mentions him."

They climbed into Andrew's Landrover. "You ought to keep in with him, Evans. Who knows what's going to happen in the next few years? I shouldn't be surprised if they try to nationalise everything in sight. They'd still need us, of course, to keep things

149

running. But your Dipra might be the next boss."

Evans smiled. "No. He's clever in his own way but Dipra's never going to be given that much responsibility. Still, I did read he had a degree from Russia. I expect he'll get a top advisory job. We don't have another economist in the country, do we? Except the DPP chap, of course. And Malachi, my goodness, I was forgetting his degree is in economics."

"Kofi Iffekan isn't that the other chap's name? With a US economics degree. And then Malachi with an LSE degree. Both better than Dipra's, I should think."

"You're well read, Andrew. It will all depend on which party gains power. On the whole I think OBA will come out on top. But it would be stupid for a poor new country to ignore all the talent in the other party, wouldn't it?"

"Politicians *are* stupid, Evans. Look at those in the 'mother of parliaments.' Did you ever see such a crowd of braying asses?"

"Mother of Parliaments?"

"Ours, my friend. The UK, oldest parliament in the world, we like to think. Took a nasty civil war to get its power and then what does it do with it? Rip off the public purse and spend all day slagging each other off."

"You don't seem to have much respect for the UK government."

"Churchill once said that democracy was the least worst form of government. And damn right he was, too. Where shall I drop you, Evans, at your flat?"

"No, at the office please."

"But man, it's Saturday."

"I want to walk round quietly and get a grip on the place. You understand?"

"The King surveying his lands while the peasants are all away enjoying themselves, eh?"

Evans gave Andrew a playful punch. "Something like that. But I still feel like the Prince Regent."

Andrew nodded. "King on Monday morning, Evans. Just time to get your crown on straight. Here we are. You sure you don't want me to stay?"

"No. Go home to your family and enjoy your weekend."

He walked around to the hangar door as Andrew pulled away, feeling for his big bunch of keys. But the personnel door to the hangar was already ajar. Now what fool had left that open?

*

Triggered by Celine Brandt's departure, Chief Superintendent Holland was having another look at the information file on the Brandt burglary, as the case was known, when he received the phone call from Evans.

"Mr. Holland, I think my machine hangar may have been burgled – it's even possible the burglars are in there now."

"What? For God's sake don't try to tackle them. Where are you?"

"In Celine's – no, in *my* office. When I saw the hangar door open I decided to phone you first."

"Couldn't one of your people have left it open by mistake?"

"I thought of that first, then I remembered it was locked before we had our farewell party for Celine. We all left by office doors. Can you get here quickly?"

"Like a shot, my son. Just stay put in your office; lock the door if you can. We'll be there in minutes."

Evans dutifully locked his door, wishing he could see the hangar door from Celine's office – my office, he again forced himself to say.

Three cars pulled silently into the compound and a dozen burly policemen got out, leaving doors ajar so as to make as little noise as possible. Evans recognised Holland leading them, with his faithful Chief Inspector Padmore Watabenje in close attendance.

Evans let himself out and joined them. "I can't be sure they're in there," he whispered to Holland.

"Better we find out than you," muttered Holland. "Is there a way out at the back?"

"One personal door in the back corner, to a yard, one in the side opening into the offices."

Holland quietly despatched two men each to guard them.

The rest gathered around the hangar door, from which sounds of demolition were now emerging. At a signal from Holland two of the constables heaved the main door back while the Chief Superintendent bellowed, "Armed Police, don't move!"

The three men engaged in demolishing the cab of the biggest machine as best they could with large spanners froze with weapons poised in mid-air.

"Drop your spanners and come down, gentlemen. My chaps will assist you."

A moments hesitation ensued while the three considered their options, then deciding they hadn't any, they dropped the spanners with resounding clangs into the vast bucket at the front end. And made their way down, each to be seized by two policemen who promptly handcuffed them.

"Good," said Holland, "very sensible decision, Mr. Adunbi." He addressed the remark to all three men but the surprise on all three faces didn't tell him much.

"Which of you is Mr. *Micah* Adunbi?" The taller of the three touched his heart, fingers splayed.

"And you are?" Holland challenged another.

"Steven Adunbi."

"Brother? Cousin?"

"Cousin. My brother Thomas." He indicated the third man.

"Good. Well I think we need to go down to the station and have a little chat about this morning's adventure and the burglary a few months back of a certain house in Woodlands."

"It was not me," immediately protested one of the cousins. "I was not there that night."

The other two turned to him with looks of evil. "Shut yo' mouth!" commanded Micah Adunbi.

Holland noticed, as they walked past Evans, that none of them showed any sign of recognition. This had clearly been a mission of revenge without the participants even knowing the victim.

*

The Sunday papers were full of the return of 'The Freedom Delegation'; though only one was fortunate enough to be able to print a

few fuzzy photographs of figures entering taxis at the airport. Even a picture of one delegate shaking hands with someone in the crowd though neither figure was identifiable. Evans thanked his luck. The last thing he wanted was a crowd of journalists haranguing him just as he was trying to get to grips with his new responsibilities.

The Henry City Journal, the serious newspaper largely read by expatriates had a small item on its business page recording the departure of Miss Celine Brandt and the succession of Mr. Evans Watanero, the first African to head up a major UK company here. To Evans's enormous gratification, it even added, "We wish him well," in its final sentence. After which, nothing.

Evans noticed that not a single newspaper had got wind of the break-in and he silently thanked Chief Superintendent Holland for handling it so quietly. Of course it would all come out in court but thank Heavens the wheels of justice ground quite slowly.

The Freedom Delegation, as all the papers called it, had been whisked off into oblivion and in the next week there was considerable speculation where it might be. A rumour that it had taken over the top floor of The Tropical House sparked an invasion of journalists, requiring the manager to come out to assure them he had no such guests.

The smart money was on the Governor's Mansion and a little group of photographers gathered outside its gates but only the Governor moved in and out at high speed in his Range Rover and during his official engagements he merely smiled at all questions. The press soon found more interesting stories to pursue.

Nevertheless after four weeks Evans had a phone call to his new home.

"How did you get this number, Dipra?"

"In de book, man. General manager of InterEarthMove,

residence, it says. Dat's you now, not so?"

"Yes, that's me, Dipra. Where are you?"

"Not allowed to say. But we coming out soon now, Governor will announce new body, some British, some Bishgadi, to act as interim government. Should have been done before we come, but office cock-up. Anyway, I get responsible for Industry, just like I want. Public Works Director work alongside me. But I want you in too, Evans."

"Dipra, I've got a big job here. I can't just stop it to work for you!"

"Not what I mean, Evans. I want you to sit on committee to advise me. PWD man British, won't understand our ideas. You Bishgadi, help me make right decisions. We meet first, after announcements, probably next week. You doin' OK in new job?"

"I'm managing, Dipra. My chief accountant Andrew Maitland is a great help."

"Malachi would be better."

"No, I don't think you can say that. Andrew is first class. Malachi was good but still had much to learn."

"We talk about that when we meet. I call you from office when I get one. Probably present director's office, but then I have to find place for him too. Goodbye Evans."

Evans found that conversation vaguely troubling. He hoped the new government was not going to be too aggressive, too radical. Was Dipra's thinking influenced by his time in Russia, perhaps?

*

Fiona Maitland and her children were dying to visit the Lombe National Park. The brochures showed wonderful pictures of lion and antelope, giraffe and rhinoceros. And elephant and hippo happily mud bathing in the river Lombetenga. Couldn't they take the long wheelbase Landrover and go down for the New Year?

Evans explained what had happened to Roger Waddell and his family. "You're welcome to go, of course, but try not to drive in the dark, Andrew. The road is very poor. And don't build up your hopes too high about seeing animals. I always think those pictures in the brochure were taken years ago."

"By a photographer who waited three months for each photo, eh?"

Evans grinned. "Something like that. Still, you may be lucky. Take plenty of water for the kids and make sure the Landrover's all kitted out – spare wheel OK, can of petrol, water for the radiator, etc."

"You sound like a veteran."

"No. I've never actually been down there! But I've heard friends talking. Must go myself sometime, though to be honest, wild animals have a pretty limited appeal. In my village, they were considered a terrible nuisance, always destroying crops. You'd be amazed how much damage a herd of Lechwe can do."

"Well, it's the wife who's so keen, so I've got to go, Evans. Scottish women have a knack of getting their own way."

"That's Scottish? I thought it was just women!"

FOURTEEN

With his family on board, Andrew Maitland sped off in the Landrover down the broad highway out of town. After thirty miles it narrowed down so that when a vehicle came head on, each had to put the nearside wheels off the tarmac in order to pass. Large lorries seemed less inclined to move over and on one occasion Andrew deemed it wise to pull off altogether and just let the juggernaut pass. He had long ago become used to the idea that nobody slowed down, even in the face of obvious hazards.

Coming to an open, straight and empty section, he put his foot down. "Maybe I didn't allow enough time to get there," he explained to Fiona. "Difficult to judge from the map. We may have to overnight in Sendova. Pity, though, I quite fancied my first night in a thatched rondavel."

Twenty minutes later, a policeman stood out in the middle of the road and flagged them down.

"Now what does *he* want?" exclaimed Andrew irritably. "It'll definitely be Sendova if he wastes our time."

He obediently pulled the Landrover in, finding a patch where he could get clear off the road. "Yes, constable, what can I do for you?"

The man was all smiles. "Exceeding speed limit, sah!" he proclaimed. "On de spot fine."

"What speed limit? We're in open country."

"See up dere?" the man asked. "Village huts, not fifty yards up hill?"

Andrew focussed on the smudges just poking above the near horizon. "OK, yes, I see the village, but there's no speed restriction down here."

The big smile appeared again. "Come wid me." He led off back down the road, so far that Andrew began to wonder if this was some kind of trap. He'd left the family in the truck. Should he just refuse to go any further? Was this a real policeman?

Then the constable stopped and took a great armful of the

156

tall grass which lined the road and bent it outward. Andrew came up to him and saw what he was exposing: a speed sign, with a faded 30 writ large.

"Well, how was I supposed to see that?" he demanded.

Only the smile answered him. "What speed you t'ink you doing?"

Andrew shrugged his shoulders. "Fifty, perhaps?"

"I t'ink nearer seventy, sah."

It appeared to Andrew he was now in a negotiation.

"Can we agree sixty, perhaps?"

The constable thought for a moment, then allowed his smile to break out. "OK. Sixty will do. One hundred shillings for breaking limit, doubled for each extra 10 miles per hour. Dat makes.." He took out a notebook and pencil. "Two hundred, four hundred, eight hundred shillings. I hope you got dat on you."

"What if I havena?"

The policeman puzzled over this for a few seconds, then returned to the attack. "Police station, up dere. Must hold you till someone comes to pay. But I t'ink you got 'am."

Andrew knew when he was beaten. "You going to give me a receipt?"

"Of course, sah." He tore a sheet from his notebook and wrote in it '800 shilling from Mr....' "What your name, sah?"

"Maitland, Andrew Maitland, InterEarthMove. On our way to Lombe."

"You never get there tonight, sah." He took the 800 shillings Andrew proffered. "Should stay Sendova." On the bottom of the 'receipt' he wrote 'Daysprings Hotel.' Very good hotel, main street in Sendova. Only hotel. Belongs my sister; you tell her I send you, she look after you too well. Loves piccins too. How many in dere?" He gestured to the Landrover.

"Two," said Andrew. "Thank you for your help."

"No trouble, sah. Wish you good time in Lombe Should visit Duke of Dorset falls, very pretty. I on duty all over holiday, but perhaps I will be at Station party for a few hours."

Yes, thought Andrew, now that I've provided all the booze, I hope you enjoy it.

*

Evans was furious when he heard about it.

"Extortion, that's what it was! Simple blackmail."

"Oh, come on Evans, it's not such a big deal. Eight hundred shillings isn't a matter for suing the police over. He was quite a jolly bloke and as it turned out his sister's hotel wasn't too bad, a bit well, scruffy, but decent beds and edible food. Better than travelling by night, certainly."

"Andrew, it's a matter of integrity. I haven't personally come across a corrupt policeman before though I've heard rumours. But to go for a European – that's unheard of."

"Would it make it any better if I'd been African?"

"No of course not, it's just that we've always been respectful of expatriates. Anyway, the point is the police are there to enforce the law, to bring fairness, not to exploit their position. I could mention it to Chief Superintendent Holland."

"No, don't do that, Evans. You could say he *was* upholding the law. After all, he did show me the speed restriction sign."

"Yes, and he should have kept the grass cut so motorists could see it. At least I'll tell Mr. Holland *that* needs doing."

"OK. But dinna tell him I was taken for a ride, will you? I have my professional Aberdonian reputation to maintain."

Evans looked curious. "What?"

"Sorry, not in your culture. Scots are supposed to be careful with their money and Aberdonians the tightest of all. Lots of jokes about us."

"I don't believe it, Andrew."

"Good, because it's nae true. But some of the jokes are quite good. Sad world with no jokes, ye ken. Even if they are at your expense."

"I'll bet the British have some about us."

"Aye, they have. And you about the Brits?"

"No, I don't think so. Perhaps we're too respectful."

"That'll change, with independence. You watch."

"So tell me one about us."

"You might find it offensive," said Andrew, warily.

"Oh, come on, try me. I'm pretty broadminded now, aren't I?"

"Right." He took a breath. "A British airliner is coming in to land at.. let's say Lagos. And the captain announces they'll be down soon and as there is a time difference, would passengers all please adjust their watches, by setting them back ... three hundred years."

Evans laughed out loud. Andrew watched with a quiet smile.

"You think," said Evans, "I would have been offended if you'd said Jamestown?"

"Plenty of your people would be."

"Yes, I see that. It's the grain of truth which is hurtful, isn't it? Is there just a grain of truth in the Aberdonian special care with money idea?" he asked mischievously.

"Touché," said Andrew.

"And I even know what that means," said Evans proudly. "But none of that gets us away from the cheating policeman. Sometimes I worry about the way this nation may go when we get independence, Andrew."

*

The announcement of the new interim administration was a fairly low key affair, but the picture of the expatriate and the 'Bishgadi' executives all in one big smiling group on the steps of the Governor's Mansion made the front pages of all the papers. Even the Director of the PWD had managed a smile alongside Dipra Forfpi, the new Executive for Industry, who would now be his boss.

"You see my picture in paper, Evans?" Dipra demanded on the telephone next day. " I take over PWD Director's office, he move to share with Assistant Director. But he going home in few weeks so my new friend Steven get office to he-self again. We get along OK but I need your help."

"Dipra, I already told you, my job here takes all my time.

Michael Savage is a very good man, I know. I'm sure he will help you all he can."

"Evans, I am setting a committee of top people to help me. You have to be on it. You get letter in a few days, tell you when first meeting will be. Letter will be an order, Evans. Important Government work. I expect

see you dere. I wanted see you before formal meeting but got no time. We talk after it."

*

The letter came a week later.

You are required to attend the first meeting of the Interim Administration's Industry Committee on Wednesday 2nd December at 10.30 a.m. The meeting will be held in the conference room of the Tropical House Hotel. Lunch will be provided and this first session is expected to finish around 3 p.m. You will be advised of your future responsibilities during the course of the meeting. We look forward to your presence. Dipra Forfpi, Executive for Industry

Evans was disturbed. He took the letter to Andrew for advice.

"Well, he's *your* friend, Evans. Funny wording to the letter, sounds like something the courts would send out. But its probably been drafted by a British civil servant. Perhaps Forfpi asked him to make it as formal as possible. I don't know if you can be *made* to attend, but shouldn't you just think of it as part of your responsibilities now, in your new position? I expect Celine would have gone. Anyway, aren't you proud to be called on for Government service?"

"Maybe. There's something in what you say. But don't I remember an English saying about having two masters?"

"Masters two will never do," quoted Andrew. "Cornish, I think. Yes, you're right. But Forfpi won't *be* your master. He's only looking for advice. And you have to stay in with him for the sake of the company, don't you?"

Evans pondered the matter. "True, I can't make an enemy of Dipra. Not that I want to. We were good friends back in the village. But now he's a bit ….well, a bit too cocksure, perhaps."

"Cocksure? Now there's an interesting word. A lot of your people must think that about young expatriates, don't you think? Look, if the legal aspect worries you, why not talk to James Holland? He's probably having to deal with a similar problem himself."

It was true. While Holland still reported to the Governor, he did have the young Joseph Amass trying to breathe down his neck every day. Holland was now grateful for the protective screen Padmore Watabenje managed to erect around his boss. Padmore devised exercises which took Amass off with 'routine patrols' for much of each week, 'learning what real police work was all about' as he put it. Amass was distinctly doubtful but was too young to take a stand over it and in any case he found his leader Abel Iffeled approving of this 'basic groundwork' – and it was important to satisfy the party leader.

Holland wasn't quite sure what the legal situation was but he counselled careful co-operation with the new authorities. "I'm just keeping my head down, Evans, but *you* need to be seen to be *actively* co-operating. I'll be off home a year after the elections, if not sooner, but you have a lifetime here."

"Mr. Holland, I've heard that Dipra talks about the need to have *more* expatriate policemen here following independence. Surely they'll want you to stay on?"

"James, please. They may want it, but somehow I don't see it being very comfortable. Not for expatriates. No, it's your country and you have to find the people to run it. You'd make a good minister yourself, Evans, educated, experienced, articulate, ever thought of going into politics?"

"Absolutely not. I'm an engineer, that's where *my* service to the nation will be."

Holland shrugged. "OK. I wish you luck on your committee. By the way, I am charging the Adunbi clan. Two of them with the house burglary and all three with criminal damage and a few other things for the sabotage of your machines. We might need you to testify."

"Oh, God that will make Benson Adunbi hate me even more!"

"No way we can get round it, my son, you'll have to be chief prosecution witness. Benson is well guarded; he's not going to get out. And I will have words with the family to tell them this nonsense has got to stop. The mother is a sensible woman, and she rules the roost."

"Rules the roost?" asked Evans.

"Sorry, it comes from the idea that cockerels rule all the chickens. But in Africa, it *is* often the mother who rules, not so?"

Evans grinned and nodded his head. "You know much about our society."

"Should do, Evans. I've been here twenty five years."

"Long enough to pick up African mores, not so?"

Holland smiled and inclined his head in acknowledgement.

*

They were gathered in the conference room at twenty past ten, drinking coffee when Evans entered. He searched the room for Dipra but couldn't see him so helped himself to a coffee. Then he caught sight of Charles Teng in earnest discussion with the Director of the PWD, whom Evans knew from his work. He wandered over.

"Evans!" the Chinese man greeted him. "How are you settling in to the job? I expect you know Michael Savage, PWD?"

"I do." Evans shook hands with them both. "The job's OK thank you, Charles, but I'm not sure I have a lot of time to give this committee. Where's Dipra ..I mean Mr. Forfpi?" he corrected himself.

Charles wasn't the man to miss a slip like that. "An old friend, is he?"

"Yes," Evans admitted. "But that won't make it any easier to find the time."

"Your Mr. Forfpi is actually in the games room finishing off a game of snooker. I just hope he finishes in time. He's mad about it, you know, and he waylaid an innocent observer watching him do trick shots." There was a certain edge to Michael Savage's voice, not lost on either of his companions. "But he's so good, he should demolish the poor devil."

"Snooker? Where'd he learn that? Do they play in Russia?"

"Don't know about that. But I expect they play in prison in UK."

"Here he comes," warned Charles. "Proper respect now."

Dipra Forfpi sailed into the room. 'Sailed' was the word that came to Evans, suiting it to Dipra's flowing national costume and consuming bulk.

"Right, people. Let's get started. I sorry to be little late – very important matters in anudder part of hotel. Michael, you goin' to be secretary?"

It was a rhetorical question. Savage took a notepad from his briefcase and laid three carefully sharpened pencils alongside it on the table. "Ready, Mr. Forfpi."

*

At the end of the meeting, Dipra waylaid Evans. "You play snooker, Evans?"

"No. My sport is more active, Dipra."

"Hmph. I could teach you, I pretty good player."

"So I heard. But I simply have no time. Running InterEarthMove is a pretty busy life, you know. I'm glad our next meeting here isn't for a month. Still, this one did seem quite useful."

"Ver'good for me. But you must relax sometime, Evans. Always your problem, too serious. I hear you seein' that pretty doctor Malachi was with years ago."

"You're well informed, Dipra. We do see each other a bit. Nothing too heavy yet. We both have tough jobs."

"Don't let it get too heavy," said Dipra. "She is niece of OBA leader."

Evans was taken aback. "What's that got to do with anything? Anyway, she isn't his niece, he is a cousin of her father, who is a well respected surgeon in Karle Mo"

"I know dat. He good man. But his cousin leader of party

I t'ink may lose election. You want to go up ladder, you drop Grace Endoman."

Evans was incredulous. "Dipra, is this the brave new world your party is planning for us? Where you are going to interfere with personal relationships? As it happens, Grace and I are not planning to take our relationship any further for some time but I wouldn't want to think some politician is able to tell me what we should do."

"I not telling you what to do. I telling you if you want get ahead it sensible not to be friends with opposition."

"But *your* party might be the opposition, Dipra. Anyway, I'm not sure which party you do support. Who knows what will happen when there is an election?"

"DPP will win, I know. And everyone will want be on our side den."

"But I'm the head of a major company, Dipra. I don't want to get into politics, never have. My role in the new Bishgad will be to make sure development is properly supported. Just that. You're not telling me that being friends with Grace would harm my company are you?"

Dipra looked away. "No," he grudgingly admitted. "But…"

"But what, Dipra?"

"But your company may not always belong to the British."

Before Evans could protest he added. "'Course you still be manager, but perhaps government will own it. Den it would be silly if you married into opposition party family."

"Dipra, this company will be worth millions! Why would government waste money buying something already there, already doing good for the country? My plans are to ask InterEarthMove for much more investment when the new Bishgad comes, because there will be all kinds of development money coming in to the country and so lots of work for us. You think they'll invest if you force them to sell the local branch?"

"We may import machines from other countries. Russia has good earth moving machines. Your company could handle many kinds. Competition would push prices down."

"You don't know what you're talking about, Dipra. The service back-up is very important with this equipment. OK bring the Russians in to provide competition but make them promise proper back-up too, otherwise there will be chaos."

Dipra looked disgruntled and Evans was suddenly sorry for him. He knew so little about the real world and here he was a Minister, almost, responsible for a major part of the new country's development.

"Dipra, why do you want me on your committee? If you really want advice, you have to face up to realities. I don't want us to quarrel but it seems I won't agree with some of your ideas. I never said I want to marry Grace, but if I decide I do, I shan't ask permission from you or anyone else except Grace herself. Now I must get back to the office. And you to yours."

Evans turned and walked away to avoid any further dispute.

FIFTEEN

The Adunbi boys were duly charged and brought to trial. Evans was called on to appear as a witness for the prosecution, as were Holland and Watabenje. The defence somewhat half-heartedly produced two members of the family who swore to all three of the men's presence at home when the house burglary took place, but a swift raid on those homes by Watabenje and a few constables produced a number of cheongsams which could only have come from Celine's wardrobes. The story that they had been bought in the market sounded highly implausible to the judge and he spent little time finding the Adunbi boys guilty of both the burglary and the attack on the warehouse of InterEarthMove.

He would pronounce sentence in a week and in the meantime the boys were to be detained in custody. The case was reported in the local press but little importance was attached to it and Evans's appearance not specifically mentioned.

*

Chief Superintendent Holland now found himself invited to meet Abel Iffeled in his offices within the Governor's Mansion.

"Can you tell me what this is about, Mr. Iffeled? Might I need some files?"

"No, just come. Something I want to discuss with you."

Puzzled, Holland drove up the hill with his faithful retainer, Padmore Watabenje. "You've no idea what this is about, Padmore?"

"No, Sir. Perhaps Iffeled thinks he will be candidate for Minister of Interior, so perhaps he wants to sound you out about the future – will you stay on and all that. But where will that leave Amass?"

Iffeled greeted them cordially but then asked Watabenje to wait while he spoke with Chief Superintendent Holland. They were both somewhat abashed.

"Chief Inspector Watabenje is my right hand man, Mr. Iffeled!"

"Yes, I know, but this is a private matter, Chief Superintendent."

Watabenje shrugged and Holland gave way, following Iffeled into a spacious office with a view out over the beautiful lawns.

"You been in here before, Chief Superintendent?"

"In the Mansion, yes, in this office, I don't think so. Splendid views you enjoy."

"Yes." Iffeled paused and busied himself pouring coffee. "Tell me about the Adunbi trial."

Holland looked surprised. "Adunbi? All cut and dried. Caught in the act as far as the criminal damage charge is concerned, and very strong evidence in the case of the burglary. Stolen items recovered from their own homes. I should think they'll get five years, perhaps only two for the younger cousin who was not at the burglary."

"Yes." Iffeled went on stirring his coffee. "Could InterEarthMove drop the charges at this stage?"

Now Holland was genuinely startled. "Drop them? The charges don't come from InterEarthMove. These are criminal charges, brought by the Police."

"So *you* could drop them?"

"No, I don't think so. Judgement has been made. Why on earth would we want to drop the charges anyway?"

Iffeled was silent. "If you found new evidence?"

"Are you saying you *have* new evidence Mr. Iffeled?"

"There might be some. Perhaps the judge would look at the trial again if…."

"I very much doubt that. Judge Ainsworth is a man of very considerable experience who would be unlikely to change his mind without really substantial new evidence. And as I told you I myself, in company with Padmore Watabenje and some six police constables, caught these boys actually in the act of destroying equipment in InterEarthMove's hangar. Also, we have established strong motive for the two crimes. I'm really not sure why you are raising this matter now. All we are waiting for is the sentence."

Iffeled poured more coffees. "I see. And you think five years is planned?"

"Not *planned*, I can't plan anything. That's just my estimate of what the judge will consider an appropriate sentence. Judge Ainsworth will decide, of course. It could be more."

"And it is quite impossible to withdraw charges?"

"Absolutely impossible. What is your interest, Mr.Iffeled?"

"Oh, no personal interest. I just want to see justice done, that's all. Maybe I have a word with Judge Ainsworth." He rose to indicate the meeting was over. Holland took the hint, shook his hand and left.

In the car he asked his Chief Inspector, "What's the likely relationship between Iffeled and the Adunbis, Padmore?"

"The Adunbis? I can't think." He was silent for a moment. "Someone trying to get at you, Sir?"

"Yes, I rather think someone has been. And I may have to warn Judge Ainsworth. Of course nothing Mr. Iffeled can say is likely to influence the judge at this stage, but I worry for the future of justice in this country, Padmore, if politicians start interfering."

"The men seem to think OBA will win the election so Iffeled may not be in power."

"And you think OBA will be better?"

"At least they have an educated man at the top."

"Yes, there is that." Holland pondered the matter. "The question will be whether he can maintain firm control. Whether either of them can. I think I'm going to have a little chat with Sir Joseph."

*

It was on a short trip to Nigeria that Holland picked up a clue why Iffeled might be interested in the Adunbis. While having coffee in the airport, awaiting the driver promised by the Nigerian Police, he idly scanned a local paper left lying on the table by the previous occupant. A small article on the front page made reference to one Joseph Adunbi, the well-known chairman of Edu Abange Motors; he had been introducing the latest Landrover to the market at a spectacular reception staged in Tinubu Square.

Unlikely to be a relative, Holland thought. Sounded like a millionaire. And anyway, how would Iffeled be connected?

Later that morning, during the break in discussions, he asked his friend the Assistant Chief Constable if he knew of a Joseph Adunbi.

"Who hasn't, old boy? He's one of the richest men in Nigeria, even if he isn't a native."

"Not a native?"

"No, he was originally one of your lot, but he obviously saw Nigeria would be well ahead of you and he came across here when he was twenty. He's just turned forty, I believe, so he's done pretty well, don't you think? What's your interest in him?"

"Just that I've met the name in Jamesland. That's why my eye picked it out on a newspaper."

The DCC paused to contemplate. "Of course he's a complete rogue, but I shouldn't think he's ever done anything illegal; just business sharp practice. Landrover is just one of his marques; he's got a dozen Japanese, Korean, Italian and French brands. Then there's his separate air-conditioning business. All in all, a pretty slick operator and well connected politically; of course, you need to be in this country."

"You think he's still interested in his own country?"

"Shouldn't think so, but you never know. He's a Nigerian citizen, well respected, lives the good life here – and in London, from what I gather – not likely now to spend sleepless nights about the fate of Jamesland, or Bishgad, as I think you're going to call it."

"Bishgad will have only two motor vehicle distributors, both British. On independence, the market might look quite attractive to your man." Holland made an internal resolution. "I'll have to keep a lookout for him."

"How long are you going on there? They'll want to retire

you as soon as Bishgad comes, old chap."

"Well, Nigeria hasn't retired *you*."

"No, but they made jolly sure there was a Nigerian above me. Not that I mind; he's a decent chap, quite willing to learn – unlike the arrogant politicians – and my final retirement will be on quite generous terms. Look out for yourself, James. Watch those pension rights. Can't you get ranked up a bit before you go? At least to *ACC*. You are the boss man, after all."

"Sort of," muttered Holland. "Maybe I will raise it with the Governor, thanks for the tip. You know, quite apart from that, this has been a very useful little conference for me. I hope African governments will keep the exchange of ideas going, when they're all independent."

"Not a hope, old chap. They all hate each other like fury!"

*

As Holland had forecast, Judge Ainsworth was soon politely invited up to the Governor's Mansion to meet Mr. Iffeled. He listened carefully but with increasing incredulity to what Iffeled had to say about justice and the tendency for powerful companies to ride roughshod over the little man.

"Mr. Iffeled, justice takes no account of the relative positions of defendants and accusers in society. In any case this was a criminal matter, Jamesland's most senior police officer himself was actually present during one of the offences, with possibly the most senior African businessman present. The case was unanswerable. I have only to pass sentence tomorrow."

"And your sentence will be?"

"Mr. Iffeled, I am not at liberty to divulge the details except in open court. Perhaps you were unaware of that."

"But I am the leader of a party which is likely to form the government! You could tell me."

"No, Sir. Even when, and if, you are the first President of Bishgad, you will have no power over the judiciary, except of course, the power to dismiss a judge, which I understand will be incorporated in your constitution. It isn't like that in UK but

170

constitutions should be adapted to the society they are meant to serve."

This little speech left Iffeled rather fazed. He sensed he had been put down, even though the last sentence seemed to show some sympathy with the new cause. He tried just one last gambit.

"I do hope, Judge Ainsworth, that when passing sentence, you will take into account the poverty and misery you may be inflicting on the innocent families of these men."

Ainsworth looked at him and rose from his chair. "My sentence will attempt to balance the needs of justice with the wider concerns of society. Goodbye, Mr. Iffeled, I can see myself out."

*

Chief Superintendent James Holland thought carefully how to approach the problem. It was when he happened to see Evans Watanero loading groceries from the supermarket into his car that the idea occurred to him.

"Evans, time you got yourself a decent motor, surely?"

Evans looked up. "This was Celine's. If it was good enough for her I suppose it should be good enough for me."

"But it's a woman's car, Evans. Surely you could put on a bit more style? Budget a bit tight?"

"No, no, I do not think London would object to my replacing it. We allowed Andrew to buy a pretty good Landrover."

"A big beautiful Peugeot Estate would look more appropriate. Go anywhere, they will. Mine's a bit long in the tooth now, but I can't see the powers that be authorising a replacement for an old boy who'll be on his way in a few months."

"On your way? Surely you'll stay on for a bit after independence? And how long will that be?"

Holland shrugged. "Who knows? I should hope to survive until the great day, perhaps, but after that … What about this car of yours? Fancy the idea?"

"You know, I've never actually bought a company car for

myself. Funny, isn't it, I've bought huge pieces of equipment worth thousands of pounds, but only from my own company, of course, and then I've had to justify the purchase in terms of its resale potential or its earning power in rentals. But a car..."

"No problem, Evans. Why don't I come with you to help out? Not that you can go far wrong with a *new* car, it's when you're buying old bangers you have to watch out."

"Old bangers?"

"Sorry, slang expression for second hand cars. I suppose it refers to the noise their engines might make. A new car will have a guarantee, of course. An estate would take the groceries much easier," said Holland, observing the difficulty Evans was having. "What do you say?"

"Well, I could look, couldn't I? Better ask Andrew first, he'll know if it might raise any problems."

"You do that, Evans. There must be a budget for the GM's car and I'm sure Andrew will encourage you to get something more in keeping with your position."

*

Evans asked Grace first. She was amused.

"Lucky you, being able to buy a new car just like that. Mr. Holland is right; your present car isn't very dignified, for a man. Why ask *me*?"

"I wouldn't want people to think I was getting ...."

"Stuck up?" volunteered Grace.

"It's difficult to justify grand cars when half the population can barely make ends meet and my own workforce is...."

"I think your own workforce is very happy to see your success. A new car would be a proper symbol of achievement. Mr. MacDonald always drove a good car and Celine got one that was, well, smart – I think it's a lovely car but I understand Mr. Holland's view that it really isn't a top man's car. Celine wasn't looking for dignity, she wanted to make her own impression, unique, clever, sexy, I think they call it zip in UK."

A thought suddenly struck Evans. "Would *you* like it? You

are unique and clever...and...it would suit you," he finished lamely. "We could sell it to you if I get a new one."

"I meant the car is unique; but then so was Celine. So I'm not sexy then?"

Evans turned his face away. "You are ... you are beautiful and very clever and...."

"But not sexy?"

"OK. I give in," he laughed, at the same time blushing furiously, "yes, you're sexy too."

"Nice," she said. "Go and buy yourself a new car, Evans. And tell me how much your present car will sell for."

*

Next he approached Andrew, reporting his conversation with Holland.

"About time, man. I was on the point of mentioning it. Go and buy the car James Holland suggested. We can sell yours on the market."

"Grace is interested."

"Is she, then? We could offer it to her at book value, couldn't we? It's worth more because it's been so well looked after, but for a friend ..."

"I'll talk to James Holland about a visit to City Cars. You want to come?"

"No. Just make me jealous! Seriously, James will be a very good adviser. And he'll frighten a good discount out of them!"

From among the range in the showroom, Evans chose a luxurious Peugeot in what the brochure called 'Thunder Grey'.

"Very dignified," commented Holland. Then turning to the salesman, "Who is the Merc for?" He gestured to a splendid drop-head coupé in a particularly bright red.

The salesman seemed embarrassed. "Special client, Sir."

"The Governor, perhaps?" asked Holland with a lift of the eyebrow. It didn't seem the Governor's style to him, but who else could afford such a beast? "Must be a very wealthy gentleman."

"It is…partly…a gift. Somebody our Board wishes to pleasure."

Holland abruptly changed the subject. "Good discount, eh? What discount can you offer my friend?"

"Five percent," responded the salesman, far too quickly.

"You a UK owned company?" enquired Holland innocently.

"Mostly. I might be able to stretch to ten."

"Good margins in your business, I expect," chipped in Evans. He was beginning to enjoy this.

"Why don't you try twenty?" asked Holland. "Some local capital in here, is there?"

"Some shares held by a Nigerian. He'd kill me if I went to twenty."

"So he's the majority owner?"

"Just. Would you settle for fifteen?"

"Seventeen and a half," pronounced Evans. "Your Nigerian will allow that, I'm sure. Cheque from InterEarthMove – and the prospect of more sales as we grow."

The salesman busied himself with calculations on a scrap of paper. "Well," he eventually conceded, " I can get close, let me at least round it up…I could suggest this to my boss." He showed them the figure he proposed.

"OK," said Evans. "Put that in proper written quotation form and I'll let you know."

The salesman hurried off into a back office, while James Holland carefully examined the glossy brochure. At the foot on the inside of the front cover were the full details of the importing company and he had what he'd been looking for. He pushed it in front of Evans with a warning finger to his lips.

"See that?"

In very small print were the directors' names. And tucked away in the middle was Joseph Adunbi (Nigerian).

*

The Adunbi boys were given three years for the burglary and two for the criminal damage, the sentences to run concurrently. Thomas Adunbi was charged only with the criminal damage and got just the two years.

"Five years!" complained Micah Adunbi to the policeman who took him away.

"No, no, you wrong. If dey concurrent, dey overlap. You only got three years ahead. Maybe less if you good boy."

"How does Judge think our families will survive widout us?"

"You should t'ink of dat before robbing people. You lucky not get five years proper, I think."

"When freedom comes, we all share same wealth, not some rich some poor. Maybe if freedom comes soon I get out early. Maybe all prisoners go free for new start."

"Never! Criminals got to be punished, stop dem doin' it again."

"We not criminals! No gang, no violence, just steal a few dresses."

"And smash up few machines. How you like your wife's dresses stolen? Your car smashed up?"

"My car already smashed up," said Micah, "ten years old when I buy it. Dis a very unfair world."

The policeman scratched his head. "Some people more clever, work harder, dey get rich."

"And some people have white skin. Dey gets rich. You t'ink dey all rich in Engaland?"

"No. Some prisoners have been and dey see poor people just like us."

"DPP says it will not be like dat in Bishgad."

"So does OBA, but I don't believe any of dem. Get in de wagon."

*

The Governor was not pleased with the progress of the Interim Administration. He had reports of attempts to wield influence by party leaders and others, on the police, on some top businessmen, even on the judiciary. He determined to raise the matter with his masters in London.

"They're all the bloody same in Africa," commented the

Foreign Secretary. "What do you expect? They'll be at it the minute we depart anyway, so why worry?"

"With respect, Foreign Secretary, we owe them a duty to hand over a strong and fair administration; to depart with clean hands at least."

"So what do you want to do?"

"Postpone the elections for eighteen months, give me time to talk some sense into them."

"What? There'd be hell to pay in the House. The PM's keen to get shot of them. And the opposition would crucify us for hanging on to our colonial past. Not to mention the anger you would face locally."

"I can deal with the local anger, Foreign Secretary. I must advise that if we leave a shaky foundation, we shall inevitably get the blame in future years for any problems which may arise. You will be bombarded with questions after the first coup. You've seen that in other countries."

The Minister propped his elbows on the vast desk and rested his face in his hands. He looked across to his Junior Minister. "What do you think, Rodney?"

"The Governor has some legitimate concerns, Sir. Can we have a view from the Under Secretary?"

"Oh, I'm not as intimately concerned with Jamesland as young Willoughby here," protested Sir Humphrey. "What do you think, Peter?"

Peter Willoughby took a deep breath and looked around the distinguished gathering. This was his great chance. Muff this and his career would be in tatters. Make it work and he'd be a hero. But who should he back? The temptation was to back the FS and get into his new High Commissioner Post as quickly as possible. But then if there was a coup, he'd be on the ground in the thick of it. With the ex-Governor telling everyone, 'told you so.' No he'd better back the Governor. Sir H would clearly go along with whatever was suggested, he was too near retirement to want another battle. And junior minister Rodney Forsure was just a cipher; everyone in the Office knew that.

"I think the Governor's plan, which will require great courage on his part, must be the best for the country, Sir."

"Right! On your head be it, Governor. Let me have a Statement to read to the House a.s.a.p. I'll check it with the PM. Have copies ready for distribution as soon as I make the announcement. We must all sing from the same song sheet on this, gentlemen. All right, off you go."

In the huge corridor outside the FS's office the group paused.

"Right. The boss has spoken. I'm sure I can leave this little matter to you, Rodney, to sort out with the Governor and Willoughby. Let me have your final draft by noon will you?" The Under Secretary swiftly entered his own office and closed the heavy door.

"My office or yours, Minister?" queried Willoughby.

"Mine, of course. I'll get some coffees laid on. The FS was never one to consider human comforts."

The three charged with the destiny of seven million people made themselves comfortable in the vast black leather arm chairs grouped around a beautiful inlaid coffee table in a huge, close carpeted office with pictures of grand Victorian gentlemen on every wall, to be served coffee by an exquisitely lovely young lady who had been celebrating her double first at Oxford only six months earlier. Willoughby tried not to be distracted from the business in hand.

*

The Governor was safely back in Henry City before the day of the House announcement. He called the leaders of DPP and OBA and five each of their top aides to an urgent meeting. And let them have it.

"Gentlemen, I'm sorry to have to tell you that I am very disappointed with the conduct of the Interim Administration."

Their eyes showed startled whites. Mouths began to open in protest but the Governor raised an admonishing hand and they fell quiet.

"Some of you have sought to influence matters which are

not within your powers. Some of you, I regret to say, may have accepted inducements to use such influence. If Bishgad is to be a law-abiding democracy, where the rule of law is paramount and the rights of the individual are fully and properly respected, these practices must cease."

There was silence as they waited for the consequences.

"My government has decided to delay independence by eighteen months."

SIXTEEN

Sir Joseph sat quietly through the uproar that followed, looking from side to side as he listened to the accusations people were hurling at him and at each other. At one point he even got up and walked over to the sideboard to pour himself another coffee. Gradually the noise died down, as they realised he had not responded to a single one of their protests.

"Gentlemen, are you now willing to listen?"

The silence and wondering faces reassured him.

"Good. If you are to achieve your cherished ambition of an independent Bishgad, you will need to follow the rules, which I am about to explain to you. You will not like these rules, indeed some of you will clearly hate them, but you have no choice in the matter."

A lone voice struck in. "You may be asking for an armed insurrection."

The Governor looked coolly at Joseph Amass. "That seems to me a peculiarly inappropriate response from the Executive currently responsible for the maintenance of law and order. Does anyone else around the table contemplate joining Mr. Amass's terrorist army?"

"I didn't say terrorist, I said armed insurrection."

"I doubt, Mr. Amass, if our military forces would be able to distinguish the difference." The Governor gave a short sigh of dismissal and resumed his air of headmasterly command.

"For the next year, I need you to drop all references to Party and to welcome the creation of the Interim Government of National Unity. IGNU for short."

IGNU fortunately meant wisdom in the local dialect. Whitehall had very nearly saddled him with the ridiculous title of Provisional Interim Government for his new administration. It would have been, he acerbically pointed out, a PIG of a mistake.

There were murmurs around the table but he ignored them.

"Some of you will be appointed to Posts in this administration and if you can be seen to be handling them responsibly, you will remain in post after autonomy is granted, until the first election. Before that we shall hold an election only for the post of Interim First Minister. I need one popularly elected minister to advise me on day-to-day matters. Candidates for that post will have to demonstrate support from all ten regions of the country, in order to ensure that selection will not be based on tribal affiliations. All clear, so far?"

"When will parties be allowed again?" asked Dipra Forfpi.

"Just before independence, but no party will be registered unless it can demonstrate support across all ten regions again. The details will be in the revised constitution, which is being printed in London at this moment.

"Meanwhile the new Interim First Minister will have no party affiliation. Elections to an Assembly will be held six months after the formal declaration of Autonomy, and they will be on party lines so that at Independence there will be a strong government ready to take over. After that you will be on your own, to structure your own government and appoint your own ministers. I shall be conducting interviews over the next few days to make the Interim appointments, and not all of them will be from this group."

There was a clear menace in this last statement and more than one of them felt a chill.

"How can you force this on us? We shall appeal to your Prime Minister in UK."

"My PM is of course fully aware of these plans, which have his total support, Mr. Amass. Indeed he is making a statement to the House in London at this very moment. We came to the conclusion that there were enough level headed leaders in Jamesland to see the benefits of this policy and to make the arrangements work."

"But it means all the power is in your hands!"

"Until Autonomy, yes. And even thereafter I shall retain a good deal of power until full independence. But you may *all* wish to throw your hats in the ring for the election to Interim First Minister, a post that will have considerable influence, I need hardly say. I will accept nominations of any of you who can demonstrate at least some cross country support – twenty voters in each region."

"When will that election be held?" asked Dipra Forfpi.

"You have two months to get your nominations in and then one more month to campaign, but without, let me emphasise again, without party labels. The election will be open and fair and approved candidates will be given equal radio time to argue their case."

A mad, exciting thought struck Dipra. If there were effectively no parties, he owed loyalty to nobody. He could even –

"Governor, you have my support." Emmanuel Endoman looked around the table for endorsement.

"Thank you, Mr. Endoman," said the Governor quietly.

"And mine," added Iffeled and Dipra simultaneously.

A disjointed chorus of grudging approval moved like a wave around the table. Last of all, Joseph Amass.

"It is not African, but we must accept it, I suppose."

"Good," said the Governor. "I will arrange for my secretary to call those of you I wish to interview over the next three or four days. Please do not interpret a call as a guarantee of a post. These talks will be investigative. When the final decisions are made I shall seek approval from HMG before announcing them and I shall announce the date from which these new Interim Administrators will take over the responsibilities from the present Executives. Meanwhile, please return to your posts and get on with running the country as best you can. Thank you, gentlemen."

He rose to indicate the session was at an end and they reluctantly shuffled out, each cursing that there had been no opportunity for a quiet word with the Governor before departing.

"May I have five minutes with you to discuss a matter which has arisen in my department, Governor?" It was Iffeled who had solved the problem.

"No, Mr. Iffeled. You must solve your own problems for a few more days."

181

The rebuff was quite sufficient to deter anyone else with similar ideas.

*

Evans was surprised to receive a summons from the Governor to the Mansion.

"An invitation, Mr. Watanero, not a summons." Sir Joseph was in his most emollient mood. "I have an idea to put before you which I hope you will give serious consideration."

Evans sat quietly watching the Governor.

"You may have guessed that it has a bearing on the recent press announcements about the delay in Independence?"

"How does that affect me, Sir?"

"I should like you to take on the portfolio of Public Works."

"But I am not a politician! I am an engineer."

"And one who has been in a position to observe all the works going on across the country for some years. Your reputation goes before you, Mr Watanero, a reputation for honesty and integrity and for competence. The British Public Works Director would be glad to work with you. Indeed I believe he would be happier with you than with Mr. Forfpi."

The Governor gestured to stall Evans. "I have a superfluity of politicians, Mr. Watanero, but only a handful of really competent people with which to form a government. You may say that is the Brits' fault for not training you, and I would have to hold up my hand to that, but the fact remains, competent people are very thin on the ground. In the absence of competence, I shall seek integrity, another quality which is all too often absent in politicians, but not all politicians, of course. In you I feel I have a rare combination. Will you please think about it?"

"Sir, I have a large and important company to run."

"Could your friend Andrew Maitland not take that over?"

Evans considered this. "He could run it, of course, and very well. But it would be a bad move to put another expatriate in charge after it had been Africanised, wouldn't it?"

"You have a good point there. But perhaps you have heard the expression about omelettes and eggs?"

"I'm sorry?"

The Governor smiled. "Probably too obscure to have become part of your idiom, though your English is excellent, Mr.Watanero. The saying is, 'you can't make an omelette without breaking eggs.' I have to make choices, and it is very difficult to choose between perfectly good flourishing eggs, ready to produce excellent chicks perhaps, and the golden omelette I see for the future. You see what I mean?"

Evans nodded. "I am ... honoured to be considered ... but it is a very big decision. The biggest I have ever been faced with. May I have time to think it over?"

"Of course. I need several days to put this administration together. A reply by Monday would be very helpful. Enough time?"

"I must accept that it is, Governor. Perhaps discussing it with friends would help."

"No doubt. But not, please, Mr Forfpi or Mr. Maitland. And only someone with total discretion."

Evans nodded. "Of course." He rose to go and the Governor proffered his hand.

"I hope you decide to accept. Just a last thought. Isn't your friend Malachi Goodwill due back soon from LSE?"

"In a few months."

"So an expatriate succession at InterEarthMove might be just a holding operation? Think about it."

*

"You seem to be an expert on Chinese food," commented Grace. "You always knew just what you were ordering when we came here in the group. I suppose Celine taught you."

"Yes. We ate here first when celebrating Malachi's promotion, with Lilly Bell. You had been invited but refused him, if you remember."

Grace was silent.

"There are things I want to talk to you about this evening. Things I need your advice on."

"*My* advice! Since when did brain box Evans Watanero

need *my* advice?"

"Grace, don't attack me. You are a good friend and I need a good friend's objective view on a situation. Please."

She was struck by the sincerity in his voice. He was a difficult man to know, but she had always felt he was honest. She would take him at his word. "Go on then."

"The Governor has asked me to be the Administrator of Public Works in the Interim Administration."

"But that's wonderful! So what is your problem?"

Evans waited while the waiter brought all the dishes and placed them on the spinning wheel in the table centre. "Enjoy your meal," he said and they smiled at him.

"Help yourself to the nearest items, Grace," Evans gestured. "Start with the rice, of course."

"So, Minister Watanero, eh?"

"Sshh.." he murmured. "Nothing is decided. Obviously I cannot do both jobs. It has taken me years to get to the top of InterEarthMove and I am reluctant to let it go."

"But to be in the Government is a great honour, Evans."

"Yes, I know that. But InterEarthMove has invested so much time and money in me, I am ... can I let them down now?"

"You mean, you would see it as a sort of betrayal? Of your company – and of Celine?"

He didn't answer, but steadily munched through the food. Had Grace put her finger on an aspect he wouldn't even admit to himself? Was it just the company he would be letting down? Celine had gone out of her way to reassure him that his only duty was to himself; that he 'owed' her nothing; that his position had been obtained by intelligence and hard work. But did Grace see it that way?

"I am the only African at the head of a major company here. If I go into Government I shall have to leave the company to Andrew."

"Is that so bad? You are very good friends. And you are always telling me how much you admire his ability."

"I do, I do, but he's still an expatriate."

Grace thought about this, while she carefully dissected a king prawn. "These are really delicious. Isn't there someone on your staff who can be groomed to take over very soon? How long would you be gone anyway? Surely the Governor doesn't expect you to go into politics as a career? Or do you fancy that life? Another Dipra?"

"No. Definitely not a political career. But perhaps I could be a good influence on Government policy during the early years. Moderate some of the madcap ideas Dipra has."

"It sounds to me you have already decided and won't admit it to yourself."

"No, that isn't right. I need to know what *you* think."

"Why should my opinion influence you, Evans? It is a decision you have to make for yourself. It is your life."

He was silent for a moment as the waiter collected their plates. They ordered lychees, which Evans explained left a clean taste in the mouth. When the waiter had departed, Evans looked at Grace very carefully.

"Would you consider marrying me, Grace?"

With difficulty she suppressed the smile that wanted to break out all over her face. "Are you serious?"

"You know very well I'm serious. Or are you saving yourself for Malachi?"

"Ridiculous, Evans. About as likely as you marrying Celine."

He flinched.

"Yes, I know you had hopes, even though you could see it was completely impractical. She was lovely, and very intelligent, and happy ... and in another society perhaps you could have ... but here ...

"Celine is in the past, Grace. Will you marry me?"

She sighed. "Well, I suppose I can't expect romance from a cool calm analytical engineer, can I?" She paused. "Yes, I'll marry you." Now she let the smile loose.

He was filled with the sudden joy that comes from the conviction   that everything in the world is *right,* that he'd just done the most sensible thing in his life. It was all he could do to suppress a whoop.

Instead he stretched his hand across the table and said, "Thank you, Grace. You have just made me the happiest man in Jamesland. *Now* will you help me with my decision? Now that it's *our* life. What do you advise for your husband?"

"Not quite yet, Evans. But go for it, of course. Accept the Governor's offer. But don't join a party; just be yourself. You are better than all of them."

*

The Governor was delighted by Evans's decision and suggested he should now talk it over quietly with Andrew Maitland, but not, for the time being with Dipra Forfpi. The make-up of the new Interim Government of National Unity would be announced on Friday. That was quite soon enough for Mr. Forfpi to know. Forfpi would in any case have a suitable role; he would not, the Governor thought, be too disappointed losing Public Works.

For once, Andrew Maitland was taken aback. He absorbed the news in silence, while Evans explained the probably temporary nature of his new role.

"You will need London's approval for me to take over, Evans. They may have other ideas. I have no experience of General Management. They may want to fly someone out."

"Yes, I know. But I want *you* to take charge, perhaps just until Malachi comes back. Perhaps until I'm released from the Government. I don't know. But surely you'd like to grab it?"

"I would so. I'm grateful to ye for suggesting me, but I have my doubts London will agree."

"Let's see, Andrew. I'll phone the Personnel Director and see if I can't talk him into it. One other thing I have to tell you, I'm getting married."

"Och, you've seen the light at last! So Grace finally caught up with you?"

Evans was a little shocked. "I asked *her*, Andrew! Last night, at dinner in the Flower Garden."

"Of course. I'm sure she wouldn't have had it any other way." He gave Evans a playful punch.

"You're a great engineer, Evans, but I shall worry about your political abilities. Still, Grace will help you, I expect. Give her my sincere congratulations. She's got a good man."

Evans now spent some time on the telephone to London, announcing his decision to leave the company and coaxing a reluctant Personnel Director to agree that Andrew Maitland was the man to fill the gap. It was an honour for the company for him to be asked to join the Interim Government. He would always be on hand to advise Andrew if necessary. When he came off the phone he congratulated himself on his new-found powers of persuasion. Perhaps Grace had done that for him.

The Interim Government was to be announced on Friday at twelve noon. Dipra Forfpi was to get Industrial Development, a post which pleased him, though he was very surprised to hear of Evans getting Public Works. He telephoned at eleven forty-five.

"Evans, you a sly dog! Why you give up top job for dis temporary post?"

"Because I was asked, Dipra, and I think I can bring some helpful thinking to it. After all, that's what you said yourself. I must go, Dipra, I have to talk to my staff. You are pleased with your job?"

"It OK. Good we still working togedder. I see you soon."

Evans called a meeting of all staff to speak to them before they learned the news from the radio. They all knew Mr. Aberdeen and he was sure the company would continue to grow and provide everyone with a good living. London had approved Mr. Aberdeen taking over. He didn't emphasise the temporary nature of Andrew's post, knowing it would cause uncertainty. Better they accepted Andrew simply as the new boss man.

"You handled that very well, Evans. Thank you. The Governor's clearly a fast mover, if you are to take up post in a week. Hope I can come back to you for advice now and then – I'll need it."

"I had to promise London I would stand by you."

"Good. Tell me, what are the other posts?"

"Dipra gets Industrial Development, so you bet he'll be a regular visitor here."

Andrew made a face.

"Sorry Andrew, you'll get used to him. I am not entirely sure how the other jobs have been distributed, but I know Iffeled and Endoman are looking for nominations as Interim First Minister. The Governor didn't offer Iffeled anything, I believe, but Endoman he offered the Interior post; he declined it in favour of running for First Minister. Of course neither can use a party ticket, but people will remember DPP and OBA."

"You didn't consider running for the top job yourself?"

"Me?" Evans was startled. "Of course not. What experience do I have of politics?"

Andrew Maitland shrugged. "What do Iffeled and Endoman know? I admit Endoman seems a good guy but *nobody* here really knows what they are getting into, do they?"

"Perhaps not. Don't say that to Dipra, will you? Not if you want to keep good relations going."

"I shall be discretion personified." Andrew gave a little wink.

SEVENTEEN

Grace and Evans decided on a quiet family wedding.

"We shall have to keep all your new contacts at Public Works at bay," said Grace. "After what you told me about Dipra's attitude to your marrying into the 'opposition', you had better keep quiet about it until afterwards."

"Yes, Grace, but surely your father will want Emmanuel Endoman to come?"

"I'm sure he will, but we'll tell him to keep it quiet. Our wedding has nothing to do with politics."

So the wedding took place in the tiny Baptist Chapel on The Cantonnements, attended only by Grace's family, Evans's ancient but proud parents specially brought down from his village and Andrew Maitland and family.

"We are really honoured to be invited, Evans, and you and Grace must come to us for your first social engagement as man and wife." Fiona Maitland was touched to be included. "Am I allowed to ask where the honeymoon will be?"

Evans smiled broadly and put a finger to his lips. "Sshhh.....
Actually Kenya, just for a week, but it's a state secret of course."

"Lovely for you. I wish you a long and happy marriage."

"I overheard that," Andrew muttered as Fiona moved away. "Grace drew the line at Hong Kong then?"

"I didn't like to even suggest it. But I've stored it for a future holiday."

Andrew nodded. "Give it five years, Evans. Maybe Celine will be happily married by then."

*

Dipra read about it in the Henry City Journal. He now regarded this newspaper as essential reading, primarily to keep him up to date on business and the activities of the expatriate community, the two things intimately connected. And there it was, the wedding of Dr. Grace Endoman of Karle Mo and Mr Evans Watanero, formerly chief executive of InterEarthMove and most recently appointed Administrator of Public Works.

Guests included Mr. Emmanuel Endoman, candidate for the Interim President and cousin of the bride's father, the distinguished surgeon from Karle Mo hospital.

Dipra shook his head in disapproval. First Evans hadn't invited his oldest friend and second he'd married into the wrong party. Because the parties would come back, he felt sure. He felt strongly enough to speak his thoughts out loud, to an empty office.

"Bad move, Evans. I think you de clever one till now. When Iffeled President, you get nothing."

*

Strolling along the white sand beaches of Mombasa hand in hand with Grace, Evans was unlikely to worry too much about developments in Jamesland, least of all about Dipra's concerns.

He had enjoyed proving to himself that he could swim in the ocean as well as in his pool; well, if not exactly in the open ocean, certainly in the bay so neatly enclosed by the coral reef marked by the crescent of white froth not half a mile out.

They had been out in the glass bottomed boat to marvel at the colours below and to watch the small boy in his goggles and flippers exploring close up while the boat gently swayed until someone implored the boy's mother to bring him up 'before we all bring our breakfasts up.'

They read ridiculous novels in the shade of coconut trees, occasionally paying a boy to swarm up and collect for them a fresh coconut which he would decapitate as easily as a boiled egg with a single swift stroke of his panga, allowing them to drink the cool fresh milk directly from the nut.

They walked the beach from end to end in the twilight, calling at each of the hotels' beach bars in turn to sample cool speciality fruit juices, made from endless permutations of mango, paw-paw, grapefruit, oranges, limes, banana, passion fruit and grenadines, topped with sprigs of mint.

And finally the ecstasy of the bedroom, the beautiful dark bodies carefully exploring each other, tenderly stroking with sensitive fingers, gasping their love in the moment of release.

"I don't know where you learned all this," Grace said. "But you must have had an excellent teacher."

"It is you I am learning from," said Evans. "Nothing that went before matters any more."

In the foyer of the Sandyman Beach Hotel next morning, Evans caught sight of a minor headline in the day's newspaper. ' First Minister Candidates Begin Campaigns in Jamesland.' He just couldn't be bothered to buy the paper.

*

Three months later Emmanuel Endoman was declared First Minister of the Interim Government of National Unity. The Governor prayed he would take the title seriously. Yet he was astonished when his prayer was answered so fully and quickly.

Endoman suggested that Mr. Iffeled might be offered a special role in the Administration, 'to keep him in the public eye pending independence' and to ensure he would not be a focus for dissident politicians of his former party.

The Governor seized on it as a sign of Endoman's excellent political sense. He quickly summoned Iffeled to a meeting with himself and Endoman at which they suggested Mr. Iffeled might consider taking a senior advisory position in the First Minister's office.

Abel Iffeled was even more astonished than the Governor, but quickly recognised the wisdom in accepting this hand of friendship – or was it just an outer filament of a spider's web? At any rate he felt he had to accept. And braced himself for the challenges he would meet at the secret meeting he was to have later in the week with colleagues in the party which he was no longer allowed to mention by name.

Curiously, despite the careful arrangements they had made, not a single former colleague turned up to the secret meeting. Iffeled began to wonder if his old party did indeed still exist, even in the minds of his old friends. Perhaps Bishgad should turn its back on party politics. He resolved to spend more time with Endoman discussing the future.

Dipra Forfpi observed the move of Iffeled into the First

Minister's office and also gave some deep thought to the future. Could he have been   wrong? Maybe Evans had made a smart move marrying into the Endoman family. Once Endoman had established himself in the interim role, wouldn't he be well placed to become the first proper, fully elected President of an independent Bishgad? And wouldn't he then have executive powers? Dipra thought it was time to mend his fences with Evans – if indeed he had broken any. He would demonstrate his full approval of the marriage. And he thought of a good way to do just that.

"Evans, long time since we spent time together." The phone call interrupted their evening meal but Evans thought he had better listen. What did Dipra want now?

"Yes, we are both busy men, I suppose."

"Of course, but we could spend an evening out sometime, couldn't we? What about Kakadu, where you used to go wid Malachi?"

"How do you know about the Kakadu, Dipra?"

"I talk to Malachi in London, he tell me what good times you had. I never see you relax like he tell me. Dat mad taxi driver in prison now, not so?"

"Protective custody, Dipra. You think you would enjoy the Kakadu?"

Grace had by now identified the caller and was making negative gestures. She rather ostentatiously collected Evans's plate and took it through to the microwave, their latest acquisition.

"Of course. You 'tink Grace has a friend at Karle Mo who could be my partner?"

"I don't know, but I could ask. Look, Dipra, we're in the middle of dinner, can I ring you back later, please?"

"OK I leave it wid you. Don't forget." He rang off.

"What was all that about the Kakadu, Evans? You *haven't* promised Dipra we'll go with him!"

"No. Can I get on with my dinner now?"

Grace retrieved it and placed it in front of him with unwonted ferocity. "It is not good to get mixed up with Dipra again outside the office work. The man is a …"

"A what, Grace?"

"A crook, probably. At the very least a man of little integrity. A politician, always on the look out for his own interests."

"But Grace, I'm a politician now and Dipra's an old friend. A senior man in government with heavy responsibilities, just like me. You can't dismiss him as a crook, just because you don't like him."

"OK what did he want with the Kakadu?"

"He was suggesting an evening out with us and hoped you might be able to bring a friend from the hospital. I expect he's just lonely."

"No friends, eh? Now I wonder why that is?"

"He hasn't had much time for a social life and he's only been in the country for -"

"Two years, is it?"

"Grace, let's not quarrel over this."

"But you have to ring him back, I heard you promise,"

"Yes." Evans lapsed into silence.

"You are too kind, too forgiving, Evans." She saw the misery on his face. "OK, tell him just this once, though why *I* should forgive him for telling you not to marry me -"

"Yes, he got that wrong. But he was trying to help … now he's trying to make up for it."

"Trying to make up to you, you mean. He wants to get on your right side, now your relation heads the Government."

"Interim Government, remember." Evans gave a wry grin. "Possibly. But why not be friends? I'm not going to be in the government of Bishgad for very long. If we are friends we shall work together better. You going to help?"

"I suppose I'd better get used to being a politician's proper wife. Yes, OK I'll join in on a Kakadu night."

"And bring a friend for Dipra?"

Grace sighed. "I'll ask around the nurses."

"I'm sure they'll jump at the chance of an escort like Dipra, big man in Government."

"Yes, that's what I'm afraid of. It needs to be someone with her head on tight. A mature nurse. I'll give it some thought."

"Good, can I ring him and tell him?"

"I suppose so," she conceded. "Tell him I'll try."

*

The nurse Grace came up with was a pleasant young lady around thirty years old. Ruth was a senior ward sister, according to Grace, originally educated in a convent school, so very well brought up.

"Warn Dipra," Grace said. "He'd better not try anything on. I don't know what sort of girls he's been seeing in Russia and England, but Ruth is a *good* girl."

"Right," said Evans, suppressing a smile, "I'll tell him to have a strong dose of bromide before coming out."

"I mean it, Evans, Ruth is my responsibility for the evening. I don't want her upset. And he's *your* friend. And supposed to be a responsible member of government!"

"OK, OK. You've made your point, love. I'm sure Dipra will be the soul of discretion."

"He's not very refined."

"No, I have to admit that, but as Andrew would say, his heart's in the right place. Hey, that's a good idea; I'll ask Andrew and Fiona to join us! What do you say?"

"Now that's the best idea you've had for some time. Does Andrew know Dipra?"

"Only from a conference we had a couple of weeks ago. But I'm sure they'll both welcome the chance to establish stronger links. After all, Dipra's responsibilities cover Andrew's area."

"So you men will spend all evening talking shop."

"No. I'll extract promises from both of them."

*

Evans should have guessed. It was the three women who 'talked shop' all evening, but he didn't mind. It was good to see them all getting along together so well, with Grace acting as the bridge between Fiona and Ruth, knowing them each in different spheres. Yes, this had been a good idea. It was still something of a novelty for other groups to see two African and one European couple so obviously at ease with each other, though in truth Dipra was still feeling his way in expatriate company outside the office.

"You play snooker?" he asked Andrew.

"Ay, I've played a bit. Of course, being Scottish, golf is my first game, but I've played a wee bit snooker here and there. Do you play golf?"

"No. Not yet. I do deal wid you. You teach me goluf, I teach you really good snooker. I pretty good, not joking, very keen."

Evans wondered whether to intervene. But Fiona beat him to it.

"You cannot be more keen on snooker than Andrew is on golf. A few more years out here, where the weather is so good he can play all the time, and I shall expect him to win the 'Open' back home."

"Open?"

"The British championship, Dipra. I've played two rounds with Andrew and he goes round in exactly half my score. But he's very patient. Will you be that patient on the snooker table?"

"If he go round in half your score, you beat him, surely?"

Somewhat to Dipra's discomfort, Evans and Grace, Andrew and Fiona all burst out laughing, while Ruth looked wonderingly on.

"The lower score wins, Dipra," said Evans, taking pity.

"Och, I'll explain it on the course, Dipra. Shall we try up at the club tomorrow morning?"

Evans shot him a grateful look.

"It sound OK to me. But I need sticks, yes? What time we go start?"

"You can borrow my clubs, Dipra. I'll send them along with Andrew tomorrow. I'm just sorry I can't come myself, but Mrs. Watanero has plans for some shopping, I believe." He glanced at Grace.

"Yes, I do." She hesitated. "I have to get some more generous dresses."

Fiona's and Ruth's eyes lit up.

"Congratulations, Grace. When is the happy event?"

"I'm saying nothing more until I've had some checks. Not a word in the hospital please, Ruth."

"Lips sealed, Doctor Grace."

Andrew clapped Evans on the back. "A real family man soon, eh? Come round for a dram sometime and I'll initiate you into the mysteries of fatherhood."

"Oh, no, don't let him, Grace. He'll be out on the golf course at the first whiff of a nappy."

"I t'ink I get my goluf training in before I get married," announced Dipra.

*

"So how is your snooker, Andrew?"

"Mine's still pretty awful, but the man's a genius – I'll swear he can make the balls talk to each other in passing!"

"Perhaps he puts a juju on them."

"Yes, now I begin to *believe* in juju. Seriously, I really think he's world class, though I don't know much about it. Perhaps he should try his luck back in UK."

"Now you're just trying to get rid of him! Anyway, never mind his snooker, how's his goluf?"

"You think we'll ever teach him how to say it? Anyway, nowhere near as good as yours, but he perseveres. You'll have to watch out, he's a pretty determined character. Buying expedition successful?"

"Yes, I think so. Grace bought three dresses and each one took an hour to choose, more time than we need to decide on a dragline."

"Oh, come on Evans, give her a break, this is the most important event in her life. Just be grateful I managed to steer Fiona away from joining you as an adviser – then it would have been two hours per dress. You got a timing for the happy event yet?"

"Sometime in February, she thinks. I hope to persuade her to stop work at Christmas."

"Devotion to duty, eh? That sounds like your Grace all right. Fiona will be happy to help any time you know. She asked me to emphasise that to you."

"Thanks. I'm sure she's told Grace, but I'll repeat it. You are good friends to have at times like this."

"I just hope it isn't catching, Evans!"

*

The Kakadu became a regular feature of Friday nights for the six, the women using it as an opportunity to talk babies and the men an opportunity to talk business. In respect for Grace's condition, the dancing was rather limited. They enjoyed the music, the food and the conversation.

Evans and Andrew were surprised at Dipra's increasing grasp of the complexities of industrial development.

"Nearly as good as his snooker and a damn sight better than his goluf," joked Andrew, when Dipra had left the table temporarily. "Incidentally, my snooker's coming along pretty well now. Why don't you join us up at the club sometime?"

"And give you another game in which to beat me hollow? No thanks. Anyway, I shall have to spend more time with Grace now. But you're right about Dipra; he's begun to take things seriously at last. I think the appointment of Endoman and Iffeled co-operating has chased away his simplistic view of politics. Perhaps he really will be a big man just as he forecast all those years ago. Even Grace has come to respect him."

The girls returned to the table, providing Fiona with the opportunity to say to Evans, "Your wife is looking really splendid. I'm sure the baby will be the most beautiful in Jamesland."

"Very slow cooking for best results," joshed Grace.

"The most beautiful in the world," corrected Evans. "Especially if it's a girl."

"You don't know yet?" queried Ruth, turning to Grace.

"I don't want to know before it is born. Perhaps I'm superstitious. And if you find out, you must keep it a secret!"

"I promise," said Ruth. "And we'll give you all white baby clothes."

Grace smiled and Fiona laughed, "Then we'll be able to send the men out to buy them!"

"Oh, no, mercy!" pleaded Andrew.

Later, as Evans and Grace took the opportunity to dance slowly to a very sedate tune, he wondered if she had formed an opinion on Dipra's relationship with Ruth.

"She's a bit potty about him, Evans. I'm not so sure he's right for her. But he has improved in recent months."

"High praise indeed! He's almost acceptable now, is he? He will be a powerful figure in the new Government, you know. He's not as stupid as his unfortunate lack of articulation makes him seem. Anyway, you think he and Ruth...?"

"Let's not jump the gun, dear. At least he's a proper gentleman, from what she tells me. That's quite a good sign, isn't it?"

"Is it? Am I a proper gentleman?"

"You were born a gentleman, Evans. If I'd let you stay a gentleman we wouldn't be married even now. Then I realised that if I kept on being a lady, we wouldn't get anywhere."

"Malachi wasn't a gentleman, according to your definition?"

"No, and I wasn't a lady, and I'm ashamed of it. When will he be coming home?"

"You want him back? Shame on you."

"Don't be silly, I just wonder how he will fit into the system back here. In the summer?"

"Yes, I should think so. And he'll have no problem. Dipra will be looking out for him. I just hope they won't somehow move Andrew over to make room for him."

"Andrew will have a career back in UK, won't he? Surely you expect a Bishgadi to take over some time?"

"Yes, long term. And Malachi is the only qualified local at this stage. Still, I hope they don't push Andrew before he's ready to go."

EIGHTEEN

First Minister Endoman and his senior advisor, Abel Iffeled left the Governor's reception together, a very good sign in Sir Joseph's view. Could they be persuaded, when the time came, to jointly head a single party, at least for the first few years?

He watched them get into Endoman's Range Rover. Had Iffeled sold the Merc or was he just keeping it hidden in his garage? The driver screeched away down the drive. Why so fast, was the driver drunk? Mansion staff had been given specific instructions – no alcohol for any of the drivers. Perhaps he just drove like that all the time.

In the car, Iffeled was alarmed enough to murmur to Endoman.

"Shouldn't you slow him down?"

Endoman leaned forward. "Take it easy, Amos. There's no hurry."

"Right, sah." The Range Rover slowed suddenly enough to cause both Endoman and Iffeled to pitch forward in their seats.

"Amos, for goodness sake! Drive softly."

"Yes, sah."

They proceeded at a more leisurely pace until joining the new Ring Road highway. Now Amos could not resist using the car's awesome power to accelerate away. Endoman looked at Iffeled and shrugged resignation. Five minutes later, he realised Amos would miss their exit if he did not slow down.

"Next exit, Amos, slow down for it."

But he had left his warning too late. Amos swung the heavy vehicle into the minor road at speed and met a small open-topped sports car trying to join the ring, head on.

*

Evans reached hastily for the telephone hoping it was Grace. She was working far too late, even for a Karle Mo management meeting. He'd been home from the Governor's reception for at least an hour.

It wasn't Grace. It was Ruth.

"Evans, you'd better come to the hospital. Grace...."

"Her car broken down?"

"Evans she left an hour ago and now she's back ... in an ambulance. Please come quickly, Evans."

"She's hurt! How badly, Ruth?"

"Pretty badly, please come, Evans." She broke off in sobs and the telephone went dead.

He drove like a madman. In three minutes he was on the Ring Road and speeding towards the coast. The familiar blocks of Karle Mo hospital loomed out of the mist, above the new sodium lighting. He fought the car onto the slip road and roared into the car park.

Racing into A&E, he demanded of the duty nurse, "Dr Endoman?"

The look of fear in the nurse's eyes told him too much. "Both in the theatre," she said. "Our top team are working on her."

He drew a deep breath, forced himself to calm down. "Road accident?"

She nodded, mute, her eyes full of tears. "Her father is in there and Sister Ruth too. They are doing everything ..."

He slumped onto a bench and closed his eyes. The rattle of a cup, tendered by the duty nurse, brought him to attention.

"Some sweet tea may help." She turned away, unable to maintain optimism in the face of his despair.

*

They had got the woman into an ambulance. One policeman recognised Iffeled and Endoman from the pictures he'd seen in the newspapers. The sergeant contacted his station and Chief Superintendent Holland was quickly on the scene. Perhaps the woman would survive, they told him. The two 'big men' were certainly dead. Only the driver in the Range Rover was unharmed. He was over there throwing up into the bushes.

"Arrest him and hold him at the station until I get back," commanded Holland, quietly. "Call Chief Inspector Watabenje in and say nothing to anyone else until I see you. Nothing to anybody. You understand?"

"Yes sah."

Holland drove away to inform the Governor. He wondered who the woman was. Obviously it had been a small car but the wreck provided few clues, especially since it had burned out shortly after impact. Poor girl, meeting a drunk driver at this time of night. How could he have got drunk waiting up at the Mansion reception?

*

Sir Joseph was horrified. "You quite sure it was...."

"Quite sure, Sir. I've given instructions that the two policemen at the scene are to tell no-one but Padmore, pending your decisions."

"Very sensible. But we must put out a statement tonight. Who the hell am I going to ask to take over? I had high hopes for the spirit of co-operation which was emerging between those two."

Holland was silent, leaving the Governor to ponder.

"Who was the woman, Holland?"

"My men didn't know, Sir. They just called an ambulance and sent her off to hospital. They didn't give much for her chances, I'm afraid."

"Forfpi, it will have to be Forfpi." Sir Joseph was off on his own train of thought again. "He's a bit crude, uncultured to say the least, but he's nobody's fool. I used to think him a bit of a firebrand but he's settled well in recent months and does a good job in industrial development. What do you think?"

"I hardly know the man, Sir. But I have heard.." He paused.

"Heard what?"

"It seems he's an ace snooker player," Holland said with a smile. "I suppose that's an indication of something."

"Control. And a certain level of cunning. Just what we need. I'm glad you mentioned it, Chief Super."

Holland looked gratified. "This may not be the most appropriate moment, Governor, but I get so few chances to talk to you…"

"Something on your mind?"

"Yes, Sir, the possibility of a step up in my rank."

Sir Joseph nodded. "Yes, you have a good case. I suppose you realise I am myself the Chief Constable, by virtue of my Governorship?"

Holland smiled. "Yes, Sir, I am aware of that."

"So ACC would be acceptable to you?"

"More than acceptable, Sir."

"I'll have it gazetted. You've been doing a good job here for some years. Congratulations."

*

Dr. Endoman and Ruth emerged from the theatre, his face a dark cloud, hers bathed in tears. Evans did not need to ask. His heart a lump of stone, he embraced the older man until the tears flowed for both of them. Gently leading Endoman to the bench he sat him down and turned to Ruth, leaning against the wall, gasping sobs. Evans embraced her in turn.

He now looked down at Endoman. "May I see her?"

Endoman sighed and gave the faintest of nods. "Ask the staff in there… if she is ready."

Despite himself, he was shocked by the grey, lifeless body. It wasn't possible this was his Grace. The little hump in the centre of the bed could not be his dead child. There was no God. He'd always been doubtful, now he was sure. If there was a God, Evans did not wish to believe in him. Because he was a cruel, sadistic God, a God who gave and snatched back life in the course of a few months. You might expect that of the old village gods, but not of the one true God, whether Christian, Jewish or Islamic.

A great shuddering sigh escaped him. He knelt by the bed and kissed that perfect cheek. "Goodbye, Grace," he stammered between sobs, "even if there is no God, you must surely be in heaven."

A hand on his shoulder brought him back to the real world. "She was a wonderful lady, Mr. Watanero."

He looked up to see a young English nurse holding back

her own tears. "We are so sorry…."

Ruth had contacted Andrew, who was waiting patiently in Reception. He approached with his arms wide. "Evans…"

They sat together for some minutes, Andrew waiting for the heaving to subside. "You can stay with us, Evans. Fiona is making things ready for you."

Evans looked up through unfocussed, puzzled eyes.

"The staff have given me some pills for you which should help a little. Here's the water. Come on my friend."

Evans obediently swallowed the two proffered pills and leaning heavily on Andrew Maitland, made his was through the double glass doors, out into his new, devastated world.

*

Dipra Forfpi could hardly believe the voice emanating from the telephone. It was the Governor, Sir Joseph, he felt sure. But the message was ridiculous. Would he go up to the Mansion immediately to talk things over? What things? At midnight?

"Mr. Forfpi, I prefer not to go into detail on the telephone at the moment but it is *essential* you come straight away."

"Why you never talk to me during Reception?" At the back of his mind Dipra knew this was less than respectful, but he was tired and this call had interrupted his sleep.

Sir Joseph exercised his well-respected calm to its outer limits. "Things change, Mr. Forfpi. I shall expect you here in twenty minutes."

Could the Governor order him about like this? It was an order, without doubt. But the Governor was not a man to issue unnecessary orders. He had kept a watch on Dipra's ministerial responsibilities and guided him from time to time, but always with a light touch. Dipra reluctantly fell out of bed onto his knees, reflecting how much easier this procedure was than getting out of the bucket years ago.

On the way to the Mansion he passed the wreckage of a motor accident, one large vehicle upended in the ditch, another small one burnt out nearby. "Foolish people," he said to himself.

To his surprise, the Governor met him on the front steps.

"Sir Joseph, 'dis strange time to do business."

"Mr. Forfpi, even I have no control over the timing of strange events. I have to tell you that a tragic accident has occurred. I have some coffee prepared inside for us. We shall need it before the night ends, I believe."

Dipra sat on the sumptuous chaise longue and accepted the coffee Sir Joseph meticulously poured for him. He could not understand why no servants were present but a growing feeling of anticipation mingled with fear assailed him.

His mouth dropped open when the Governor recounted the accident to Endoman and Iffeled. "The wreck I just seen on Ring Road?"

"Probably, I have not been there myself. Chief Superintendent Holland reported it to me. There is no doubt the two men are dead and a young woman is in hospital with very serious injuries."

"Who dis young woman? She drunk driving?"

"No, I rather think it was Mr. Endoman's driver who was drunk. We do not yet know the identity of the young woman. Mr Holland will inform me in due course. Meanwhile…

"I need someone to head up the administration, Mr. Forfpi. Are you up to it?"

Dipra's poached egg eyes and sharp intake of breath betrayed the shock. "Me? First Minister?"

"Of the Provisional Interim Administration, yes, Mr. Forfpi, on certain conditions…."

*

Dipra was desperate to tell Evans Watanero of these latest developments. He telephoned the house several times without response. Perhaps the phone wasn't near enough to wake them at night. He would go round first thing in the morning.

Pulling into the Watanero driveway at seven the next day, Dipra found the house strangely quiet. He roused the houseboy from his little shack in the garden. "Your master no dey?"

"He leave late last night sah, never come home. I not know where he be."

"And madam?"

"Never come either. Maybe they stay with friends."

Puzzled, Dipra drove away. He would check in Evans's office. But Evans was not there. Frustrated, he turned his mind to the new job. He gathered his staff for the nine o'clock news on Radio Jamesland.

"Dis will save me trouble telling you all happenings," he said. "Listen carefully."

They heard the announcement from the Mansion with astonishment and began to jabber among themselves until Dipra shushed them for the end of the message.

"It is with very deep regret that we must also report the death of the driver of the second vehicle involved in this tragic accident, the much loved and greatly respected Dr. Grace Endoman of Karle Mo hospital, wife of Mr. Evans Watanero, Administrator of Public Works."

Dipra was shocked to his core. But now he understood. So where *was* Evans now? What friends did Evans have, now that Malachi was in London? Andrew Maitland, of course. Where did he live? But no matter, Dipra would find him at the InterEarthMove offices.

Forgetting all his new responsibilities Dipra set off for the works compound. Maybe there was something he could do for Evans.

*

Andrew Maitland's car followed Dipra's into the yard. As both men got out, Maitland betrayed his astonishment. "Dipra! I must congratulate you on your new appointment. But what are you doing here?"

"You got Evans at home?"

"Yes, he is quite distraught. You know of course about Grace?"

"Yes. You think I should see Evans? If I can help...."

"Evans will sleep most of the day, I think. The doctor has given him some pills to calm him. Fiona will keep an eye on him."

"Dat good. I very sorry for him. You good friends to take care. Not many English…" He corrected himself, "Scottish, I t'ink. Anyway, you keep me informed, please?"

"Yes, Dipra. Ruth will need comforting too, you know; she was in the operating theatre when Grace died."

Dipra's eyes widened. "I never t'ink of dat. Was all night wid Governor and straight to office dis morning. Terrible! I must go to her now. Thank you, Andrew." He turned to get in his car. "Good luck with Evans. He very important for de future of Bishgad."

Andrew nodded. "We shall all be as supportive as we can; he is very popular and well respected here. I will tell him you called."

"Was that Mr. Forfpi you were talking to, Mr. Aberdeen?" asked Joshua as Andrew passed. "The new Minister?"

"Yes, Joshua, he is very concerned about Mr. Watanero."

Joshua nodded. "I remember when he and Evans and Malachi all slept in the buckets of big loaders. I knew he would be a big man in the new country, but not this soon. What can the staff do for Evans? When will Mrs. Watanero's funeral be?"

"I don't know yet, but on that day I will close the plant. Then you can all attend. Evans would like that, I know."

*

The funerals of Endoman, Iffeled and Grace Watanero were held together in the tiny Anglican cathedral on the crossroads. The Governor declared a day of mourning and himself attended the funerals with Forfpi and the entire interim administration.

Andrew and Fiona Maitland flanked Evans along the aisle to view the three coffins covered in a profusion of flowers and notes, Grace's the most heavily garlanded with many bouquets from InterEarthMove and Karle Mo staff. Dipra left the official party to come across and embrace his old friend, both in tears as Andrew and Fiona stood by. Going back to their pew, Fiona put an arm around Ruth.

"Be brave, Ruth. Grace would have wanted that."

The service proceeded; the Governor made a valedictory

address and they all kneeled to pray. At the end of the prayers, Evans remained kneeling, Andrew and Fiona on either side placing a hand each on his shoulders. Ruth was overcome and knelt again to have Fiona use her other hand to rest on her head.

The four remained like that as the church emptied and Dipra came back to join them, sitting in the pew behind them. A few minutes later Chief Superintendent Holland sat alongside Dipra in silence. No words were needed and none spoken. Nobody moved until Evans himself looked up.

"I think I am ready to go now, Andrew. Thank you."

NINETEEN

"Mr. Forfpi, I have in mind to delay Independence a little as a mark of respect for Mr. Iffeled and Mr. Endoman and also as an opportunity for you yourself to get a firmer grip on the Interim First Minister role."

Dipra stayed quiet, a skill he had only in recent months acquired. Maybe he could still learn a thing or two from Evans.

"However," the Governor resumed, "the sooner we announce a firm date at least for what we can term autonomous government, the less unsettled the political atmosphere will be. If I were to propose next April , not the first because that has unfortunate implications in UK, but perhaps the fifteenth."

"What dese implications, Governor?"

Sir Joseph took a second to relate the question to his statement.

"Oh, in England the first is called All Fool's Day. It is all nonsense of course, but people try to spring surprises on that day so we try to avoid timing important events on it. Now, assuming you do a good job in the next nine months – and I have little doubt concerning your ability or commitment - you would move forward with the title Acting President and all the interim Administrators will go on as Acting Ministers.

"A month later we can begin the registration process for political parties. As I pointed out earlier, parties will need to demonstrate support across all regions. Perhaps fifty voters in each might be a suitable minimum."

Dipra merely nodded his agreement.

"Then we could set the date of the elections for say July 31st and have a proper celebration of full Independence on 15th September, time to ensure all results are in and checked."

"Dat sounds OK to me. You goin' to announce it soon?"

"I must get the details down on paper and submit them to my masters of course, but having your support should ensure there are no hitches. Can I make a few suggestions regarding the future?"

Again Dipra simply nodded.

"First, try to persuade your friends not to use the old names for the parties. It would be better to choose new names, allow for new alignments and most importantly, the new parties must try to formulate some practical policies and promote them. They cannot simply rely on a call for freedom, remember; they need to have ideas on development, whether you want a capitalist or socialist society or something in-between."

"Evans could help me work t'ings like dat out," Dipra involuntarily exclaimed.

Sir Joseph smiled. "Indeed, but you cannot be sure he would join a party. Two things I could say to you personally, Mr. Forfpi."

He looked keenly across at Dipra. "You must not be offended, I intend only to help."

Dipra wondered what was coming, but kept silent.

"First, perhaps it would be a good idea if you took some … some English lessons, both grammar and pronunciation."

Dipra was astonished. "Where I get such things?"

"I believe I could arrange for an English lady from the Technical Institute to coach you privately, if you were willing."

Dipra thought about it. "How much time it take? I busy with work."

"I know that very well, of course. But an hour every evening after work …"

"Every day?"

"Perhaps every weekday. Would you agree?"

"What good it do me?"

Sir Joseph pondered the question, carefully formulating a polite reply. But Dipra beat him to it. "I know, make me talk like Evans."

The Governor smiled. "Much nearer to him, anyway."

"OK. What de second thing?"

"When the time comes for elections…" Sir Joseph paused. "If you seriously wish to remain in the Presidency, it might be quite a good idea for you not to belong to any party, to campaign as an independent."

"I got to get fifty supporters from each region too?"

"Yes. But you might be in quite a strong position after your time as Interim First Minister and then Acting President. And the President has to be re-elected every seven years, you know. Party strengths and popularity can change in that time. After a successful term, I doubt any party would want to put up a candidate against you."

Dipra's eyes narrowed. "Why you want to help me? Yesterday I a rebel. Now the Governor is my friend?"

Sir Joseph gave his broadest smile. "Mr. Forfpi, I am interested in leaving behind me a stable country with a stable government. I have already spent far longer here than I had intended and the least I can do is ensure a sound legacy after all the upsets."

He leaned forward confidentially. "When you have spent some years in government roles such as mine, you develop a gut feeling for the competence of people. I have come to respect you and have faith in your abilities. But I have had to make a positive effort not to be distracted by your speech. It disguises a good brain. Which is why I suggest the English lessons."

Dipra sat back and digested this long speech while the Governor watched him carefully.

"You right. Both things. OK I take your advice. Evans say it many times but I think he just a snob. Now I see what he mean."

"Good. So we can be friends and drive this thing forward to a successful conclusion?"

Dipra extended a hand in reply.

*

Evans was at the airport to meet Malachi. His heart surprised him with a little lurch as the tall figure of Malachi came into view through the exit doors of the Customs Hall. Wordlessly, they embraced.

"You are a minister now, Evans!"

"Interim Administrator is the correct term, Malachi. And

you have a first class honours degree from LSE, the most educated African man in Jamesland."

Malachi grinned. "Better than Dipra, eh? But he's the President, which is a bit more important. I have to find a job."

"You must have picked up understatement and perhaps even some modesty in England, Malachi! No, Dipra is the Interim First Minister. And I think he may have some ideas for you on the job front."

"I was very sorry to hear about Grace, Evans."

A spasm crossed Evans's face but he turned the conversation. "No wife or girlfriend from England, then? You must have had chances."

Malachi heaved his bag into the boot of Evans's car. "I'll tell you all about it on the way."

Evans weaved through the traffic.

"Many more cars than before," exclaimed Malachi. "Jamesland must be booming."

"A lot of inward investment by foreign companies, trying to ensure they are established before independence. Does that surprise you, Mr. economist?"

Malachi smiled. "They expect us to do better on our own. We may not have the expertise but we have the *desire* to progress. The British were content to let things drift, just so long as their companies brought out good profits. Now we must push for *growth*."

"InterEarthMove has grown, Malachi. And London has put in a lot of capital to meet future demand. But I shall leave Andrew to explain all that. Tell me about London."

"There *is* a girl. But she has the same problem as Celine...."

"She's Chinese?"

"No. She's Indian. Well, she would say Asian. Her folks were kicked out of East Africa. She is reluctant to come here because of that."

"She knows you are a friend of the First Minister – Interim First Minister?"

"Yes. She knew I was meeting Dipra in London in my first

year. I have promised to write to her to explain how things are here, when I know for myself."

"And you love her?"

Malachi was silent for a moment. "She is as beautiful as Celine, darker skinned, long black hair, deep brown eyes ... and as quiet as Celine was extrovert. Yes, I love her. Am I fated to love outside my own race?"

Evans touched Malachi's hand. "Big word, Malachi, extrovert. Lighten up. You are old enough and well educated enough to marry whomever you want to now. Kwame Nkrumah has married an Egyptian woman."

"Well. Tell me your news, Evans. How is Dipra managing?"

"He is good in the job. And the Governor has persuaded him to improve his English, something I have been trying to do for years. You will probably get a call from him this evening. I told him you would be staying at my place for a few days, while you sort yourself out."

"Just like the old days, eh?"

"A bit, yes. But I have a nice bungalow now. After Grace ... I had to move somewhere new. Anyway, it is out in Woodlands. If you want to go into town this morning I can send the car back with a driver-"

"No, I will just unpack a bit and ... will you be home for lunch?"

"Yes. And we can talk more this afternoon; I have arranged to take it off to spend time with you. Perhaps we could visit Andrew, too."

"But won't he think...."

"That you have come back to take over? Possibly. He was aware it might be a temporary arrangement and he knows you would be first in line. But he won't mind, honestly. He and Fiona have been good friends to me since ..."

"I shall be glad to visit him. And look forward to Dipra's call. Is he still fat?"

"Well, not *very* fat. Well covered is the polite term in UK

I think."

"Still smoking?"

Evans showed his surprise. "Did he ever?"

"Just putting on a show, perhaps, while he was in London. Trying to look sophisticated. I told him you would not approve."

Evans laughed. "And you think he gave up for me? I don't have that much influence on our Interim Minister, Malachi. But I have never seen him smoke. Not even in the Kakadu."

"You used to go there again?"

"Yes, Dipra and Ruth, Andrew and Fiona, Grace and myself. But not since... You know, we were fully accepted, two African and one European couple. Why should your Asian lady not settle here?"

"Her name is Reeta. I will tell her what you say."

*

Evans had exchanged houses with Andrew on taking up his governmental post, arguing that the company chief's house should now go to Andrew and moving to his place would save the government some money. Abel Endoman had been appreciative of this gesture by InterEarthMove though Dipra had taken the view that government should provide proper prestigious accommodation for its senior people.

With the death of Grace, however, Evans felt he could not stay in the house they had shared so he took advantage of the Governor's offer of a new property on the further side of the city, a property with no hurtful associations.

Malachi liked the place and enjoyed sitting around the pool in the cool of the evening with Evans, supping a Planet beer like old times, while the steward prepared their dinner.

"You have the good life here, Evans. Nice house, top job, good money, what more could you want?"

"A live wife," exclaimed Evans and seeing the shock on Malachi's face, "sorry, I'm still a bit-"

"My fault. Stupid of me. Must learn to keep mouth shut."

The telephone rang in the house, distracting them from the embarrassing situation.

"For Mr. Goodwill, sah," said the steward, his eyes rolling. "It be de Minister."

Malachi glanced at Evans who nodded.

"It's the call I told you to expect. Go on. Mustn't keep the Minister waiting."

*

"He wants me to go up to the Mansion tomorrow morning. Says there are things to discuss. And he wants you with me."

"Me? What for? I have a big workload tomorrow."

"Maybe, but you mustn't keep the Minister waiting." Dipra gave Evans a light shoulder punch. "Now it really will be like old times, the three of us together again."

"Yes. I shall be interested to see what he has in mind for you."

*

They sat in the suite the Governor had allocated to the Interim First Minister, overlooking the fine lawns dotted with Jacaranda and Flame trees and surrounded at a distance by a high hibiscus hedge.

Dipra himself did the honours with the coffee. "You want sugar? I never take it now. Notice how slim I be getting?"

"I *am* getting," murmured Evans, to Malachi's astonishment.

"Right. I am getting. But my English is getting better, don't you think? All down to Mrs. Mitchell, my tutor. She very fierce with me." He burst out laughing. "Not many people tick off the First Minister like she. Except Evans. We three have chance to make Bishgad very good country."

They supped coffee while Dipra pushed the biscuit plate across to Malachi. "I don't eat biscuits either. But you pretty thin, Malachi, you could do with some nourishment."

Malachi took one and looked enquiringly at Evans who waved the temptation away.

"Did your London degree cover banking?" asked Dipra.

Malachi shrugged. "A little. The theory of course. Why do you ask? My practical experience was in accounting, for

InterEarthMove."

"My degree never touch banking. We shall need a new currency when Bishgad comes, with a central issuing bank, taking over from the present arrangements. I can get top man from London to help us with it but we must have a Bishgadi in control."

Malachi and Evans sat quietly, waiting while Dipra took another swallow of coffee.

"You could be my economic adviser for now, working inside the Presidency when it comes. When the time comes you would be responsible for the new bank, appoint the Director and so on. Meanwhile you could begin to compile a proper record of all the businesses in Jamesland. There are lots of booklets of companies in particular industries but I want to see an official guide to Bishgadi Commerce, with all the details of companies, directors, capital, sales and all dat. Evans can help a bit. You take the job?"

"But haven't you got a Minister of Industry already, Dipra?"

"Yes. Me! I never give it up but it mostly run by the civil servants now. Two good men, even if they are English. But part of your job would be to train Bishgadi to replace them."

"And what would my title be?"

Dipra roared with laughter and looked at Evans. "He not like you, Evans. He worries about titles." Then he turned to Malachi. "I just teasing. Economic Adviser to the First Minister, for the time being. OK? Same salary as Evans - for the first time since we all slept in the buckets, eh? Now you want the job?"

"Yes. When can I start?"

"Officially on Monday. I will get it Gazetted in Saturday's issue. But Evans can start showing you around straight away. Introduce you to the various administrators, that sort of thing. You look after him, Evans?"

It sounded like a question, but Evans recognised an order when he heard one.

TWENTY

Despite an enormous workload, time seemed to drag by for Dipra. The ultimate prize, which seemed so firmly in his grasp when the Governor first approached him, now seemed like a mirage. There were so many hurdles to overcome, so many months to wait. October, November, ground along towards Christmas and he looked forward to the holiday break. He would ask Malachi and Evans to join him for a slap up meal in the Tropical House and perhaps go on to the Kakadu.

Yes, he would include Andrew Maitland too, and that splendid wife of his, Fiona. Ruth would come but who could he find for Malachi and Evans? Malachi was curiously reticent about women; maybe he'd met someone in London. If he had, he wasn't telling anyone about her. Perhaps she was British. Would that be good for a senior government man? Perhaps it would bridge gaps of understanding. But would the population like it? Even if Nkrumah had taken an Egyptian wife; at least she could be described as African in some way. But a white girl?

He dismissed the speculation. He'd get Ruth to find a friend, friends, for both Malachi and Evans. Surely Evans should be getting over Grace by now? He put the idea to the two of them.

Evans sat silent while Malachi looked embarrassed.

"I sure Ruth can find friends for you. Come on, let's celebrate. Next year we shall have our independence. Life is looking good, not so?"

"Isn't it?" responded Evans automatically. "Independence does not seem so very important to me now, Dipra. Nor does a holiday, to be honest. Maybe I'll just quietly work through it."

"You can't do that," protested Malachi. "You already work too hard. Yes, find me a companion, Dipra, but tell her there's no prospect of the evening leading to anything. I'm committed."

Evans watched him carefully.

Dipra was intrigued. "You goin' to tell us about this commitment, Malachi? In London?"

Malachi looked to Evans. "You tell him."

"Malachi has met a beautiful Asian girl in London, a girl whose parents were thrown out of East Africa. He couldn't persuade her to come back with him because her experience of African governments makes her nervous. She's waiting for him to tell her what it will be like here for her."

"What her name? What she do?"

"What *is* her name, Dipra. What *does* she do for a living? Her name is Reeta and she's a student nurse, but will be qualified very soon. Come on Malachi, *you* do some talking here."

Dipra interrupted. "You were worried about an Asian nurse in our society?" he asked Malachi. "Didn't we accept your Celine Brandt in InterEarthMove? It no good to replace the old race barriers of the British with new ones of our own, is it? Andrew Maitland is a good friend to all of us now, isn't he?"

"Not the same as marrying across race, Dipra."

"You want to marry her, you marry her. I will be your best man if you don't want Evans. In any case I want to be honoured guest."

A thought struck him. "Maybe I persuade Ruth to marry me same day. Evans be best man for the both of us. Yes, brilliant idea. What you think, Evans?"

A smile crossed Evans face even as tears came to his eyes. "That should certainly reassure Malachi – and Reeta – to have the First Minister marrying alongside them. You sound very sure Ruth will have you, Dipra." He hesitated and then said, "But if Malachi agrees, I should be happy to be best man."

They turned to Malachi, who was biting his bottom lip. He took a deep breath before answering. "It all depends on Reeta. Can I offer … what you suggested … to persuade her to come out?"

"Of course. We want to meet her. You met her, Evans?"

"No."

"You got some photos, Malachi?"

Reluctantly, Malachi pulled out his wallet and extracted two well-worn photos with ragged edges. "Taken in Spring."

He handed them across.

"Wow!" said Dipra. "Now we got to meet her." He laughed. "So what about you, Evans, when you coming back on to the market?"

*

Andrew carefully explained to Fiona why the four men were going out for a meal without the girls – because two of them *had* no girls at present.

"It's Christmas, Andrew, we should be together as a family."

"Aye, but it isna Christmas proper. It'll be the night before Christmas Eve. I feel that as they've included me I really ought to go. The Kakadu I've vetoed, but the meal in the Tropical House's OK, isn't it?"

"Well, I suppose so, but it leaves me alone with the kids. I suppose I could ask a girlfriend or two in for a meal. If any of them are free. Hey, why don't I invite Ruth?"

"A brilliant idea, my love. It might save Dipra getting into trouble too."

*

"You know about Malachi's girlfriend in London? An Asian nurse, Dipra says."

"Gosh. Is he going to bring her over, Ruth? The hospital could do with some more trained staff couldn't it?"

"Absolutely. You think we can make an Asian girl happy here? I expect her culture is very different, Fiona."

"So is ours, Ruth. I think a shared love of nursing will go a long way to helping understanding. You think Malachi's going to marry her?"

"That is the plan." Ruth looked away, suddenly shy.

"What is it, Ruth? Don't you like the idea?"

She looked up again, her eyes shining. "Dipra says we should have double wedding, me and him, this girl and Malachi."

Fiona moved across to the sofa and gave Ruth a big hug. "That will be lovely for you. Do you know Malachi's lady's name?"

"Reeta. Dipra says she is very beautiful. I got quite jealous when he described her from a photo."

"Nothing to worry about there, Ruth. Did you ever meet Celine? Andrew's descriptions of her after his first interview made me think he was already looking for flats in Hong Kong. It's just the way men are. But I wish Evans would find someone now. We could go out like we used to, Dipra and you, Malachi and Reeta, Andrew and me and Evans with his new love. Wouldn't that be fun? Three races all mixed up in public. Shame we can't get Celine back for Evans. Do the old buffers from the Tennis Club the world of good."

They had a shared giggle.

"If it all works out, Reeta agrees and all, Evans will be best man. For both weddings. Is that possible?"

"Why not? Oh, I do hope Reeta will agree. I thought Malachi might take over from Andrew, but Dipra found him another job. That's good. Andrew wants to stay here for a few years if he can and being the boss man is good for his career. Not the boss in *this* house, though," she laughed.

"If Reeta works at Karle Mo, I might be *her* boss, you know. You think that would be difficult for us?"

"Wait till you've met her, Ruth. She may just be a smashing person, someone we'll all love. Malachi's not a bad judge, is he?"

"You know we don't *judge* when we fall for someone. Except perhaps Evans. He's a very careful man."

"Ruth, I could almost think you fancy Evans."

Ruth sighed. "Wrong time, wrong chance. I loved Grace. Never could hurt her. And Dipra is good man, too. He is going to be President," she added defiantly.

"And you are going to be very happy, I'm sure. Just so long as you can make him relax for an hour every week or so. That's Andrew's problem, and I'll bet it's Malachi's and it certainly is Evans's. How are we going to find him a wife when no-one can get him away from work for more than an hour? We ought to plan a campaign, you and me, to sort him out. Unless you want to grab him while you and Dipra are both still free?"

They smiled at each other.

"No chance. I'll find him another nice nurse from Karle Mo."

*

"Another letter from the heart-throb, Reeta?" Daintree handed it across. "You can't keep him dangling forever, now, why don't you go for broke?"

Reeta moved to a chair in the far corner of the room and carefully slit the envelope. She read the contents with growing amazement. Daintree, slyly observing while still buttering toast, whispered to the other two, "Looks like our Malachi has hit the right button this time."

"I heard that," called Reeta.

"Well?" All three spoke together.

"He wants me ... he wants me to go out and marry him."

"We knew *the*t Reeta, what's new this time?" Winnie was always up-front with her questions.

Reeta looked up shyly. "You aren't going to believe this ..."

"Try us, Reeta, we're willing to believe anything." Janet was smoothing the path for Reeta.

"Well, he says if I will marry him we could have a double wedding with Dipra Forfpi, the man he contacted when he was here."

"But he's the *President* now, Reeta!"

"Not yet, but quite likely, yes."

They all fell silent while they digested the news. Then Daintree could no longer hold herself. "Wowee! Our little Reeta marries a top government man, alongside his president getting hitched at the same time. Champagne time ladies."

"I haven't said yes yet." Reeta's soft tones brought them back to earth.

"Don't you dare turn him down. He loves you like crazy and you love him back and his President obviously fully approves the marriage and you'll be at the top of society in a brand new free country and - "

220

"OK, OK, Winnie, I get the message. I'll marry him. But only," she added shyly, "if you three will come out to support me."

"Chuck, we'll come if we have to row the whole bloody way." Daintree gave her a big hug and the others joined in.

"Right," said Janet, "where's the nearest off-licence for that champagne?"

*

David Berry treated his visitor with great caution. "The best educated African in Jamesland," the Henry City Journal had called him. The First Minister had asked him to make a survey of all business enterprises and he was taking the job very seriously. It was said they'd imported some high-powered technology for him to enter all his findings. Something like Berry's airline was using now to keep track of bookings.

"Coffee, Mr Goodwill?"

"Thank you. Tell me all about your airline's operation here."

"Well, we now run four flights a week to London, up from three just two months back, and business is growing so fast we think we'll have to go to a daily schedule soon, but I need a couple more expats to cope with that."

"Why not use locals?"

"Not enough trained people yet, but we have two training in London already and two more will go in a month. The airline business is quite complex, Mr. Goodwill."

"OK, tell me more. Excellent coffee that."

Berry took the hint and poured another, then began a comprehensive review of the airline's activities, equipment – aircraft, he explained – staffing, route control, planning slots at Heathrow … While Malachi made copious notes in his book.

"When we are independent," Malachi interjected, " we'll probably want our own airline, you know. Will you help us with that?"

Berry swallowed. "That's really a question for my board

of course, certainly way above my level. A lot of factors to consider."

"Including perhaps," Malachi shot back, "the possibility that we might ask say Air France or Lufthansa to help."

Berry inclined his head. "You'll be free to choose of course. But I expect my governors *will* want to be involved. That's just a personal opinion you understand. I can't commit us in any way."

"OK." Mr. Goodwill seemed satisfied with that answer. "Now one last thing; a favour I want to ask you."

Berry's antennae immediately stretched to maximum, along with prickles. "Ask away, Mr. Goodwill."

"I am going first to tell you something which very few other people know yet and which you must promise to keep absolutely secret for some weeks."

Berry's prickles subsided a little and he nodded assent.

"The First Minister and I are planning a double wedding in the very near future."

Berry was astonished. He recovered enough to say "Congratulations, Mr Goodwill."

"Thank you. Now, my fiancée is in London and she has three very good friends, ladies I know well myself from my student days. There is also my landlady from those days. These people are not very rich but I would very much like them to be able to attend the wedding." Malachi left the statement hanging while Berry considered the implications.

"I will put certain suggestions to my management in London, Mr. Goodwill. I can do no more than that."

"It is enough, Mr Berry. I know you will present your ideas with enthusiasm. Both the First Minister and I will be extremely grateful if you are able to help us in some way. Now, I must be off. Thank you for the coffee, for your very illuminating explanations, and for your promise of help. When you are talking to London, do remember the wedding is a secret, won't you?"

Berry rose with him, pondering how to interpret the 'promise of help,' and ushered him to the door. Well, it could do no harm to ask. Or to remind London of his long forecast likelihood of a national airline being among the new government's priorities.

*

The date was set for 1st March. The Governor had advised getting the weddings well out of the way before the announcement of Autonomous Government, now agreed for April 14. Dipra himself put a call through to David Berry.

"You know about the double wedding from my friend Malachi Goodwill?"

"Yes, Minister."

"So what can the airline do for us?"

"I have put suggestions to London, Minister, and I am waiting for their decision."

"OK, but you have to press them. If you not going to help I shall have to approach Air France."

"But they have no service here, Mr. President."

"I 'spec they would organise a special flight on from Astrica if it was needed." Dipra had no idea whether such a move was possible but it seemed worth a try; at least it would bring some pressure on the British airline.

"Minister, I will chase up London today. I am sure we can get a decision within a few days."

"Good. Let Mr. Goodwill know as soon as you can please."

"Yes, Sir." Berry put down the phone and started to dial the long, long number needed to contact the direct line of the Commercial Director.

*

"Mr. Goodwill, I'd like to talk to you about the matter we discussed when you visited me."

"Good news?"

"Yes, I think I can say that. But we need to meet, either here or at your offices."

"OK. You come to me. Eleven o'clock, at the Secretariat?"

"I shall be there, Mr Goodwill."

Berry was there a few minutes early, delighted with his

success. Four Business Class returns and one single could be provided for this special occasion. Could Mr. Goodwill give him dates?

*

Goodwill's letter caused enormous excitement in Wandsworth. It spelled out the flight dates and asked Reeta to contact 'my dear old landlady' on his old phone number. *She will probably be very surprised, and you may have to persuade her to come but when you tell her you are all coming I'm sure she'll agree to join you.*

And so it proved. Mrs. Baldock was overwhelmed and very gratified and all of a dither at the prospect of going out to *darkest Africa.* She would have to buy some new dresses. What do they wear out in that heat, dears?

The younger women took her along as they chose their own outfits and five very well turned out ladies checked in at the Heathrow desk on the appointed day, each carrying just about the maximum baggage allowance. Reeta's wedding dress occupied its own special case, a gift from her loyal house-mates.

Meanwhile, in Henry City, quiet preparations were proceeding under the management of Fiona and Ruth, the vicar and all contractors sworn to secrecy until the great day.

Now time seemed to Dipra to be rushing forward. How could he maintain the pace towards autonomy while getting ready for his own wedding? Evans and Malachi reassured him he was doing a great job.

"I never been married before," Dipra exclaimed.

"Nor have I, Dipra. We're bound to feel a bit nervous. But you are the First Minister of the country, Dipra, and soon to be President; you have nothing to be nervous about."

"Interim President."

"Nothing interim about being Ruth's husband, Dipra." Evans butted in. "On the day, you'll all be very proud of each other. And I shall be proud to be your best man. We are going to fill the country with love, an ideal atmosphere for independence when it comes."

Dipra beamed. "Yes. We show them family values, all the good things Bishgad will champion."

*

Malachi and Evans met the ladies off their plane, with a minibus from the PWD's garage. Taking a look at their baggage, Malachi joked they should perhaps have brought one of InterEarthMove's forklift trucks.

He wrapped himself around the diminutive Reeta, leaving Evans to introduce himself to the other four.

"So you're the famous Evans," said Daintree in her usual forthright manner. "The brains of the outfit."

"I don't know about that," said Evans. "It's that chap who is 'the best educated African in Jamesland' according to our local newspaper." He gestured to the couple still in a tight embrace. "Let's get your baggage loaded and perhaps he'll come up for air by then."

They all had a little laugh and Janet protested, "Well, he *is* going to marry her."

On the way down the Great East Road, Malachi and Evans pointed out the buildings of interest, many of them newly constructed, and the rising grandstands being prepared for Independence Day in August.

"Hey, Reeta, you'll be here for that. I'd give my eyeteeth to be here. Who'd have thought Jamesland would beat South Africa to it?"

"But South Africa's already independent," said Evans.

"Already a police state," spat Winnie.

"You think they might want more nurses here after Independence?" Daintree broke in. "Malachi here's been telling Reeta he might get her a job in a hospital … Barley Mow or something, sounds more like a pub to me."

"Karle Mo, k, a, r, l, e, m, o. You can enquire. Dipra Forfpi's wife to be, Ruth, works there."

"Hey, I'm looking for a job in catering. I wouldn't mind a job in a newly independent African country. Maybe some of your new government departments will need top quality services." Winnie wondered if she'd pushed too hard. "And Doris here wants to pioneer bed and breakfast in Bishgad, don't you Doris?"

Mrs. Baldock recovered quickly from her surprise. "At least it would be nice and warm and sunny, wouldn't it? But I don't know what people eat here for breakfast."

"You girls are impossible, teasing our hosts so soon," broke in Reeta.

"Oh, that's all right," said Malachi. "But I must say, the Catering Rest Houses which colonial government set up mostly for its travelling civil servants will probably fade away and there will be opportunities for small hotels in the main cities."

"See, Doris? You and I could go into partnership here."

They were interrupted by Evans. "This is your hotel, the Tropical House. Let's get you settled in."

TWENTY-ONE

Word had got out, of course. Even those who knew nothing could hardly fail to notice the large cars turning into the Cantonments for the Baptist Chapel. Someone recognised the First Minister's car and a small crowd began to gather. This looked like a wedding. But whose was it?

Simon Benson, the mixed-race Henry City Journal reporter was the first to arrive on the scene but because he could not raise a photographer before leaving his office he brought with him just a small 35mm camera and hoped to get some reasonable pictures of whatever it was going on. That was certainly the First Minister who'd just gone in and he thought that was the new man from London who'd become the Minister's adviser. Malachi Goodwill, that was his name.

It was when Evans Watanero arrived that Benson put things together a bit; Watanero and Goodwill had been friends from their youth, he remembered reading somewhere. Yes, it was when Goodwill was going off to London, quitting a good job in InterEarthMove. So was it one of them getting married? Not Watanero, surely, it didn't seem that long since his own wife had died in the terrible car crash that killed the previous political leaders.

Benson's attention was diverted to a large limousine carrying two ladies in white, sitting side by side on the back seat. He flashed his camera quickly. Now *this* was a story, surely. *Two* brides?

While he was still pondering this, another car drew in through the gates, packed with ladies, three white and an African girl. He couldn't see all that well, but formed an impression of an older white lady in there with younger girls. He'd have to get closer than this to do the story justice.

*

"Nervous, Evans?"

He smiled as Fiona laid a hand on his arm. "I can't think why I should be, but it is a big day for all of them, isn't it? I would have liked more of a rehearsal, but I expect I'll manage. I owe it to my friends to do it well, don't I?"

"You'll be great, Evans." Andrew had detected the moist eyes of his friend and wondered if this was too much for a relatively recent widower.

Evans took his place between Dipra and Malachi in the front pew and quelling the butterflies in his own stomach, counselled them to be patient. "Brides are supposed to arrive late, you know. Mine did." He tensed his stomach against the rising tide of emotion as his own words knifed into him. Bowing his head and closing his eyes, he was relieved to hear the organ start up and turned his head along with the others to glance back down the aisle.

Ruth and Reeta were progressing slowly forward in almost identical white dresses, an idea first mooted by Fiona Maitland in an attempt to avoid any possible rivalry. That had taken some organising but Jamesland tailors and seamstresses were renowned for their skills and they'd produced for Ruth a very good copy of Reeta's dress, just working from a photograph.

The light copper tones of Reeta and the flawless shining black of Ruth just penetrated their veils. A little gaggle of children followed, carrying the trains; the Maitlands' two, a niece and nephew of Ruth, and two small Asian children borrowed from one of Andrew's managers for the occasion to make this a celebration of the multi-cultural society Bishgad would promise.

After the ceremony, they all came out onto the steps of the little chapel and confronted the crowd which had now gathered. Dipra spotted the reporter from the Henry City Journal and invited him to come inside the grounds for better pictures.

Benson couldn't believe his luck. Here was the First Minister marrying his girlfriend at the same time as that Mr. Goodwill was marrying this beautiful Asian lady.

He wormed his way alongside Andrew Maitland. "Can you give me some names? Who are these guest ladies?"

Malachi had prepared Andrew for just this question and Andrew passed across a typed sheet providing the names of all participants and a potted biography of each.

"And Mr. Watanero was best man to both?"

"He was. He is a true friend of both men. And I am proud to have him as my friend too."

"He has recovered from his wife's death?"

Andrew looked at the man. "You married?"

"No. Not easy here, being neither black nor white. You think Mr. Goodwill's children will have a difficult time?"

"Doesn't the mix of bridesmaids and squires tell you something? Anyway, Evans still grieves for his wife of course and I'm sure he has had to keep a careful check on his emotions amid all this happiness. You won't print that, will you?"

"Of course not."

"Malachi's children will be born into a new world, the world you already inhabit. Think of yourself as a pioneer, my son. Did you notice two lovely European girls and one African from London, on the list? You even know their names, man. What are you waiting for?" Andrew grinned at Benson. "I'll suggest to Dipra – the Minister," he corrected himself, "that you come into the reception to get some more photos. Strictly for professional reasons, of course."

"Of course," said Benson. "And thank you very much."

*

Benson filed his story and his editor inevitably gave the event front-page coverage plus two extra pages to accommodate all the photos with their captions. The paper waxed eloquent about the little helpers from different races and lauded the brides and grooms for this display of the best trends in society. The Henry City Journal didn't go in for lauding much so Dipra and Malachi were gratified by the coverage, which in truth had been one of the ideas put forward at a planning meeting between them all. It was either Evans or Andrew who had suggested it, but they thought at the time that they would be providing the information after the event. With the fortunate arrival of Benson they were hot news.

The other newspapers were a day late but the Journal

generously made available its pictures so they could reach a wider readership. Dipra could not have been more pleased. He rang the editor to express his appreciation and asked especially for that man Benson to be commended for his coverage. Benson was meanwhile trying to decide which of the young ladies from London he might invite to join him for dinner.

"I believe you were Mr. Goodwill's landlady in London?" he asked Mrs. Baldock in the hotel foyer next day. "Yes, he was with me for over three years, you know. I remember him going off to meet Mr. Forfpi several times when they were holding those talks at Lancaster House."

"Oh, of course he already knew the Minister from his youth. What was he like as a tenant? Mr. Goodwill, I mean."

"Oh, a very diligent student, I think. He spent hours in his room studying. Well, he got a brilliant result didn't he? He used to eat me out of house and home you know, an enormous appetite. Still it was nice to have my cooking appreciated. I used to give him plenty of fish, for brain power, thinking he needed that. But of course I had no idea that one day I would be out here for his wedding. I've never been further than Majorca before."

Simon Benson made notes in his book. "And the other ladies? How did he meet them?"

"Well, he used to go off every week to watch the television in their house; it was when he was trying to speak better English and that Janet was coaching him for a play his college was doing. I told him not to pick up Daintree's accent when I heard there was a New Zealander in the group. Anyway, I invited him downstairs after that to watch the telly with me in my living room, but he still went across once every week to see his friends. Now I realise it was really Reeta who was the main attraction!" Mrs. Baldock burst into a great guffaw.

"So Daintree is the tall white girl?"

"Yes. A nurse like Reeta. The little English girl – well, she's actually Scottish- is in the theatre and the tall black girl's a cook. She's from South Africa. She tells me it's awful there for her people."

"And how long are you all staying?" asked Benson, still scribbling in his notebook.

Mrs. Baldock looked at him shrewdly. "The President has suggested we stay for an extra week, to see some of the country. Which of the girls interests you?"

Benson bit his lower lip and shrugged his shoulders in resignation. "I don't suppose any of them would be interested in me."

"What? Good-looking fellow like you, lovely colour, too? Just what any of them might look for. Try the little Scottish lass. She's used to drama and she's trying to write, so you'd have an interest in common."

"You think so?"

"I know so, young man. You want me to ask her for you?"

"No, no," he said hastily. "I'll pluck up courage and ask her myself. Wish me luck." And Simon Benson plunged into the fray to find Janet, the Highland lass.

*

Reeta had accepted Evans's assurances that an Asian girl married to an African man would encounter no problems honeymooning on the Kenya coast so Malachi whisked her away for a week. Dipra pleaded pressure of work and took off only two days, in which he and Ruth visited the local game park and spent the rest of the time on the snooker table, where Ruth showed great promise, according to Dipra. Ruth herself began to work out ways in which she might free herself from having to stand for hours watching Dipra achieve his wonderful strokes. It was marvellous, of course, what he could do, but there were limits to its entertainment value.

She resumed her work at Karle Mo hospital and made discreet enquiries about the possibility of Reeta joining the staff. The management, anxious to please the Minister's lady, were immediately co-operative and shortly after she returned from

Mombassa, Reeta was to be invited to a meeting of the management committee.

Meanwhile, the other ladies had made several short trips up-country and they had all spent a couple of evenings with Benson at the Kakadu. Somehow he didn't seem able to detach Janet from the group. Now there were only two days left, Janet seemed less keen than the others to get back to London but recognised she could not outstay her welcome, financed as it was by the Government.

"We'll be back, sport, you watch. I made noises to thet Evans chap about how good it would be for us all to be here for the Independence celebrations. You know, big leader's landlady and friends from London, one of 'em keen to see a really free African country get its spurs, one of 'em from a fellow commonwealth country. Choice!" Daintree winked at Janet. "I didn't mention that one of 'em's got the hots for a certain honey coloured guy."

"Daintree!" protested Janet. I haven't 'got the hots,' I've found someone with the same interests, a nice man too, educated, polite, charming company."

"And dishy," added Daintree. "Anyway, we'd all come if they invited us, wouldn't we?" She looked around for confirmation, meeting silent nods and beaming smiles.

"But you mustn't count chickens, Daintree. It would be very expensive to bring us all back." Mrs Baldock was uncertain.

"No worries, Mrs. B. Just let me work on Evans. Now, he's a nice man too, educated, polite, charming company." She winked at Janet again.

"You girls are like a bunch of piranhas," protested Winnie. "Evans is not long widowed, Daintree." She frowned to indicate her disapproval, then despite herself broke into a broad smile. "Anyway, he's more my type. Go find yourself a handsome Maori, Daintree. African Unity," she declaimed, punching her fist in the air.

"And what happened to your handsome Swede idea, Winnie?"

*

Winnie found Evans was indeed off-limits. He expressed great interest in her exposition of the political situation in South Africa, was enraged by the injustice of the system and sympathetic to her problems in London. But despite their earnest conversations over innumerable cups of coffee in the hotel foyer, he never once invited her to dinner, disregarding the heavy hints about Janet's dalliance with Simon Benson.

"Good man, Benson, I think. Maybe Janet could find him something in London to give him extra experience. Just for a short time; we need people like him to make their careers here."

"Y'know, I'd really like to be here for Independence. I suppose you couldn't fix me an invitation?"

Evans looked carefully at her, his head cocked and eyes wide in mock surprise. "And I thought," he said with a sly smile, "you were chatting me up for my brains."

Winnie had the grace to blush. "A bit of that too, Evans."

"Well, Dipra wants us all to give you a proper send-off at the Kakadu on Friday night. So you'll have the chance to ask him yourself."

"I couldn't do that! Ask the First Minister? No." She reflected a moment. "But I suppose we could put Reeta up to it."

Evans laughed. "Good move, I expect. But you haven't much time to talk to her when she gets back. I'm sure you'll find a way – of course she could have been working on Malachi already."

"Can I tell the others about Friday night?"

"Yes, I was going to ask you to do that, even before you started to chat me up."

She gave a small smile. "Maybe you're the cleverest of all three of you, Evans. But sad, still. I'm sorry you've had such a terrible experience, but the wounds will heal you know. Y'know, never mind Independence, I'd quite like to be around when your wounds heal."

She put a hand on his arm. "In case nobody's told you yet, I'm a demn good cook."

*

With an enormous ear-splitting flourish, the band signed off the first half of its programme and they all returned to their seats, sweating with the exertions of the dance.

"Man, I haven't seen many white couples let themselves go like thet before!" Winnie was full of admiration for the gyrations of Andrew and Fiona.

"Och, it only takes a few malts to get ma man going," responded Fiona. "But we'll never have quite the grace and fluidity of you Africans. Mind you, Reeta takes some beating when it comes to fluidity."

Reeta blushed a little and Malachi encircled her with a proud and protective arm. "I think we all enjoy ourselves when we let go."

"People," announced Dipra somewhat pompously, "I have a great idea." They all turned to him.

"You should all be at our Independence Day celebrations."

"My idea, Dipra, remember?" Malachi wasn't to be done out of the credit. "But how can we arrange it?"

Evans broke in. "Will the Governor and his staff be responsible for all the arrangements, Dipra?"

"Yes, in consultation wid Acting President. If dat me, I t'ink I get de last say." Dipra's speech always deteriorated when he'd had a few drinks, or when he was excited, or both, as he was now.

"It's just possible..." Evans hesitated. "Just possible you may not *be* the Acting President when the date comes, Dipra."

Dipra's eyes assumed the fried egg look. "'Course I shall. I campaign independently, nobody want to challenge me. My good friend Sir Joseph advise me.

"You all going to come." He waved his arms inclusively around the group – Ruth, Malachi and Reeta, Evans, Winnie,

234

Daintree, Janet and Simon, Mrs. Baldock and even James Holland brought in to make up the male numbers.

The Kakadu management had seated the party at a discreet distance from the rest of the diners. Just as well, thought Evans. A mildly inebriated First Minister on a night out wasn't perhaps the best way to get re-elected. Dipra hadn't mentioned his plans before. But what a good idea it seemed. He wondered if he might get elected himself on an independent platform. Or should he just step down and hope to be appointed to a similar position as a civil servant? Or should he ask to come back in to InterEarthMove? Shame for Andrew, he thought, looking across to see his successor and Fiona in animated discussion with Reeta. Anyway, could he be sure Inter would have him back?

Winnie broke into his thoughts. "You think he will get back in?"

Evans had to re-align his thoughts. "Yes, I think he probably will. So maybe you *will* come back for Independence."

"Good. I like this society. I could do a really good catering job out here. Could you help me with introductions?"

"Perhaps. I need to think about it."

"Do that, Evans. And heal those wounds. Would you mind if I wrote to you from London?" She asked the question with unaccustomed shyness, catching him off guard.

Then a ghost of a smile appeared and he nodded. "I think that might be quite nice. I get very few personal letters in my mail these days."

TWENTY-TWO

"What are you two going to do about the elections?" Dipra was never less than direct with his questions. He had asked Evans to stay behind after the 'cabinet' meeting and asked Malachi to come in for a little talk.

'Autonomy' had passed with scarcely a ripple; the Governor had held a small ceremony in the Mansion, all the Interim Administrators had become Acting Ministers and Dipra Forfpi had become Acting President. Sir Joseph had been glad to keep the whole affair low key and the short report on page two of the Henry City Journal met his wishes entirely. The general public, as he explained to the editor, were unlikely to appreciate the true significance – or the limitations – of autonomous government.

Independence, and before that the forthcoming elections, were the real news. Since the general public had also very little concept of how the elections would shape the future of the country, the Journal editor was planning an educational programme. The other papers read the Journal every day to see when the scheme would start.

"Maybe I will start a party, Dipra, why don't you head it?" Malachi had been waiting for Autonomy to broach just this subject.

"No. I tell you before, I shall campaign on my own. Now I am Acting President, I don't think I need a Party. Governor recommended that."

"Dipra, you don't have to take any notice of the Governor now. You can be your own man."

"I know dat. But he wise old man, help me a lot this last year. And he right. President above politics. You can be Prime Minister, Malachi. We run the country between us. With Evans help, of course. Evans is the clever one."

Evans smiled. "Just the little matter of winning the election, Dipra." He turned to Malachi. "Do you think you can count on some important support?"

"I talked to Kofi Iffekan. We have similar backgrounds now. He's young and clever, with some good ideas. I heard his talk at the Tech last week and approached him afterwards."

"Iffekan not one of us," growled Dipra.

Evans protested. "There is no *us*, Dipra. We have to look to the future, not the past. There would be a lot to be said for a single party state, where we can use all the talent. It seems stupid to me for a new nation with very limited resources of education and intelligence to have one half of its elite spending all their time trying to attack the other half's ideas."

Dipra looked puzzled. "We all have different ideas. It right to argue them out."

"Yes, but not across party lines. Loyalty to Party can easily blind people to loyalty to country. What do you think, Malachi?"

"Well, there may be something in that. But could we really get all the best brains into one party? Not likely, is it? Some will want to boss their own outfit."

"True, but shouldn't we try? Perhaps there could be a major party just at the start, like Congress in India. A couple of minority parties would do no harm, but the aim should be to create one really major party, with all the best people in it."

"So you lead it. People respect you, first African chief of a big British company, member of cabinet...."

"No, I'm not getting into politics, Malachi. Except to endorse Dipra's campaign, not that he'll need any endorsement from me. I just hope the new government might find a job for me somewhere. Or perhaps I'll go into consultancy. I could pick up work for the contracting companies and perhaps for government departments too."

Dipra was intrigued by the idea. "You going to try it, Malachi? Get Iffekan and some others along with you? What will you call the party?"

"Bishgad Independence Party, I think."

"No, no, Malachi, that's all wrong. We shall *be* Independent. You'd be fighting under yesterday's banner. Emphasise the future. How about Forward Bishgad?"

"Maybe. But it's too short. Bishgad Forward Party?"

They stayed silent for a moment. Then Evans had an idea.

"Bishgad Forward Peoples Party. Then it means the party for forward people as well as for a forward country."

"Brilliant," said Dipra. "You always clever with words, Evans. But I still won't join."

"OK," said Malachi, "but you won't mind if we endorse you, will you? It will be good for both you and the new party, don't you think?"

"Ver' good," conceded Dipra. "But work on Evans to join you. You won't find a better Minister of Public Works anywhere in Bishgad."

"Never mind that, Dipra, Malachi has to work on policies, ideas to put before the public. There has to be a manifesto, setting out your aims. It's time we asked for votes for ideas instead of for personalities. The personalities business bedevils politics in every country, as far as I can see. Maybe the Presidential election has to be about personality, and you don't need to express policies, Dipra, because your job will be to act as a balance to government, a bit like the House of Lords in UK. But let's have a party, or parties if we must, that stand for something, for fair shares, or improved education, all that sort of thing."

"Will you help us draw it up, this Manifesto?"

"Yes, Malachi, if you promise not to publicise my role in it. Maybe that will be the start of my consultancy practice," he laughed. "But as you'd be my first customer, I won't charge you."

*

There was something Evans had to do for Dipra first. He contacted Simon Benson and suggested that an approach to the Acting President for an exclusive interview might not be rejected.

Benson was thrilled to be invited up to The Mansion for the purpose. And even more thrilled when a well briefed Dipra Forfpi gave him the news that he would be campaigning entirely independently of any political party that might be formed. Not that he'd heard of any yet. But there were bound to be some.

Better to keep the Presidency independent, Forfpi thought. Under the new constitution the President shared power with the Prime Minister. That would be good. Forfpi would be happy to work with whoever the people chose. He was sure every leader was now determined to help Bishgad succeed and grow.

The Henry City Journal editor was sufficiently impressed to run the interview on the front page. It sat well with his plan to outline the electoral process to his readership. And it would boost his circulation nicely. And make him popular with the President. His rival newspapers could only read the words of wisdom with envy. Three of them approached him for permission to reproduce material. Yes, of course, he murmured sweetly, all the electoral process stuff you can do the day after us. But not the President's interview. Nobody can stop you referring to it, of course, providing you acknowledge its source.

Sales of The Henry City Journal quadrupled and Simon Benson took home a substantial bonus.

Reporters were now buzzing all over the city harassing business leaders to see who was or was not going to announce a party formation. Slight references to the need to gather support from all the regions were taken as proof that Mr. A would be launching a party. But Mr. B would get there first, claimed a rival newspaper.

Evans pressed Malachi to announce. "Pre-empt them all, Malachi. I'll get Benson in for you. We're nearly finished on the manifesto – and none of the others will have one, I'll bet."

So Simon Benson had a second exclusive. Mr. Goodwill had secured the support of a dozen leading figures for his Bishgad Forward Peoples' Party and they were gathering signatures throughout the regions. The party would be publishing a manifesto next week and invited all forward thinking people to join. All views and opinions would be treated seriously in the BFPP; it would be a truly democratic organisation.

The Henry City Journal swept all before it. The printing presses ran wild and a rival paper withdrew from the market and offered its capacity to The Journal, which snapped it up. Lorries could be seen every morning departing for the regions loaded with newspapers. The editor contemplated changing the name to Bishgad Journal, now that it was a national newspaper, the first the country had ever had. He even asked Benson's opinion.

"You could ask Mr. Watanero what he thinks, Mr. Whitman. He's the brains."

"You mean he wrote this manifesto?"

Benson wondered if he'd said too much. "No, I just mean he's clever. If you want to go national, he'd be good with ideas, I think."

The editor looked quizzically at Benson. "He's your go-between, isn't he? Have you asked him what his own plans are?"

"Not politics, I gather. But he knows the whole country from his work with InterEarthMove and with Public Works. Shall I invite him in?"

"Yes, do that."

Evans thought The Journal could well go national but it would need correspondents in each region to keep abreast of developments there and to give local readers extra points of interest. There was an exciting time ahead, and it wasn't only for Jamestown. Covering the election in the regions would be important too.

"I ought to pay you for this advice," said Whitman.

Evans grinned. "Just give me a good press when I start up my consultancy, would you? I wish you success. And this young man." Evans gestured to Simon Benson.

"Yes, thank you, Mr. Watanero. If we are going to have correspondents all over the country, Simon must be our new Chief Reporter."

Benson looked startled and then gave way to a broad smile.

"You two are the first to know," said Whitman.

*

"So Evans won't join a party, not even Malachi's? He's following your lead, Dipra."

"No Ruth, Evans never followed anyone. He the only one

240

I might worry about standing for President, but I think he too soft."

"Keep him happy, Dipra. We all know he is clever and he's going to endorse you anyway. That will be good; people respect him. But he is still sad, isn't he? I thought that South African girl Winnie might catch his eye but nothing happened."

"Maybe it will when she comes back."

"You meant that? I thought it was just because you were...."

"Drunk?" Dipra laughed. "Yes, I was a bit, but I going to make sure those ladies come back. It only right for them to support the new Prime Minister."

"Dipra, we haven't even had the elections yet! It said in the paper today that one Joseph Amass will start a party too."

"Yes, but it no good. You watch. When Malachi's party get going, Amass will ask to merge them. An' Malachi should say no, den offer for Amass to join the BFPP. He will join." Dipra giggled. "Malachi's push and Evans's brains will certainly win dis election. When I President, I get de snooker table in Mansion House, get plenty practice. You an' me got great future, Ruth."

Ruth kept her own counsel about this prospect.

"And you sure you can fix it for those girls to come back?"

"Of course. Governor and me, we soon going to make up guest list for official celebration. UK Government Ministers, Commonwealth country representatives who will be High Commissioners, all those sort of people and personal guests wid some connection. Malachi will nominate his professor from LSE and the ladies, perhaps Evans will want to ask dat Chinese girl back, used to run InterEarthMove."

"May not be a good idea, that, confuse Winnie."

"Why it confuse Winnie?"

"Oh, Dipra, you are a nice innocent man."

*

The BFPP manifesto gave the people plenty to think about. Evans had carefully gone through the manifestos of the Labour, Conservative and Liberal Party manifestos from England and tried to envisage their proposals against a background of Bishgadi society. He felt he'd got it about right, a just left-of-centre thrust that didn't promise too much too quickly.

Malachi wasn't precisely sure what left-of-centre meant though he'd seen the term in use in London. It seemed to him that people could be left- of-centre on some things and right-of-centre on others. However he understood very clearly Evans's wish not to give 'too many hostages to fortune' and he even made a few useful suggestions that Evans incorporated in the document.

They leaned on The Journal's editor to provide a big print run at minimal cost and interleaved it with the paper. Mr. Whitman was at pains to point out in his editorial that this by no means meant the paper was supporting this particular party; The Journal wished all parties well in the coming elections. The insert was a purely commercial transaction.

Joseph Amass was nevertheless furious and took a strong complaint to The Governor.

"Have you approached The Journal yourself, Mr Amass?" queried the unflappable Sir Joseph.

"No, but you can see this is a cheat."

"No, Mr. Amass, this is politics, democratic politics. Do I take it you are forming your own party?"

"I am trying, now, I got signatures from six regions already."

"Then get the other four, Mr. Amass and ask the Journal to carry *your* manifesto. They will charge you, of course."

"Dipra Forfpi has not published a manifesto."

"No, he has opted not to belong to a party. He will campaign on his own name. He already has all the necessary signatures from all regions and nobody else has bothered so far. Have you considered running for President yourself?"

"He is cunning. Got that all wrapped up. But Goodwill is his great friend, so I know they will co-operate. It is a cheat, dey have fixed it."

"Mr. Amass." Sir Joseph gave a resigned sigh. "If you have read the BFPP manifesto you will see that it offers to listen

242

to all points of view. It seems to me to hint at a one-party state, which I am opposed to in principle but on the other hand there is an argument that a young country with few educated resources needs to use every bit of talent in government rather than waste energy on party squabbling.

"I should guess that your own views tend towards socialist concepts. If you feel a BFPP government is inevitable, perhaps you should consider joining that party to get your viewpoint recognised. There will be plenty of opportunities for clever people like yourself."

Sir Joseph waited for the compliment to sink in before continuing. He could see he had Amass confused.

"And with your previous experience as an administrator, you should be well placed."

"You sacked me!"

"Only because you broke the rules, Mr. Amass. That does not disqualify you from government forever, you know. This country has Autonomy and can make its own decisions now."

The Governor rose to indicate the audience was over. "I shall be interested to see what course of action you take, Mr. Amass, whether it be forming your own party or joining another."

"Evans Watanero in this BFPP?"

"No, he does not wish to pursue a political career." Sir Joseph maintained an expressionless face.

"And you did not write this manifesto?"

"Good lord, no, that would be quite improper." Sir Joseph's urbanity temporarily deserted him.

"Then Evans wrote it," declared Amass, with some venom. "He is the fixer behind the scenes. Goodbye, Sir Joseph."

He turned and stalked away.

TWENTY-THREE

"I think I will go on with my idea to form a proper socialist party unless the BFPP brings some of its manifesto into line. You have to make some choices."

Joseph Amass was putting his case to the Acting President and his adviser Malachi Goodwill.

"Why should we take any notice of your ideas, Joseph. We are going to win this election hands down."

"We? You mean you and Malachi? I thought you were independent, Mr. President."

"The Bishgad Forward Peoples' Party. Malachi's party. You know what I mean."

Amass smiled. "I know. You and Malachi's and Watanero's party. But I have plenty of support. I can get enough seats to make a coalition necessary."

Malachi butted in. "Surely you can see that it will be better we have only one party. Talk to us. We should show the people their leaders are united."

"I *am* talking to you, Malachi. I come to tell you what I want to join your party. You going to listen?"

"Tell us."

"Four things, only."

He paused for dramatic effect and they sat forward on their leather armchairs. Then he spread his left hand with thumb tucked across the palm and touched the little finger with his right hand middle finger

"One, a commitment in the manifesto to ensure more state ownership of companies. InterEarthMove for a start."

"But the manifesto has already been printed," protested Malachi.

"OK, but a commitment from you to make it happen."

Amass continued to hold out his hands, implicitly threatening. Malachi and Dipra exchanged glances. Amass made his own interpretation.

"OK, I know, you have to ask Watanero first. You do that.

Second," – he touched the ring finger – "you put the word National in the party name. Bishgad Forward Peoples National Party. I can't bring my supporters in unless it is clear this is a truly national party."

"That doesn't sound a problem to me," said Dipra. "What you think, Malachi?"

"Maybe. We can't alter the manifesto but the change could follow later, perhaps before the election itself. I shall ask Evans."

"Third," – his middle fingers touched – " you, Mr Forfpi, become the leader of this party."

Dipra was astonished. "Why? I got plenty support on my own."

"A national party has to be headed by the President. We all in this together. People will understand that better. Maybe we are only feeling our way but if your idea of a dominant party is to work, it needs everyone important to be involved."

Dipra scratched his chin. "Have to think about that. Party makes bad decisions, I get blame. Party loses power, I lose power."

"Exactly. A *responsible* President. Tell Evans Watanero about it."

"And your fourth idea?" Malachi sensed Amass was playing his cards carefully. Was perhaps saving his trump card.

Amass touched his left index finger and looked directly at each listener in turn.

" I become Prime Minister."

*

Evans looked coolly at his two friends. "I read somewhere that politics often meant choosing between two evils. Amass can be a real problem if he starts his own party. On the other hand, I don't like the idea of nationalisation. Especially InterEarthMove. It's too good a company to ruin with inexperienced management. And nationalising it would put off other investors."

"We only have to *promise* him, not necessarily do it."

"And will you be able to stop him if he's PM? How do you

feel about that, Malachi? Is he effectively hi-jacking your party, putting Dipra at the head and taking number two place himself?"

They fell silent.

"What about the party name?" demanded Dipra.

"Oh, I don't think that's any problem. You could at least agree on that. Will you give up your independent role, Dipra?"

"Will you come inside the Party yourself, Evans?"

They fell silent again, each man contemplating the various courses open to them. "You could be compromise PM, Evans," Dipra suggested. Evans shook his head and the silence resumed.

It was Evans who broke it.

"OK. Let me outline a possible arrangement. Some of Amass's arguments have merit. If you lead the party, Dipra, I will join it. But I have to tell you I want only a ministry concerned with infrastructure development. If Amass has to be PM and Iffekan is a strong candidate for Minister of Finance, Malachi should be Minister of Commerce and Industry which will put him in charge of nationalisation, if any is going to happen."

"Not bad, I suppose. Dipra and I could make sure between us that nothing bad happens, nothing too extreme. Iffekan is a capitalist by inclination. Training in USA probably makes sure of that."

"And does training in Russia make Dipra inclined to state control of everything?" Evans smiled at Dipra as he said it.

"I see some bloody good things and some bloody bad ones. Some things good to nationalise, others a disaster. Especially when they get corrupt."

"Hang on to that idea, Dipra. Let's think carefully what's best for Bishgad, not best in Russia or USA. We can at least learn from their mistakes. But what do we tell Amass?"

Goodwill punched his right fist into his left hand and leaned forward. "We agree his four points. New name is OK, no problem. But not too enthusiastic about InterEarthMove. Promise to look at it in two years when the new government is settled in. Must learn to walk before we run, we tell him. Dipra heads the party but Amass gets the PM job."

"*Very good*, Malachi. You have all the makings of a really astute politician. You agree, Dipra?"

Dipra nodded. "We have to pay subscription or something to join this party?"

"Ten pounds a year for ordinary membership, fifty pounds for life membership. Evans worked out the fees. That will be twenty Gadi and a hundred Gadi when it comes in."

"OK. Evans and I will take out life membership, not so, Evans?"

"Shouldn't we," corrected Evans, automatically.

*

The election was a foregone conclusion.

A high profile public statement from Dipra Forfpi announced that he had carefully considered the manifesto of the BFPNP and found himself so totally in agreement with its aims that he was honoured to accept their generous invitation to lead it. The Journal gave him full coverage and carried the news also that Evans Watanero had also decided to run for parliament under the same banner. Then Amass joined in and the bandwagon began to roll.

Ambitious young men all over the country hurried to join. Malachi's committees, set up on Evans's advice, selected candidates for each of the sixty-nine seats not allocated to Malachi, Evans, Amass and Iffekan. Only in five outlying seats did the BFPNP fail to win. A handful of chiefs exerted their traditional powers to persuade their people to put them 'in government,' even though they had no party and no policies other than to get paid for talking 'in dis new chiefs' place.'

While his friends exulted in their victory, Evans thought deeply about the advisability of establishing a proper 'House of Chiefs' as an advisory body. It shouldn't have any real power, he explained to Dipra, but it would provide an outlet for the views of traditional chiefs and give the government an ear to the ground. That might be very useful when some of the reforms they would need to institute came along. Get the chiefs on your side and you'd get the people.

Dipra and Joseph Amass agreed a raft of ministerial appointments and a cabinet of the senior posts, which Evans reluctantly agreed to join. A leaflet was hurried out amid the preparations for Independence Day, with short profiles of the ministers and their responsibilities. Dipra's photograph occupied the whole of the front cover and if few people bothered to read the contents, many indeed unable to, every home and business in the country hung the picture on the wall, some in ornate frames, most attached only with sticky tape. Dipra had become the icon of Independence.

*

In London, Janet, Winnie and Daintree invited Mrs. Baldock to come round to discuss these exciting invitations to Bishgad's Independence Day celebrations. The letter came from the President, Dipra Forfpi.

"Almost our brother-in-law," commented Daintree.

"And just how you figure thet out, Daintree?"

"Reeta's nearly a sister, and Malachi and Dipra are like blood brothers. Almost in the family, we are."

Winnie found the idea appealing. "Man, I wouldn't mind taking my place in thet line-up; there's still Evans on the loose."

They looked at her astonished at this frank outburst. "Right," said Daintree, "and Janet catches her Simon Benson, which leaves just me and Mrs. B. to find Prince Charmings on this visit and we can all live happily ever after in beautiful Bishgad. God, I could manage a few years of that sunshine."

"I rather think I'm past Prince Charmings, Daintree, and anyway I'm happy meeting the world through my students in Battersea. But you girls could do a lot worse. Look at Reeta, married to the Minister of Commerce and Industry and with a good job in the country's top hospital. She's obviously thoroughly enjoying life out there."

"Yeah, well, the Minister of Public Works and Infrastructure might not be too bad a catch, at thet!"

"Winnie, you mercenary bitch!" Daintree feigned shock. "Marry for money, would you?"

"No. But if a bit of money came with the passion, I wouldn't let it put me off. Evans is a pretty nice guy, man. But how long will I have to wait before his wounds heal?"

Mrs. B tactfully intervened. "Did Simon ever write to you, Janet?"

"Oh, yes. He's had some promotion too, you know. Chief Reporter for The Journal now. He tells me the paper has grown enormously on the back of its coverage of the election and his editor is over the moon about it. Simon's contacts with Evans made most of that possible. But anyway, he's a very clever reporter, he writes great reports because he is so well read."

"Sounds like you're keen, Janet."

"Well… He is pretty nice. But *I'm* not counting chickens," she added hastily, seeing Daintree about to make some remark.

"OK, OK, let's get on with discussing plans for the visit," broke in Winnie. "We going to get a taxi up to Heathrow, do it in style? With First Class tickets, ladies, thet's the least we can do."

"Yes, between the four of us, it won't be too expensive. We'll need an estate car to carry all our baggage, thirty kilos allowance, remember. I'm going to lash out on some swanky new dresses this time, now I know what the climate's like." Daintree was enthusiastic. "And I might even see if there's any possibility of a job at Karle Mo alongside Reeta."

*

In Jamestown, preparations for the big day were continuing apace. A whole area of shanty dwellings down by the sea had been cleared and shiploads of cement brought in to provide a concrete base for the new square and the series of grandstands that would surround it. People who had spent their lives in straw huts or the more affluent in converted sea containers now found themselves relocated into tiny prefabricated houses with electricity and water laid on, clinging to the hillside to the West of the city. Evans's ministry organised the construction of the square and the assembly of the houses and screwed the money out of the British government to pay for it all. Bishgad would have a great debt to its new British High Commissioner, Evans commented to Peter Willoughby.

InterEarthMove provided all the necessary machinery at half its usual rental rates as a gesture of goodwill to the new country, to the development of which it would be proud to make its contribution. A full-page advertisement in The Journal emphasised the point, to Evans's quiet amusement and Joseph Amass's fury.

"Could we not have got more money from Britain to pay proper rates?" he demanded. "We should not be beholden to a commercial company."

"Joseph, just be grateful the company has a social conscience. Britain is not a bottomless pit of money. The money they give comes from British taxpayers. Ask Kofi to explain it to you."

"I know that as well as you, Evans. It is right for one of the richest countries in the world to give to one of the poorest, especially when some of their wealth was robbed from us."

"Robbed, Joseph? You know what this country looked like before the British came? Are you going to give up some of your own wealth to help the poor get education?"

"I shall pay my taxes."

"And give to charity too? Better practise, as well as preach, socialism, Joseph. The new government will come under great scrutiny you know. Nobody in more detail than the Prime Minister. You need to be seen as a caring politician, not just a combative one. You may not like some of Kofi's ideas, but you have to listen to them carefully. He is a very clever economist, a very practical man."

"A very capitalist man! Am I the only socialist in this new government?"

"No, I'm sure you're not. Let's hope we've got the right combination for a young nation. But we'll have to use capitalism if we are ever to develop ourselves economically. You know I'm not opposed to your ideas of fair shares, nor I think is Dipra or Malachi. But we are all, all of us including you, Joseph, the result of some judicious preference in our past, aren't we? Countries need elites to lead them. We were the lucky ones. Let's be grateful and continue to look for bright young people for preference, so we can build tomorrow's leaders."

"That can be done under socialism!"

Evans put a hand on his shoulder. "Stalin? Khrushchev? Not a good record, Joseph. The British do know a thing or two about balancing both socialism and capitalism with democracy. Now, what did your committee decide about the new name for the city. Everyone is dying to know."

Amass knew he had been sidetracked but could not resist it.

"We think Feralode, my idea, from the old iron mining which used to take place here."

"Brilliant, Joseph. Two 'r's I suppose?"

"No, only one. We don't need to stick too close to English ideas of spelling. Our people will be happier with one."

"Yes, I think you're probably right. Feralode, good. I'm sure Dipra and Malachi will be very happy with it."

"They must be. The committee," said Amass with as much cool dignity as he could muster, "approved it unanimously."

*

"It is very good you are making Dr. Endoman Minister of Health, Dipra. Everyone at Karle Mo is very pleased. Was it your idea?" Ruth was enthusiastic.

"Well… actually it was Evans suggested it. He said the Endoman family deserved to be integrated into the new government and Dr. Endoman is very respected even in Britain."

"Yes, good. We have another idea on the staff, you want to hear it?"

Dipra looked cautious. "What staff?"

"The nursing staff at the hospital. We wondered … The idea that we are going to get a new wing just for children if the UK government come up with the funds…"

"We don't know yet. But it could be. What about it?"

"You could suggest it should be called the Grace Endoman

251

wing. We would all like that. And Evans would be pleased, I'm sure."

"You don't think it look too .. too much all in the family, you know? Minister of Health opens new wing in his own name? We need to be careful, Ruth."

"Not his *own* name, Dipra, his daughter's. Maybe we should use her married name. Grace Watanero Wing?"

"Yes. Better, I think. You want to ask Evans yourself?"

"No. It nicer if it comes from his old friend Dipra. Maybe it will help to heal his wounds from losing Grace. And it would show how sorry you are, in a way, to benefit from Grace's accident."

Dipra nodded. This wife of his was a very clever woman. She understood people. She was beautiful to stand alongside on a platform and good fun to live with. If only he could get her to take snooker more seriously. She could be so good at it, if only she would practise more.

*

My dear Evans,

I was really pleased to hear from you and delighted to receive your invitation to attend the Independence ceremony for Bishgad. And you now, the Minister for Infrastructure and Development, wow!

I had heard, of course, that you'd left InterEarthMove and that Aberdeen had succeeded you. Good man, I know. We made a good choice there. It seemed surprising to me that you'd choose to go into politics, you're not devious enough to make a real go of that, I felt, but you seem to be proving me wrong! Perhaps Bishgad politics are easier than in more developed countries and you don't have to be devious. Well, I hope you don't, that wouldn't be you.

Yes, of course I will come. But no 'partner' as you so discreetly put it; there isn't one yet. Maybe I've left it too late! My business career, you might have heard, flourishes, and I am now Vice President East Asia, almost on your level! Perhaps you can't have a really successful business career and home life too, at least women don't seem able to.

You didn't mention Grace in your letter though. I hope she's well, any children yet?

I shall arrange to fly out on 12th August, arriving 13th so as to give me a day to acclimatise and sort things a bit before the great day. So if you could reserve a room at the Tropical House for four nights – I shall have to fly on to London on 17th – don't send me tickets, I'll do my own – I should be very grateful. It will be so exciting to see you and Grace again, and Aberdeen and Malachi in his exalted new position and even James Holland if he's still in Jamesland.

It really was very kind of you to include me on the guest list and I should remind you and Grace that you still haven't visited Hong Kong. Yes, I run my little empire from the same flat I've had for years. Mind you, it does have one of the best views in the colony.

See you soon, Evans,
Much love, Celine.

Oh God, he hadn't mentioned Grace's death. It didn't seem appropriate in an invitation to a formal ceremony. Evans felt a twinge of guilt at not having informed her a year ago or more. She had not been able to make the wedding, but had sent a beautiful gift of delicate china, to which Grace had responded with a very charming thank you letter.

He had to write again. He couldn't let Celine arrive expecting Grace to be there. The shock would be unkind. But she was still unmarried. He pictured her again in his mind and relived the moment of their parting, when he wanted to cry on Andrew's shoulder. That ridiculous 'burglary' had diverted his mind. That, and Grace, and the Governor's offer … had he gone completely down the wrong path in all that?

He would seek some advice from Andrew. This wasn't a matter Dipra or Malachi could help him with. But he needed a woman's advice too; perhaps Fiona would help out. What do you say to an old lover, your first love, when she comes back into your life? Why had he kept Grace's death a secret? No, it wasn't a secret, but it was from Celine.

Malachi came into his office just then and saw the air-letter with the small neat script he remembered from years ago.

"Celine? Is she coming?"

"Yes, she is. And mentions you and how she's looking forward to meeting all the old gang."

Evans folded the letter and put it in his pocket.

"Can't I read it?"

"It's private, Malachi."

"Oh ho! Romance coming back into your life, Evans?"

"Nonsense, Malachi, you know there's no future ..."

"I know Reeta and I have made a go of it."

"But there's not an eight year reverse age gap between you and Reeta. And she's happy at Karle Mo. No prospect of Celine settling down here. She's Vice President East Asia now. And I'm committed to Bishgad's first government."

"Crazier things happen, my friend. So she never married her boyfriend?"

" No. She's a career woman. You could see that when she was here."

*

Andrew read the letter and passed it to Fiona.

"What is it you're worried about, Evans? I doubt she's going to make a dead set at you."

"No, he isna worried about that, he's worried that keeping Grace's death quiet will seem like deceit, isn't that it, Evans?"

Evans nodded. "I should have said something in my original letter. To be honest, I'd forgotten she might not know. I suppose it was such a big thing here I sort of assumed she'd hear about it, perhaps through the InterEarthMove grapevine."

"Well." Fiona poured him another coffee. "What is certain is that you must write now and explain. She'll understand, Evans. I know you loved her. Did she love you?"

Andrew looked sideways at Evans, wondering how he

would answer this direct question. Not like his Fiona, really.

Evans hung his head a moment. "Yes, I rather think she did. What did you think, Andrew?"

"*Then*, I would say yes. *Now* may be different. People change. She's now a very senior international executive. She's probably got a dozen admirers in Hong Kong, they worship success there, it seems. Her letter doesn't sound as if she's changed, but you don't know."

"I always thought her a nice lady, really nice," put in Fiona. "And you owe her an explanation, Evans. You're good with words and will be able to write a properly contrite letter excusing yourself because of the circumstances. And welcoming her again, without overdoing it. You don't want to frighten her off. She could go on being a good friend."

She glanced at Andrew. "Shall we..?"

Evans looked up. "Shall you what?"

Andrew straightened his posture a little. "Something to tell you, but it's a bit premature."

Evans was now intrigued. "Never mind, tell me."

"We have told London we want to finish out here at the end of this tour. We ought to get back for the kids' education. I've asked if they can find me something at home in eighteen months' time. That's for your information only, of course."

TWENTY-FOUR

So Andrew would be leaving. Eighteen months. Should he ask London to think about having him back? Would an eighteen-month stint in Bishgad's first government be useful, either to the country or to himself? Should he back out now, leaving Dipra and Malachi to handle Joseph Amass on their own? He could fill in the eighteen months with consultancy work, surely? But would he get any?

The conflicting ideas circulated so quickly in his head he needed paper on which to write them, to see any one clearly, its advantages and disadvantages, its risks and opportunities. Did he really want to go back into InterEarthMove? Or was that a backward step for him? It was certainly a much bigger company now than when he'd left it. Would the spirit of the place feel different? And anyway, would London even consider him?

He put his confused thoughts to the back of his mind as he came into the cabinet meeting. Everyone was present except Dipra. When would he learn to get his timings right? Evans discreetly despatched a messenger to the snooker room to dig Dipra out. One day, Evans thought, Dipra will abandon the Presidency to become a professional snooker player. But not yet. The table in the Mansion was too great an attraction.

Another five minutes and Dipra came into the room, slightly out of breath. "Sorry, people. Something I had to finish first." And in an aside to Evans, a fiercely whispered joy, "Hundred and Forty Seven break – my first ever!"

Planning for the great day took up most of the cabinet's time. The Minister of Transport announced the agreement of the British Government to supply five hundred vehicles for the day, all painted black and gold, the country's new colours, and ranging from Ford Fiestas through Land Rovers to Jaguars.

"And one Rolls Royce for President," added Dipra.

"Couldn't we have some Mercedes for senior members of cabinet?" enquired Amass.

"Joseph, these have to be British cars. HMG is not going to pay for German cars to come in here," Evans was moved to protest. "You will get a splendid Jaguar."

"Hmm. And what will you and Malachi get?"

"I shall get whatever Dipra allocates to me. A Range Rover might be the most sensible car for my job."

"More important things than cars to discuss, Joseph. Tell us how the plans for the stands are going, Evans."

"The erection team from UK started on the stands proper yesterday. They build up very fast, they'll be all ready in good time. The planning man from the British Foreign Office has been given the lists of guests and he is now allocating seating. I have asked him to ensure personal guests of cabinet members get clear views of the parade. After that, we should rely on his knowledge of protocol to put all the official guests in order. He warns me there is never an occasion like this when somebody does not object to his seating but he expects complaints to be very few. He says the disputes always come from middle rank countries. We'll just have to live with those."

"African countries should get priority," claimed Amass.

Dipra looked to Evans for guidance.

"I believe these matters are all fairly well understood and protocol rules are very widely accepted among the diplomatic corps. We should not try to change things too much."

"Hmm. Whites at the front, blacks at the back."

"No, it won't be like that at all, Joseph"

"We getting some ANC people from South Africa? We should show solidarity with their struggle."

Evans took his time to reply. "My friend from the FCO suggests we have one representative each from ANC and from Inkatha. Low profile seats, I'm afraid, but he says they will just be pleased to be invited."

"Inkatha is white man's stooge party."

"We can't interfere in their domestic politics, Joseph. Inkatha, as I understand it, represent the Zulu nation. Let them sort out their own problems, we have enough of our own."

"Hmm. After Independence, maybe we look at that again."

*

The vehicles began to arrive and caused a considerable stir of interest, with their unique black and gold livery. Arrangements were made for them to be safely stored until five days before the event, in a compound owned by City Cars, the firm from which Evans had bought his own vehicle years before. Storage was free, the Transport Minister explained to cabinet, in return for an opportunity for City Cars to bid for those vehicles not wanted after the celebrations.

"At what price?" demanded Malachi.

"That depends on the condition, of course. For good condition we get thirty percent of the full retail price in England. Because we not paying, it will all be profit of course."

It sounded reasonable. The firm had to make a small profit too. The Transport Minister did not feel the need to mention the two percent he would make on each vehicle sold. After all, he had negotiated the man up from a quarter of the retail price. And he had insisted the man should not mark any car up by more than ten percent when he sold them. Especially the small cars. Bishgad would have a car-owning urban population from the word go. And a lot of people would be grateful to him.

As soon as the drivers returned from their UK driving training courses, the cars were released in order of seniority. Dipra's Roller was parked gingerly and condescendingly alongside the Governor's Range Rover in the basement garage of the Mansion, by a driver newly outfitted in a dark grey uniform complete with peaked cap with Rolls Royce insignia. Joseph Amass, Kofi Iffekan and Malachi joyfully took delivery of their Jaguars complete with Jaguar-trained drivers in similar uniforms.

Evans, fully au fait with the Range Rover, dismissed his allocated driver, back into the pool. He saw no need to waste money on a driver who would probably know less than he did himself.

"It is shameful to drive yourself, you are a minister,"

declared Joseph Amass.

"Rubbish, Joseph. Nothing shameful in driving yourself. I've been doing it for years. Even in InterEarthMove, when I was GM, I usually drove myself."

"Ministers are different," claimed Amass. "You have no style."

"I'll leave the style to you, Joseph. But don't you think you might like to get your hands on that lovely Jag? All that power, man!"

"Maybe, some time," Amass grudgingly admitted.

The sometime was not long coming. "Drive me out to the Lambada Botanic Gardens," he instructed his driver.

"Yes, sah." Drivers never showed too much interest in destinations. Maybe this minister had a girlfriend in one of the villages out there. He set off North out of the city and gunned the car to seventy on a straight stretch after leaving the traffic behind.

Amass leaned over the front passenger seat to observe the speedometer. "Will it do a hundred?"

"I think so sah, but nowhere in Jamesland. Soon, de road get windy and dere are some big holes."

"OK. Pull in and let me have a go. No traffic here."

"Yes, sah." The driver showed Amass how to put the car in neutral and keep his foot on the brake before the ignition would fire, how to select Drive, gently release the brake and let the car roll forward smoothly, then just a touch on the accelerator ….

The car zoomed off. "Gently!" shouted the driver, all rank forgotten in the panic of the moment.

"OK OK, I got it. Nice steady sixty, very smooth, don't seem to be many bumps around here. How far to the Gardens now?"

"About thirty miles, I think. We done maybe twenty since leaving city."

"Good, let's see what she can do."

Amass added ten miles an hour and wound the car around the bends at the maximum speed he felt he could manage until another long straight stretch appeared. "Good. Now we see her go." He gradually pressed down, hardly noticing the build up of speed except for satisfying movement of the indicator.

"Need to slow now, for de corner," warned the driver, now luxuriating in the front passenger seat.

Amass lifted his foot but the gentle downward incline maintained the car's speed. "Must brake it down," called the driver as the bend came up fast ....

The huge oncoming Volvo truck, loaded to its maximum with tree trunks, occupied most of the road.

*

Dear Celine,

Please forgive my writing to you again at the very last minute like this but I do hope this letter reaches you in time. Your hotel room is booked as you asked and I shall meet you myself at the airport. It will be wonderful to see you again after all these years.

However I am writing because in the rush of all the preparations I forgot to tell you something I had assumed you would have heard through the InterEarthMove grapevine. Grace was killed in a road accident over a year ago. She was several months pregnant.

A car coming from a big reception at the Mansion, carrying our two most important politicians hit her head on. They too were killed. The driver was certainly drunk and is now serving seven years in prison. As you can imagine, I was devastated but by throwing myself into work and later getting very involved with the party which now governs the country, I have survived.

Putting this in a letter will save me the embarrassment and you the shock at the airport. You will be an honoured guest at our celebration, with your contribution to our economic development fully acknowledged. I have said something about it in the brochure we have published about the government and the guests so that people will know who all these strangers are on the day.

Have a safe and pleasant flight and look out for me at Jamestown. (I'll be the little chap at the back!)
Kind regards, Evans.

Evans drove in to the main Post Office to despatch this, he would take no chances. While there he looked in the Private Mailbox he rented, not that he was expecting anything but he liked to keep such private mail as he did receive away from the prying eyes of office staff.

To his surprise there was a chatty letter from Winnie, saying how excited all the girls were about their forthcoming trip; even Mrs. Baldock had lashed out on a lot of new clothes. How was Malachi? It seemed amazing they knew so many high-ranking people in Bishgad, two ministers and even the President. Did he know Janet was really rather keen on Simon Benson, who seemed to be doing well in his career though Winnie knew that part of that was down to him, Evans, and his introductions. Daintree seemed quite interested in looking at the possibility of a job at Karle Mo but that might be a passing whim, you never knew with Daintree.

For herself, Winnie was really looking forward to seeing all the gang again, especially Reeta of course, though she didn't imagine they'd have a lot of opportunity to talk with ministers, they'd be too busy with all the arrangements. Winnie had been down to a specialist flag-maker's shop and guess what, she'd found a few of the new Bishgad flags, so they would come out equipped. But she supposed there'd be millions on sale in Jamestown by the great day.

Evans folded the letter and carefully stowed it in a button-down top pocket. As he drove back home he tried to picture Winnie, remembering how tall and long-limbed she'd been, what a contrast to petite Celine. Then he wondered why he should have compared them. He switched off the thoughts and considered Daintree, perhaps she'd be an asset at Karle Mo, she had apparently always got top grades during her training. And little Janet, who had made such an improvement in Malachi's speech; actually rather better than Mrs. Mitchell had achieved with Dipra. But he'd made some progress, certainly. It was just that he forgot a lot of it when he got excited. The answer was not to get excited so often. Evans smiled to himself. Nice of Winnie to write to him. But then, she had promised.

His phone was ringing as he entered his flat.

"Where you been?" demanded Dipra. "I been ringing you all evening."

Oh dear, there went Dipra's correct English.

"What is it, Dipra?"

"Amass done killed himself. I need your advice."

"Killed himself?! Why should he do that? I thought he was very happy with his new job, new car and all."

"Road accident. Silly fool take over from driver and lose control of new car, I think. Out on the Belaradi Road this afternoon. Dat's three big men we lose in road accidents. You coming over now?"

Evans considered for a moment . "Yes, I think I had better. Have you called the Governor?"

"Not yet. You think I should?"

"Yes. And Malachi. Tomorrow you must call a Cabinet meeting, Dipra, but you need to have a policy thought out. Ten days to Independence Day, it is very unfortunate. I'm on my way. Talk to Sir Joseph and Malachi now."

*

It was a hot night but the beers were cooled ready. They lounged in the wide wicker chairs on the fly-screened balcony running outside the Governor's private apartments.

"We can be reasonably certain of privacy here," offered Sir Joseph. "You may find this a very useful meeting place, Mr. Forfpi, when you take over. Who reported this accident to you?"

"Mr. Holland. A motorist saw the wreck and rang the police. A gold and black Jaguar, he said. It lucky Mr. Holland overheard. He went out himself, kept everyone away."

"Good. The immediate question for you, Mr. President, " Sir Joseph continued, "is who you want to be Prime Minister in Mr. Amass's place. Not that I am clear I have any right of nomination. I fear we have blurred the constitution by taking Mr. Amass into your party and of course by your joining the party yourself. However, let us be practical, am I right in supposing it is likely to be one of these two gentlemen?"

Dipra looked at his two old friends. His mind raced. Malachi was the one with political ability and he had after all started the party. On the other hand, Evans was the clever one and the one people trusted most. Would one of them give way, to make the job easier? Or could he suggest Kofi Iffekan? He was also very clever, but mostly with figures. Who would be finance if Iffekan moved up?

"What do you think?" he suddenly asked them.

"I don't want us to quarrel over this, but it was me that began the party and but for Amass's intervention I should have led it to victory in the polls and so been Prime Minister." Malachi had the grace to blush as he made his bid. "But I would want Evans to be in Cabinet still, very senior, perhaps Minister of Interior."

"No, no," Evans shook his head. "No quarrel, Malachi. I am content with Infrastructure and Development. I thought this meeting was about how we announce it tomorrow. Do we tell the truth about Amass's accident? You tell me the driver was killed too, poor man. But James – Assistant Chief Constable Holland – seems sure Amass was driving. Are you going to let Amass take the blame? His supporters will not be happy."

This man, thought the Governor, is no fool. What a pity he could not be President. It would be convenient to have the driver responsible. They could rely on James Holland to see the story was clear, even if it wasn't true. But the least they could do would be to compensate the driver's family adequately. He voiced all but the first of these thoughts.

"We should get James Holland to give a statement to Simon Benson tonight so he can get it into his Stop Press for tomorrow.

Before speculation builds up." Evans had put his finger on the solution.

"I have James's number programmed into my telephone," announced Sir Joseph.

"Programmed?" Evans looked across enquiringly.

"One touch button. Number six. If the President agrees?" Dipra nodded.

"And Mr Goodwill?"

"Yes. We leave it to Evans. It is what happened. Poor man encountered this big lorry on a nasty bend. He had no chance. His widow should be granted ten thousand shillings compensation."

"Let us hope," added Evans, "that the lorry driver did not get a good look at them. He would have been high up in his cab, so maybe there wasn't time. I believe he wasn't hurt, only shocked."

"James Holland is waiting for a call from us, gentlemen." Sir Joseph was back to his urbane self.

TWENTY-FIVE

As Evans had correctly forecast, Joseph Amass was not a sufficiently well known figure, nor had he been Prime Minister for long enough, for his death to cause too much of a stir in Jamestown.

James Holland gave his version to Simon Benson and his editor found room for it on page two, with proper condolences for the families and expressions of deep regret for the sad loss of one of the nation's most brilliant leaders. But the front-page headlines were still focussed on the coming Independence Day celebrations and the guest list, which by chance had been released the day before. This was far more interesting – who were all these funny names? Was an earl bigger than a chief? Why was an Under-Secretary so important?

Evans visited the truck driver in hospital. The minor wound sustained when he nearly went through his windscreen was the least of Evans's worries. The man was clearly still in shock and the nurse had warned him not to upset her patient. But had he seen the passengers in the car?

"No, sah. I only just come around de corner, dat one by mile seventeen, when I see'd it. Hardly time to stamp on brakes. I t'ink I push dat car under me for hundred yards." The tears flowed freely. "I never get chance…"

"We know, Emmanuel. The police think the car was doing ninety and you were doing only forty. You have nothing to blame yourself for."

"But both men dead, one of dem big man, I t'ink."

"Yes. The Prime Minister. He must have wanted the thrill, to sit in the front passenger seat like that."

Evans leaned back and observed Emmanuel's reaction to this, to find it reassuringly accepting.

"It make no difference if he in back, sah, both men would die in accident like dat. Whole car crushed. I very sorry for wives and piccins."

"Yes. The Government will compensate them properly, so

they will not suffer badly. And you will get some compensation for the time you must take to recover. Don't worry, Emmanuel. Bishgad is going to look after people."

Evans reported the conversation to James Holland.

"Right. Only the Governor, the President, Mr. Goodwill and yourself have any inkling Amass might have been at the wheel. And even we cannot be certain. The rest of the world 'knows' that he was in the passenger seat. It is enough, Evans. Waste no more time on speculation; don't even discuss it further.

"But I do hope your new government will mount a campaign to stop the reckless driving which so many young people are adopting these days. Bring in a drinking and driving law for starters. And you could tighten up on the driving licence business."

"How so?"

"Make people attend a proper driving school before taking the test. City Cars could set up the first one – nice little sideline for them. There would soon be competitors. Don't let people drive for more than six months on a Provisional Licence, before they take another test. Devise a much more sensible and stringent test and stamp out the corruption among the examiners. Oh and rename the Provisional a Temporary Licence. Lots of people think it is a *professional* licence."

Evans smiled. "We'll be teaching people better English, you know, James."

*

Through the huge plate glass windows he caught the flash of deep blue silk and knew at once it had to be Celine. His heart lurched a little as he focussed on the spot where it had been, now obscured by so many other travellers. Then he saw it again, now standing by the baggage carousel.

He could have pulled rank to go airside but he did not want to betray such determined interest. He would meet her the minute she emerged from the exit doors. He could see her now, heaving her case on to a trolley; a tiny case for a tiny lady. But here she came. Another heart lurch. She was as beautiful, slender, tightly wrapped as ever.

"Evans! Wonderful to see you again!"

She buried herself in his arms before he could even reply and hugged him enthusiastically. Then she distanced herself, held him at arm's length and appraised his face.

"A little older, much more experienced, but still gorgeous," she pronounced.

Evans smiled resignedly. "You weather far better than I do, Celine. Good flight?"

"Excellent. But I'm still keen to have a shower a.s.a.p. I'd forgotten how humid Jamestown can be. Has the air-conditioning broken down?"

"Has it ever worked?" joked Evans. "Let's get you to your hotel."

They settled into the black and gold Range Rover. "I thought you might have a Merc', Evans."

"No, this is more practical for my job. Anyway, we are more or less obliged to have British cars at this stage. Malachi will have a Jaguar. By the way, he's the new PM, you won't have heard that Joseph Amass was killed in a road accident."

Celine was silent for a moment. "Then *you* should have been PM. Road accidents seem endemic in Jamesland – sorry, Evans, I really was very sorry to hear about Grace." She laid a hand on Evans's arm. "You recovered? Silly question, sorry, I hope the pain is diminishing now."

He nodded. "You never married."

"No. I think I am going to upset all tradition and die an old maid." A small giggle escaped her. "Well, perhaps not an old maid, exactly, but certainly an unmarried lady. A rich old lady, I'd have to say. If you retire as a crusty old bachelor, I'll be able to support you in Hong Kong." She lowered her head and looked at him sideways over her glasses.

Evans laughed. "You are still an exciting woman, Celine. You don't need to plan our retirements just yet. How long have you worn glasses?"

"A couple of years now. I hated them at first, till someone told me they looked sexy. Now I'm reconciled!"

"They do look good on you. Here's your hotel. I have to go back to meet the London contingent. Would you like to join us all for dinner tonight? In the dining room of the hotel, I think, to save further travel."

"Ah, these are the people Malachi met in London? Didn't I hear he married one lady, an Indian girl?"

"You did. They all shared a house in London. Reeta is now here, working at Karle Mo with Ruth, Dipra's wife."

"And isn't there one for you among them?"

Evans smiled wryly. "Tell you what, you can help me choose one tonight." He paused and then quietly added, "You did pretty well last time, after all."

*

They were festooned with airline bags and dragging wheelie cases which all looked quite large enough to take up the whole of their first class baggage allowances. He contrasted these with the modest case Celine had brought through, probably full of light silk dresses. Wrenching his mind off the light silk dresses he prepared himself for the onslaught.

Mrs. Baldock was first through. He shook her hand warmly and asked if she'd had a good flight.

"Oh my goodness, I've never had such a posh seat and such luxurious treatment! It was really very generous of Malachi."

"I'm sure he will always be grateful for the help you gave him in London as a student."

The girls now came out in a gaggle. Evans shook hands with each, with little Janet, tall Daintree and finally Winnie, who ignored his outstretched hand and embraced him vigorously, causing him embarrassment and pleasure in about equal measures.

"You're still looking good, Evans, despite the cares of the nation on your shoulders."

"Not just mine, Winnie. But we bear up. This is a very joyful time and we're all glad you are here to share it with us."

He instructed them to wait on the pavement and not let anyone lay a hand on their baggage until he got back with the Range Rover.

"No driver, Evans?"

"Meeting all of you is a personal pleasure, Daintree. I try not to use government facilities too much on personal affairs." He hurried away across the car park.

Daintree smirked at Winnie. "Personal pleasure, you hear that, chuck? You sit in front with him."

Mildly abashed, Winnie insisted Mrs. B should be upfront.

"Senior lady, eh girls?" teased Mrs. B.

Janet was intrigued by the now frequent sight of black and gold vehicles, by all the bunting and flags, the arches and stadiums they were passing. "You reckon it will be like this in South Africa one day, Winnie?"

"Please God. Whenever it is, I shall be there, if I have to row the Atlantic single-handed. How's Reeta doing, Evans?"

"Settled in very well, I think. It's good for her to work alongside Ruth, of course. How many other countries do you know where the President's and Prime Minister's wives work together in a hospital?"

"You're proud of that, aren't you, Evans?" said Mrs. B softly.

"I am, Mrs. B. I hope that's how our democracy will develop, with everyone doing their bit, whatever their position. Grace never gave up her work, you know."

The small awkward silence was broken by Daintree, as they came in sight of Karle Mo on the horizon. "Anything there for me, you think, Evans?"

"I'm not the Minister of Health, Daintree. That's Grace's father. But you could try your luck; Karle Mo may not be up to the standards you expect in London, you know."

"Maybe I'll ask Reeta to show me around. At least your climate is better than London. I can't think why they bother trying to play cricket in England. Not that they play very well, " she laughed.

"You can take the Kiwi out of New Zealand but you can't take New Zealand out of the Kiwi," Janet declaimed. "Are we in the Tropical House again, Evans?"

*

Evans wondered who had arranged the seating plan for dinner. "The one chance we'll have all to be together without formality," Malachi had declared. He guessed it was Ruth and Reeta; Dipra was probably too tired sorting out orders of precedence for the great occasion to bother with where his friends should sit for dinner. And he wasn't too skilled in these things anyway.

The two long tables had been butted up facing and with the huge linen tablecloth could have been mistaken for one. The Tropical House had made a real effort here, every place with full ranges of silver and wine glasses, every napkin standing starchly proud on each side plate.

Dipra's place would be across the table join but some material under the cloth covered the crack. Ruth sat on his left and Mrs. B., all of a flutter to be dining alongside a President, on his right. Nice touch that, thought Evans, definitely Reeta's influence there.

Evans himself sat around the corner from Ruth, with Celine on his other side, then Andrew and Fiona, with Winnie on the end. Perhaps he would have liked to be closer to Winnie, but having Celine so near …

He turned his attention to Malachi, around the corner from Mrs. B. - very appropriate - with Reeta on his left, then Simon Benson – how nice of Ruth or Reeta to invite him – next to Janet who would be delighted with the arrangement. Along the bottom of the table, James Holland maintained his suave policeman image, sitting as he was between Daintree and Winnie. No Assistant Chief Constable was going to intimidate either of them. In South Africa, Evans reflected, Winnie probably ate young constables for breakfast. It was just as well they were in the private dining room where they could all hear each other.

Evans was aware of Ruth nudging Dipra as they waited for

the first course. Dipra at first looked at her uncomprehendingly as she mimed lifting a glass, understood and lumbered to his feet.

"People," he said, "welcome on this very happy occasion. We Bishgadi are very happy to have our friends from England – and Scotland, and," glancing around the table, "New Zealand-"

"And South Africa!" shouted Winnie.

"- and South Africa, with us to help celebrate. The day after tomorrow will be a very grand formal occasion and I very glad you all here for it but tonight is all informal and I have only one toast to make; it is To Friendship!"

They all shuffled to their feet and intoned, "To Friendship."

Well done Dipra, thought Evans. The coaching is paying off. But I'll bet Ruth made you rehearse that well. Brave Winnie to speak up. He really didn't need to worry about her being down there at the end.

Celine was amused. As if reading his thoughts she said, "Your friend from South Africa is not shy."

"There are shy women left in the world, Celine?" asked Andrew, earning himself a dig in the ribs from Fiona, with a hissed "Sssh…"

Celine gave her tinkling laugh, enough to draw the attention of Malachi sitting opposite. He touched Reeta's arm as if to ward off earlier memories of London.

Janet leaned across. "I believe you are going on to London next, Celine?"

Celine nodded.

"Then if you have time, please visit us down in Wandsworth."

Winnie and Daintree joined in. "Yes, come and see how the other half lives, when it's not attending African Freedom days."

Celine smiled broadly. "Thank you. I will *make* time to take you up on that."

. Better make an effort to get Simon into conversation among all these powerful ladies, thought Evans. After all, we owe him a great deal in getting us through the last few months.

And here we all are, three boys from InterEarthMove's yard, nearly on the summit of Kilimanjaro, 'de top' as Dipra would say. Then he remembered seeing that summit as he and Grace flew down from Nairobi to Mombassa on their honeymoon. He had been surprised to see how hollow the top was. Was it always hollow when you had finally achieved your ambition? Grace had left a hollow in his heart. Could someone else fill it?

He looked down the length of the table. Winnie, perhaps?

TWENTY-SIX

The day began very early, at the Governor's request.

"Let me lower the Union Flag at the Mansion in a small ceremony at seven o'clock in the morning and then you can have the big ceremony, with the important business of raising the new Bishgad flag, without complications and fuss. It is enough that I shake your hand in the arena to signify the handover of power."

Dipra thought this a good idea. "But you will make a speech to the crowd? Promising friendship and support and all that? I anxious everyone sees we are to be good friends."

"Mr. President, I will be proud to hand over to you with proper public expressions of confidence in Bishgad's future."

And so it happened. Outside The Mansion in the cool early morning there was assembled a small group consisting of Her Majesty's Secretary of State for Foreign Affairs, The Earl of Middleshire, the putative British High Commissioner Peter Willoughby, various senior British civil servants, the Police Band, a twelve-man detachment of Royal Marines flown in for the purpose and Dipra Forfpi's inner cabinet.

The Earl of Middleshire made a pompous little speech about children growing up and parents proud to see them take their first faltering steps

just as Great Britain was now happy and proud to see this new independent nation which he was sure would uphold all the family values inculcated in her children for many centuries. The Governor cringed with embarrassment and even the Foreign Minister began to take an unwonted interest in the exotic flora of the Mansion Garden. Dipra was frankly baffled and Evans rolled his eyes at Malachi while they both fixed their faces with imperturbable respect.

But finally it was over and to the strains of the British National Anthem and the slick arms drill of the Marines the Union Flag was lowered, folded in the correct manner and presented to the Governor by the Major with due ceremony.

Sir Joseph held the flag close to his chest and made a short speech of congratulation to the assembled ministers. Then to Dipra's enormous surprise, and indeed to the slight dismay of the Foreign Secretary, he approached and offered the folded flag to the President.

"Mr. President, I think it might be appropriate for you to keep this, as a memento of good times for both our nations. It would look well in your history museum as a reminder, dare I say, of the time we have worked together, and in a sense the birth of your nation."

Dipra, like most others present, was speechless until Evans whispered in his ear that a fulsome thank you would not be out of order. "Accept it graciously, Dipra. It is a splendid token of goodwill." He then led a prolonged burst of applause to give Dipra time to think of something to say.

During this hiatus the band and the Royal Marine detachment marched smartly off and a number of servants emerged from the Mansion side door carrying trays of sparkling wine. Dipra now pulled himself together and raised his glass, "To our British friends," he declaimed. And as the glasses were lowered again, "Thank you, Sir Joseph, for that wonderful gesture, we shall treasure the flag, which will always enjoy a prominent position in the museum as a part of our history."

Full marks, thought Evans, that period of silence was well used, Dipra. That was the most impressive speech – and in perfect English too –that he had ever heard his friend make. I must remember to congratulate you afterwards.

The group now broke up and repaired to their vehicles. The Governor was to enter the arena in his Range Rover just three minutes before Dipra and Ruth made their grand entrance standing up in the back of the open-topped Rolls Royce, hopefully acknowledging the roar of the crowd. Everyone else charged off to secure their reserved seats in the main grandstand.

The Governor and Lady Whittaker stood chatting to Dipra and Ruth until the courtyard was completely clear and their own cars appeared from a far corner.

"I think our guests are likely to be waiting for us now, Mr.

President. Shall we go?"

Dipra, with very moist eyes, fervently shook his hand. "We all ready now. We remember you and Lady Cynthia for very long time." He knew he hadn't got that quite right but there was no Evans to look over his shoulder. It said what he needed to say. He would have embraced them both in the African manner but he felt that might be going too far. So he put all the emotion into that handshake.

*

Evans knew it was going to be a stinking hot day. He had advised Dipra to be sure to arrive in good time for the ceremony so as not to keep all the guests, or indeed the public, sweltering in the sun. He had wanted the ceremony to be in the evening but then it would clash with the planned formal reception and dinner. So he fought instead for an early start and reluctantly Dipra had agreed to nine o'clock.

Some shade had been erected for the most important guests but the rest in the grandstands and the public crowding around the temporary barriers would just have to sweat it out. The public of course would be in shirts and shorts and sleeveless dresses but the guests would be in formal suits, poor devils. All the Brits at this morning's Mansion ceremony had been in dark grey suits and ties. That was OK at seven o'clock, but by ten they would be sweating like boxers in the ring.

Many of the Africans would wear the newly fashionable safari suits but the cabinet ministers had stuck to the suit and tie regalia. Dipra and Malachi had been shocked to hear that Evans would wear a lightweight beige suit and no tie. "You two 'rebels' are more constrained by 'colonial' attitudes than I am," he joked. "Britain will be proud of you."

Her Majesty was represented by the Earl of Middleshire. Nobody knew quite who he was, but it was thought he must be 'royal', which was good enough for Dipra, who told anybody enquiring that Middleshire was the Queen's cousin. Several times removed, thought Evans.

The UK government's sending of the Secretary of State for

Foreign Affairs, was a very high honour, as Dipra was keen to point out, plus the putative British High Commissioner, Peter Willoughby. "A very good friend of mine," Dipra had boasted. "We shall have excellent relations with Great Britain."

"We'll need to, Dipra. But they have been pretty generous with grants for this business. Let's hope you can keep the money flowing after independence. Your friend Mr. Willoughby can be an important influence."

The crowds had begun to gather from sunrise at six o'clock. At eight forty-five the Police Band was led into the arena by James Holland and his bandmaster. Taking up position under the awnings Holland had insisted upon, the musicians began to entertain the crowd. They played a medley of locally popular tunes with some marches interposed. Evans suppressed a smile when he heard snatches of Rule Britannia coming across, a little joke from James Holland no doubt, confident that few people other than the Brits would recognise those transposed bars.

From eight o'clock the guests for the main grandstand began to arrive, many of them consular officials looking forward to their temporary elevation to Ambassadorial or High Commissioner status. They greeted each other with effusive cries of welcome, like the old friends they were, happy in their luck.

Sir Joseph had hunted out the cockaded hat and semi-military uniform he had inherited from his predecessor for the earlier ceremony and now he would parade it in full glory. Probably the last time it will ever be worn, he thought, there isn't likely to be much call for it in Lisbon. Perhaps he could gift it to some struggling amateur theatrical group back in Hertfordshire. Nevertheless, he had experienced a little surge of pride when Evans Watanero had congratulated him on a splendid turn-out. He'd always liked that Evans chap.

The front row of the stand seated the cabinet and ministers' wives and the distinguished overseas guests with their partners, with just two seats left vacant at the centre for Dipra and Ruth after they made their grand entry. In the second row were the 'ladies from London' as Celine had quickly christened them, Celine herself, Andrew and Fiona Maitland and their two children, bubbling with excitement, and Simon Benson, sitting alongside Janet.

*

One half of Simon Benson's mind was writing his report on the occasion and the other half contemplating the news he had so far kept from Janet. It didn't have to be a big thing, he told himself, any self-respecting journalist wanted a chance to work in London, after all. It didn't mean … Yes, it did, broke in his more objective self. I don't want to go if she doesn't want me there. Blow the job. I'll look for something in Manchester instead. But he ought at least to tell her, didn't he?

Yes, but not now, perhaps after the ceremony. During the applause for Dipra Forfpi's speech perhaps? He could make it sound as casual as possible. He didn't want to force her hand or anything. He wasn't proposing marriage, was he? Was he? It would make it easier to settle in London, though. But that wasn't the point, was it? He loved her. He'd better at least tell her that first. It was so good to be sitting alongside her here. Who could have forecast this from their first meeting at the wedding reception?

*

Winnie was gazing fondly at the back of Evans's head and Celine caught the look. She leaned sideways and stretched up to mutter in Winnie's ear.

"This must be especially pleasing for you, Winnie. Have you thought of living out here? Wouldn't that be nice for you, until your own country gets its freedom?"

Winnie was disconcerted. "I've joked about it, but what would I do, seriously? There'll be very few jobs at the start and they won't want a foreign caterer, will they? They'll want to train their own up."

"That's it! You could train catering students. I'll bet they don't have any black catering lecturers. You should ask at the Technical College Evans talks about so much." She lowered her voice again and put her mouth to Winnie's ear. "The chap just to the right in front could do with some good catering, I expect."

Winnie studied her face. "You think..?"

"Don't tell me you haven't thought about it! This is no time to lose your nerve. A good man can't be kept on the shelf forever."

*

Evans turned around in his seat to converse with Andrew. "All these diplomats make me wonder if you might be interested in becoming the Honorary Consul for Scotland."

Andrew grimaced. "Have to wait for Scottish Independence for that Evans. Heaven forbid! I shall certainly be home before that, so you'll have to try one of the InterEarthMove engineers, Ian MacDonald. He's a keen devolution man. Bloody good engineer but still wanting to avenge the Glencoe Massacre."

Evans looked puzzled.

"About 1700, I think. The Campbells, soldiers of King William the Third, came to Glencoe to extract a pledge of loyalty from the MacDonald clan, stayed as guests, then slaughtered them in the middle of the night. It was considered very bad form."

"I should think so too! But there seem to be plenty of MacDonalds left."

"Ay, the Campbells only killed half of them. So that's all right, eh? And it *was* three hundred years back. But don't argue that to Ian if you should meet him!"

"I think I'll try to steer clear of your politics, Andrew. Even our tribes don't act like that. Maybe we won't need a Scottish Consul!" Evans, nudged by Malachi, turned away.

*

Fiona was quite thrilled by the pageantry. "Andrew, this almost makes me want to stay on here, just to see how it all works out."

"You'll have the best part of a year to assess that, Fi. Great for the kids to be here for this, though. A little piece of history for them to recall in future years. Hope you're getting some good photos to remind us."

She took a hand off her camera to place over his. "I shall use up the whole reel at this rate. I'm very proud of you and of all your friends. But I'll be just as proud back home, whatever you get to do there. Impulsively she leaned to kiss his cheek.

"My man, special guest of the first President of Bishgad!"

*

Mrs. B. commented to Daintree that Simon seemed pretty preoccupied today. "I suppose he's having to write an article on all this. He does keep getting out that little notebook and jotting something down."

"Maybe he's got more than that on his mind, Mrs. B. Like the lady on his left."

"You think they're going to ..?"

"Let's both cross our fingers, eh, Mrs. B? Wouldn't it be lovely for them? But would she fit in here?"

"Would you, Daintree?"

"Yeah, I reckon. I've been talking to Ruth and Reeta and there seems a good chance of getting work at Karle Mo Hospital. I'm going to chase it, anyhow. Not a lot for me in London now, it's full of Aussies."

"And the Kiwi boyfriend? Where's he gone?"

"Back to Wellington, for all I know. Work Permit ran out. *He said.* Bloody liar. Still, I'm not the first girl to get dumped, am I? Probably not the first he's dumped." She laughed a short scornful yelp. "Sod all men, eh?"

"Oh come on, Daintree, nice looking girl like you can't give up on men at your age. Keep looking."

"Maybe. But I'd rather look from here than from London."

"At this rate I'll be travelling back on my own," laughed Mrs. B.

*

Nine o'clock came. The Governor's Range Rover made its stately procession into the centre of the arena while the Police Band again played God Save The Queen. All the Brits rose to their feet and with only a slight delay the rest of the grandstands followed. The little group of Marines, tactfully assembled in one corner, presented arms while their Major saluted, as did Assistant Chief Constable James Holland.

The music complete, the Range Rover pulled across to the main grandstand to allow Sir Joseph and Lady Whittaker to take their places in the front row.

Three minutes later, Dipra, keeping his promise on timing, stood with Ruth in the drop head Rolls as it purred majestically into the stadium, waving enthusiastically to the crowd, who set up a tremendous roar and waved back. The Roller halted precisely alongside the centre steps to the grandstand and as the band broke into the new and rather jolly national anthem, which very few people had yet heard, James Holland lowered his salute and opened the door.

The stand creaked as six hundred people stood to greet and applaud the new President. Ruth and Dipra mounted the few steps as regally as they could manage, but Dipra could not resist a wink at Evans and Malachi while Ruth tried not to catch the eyes of her friends clamouring their welcome. The Maitland children were clapping wildly, bringing a small tear to her eye.

Dipra Forfpi sat, allowing everyone else to regain their seats and the Governor immediately rose to begin his address.

"Your Excellency President Forfpi, My Lord the Earl of Middleshire, Secretary of State and Mrs. Wilson, Excellencies, distinguished guests and people of Bishgad. This morning the United Kingdom flag was hauled down from the mast outside the Mansion before distinguished representatives of Her Majesty the Queen, of the UK government and of the country's new leaders. I had the honour to present that flag to your new President for the Bishgad History Museum. The people of Britain salute the people of Bishgad and wish you well. We shall take a friendly interest in your development and give you all the help we can.

"But your success will depend upon the hard work you put into your country. I urge you, every man and woman here today and throughout this lovely country, to work steadily for your own future, for your children's future and for your country's future. Enough talk from an Englishman, it is now my great honour to introduce your new President, a man who has worked steadily over the years to bring about the present happy situation and who will, I am sure, lead you and your country to continuing success. Ladies and gentlemen, the President of Bishgad, Mr. Dipra Forfpi."

Sir Joseph clapped to the crowd and polite applause from the stands followed, with the crowd catching on a few seconds later and deciding they should join in. The Foreign Secretary was not perhaps as enthusiastic as he could have been and the Earl was somewhat bemused by it all. Peter Willoughby was clapping furiously as the now ex-Governor resumed his seat.

Then Dipra Forfpi rose and the clamour with him.

TWENTY-SEVEN

"My Lord, Secretary of State and Mrs.Wilson, Governor Sir Joseph and Lady Whittaker, Ministers, Excellencies, Distinguished Guests and... People of Bishgad!"

Dipra Forfpi shouted the last three words, to a roar of approval from the crowd and a little burst of clapping from the stands.

"Today we are witnessing a historic occasion. Our nation is free at last. The people of Bishgad will be responsible for their own destinies. The road to freedom has been long and hard. But thank Heaven the fight has all been around the negotiating table and not on the battlefield."

Another little ripple of applause swept the crowd.

"For this, we grateful to our former colonial masters, now our firm friends, the British."

He waited while more clapping died away and reminded himself not to omit the verb 'to be'.

"Many of those friends are here with us today. Our distinguished former Governor, Sir Joseph Whittaker."

Here he gestured to the cockaded gentleman two seats to his left, who raised that splendid hat an inch in acknowledgement. Sir Joseph was mildly comforted by that word 'former.' It at last clarified his true position. The recent months of ambiguous authority had left him quite uncertain as to where power lay in the interim period.

*"Our new British High Commissioner, Mr. Peter Willoughby, who was instrumental (*good word, that, Evans) *in our getting the very generous grants from UK Government, which will ensure we have better trained doctors, teachers and engineers with new hospitals, new schools, new roads and port facilities. You will have seen many of these projects starting up already. Thank you, Peter."*

Peter Willoughby tried hard not to allow the pleasure of this fulsome praise to be undermined by the thought that the Foreign Secretary, sitting so close, was unlikely to relish the walk-on part he seemed to have been allocated in these proceedings. Well, President Forfpi had written his own speech. Or perhaps it was that chap Evans.

"We can now look forward to a period of unprecedented development. We shall attract much new investment from overseas and we hope a lot of it will come from old friends who have been here for some years. I know I should not pick out individual firms but I cannot help mentioning InterEarthMove, the British firm that became so important to our economy, initially under the management of Mr. Duncan McDonald who sadly cannot be with us today, and then under Miss Celine Brandt, who I am delighted to see in the grandstand..."

Dipra paused to look towards Celine and she raised a modest hand to acknowledge the compliment. Another ripple of applause.

"...and then under its first African General Manager, my old friend Evans Watanero, who is now of course The Minister of Infrastructure and Development."

Evans tried to be as self-effacing as possible, lifting a hand only a few inches to acknowledge Dipra's wave.

"The company is still growing, now under the management of Mr. Andrew Maitland – what a lot we owe to the Scottish! – and we wish him every success."

Fiona seized Andrew's arm and lifted it. "Wave," she hissed, "it's only polite."

" Mr. Maitland has been teaching me an ancient Scottish ritual which they call goluf..."

He waited for the laughter to die down.

"... but I am just a piccin at it so far."

More laughter, this time even more from the crowd than from the stands. Dipra thanked his stars for the help Evans had given him with this speech. He could feel it was a great success, even if he did not himself quite understand some of the jokes. And he really must work on the pronouncement of that word.

*"InterEarthMove also provided us with your Prime Minister, Mr. Malachi Goodwill. (*Pause, it said in his notes,

awaiting crowd response – which was gratifyingly approving)
*And me!" (*Wait for applause – deafening.*)*

"Years ago, Evans, Malachi and myself all slept in the big buckets at the front end of InterEarthMove's largest machines. For nearly a year they were our only proper homes, when we first came down from our village. We thought we were very daring young men at the time but now Evans tells me that our manager Mr. MacDonald knew all about us all the time. We are properly grateful to him."

The crowd all applauded politely.

"One other person Malachi Goodwill has asked me to mention specially; his landlady in Battersea, who was so good to him for his three years at the London School of Economics, and we are proud to say is also here with us today in the grandstand- Mrs. Baldock of Battersea!"

He swept his arm and Mrs. B. half rose in her seat in acknowledgement. More polite clapping.

"London has been good to us. The UK Government and people have provided us with funds for many projects, trained both Evans and Malachi, and provided Malachi with his lovely wife."

Reeta bowed her head at this compliment. But she guessed it was Evans and Ruth who put this in. God bless them both.

"Bishgad will be a country where everyone works together, never mind their colour, creed or race. We have many Indian and Lebanese friends, good Chinese people cooking us their wonderful food in the restaurants and of course the British people like Mr. James Maitland our Assistant Chief Constable, who has served us so well in the past and has agreed to serve two more years preparing his African successor. (Yet another surge of applause.)

Some expatriates will of course be going home soon and we wish them all every success in their home countries. Many others will be staying on to run their companies and to advise our government departments and to all of them I say: Welcome to the Republic of Bishgad!"

The crowd had got into the spirit of the occasion by now and there was deafening and prolonged applause.

During this time a police detachment marched smartly into the arena and grouped itself around the flagpole. James Holland saluted the President and offered him a folded black and gold flag. Dipra walked across to the flagpole and with the help of a burly and beaming police constable raised the flag aloft. A providential breeze arose to spread the new flag to its full glory setting off renewed clamour.

Returning to his seat, through the crowd's roar, Dipra began again. *"Ladies and gentlemen, a new country deserves a new capital and it is my great pleasure and honour to announce a new name for this lovely city."*

Pause for effect, it said in his notes. A proper hush descended.

"From this moment, Henry City will become.... FERALODE."

The Earl and the Foreign Secretary, disapproving to the core, affixed false grins on their faces. The crowd renewed its clamour.

"F E R A L O D E," repeated Dipra, *" a name to recall our past and to savour for our future. An African name, chosen for us by our sadly departed friend, Joseph Amass."*

There were mixed murmurings in the crowd and much puzzlement in the stands. Now a full detachment of police in white coats and with special white covers to their caps marched to the centre of the arena and formed itself so as to spell the new name, causing a great burst of applause from the stands. People on the edges pushed to see if they could obtain a better view of what the policemen had done but soon realised it was unnecessary – the police wheeled in a fashion even the Marines major thought excellent, to display the name to every section of the crowd.

From the corner of his eye, Evans observed Andrew Maitland slip quietly from his seat. Turning his head, he also saw Celine rising to leave. Now where on earth were they going?

As the roar died down Dipra Forfpi began on his final paragraph.

"People of Bishgad, let us all be very happy on this great occasion and let us all get down to work tomorrow with renewed energy, a new sense of purpose, a new dedication to the success of our new country. But for today...let's celebrate!"

The Police Band struck up again with the new national anthem, with Dipra gesturing to the crowd to stand and wave their flags and with the Henry City Gospel Choir, which would soon have to re-christen itself, belting out the lyrics. Both band and choir gave it everything they'd got, providing three reprises so that the melody and words would become familiar to the people. It was, Evans had to admit, a very jolly tune, composed by the British lady who taught music at the Tech. Maybe it didn't have the gravitas of the Marseillaise, but then, it was *African* and very appropriate.

The choir, finally exhausted, ceased to sing and the band marched off still playing the anthem. It would be the top selling record in the shops tomorrow, Evans knew. Everyone would have to have one. And he'd insisted a sheet of the words should be included with each disc. The Kakadu, which had long since abandoned God Save The Queen as its closing number, would now revive the old custom with renewed patriotism.

As Dipra turned to gesture for Ruth to join him in the Rolls Royce, a new entrant to the arena made its appearance. A vast earthmoving machine, its every surface gleaming yellow, rumbled across to the centre, at the controls a tiny figure in deep blue silk, with a man standing on each side of her in the cab. A voice boomed from the cab in familiar Scottish tones. The crowd went very quiet.

"Mr. President, we have a small surprise for you."

Evans squinted against the sun to identify the third occupant of the cab, a wizened old man in pristine shirt and shorts...
"Joshua!" he exclaimed.

"We thought," went on the Scotsman, "you might like to make your exit with your friends Mr.Goodwill and Mr. Watanero

286

in a symbolic machine, symbolic of your past and of the country's future. And here to drive it is Miss Celine Brandt and your old friend Mr. Joshua Ademanle."

The front bucket was lowered gently to the ground to show that extensive protective railing had been welded across its front, with a simple swing gate in its centre. Dipra made his way across to the machine and up into the cab. Evans and Malachi left the stand to race across and climb up behind him. The crowd watched as six emotional people all tried to embrace each other in the confines of the cab.

"Not what I expected, young Willoughby!" ground out the Foreign Secretary.

"But very African," interjected Sir Joseph Whittaker. "There could hardly be a more appropriate send-off."

Dipra, Malachi and Evans dismounted and walked around to the front bucket, letting themselves in by the gate.

"Don't worry, people," boomed Andrew's voice again. "Miss Brandt will drive off very carefully. Please give your President and his friends the applause and love they deserve."

The bucket rose vertically three feet or so and the machine made a full circuit of the arena, passing close to the main grandstand and all round in front of the packed public slopes. Even its deep engine note was drowned in the acclamation of the largest crowd the city had ever seen. The giant machine then set off through the exit to thread its way carefully through the narrow gap in the crowd, kept open by a large contingent of the Bishgad Police Force, on its way to the Mansion.

It was followed by the creeping Rolls Royce. Quickly, James Holland asked his bandleader to reassemble his band and march behind the Rolls, again playing the new national anthem. A few metres behind the band, the two sides of the police cordon fused to allow the crowd to dance and sing to the music to its heart's content.

Dipra Forfpi, surveying the people from his elevated position, reflected that he had achieved his lifetime's secret ambition. President! Even in the wildest imaginations of his youth he had never seriously contemplated becoming *the top man* in his country. Kilimanjaro in a bucket! Maybe later he *could* be snooker champion of the world too!

Malachi Goodwill, on Dipra's left, acknowledged the waves of the crowd and quietly thought that being Prime Minister for a few years would provide an ideal base for his future commercial career. Why should he not be the biggest businessman in Bishgad, like that chap Adunbi was in Nigeria? He would have contacts all over the world.

And Evans Watanero, on Dipra's right, smiled at the waves and cheers surrounding them, and wondered if this was not his proper place, enjoying beneath him the surging power of an InterEarthMove machine. He considered the irony of a situation in which Celine was for the moment entirely in charge of his life, while he had to admit he was wishing that Winnie could be alongside him and not back there in the stands.

END